A WORD SO FITLY SPOKEN

THE SEVERED REALMS

T.A. LAWRENCE

To Mom,
for keeping every stray scrap of paper I ever wrote on as a child

ALONDRIA

MYSTRAL

DWELLEN

Veranforest

Kubii Mountains

The Bluffs

Wyndham

Adreean Sea

AVELEA

FORGOTTEN ISLE

Cvaen

The Hills

Edii Gulf

Nettlewood

Rivre

CHARSHON

Meranthi

Sea of Lythos

NAENDEN

Talens

Grythos Channel

LAEI

CHAPTER 1

ASHA

I might have been glad to be ugly, had it not been for Dinah.
All the beautiful human virgins of the land...
That particular excerpt from the herald's proclamation looped in my frazzled mind as I raced through the crowded streets of Meranthi.

"All the beautiful human virgins..." a pale-faced faerie dressed in royal blue robes whispered to her similarly clad companion as they strode arm in arm down the street.

I pushed past them, not bothering to excuse myself as I forced my way through the throng of buzzing gossipers. I wasn't exactly moving with the flow of the market traffic. Everyone else had either stayed behind to listen to the rest of the herald's proclamation, or they were still gathering around him, having just heard the whispers from their neighbors, having just noticed the congregation beginning to form.

Not me. I had heard enough.

A lanky group of faeries, their pale skin stretched over their skulls, bare despite the heat of the day, fed on today's gossip as they huddled. "Seems our king is lowering his late father's employment standards. Did you see that herald? Human as they come."

Of course, the fae would hone in on that nugget of detail, unbothered by the contents of the proclamation itself.

1

It made sense to me why the king had chosen to use human heralds to announce his decree, even though no human had ever been employed in the service of the palace. He wanted us to suffer, and what better way to shove our Fates in our faces than for the news to come from the mouths of our kinsmen?

I weaved through a group of females standing in line for produce. The vendor, a scaly faerie with beady eyes and a sunken brow, barked at a woman purchasing sunmelons. "Do I look like I'm in the business of charity?" he asked, his oversized nostrils flaring at her.

"Three coppers. That was the cost just yesterday. I apologize. I didn't know you had raised your prices," said the woman clad in dirty grey robes that bulged at the belly, forming a bump that betrayed the reason behind her need for extra rations.

"Consider it a sin tax," the faerie said. The female faerie behind the pregnant woman pushed past her and slid a few coins across the stall table with her spindly, pale fingers.

If I had to bet, I'd say the faerie only paid him three coppers before he handed her a plump melon.

The human woman—the one with a child on the way—gazed up at the vendor with wide eyes, confusion brimming under her sweat beaded brow.

She hadn't heard the proclamation. She didn't understand.

But she would understand soon enough.

Despite my empty belly's disgruntled protest, I slipped a copper into the pocket of her robes as our shoulders brushed.

I shoved myself through a gathering of male faeries, the kind that self-identified as *high fae*. As if being superior to humans wasn't enough—they had to belittle their kinsmen too. They looked human except for the pointed tips of their ears and their obnoxiously blemish-free skin. What the high fae were doing in the streets of Meranthi, I didn't care to ponder. They had probably gotten bored holed up in their mansions with not as much as a dish to scrub to keep them busy, and had resorted to gawking at the less fortunate. How entertaining we were.

Sure enough, I picked up on snippets of the conversation as I passed.

"—still finding it difficult to come up with a title for my thesis. How does, *Humans: an analysis of fidelity in a lesser spec*—Hey! Watch it!" the fae barked as I shoved him in the arm, a bit harder than was necessary to push past him. A firm grip landed on my shoulder as he whipped me around to face him. His mouth gaped with the beginnings of an angry retort, but his eyes went wide and his full lips curled into a cruel smile at the sight of me.

"What's with the veil, girl? Trying to hide from us?" he purred.

It was true. I was trying to hide something. Not out of shame, just simply for convenience's sake. While we humans of Meranthi still covered our heads to protect ourselves from our overly generous sun, women hadn't been required to cover their faces in more than a century.

He tossed my veil aside and cringed. "Oh, well, aren't you a fortunate young human? You certainly won't have to worry about being selected. No one will be mistaking you for a beauty, now will they?" he said, warranting a variety of snorts and cackles from his friends. "Tell me, what wicked being did this to you?" He scraped his fingernail over the cavern where my left eye should have been. I fought back a shudder. "I hear beauty is a requirement. But, about this *virgin* part. We might have to see—AGH!"

He yelped as I seized the opportunity to scrape the sole of my boot down his calf before slipping away into the dense crowd of headscarves. Their furious cries faded as I rounded the street corner and into an alley.

Clay walls barred either side of the alleyway, most of them textured with warped glass windows tinted with home-painted landscapes of foreign lands, where water sawed through the earth and carved a path for itself, dancing over rocks without the need to hide underground from the sun.

Windows. When we made it out of this wretched place, I would make sure our new home had windows.

Pebbled steps descended below the clay apartments, and I skipped

3

down them, pulling up my robes lest I slip, as I had done on more occasions than I would have liked to admit to myself.

That was the thing about having only one eye. Depth perception wasn't at the top of my skill set.

I didn't bother with knocking as I pushed open the wooden door at the bottom of the staircase. It creaked in protest, as if to complain that we had been using it for too long. That we should have left this apartment ages ago.

I couldn't agree more.

Father and Dinah sat on the only two pillows in our little alcove.

Two seats, despite the fact three of us lived here.

Darkness enveloped most of the room as soon as I slammed the creaky door shut behind me—not that there was much of it to hide. Dim light from a dingy lamp illuminated my father's dark, wrinkled face as he read, its pitiful rays highlighting Dinah's perfectly shaped teardrop face as she crocheted.

I'd been right to assume Dinah would be home from the market already. She ran our family's stall, weaving the finest headscarves the poor in Meranthi would ever lay their hands on. It would have been more efficient for Dinah to stay home all day weaving and for me to run the stall, except, while her face drew in customers, mine had a tendency to steer them away. Apparently, I scared my fellow humans, though what the fae's excuse was, I couldn't tell. Maybe they thought my ugliness would rub off on them if they stood too close for too long. Vain creatures. So I ran errands, and Dinah made use of the midday, when the market closed down in respect for the brutal heat, by weaving more items. She almost always made it home early, not because we sold out of stock, but because half of Meranthi knew that, if they only offered up a story about how they'd suffered a heat stroke and lost three day's pay because of it, they could walk home with a scarf for free. And probably sell it at their stall for double the price.

My sister had a tendency of forgetting that we were also poor, a quality as charming as it was annoying.

Then again, I was the one down a copper for the day's work.

Dinah tilted her head toward me, pulling her tongue back into her mouth; it had been hanging out the side of her lips while she concentrated on her stitching. That perfect, full mouth shaped into a grin as she saw me. Silly girl saw me every day, yet she still acted like every greeting was the first in years. I couldn't help but adore her for it.

"Asha." She laughed, her tenor voice echoing through our hovel. "Did you get side-tracked again?" There was no accusation in her tone. Only endearment for my less-than-convenient tendency to fulfill a whole host of tasks while I was out, only to come back empty-handed regarding whatever I was sent out to obtain in the first place.

"We really are going to have to eat at some point," my father grumbled, though not unkindly. He peered at me from behind his tattered book, the same and only book he had been reading since he purchased it twenty years ago, and frowned.

Unlike Dinah, my father had a niche for detecting when something was very, very wrong.

"What happened?" he asked.

What happened? I didn't know where to start. The herald's proclamation had been so lengthy... Where had it begun?

All the beautiful virgins of the land...

That was the only part that had mattered to me. Everything else had simply been news. Predictable. But that was not where the proclamation had begun.

If they were to understand, I needed to start from the beginning.

"The queen is dead."

Dinah clutched her chest and gasped, but my father's gaze didn't falter. He had speculated the union might end poorly. We both had. I could still see Queen Gwenyth perched on the palace balcony, round cheeks, so pale they would have charred in the Naenden sun, had it not been for the lone servant holding a leaf the size of an elephant ear over her head. I'd watched the tiny servant girl's arms tremble throughout the entire ceremony.

The queen hadn't seemed to notice.

It had been the coronation the kingdom hadn't expected ever to occur. Everyone seemed to think King Rajeen Shahryar would rule until the sun sizzled out, until a darkness enveloped Alondria that even our immortal fae king could not escape.

But then the king's envoy had journeyed to Avelea for a ball. A ball hosted for the purpose of securing a bride for Prince Kiran Shahryar.

Prince Kiran found a bride alright. Just not the one his father had expected.

I wondered what shocked the late king more: Prince Kiran choosing a human bride, or the ambush that ended the late king's immortal life, leaving the kingdom of Naenden in the hands of his son and human daughter-in-law?

Something told me it was probably the dying part.

Of course, everyone assumed that Prince Kiran had coordinated the attack. After all, what was the point of being the heir to the throne, if one's father was expected to live forever? The High Council, a committee consisting of the rulers of each Alondrian kingdom, launched an investigation, but they found no evidence of the prince's involvement.

So Prince Kiran was crowned King Kiran Shahryar of Naenden, and his human wife Gwenyth, the queen.

After his coronation, our new king had opened his mouth to introduce his bride to the crowd, but she had spoken first. She'd strode out to the edge of the balcony, that poor servant girl shadowing her, and had made an announcement.

As a token of his love for her, the king had agreed to build a sanctuary for her childhood pet to play in.

And that the people of Naenden would be blessed with the ability to contribute to the lavish wedding gift through a mandatory ten percent increase in taxes.

She'd commanded the crowd to bow after that.

Needless to say, Queen Gwenyth hadn't exactly been the mortal voice whispering in the king's ear that the humans of Naenden had been hoping for.

"I am sorry to hear that," my father said, and even though his eyes were cold as onyx, I knew he truly meant it. The queen had been one of us. A human, even if she was one of the wealthy ones.

Even if she was a spoiled brat whose favorite pet was allocated more water rations than the entirety of the Meranthi and Talens slums combined.

I supposed we had all felt safer in the keep of a human brat than a fae brat.

"What happened to her?" Dinah asked.

I plopped down on the hard stone floor and exhaled. As short as the herald's story had been, it was a story nonetheless. My magic rustled inside me, delighted for a new tale to tell. I preferred to stick to the same three, the tried-and-true narratives that still lit flames of adventure in my sister's beautiful caramel eyes. Nothing too gory. Nothing with a depressing ending. But my magic... Well, it had its own preferences.

"Oh," Dinah said in quiet realization. "You don't have to tell us. Not if you don't want. Not if—"

"No, this is clearly important. You may leave if you don't wish to see it, Dinah," our father said. Dinah bit her lip, but she didn't move.

I gulped, preparing myself for the voice that was about to overpower mine. For my mouth to reveal details my mind didn't know, details the herald hadn't shared. A shudder tapped its way up my spine. I didn't want to know. But my magic had never cared what I wanted.

When I spoke, the voice that rumbled from my throat was not my own, though it was all too familiar. My voice? My voice was as dry as the Sahli desert that surrounded our little oasis of a kingdom. It cracked whenever I found myself on the precipice of a rant. This voice? This voice was as deep and full as the Adreean Sea, as rhythmic as its violet waves and as threatening as its evening tide. I shuddered again.

I watched as the eyes of my family glossed over at the sound, knowing good and well that in a moment's time, the same expression would wash over me.

Because when I spoke, when *it* spoke—it wasn't enough to listen.

It made us watch.

CHAPTER 2

KIRAN

*H*umans lie.

The thought is bitter on my tongue, tasting of copper and bile and Ophelia's blood.

I fight back a gag as my vizier strides into my office, his forehead wrinkled with concern, judgment. That look hasn't cleared his face since I returned from Talens with the fate of my brother's wife sullying my hands.

All I had wanted was to go to Gwenyth, my wife, my queen. To wrap her delicate body in my arms and clutch her into my chest until the Flame within me quelled, to hear my defense come in the form of her melodic voice.

Instead, I had been met by the vizier, the fae old enough to have advised my grandfather. Everyone always claims that fae are immortal, but the vizier has me questioning that premise every time I lay eyes on him. His face is more weathered than the walls that surround the border of Meranthi, even with all the battering they take from the sand storms in the winter.

Perhaps we're not immortal after all.

Perhaps we're just too violent a species for any of us to manage a death by natural causes.

"The humans you recruited have issued your proclamation," he says, his voice dripping with submissive disapproval.

I knew he wouldn't approve, but that doesn't stop the disappointment in his eyes from burying a thorn into my stomach.

There were times in my childhood when I pretended the vizier was my father, because that had been better than the alternative. Better than the truth.

Humans lie with their lips, but fae lie to themselves.

I steady my voice before I speak and prop my elbows on my cedar desk as I intertwine my fingers in front of my face. That's a mistake, and I have to swallow the bile creeping up my throat as a wave of thick, clotted blood emerges from my memory and slaps at my senses. It doesn't seem to matter that I scrub my hands raw with lye multiple times a day. The stench of my condemnation has fused itself with my flesh. "Surely you're well aware why it was necessary to recruit the humans," I say, my temper slipping through the restraints I've clamped over my voice.

The vizier doesn't even wince. He only frowns, carving deeper the cavernous wrinkles on his rugged cheeks. Somehow, that hurts worse. "Surely, you're well aware that your recruitment of humans to your service is not what has me concerned."

"Pray, tell. What does have you concerned?"

The bitterness in my tone only seems to deepen the hue of the vizier's blue eyes, and they water over, glistening with a hurt I can't handle right now. "Why are you doing this?" he says, his usually stable voice matching his uneven features in this moment.

The question bounces off my calloused soul, ricocheting off the numbness that's rotted away at me since that fateful night.

Why am I doing this?

As if I haven't asked myself that very same question a thousand and one times over the past few days.

As if I wasn't asking myself that question as I killed her, as I murdered Ophelia, my brother's wife, with my bare hands. Crushed her throat until her blood peppered my fingertips and her last breath fueled my Flame. As the reins I'd tied so intricately around my magic had snapped, and the flames had burst through my fingertips, swarming her limp body as they devoured her.

Why am I doing this?

That *was* the question, wasn't it? The one I had wanted so desperately to ask my wife, the one I wanted answered from her soft lips as she melted the pain away with her kiss, her voice. As she revealed the truth in only the way a being blessed with the option to warp it could.

Humans lie, but only in the beds fae make for them.

I try not to think of Gwenyth. I try not to remember my wife. What I did to her, too.

But here the vizier is, reminding me.

"I can no longer tolerate their lies," I say.

He humphs, and I know I should punish him for his disrespect. That's what my father would have done, but the numbness has crept from my heart to my limbs, and I hardly have the energy.

"And what about you, Kiran? Can you tolerate yourself once you've slaughtered the innocent?"

A wave of heat slips from my control, and before I can catch it, tuck it back inside myself, it strikes him. I watch as his pale eyes widen, as his shock mirrors that which resides in my soul, that I would dare lash out against him. Red blotches stain his face as he stumbles backward, then coughs, straightening himself.

I might as well have slapped him.

Nausea churns my intestines at the sight, but I can't bring myself to apologize, not when even the thought of admitting I was wrong to my subordinate conjures phantom bursts of agony on my back. Not when it allows my father's voice to slip into my head, that voice I so desperately wish never to hear again, that voice I shouldn't have to hear again now that he's gone.

I don't rebuke him for referring to me by my name rather than my title, though. Perhaps he'll understand. Perhaps that is enough. "Not one of them is innocent," is all I say in the end.

He shakes his head, pinching the wrinkle that bulges between his brow. "I only wish you would take some time to think this over. Allow yourself the space for your anger to settle, for your mind to clear."

"My mind is made," I say, my temper rising again, threatening to rip through my skin and devour. It would consume the world if I let it. Then it would happily take me with it.

He sighs, then heads for the door. "Your Majesty?" he says, his hand twisted around the knob.

"Yes?"

"You're allowed to break free of him, you know."

My gut twists, and he leaves before my startled mind can think of a response.

I bury my forehead into my hands and breathe in an attempt to soothe the stinging in my eyes. I learned from an early age not to cry. My father would have beat it out of me at some point, I'm sure, but he never had to. That's one of the troubles of being gifted with the Flame. Common fae envy our power, the way the Fates gifted the royal lines of Alondria with unique abilities, specific to the type of magic that buzzes within our veins.

I'm certain they don't know about the tears, about how, as a child, any intense emotion—anger, disappointment, jealousy—would mingle with my magic, causing my tears to boil, scorching burn marks into my cheeks. How, even then, the agonizing stinging mattered little to me compared to their true consequence—that they, as good as a victim's blood on the hands of a murderer, would sentence me to my father's condemnation, to a much more dreadful punishment.

Though I mastered my Flame in early childhood, I've yet to cry since. I'm fairly certain I have the self-control now to keep my tears from boiling, but that knowledge never seems to be enough to coax my tears from their hiding places.

It's probably for the best. From what I can tell from others, from what I've read, crying has its own magical benefits, a gift passed down from the Fates. It's known for its healing properties, the way it soothes the soul and calms the mind.

I don't deserve any portion of that.

Because the vizier is right.

I don't know why I'm doing this.

My anger burns so hot, it feels as though my Flame is licking at the inner layer of my skin, searching for puncture wounds through which it might escape. And I have this dreadful feeling that if I don't unleash it, it will unleash me, consuming Alondria with me as its wick, its ember fallen upon dry grass.

One year ago, I picked Gwenyth as my bride. I can still picture her, pouring drinks in her father's house at the ball that changed my Fates. The sound still prickles my ears—the shattering of fallen glass. I can still taste the haughty declaration on the back of my tongue. The moment I announced I would be marrying the daughter of Edwan Bowen, the human merchant who had so graciously allowed us to host the ball in his mansion. I barely have to reach out with my mind to feel the heat that flushed her cheeks in that moment. Even from a distance, I could sense her fear, her excitement, her hesitation.

When I chose Gwenyth Bowen to be my bride, I had done so to spite my father, to humiliate him in front of the rulers of Alondria, just as he had humiliated my mother so many times.

What I hadn't expected was for her to steal my heart.

But that's the thing about stealing another's heart. We never seem to prosecute it like we would any other crime. Take our food, and we sue. Take our jewels, and you might lose a hand.

Take our hearts, and we'll pretend we offered them freely.

I shouldn't, but I allow my mind to slip back to three months ago, when she recommended that I visit my twin brother Fin at his estate in the province of Talens. My siblings and I have had a long history of not acknowledging our bond, the one that should have been natural if our childhoods had gone the way the Fates intended.

Our father had others plans.

My sister Lydia and I were doomed from the beginning. As Naenden law specifies that only a male may inherit his father's throne, and as Lydia committed the cardinal sin of being born first, depriving my long-infertile father of his perceived right to a first-born heir, we never had a chance. My father pitted us against one another from the moment the midwife—the successor of the one who had died at my father's hands during Lydia's birth—declared that I was indeed a male.

My brother Fin and I might have had a chance, except that he never developed any magic, and thus was shoved into the same pariah portion of the palace as my sister, while I was left to bear the brunt of the entirety of my father's attention.

I would have traded places with either of them in the span of a human heartbeat, but that didn't stop them from despising me.

Until Gwenyth.

Her name in my mind causes my stomach to reel.

Gwenyth changed everything.

And to think, I'd allowed myself to believe that was a good thing.

Humans lie, but fae lie to themselves.

When she recommended I visit my brother again, I was thrilled. Thrilled. What a ridiculous emotion, unbefitting for a king. We had already visited Fin on Starfall, for the celebration of his union with his human bride, Ophelia. I had been more than happy to give him my blessing. After all, if I had wedded a human and become infinitely happier because of it, why should I not want the same for my brother, my twin whose camaraderie I so desperately longed for? Gwenyth and Ophelia had gotten along so well—often escaping to the sitting room to whisper and giggle and share secrets—I had been shocked when Gwenyth had recommended I visit Fin on my own.

I should have paid more attention to that primal intuition, to that nagging thought, grating at my mind like a pebble lodged in a boot.

Then again, it seemed there were a great many things to which I should have paid more attention, given more credence rather than suffocating them under a thousand reasonable explanations.

Like the strange aura I sensed around the edges of my brother's wife, the thrumming of her pulse when I caught her gazing at me, or the way her breath quickened in my presence.

I had assumed she feared me. She was human, after all, and though she might have found herself in love with my fae brother, why should I expect her to trust the king molded by the hands of their cruel father?

I had assumed incorrectly, given her the benefit of the doubt.

I won't be making that mistake again. Because it wasn't fear I had sensed in her reaction to my presence. It was lust. Lust for me, or lust for my power, it didn't matter which.

If I had realized, perhaps I wouldn't have opened the door when she knocked on my bedroom quarters, clad in a sheer gown woven with my brother's eyes in mind. Perhaps I would have been prepared when she threw herself upon me, begging me to take her, when she pressed her lips to mine and whispered that she had wanted me from the night she'd laid eyes on me at Starfall. She told me that she could help me take what was rightfully mine, that she would aid me in disposing of Fin, that she had a plan to get rid of him, one that would go undetected by the Council.

But I wasn't the only one of us who had misjudged the other. It didn't matter to me that Fin had inherited a portion of my kingdom. It didn't matter that she had a plan for murdering him and securing my reign. It didn't matter that she had figured out a way to do it without any evidence that might convict me when tried in front of the Council.

What mattered was that she had ruined it. What mattered was that it didn't matter. It didn't matter that I pulled away from her embrace, that I refused to gaze upon whatever that sheer gown had revealed of her form. It didn't matter that in the moment of temptation, I had chosen loyalty to my brother, fidelity to my wife.

Because there are certain wounds that do not heal, certain bruises that only yellow, never fade.

Your wife throwing herself at your brother is one of them.

I knew that in the moment. So perhaps that was the answer I told myself when I pinned her throat to the wall and loosened the leash around my magic until it consumed her, until she was nothing but a pile of ash and a memory that would sever my relationship with my brother forever.

Why am I doing this?

I asked myself the same question when I returned to my palace, weary and ready to melt into the arms of my wife. When, instead of Gwenyth, I was met by the vizier. When he opened his mouth and uttered the words that confirmed every doubt I had chosen to suffocate rather than fodder.

"Where is she?" I had asked. By the way his weathered face had gone white, I knew in my gut something was terribly wrong. That something had happened to her, to my wife, to my everything.

Not in a million years would I have expected the conversation that transpired.

"Kiran, I need you to come with me."

"Where is she?"

The vizier's face had sunk, his words swimming through the hot Meranthi air on the way to my reluctant ears. "Queen Gwenyth has committed treason. She and her lover were caught harboring a poison deadly to the fae. Your Majesty, they were plotting to murder you."

Why am I doing this?

Maybe it's because the woman I loved is gone, and there's nowhere else to spend my wrath.

Maybe it's because there weren't enough Flames coursing through my blood to purge her of what she did when she shattered me.

I don't know why I've declared through my human heralds that, due to the treachery of my queen, I will take a bride from the humans come the next mooncycle. I don't know why I will slaughter her the following morning.

What I do know, is that I will do this every mooncycle until, at last, this wrath threatening to end the world subsides.

Maybe I'll fail. Maybe it will end me instead.

CHAPTER 3

ASHA

Once my magic reached the end of its horrid tale, it took the three of us a moment to snap out of our stupor, to remember that what we had just witnessed—down to the scent of blood mingled with ash as our king devoured the Princess of Talens with his magic—was not real, but the result of my magic infiltrating our minds, enchanting our senses to see and hear and taste and feel what it wanted us to see and hear and taste and feel.

Except this was real. Or, at least, parts of it were. I never knew just how far my magic's sentience reached, how much of the world's events it witnessed versus how much it embellished based off the limited information it gathered through my ears and eye.

As usual, I was the first to emerge from the disorienting trance, which meant I was left to process alone my magic's version of what happened to cause our king to despise human women.

My skin still stung from the heat of his rage as he crushed Princess Ophelia's throat. It had billowed off his muscular form with such vigor, I had been convinced that I was the one suffocating. For a moment, I had assured myself the princess would live, that he would spare her life. It certainly seemed that way from the horror that crossed his molten eyes. But then his hands had glowed with a gentle pulse, reminding me of a lightning bug sending a beacon to its companions. It had almost been soothing.

At least, until the light had burst.

The fire hadn't burned Princess Ophelia. It had consumed her.

But that was nothing in comparison to what it had done to our queen when her husband had been informed of her betrayal, when he'd been told of the rare poison, deadly to even the fae, that she'd purchased just for him.

She hadn't even been graced with a proper execution. Typically, anyone who committed treason was awarded with an excruciating death—quite a public one, at that.

They hadn't even presented a body when they'd made the announcement.

There hadn't been enough of her left.

I tried to block the scent of singed flesh from my mind and focus instead on Dinah and my father. Their faces had slackened, and a bead of sweat broke across my father's face. After a few seconds, their cheeks began to twitch, as if their faces had been frozen in place, and the ice had started to melt off in uneven bits.

In a moment, they both blinked, understanding washing over their expressions.

"He killed her," Dinah whispered. "He really killed her. How awful." She slumped to the pillow on the floor and sat-cross legged, dumbfounded.

My father, on the other hand, looked keen as ever. "I'm assuming our queen's untimely end isn't what has you in a panic."

I shook my head, swallowing. Of course my magic would leave that part out, force me to tell it. "The king seems to be under the impression that all human women are traitorous wh—" My father shot me a warning look and my mouth changed course, "—olly adulterous usurpers."

My father's face relaxed in approval.

Dinah rocked a bit on her pillow, but when she spoke, her voice was calm. "It doesn't excuse his actions, but, can you imagine? Having someone ruin the relationship between you and your brother? Then learning your wife was plotting to murder you with another man's help? All in the span of a few weeks?"

Leave it to Dinah to make excuses for a male we just watched burn a human woman to a crisp.

"Well, I'd rather him not take it out on us," I said, to which Dinah and my father both shot me questioning looks. I sighed, grounding myself. "He's declared that every mooncycle, he's going to take a bride from among the humans. And the next morning...he's going to slaughter them."

Dinah gasped, but the only reaction the words garnered from my father was the slightest wince. As if he wasn't at all surprised.

Of course, he wasn't surprised. I was enough of a skeptic of the fae regime, and I had only lived under it for eighteen years. My father had spent five decades as their subject, mostly under the rule of the current king's predecessor, a cruel male fond of torturing humans, the poor ones in particular.

"The first offering is in a week. We need to leave tonight. Tomorrow at the latest," I said. There wouldn't be much to pack. If we started on it now, we could be crossing the gates in mere hours.

"Leave?" Dinah's eyes went hazy, as if the thought had never crossed her mind. It hadn't, I reminded myself. As poor as we were, Dinah never seemed to notice. As far as I knew, it had never bothered her that we slept on the ground, that the fae merchants sneered at us behind their subsidized stalls. But of course it hadn't. For as long as my sheltered sister had been old enough to care about politics, a human had been queen.

My mind whirled, rewriting my childhood dreams from Dinah's perspective. Would I have dreamt of being a queen? Of ever being in such a high position? As I gazed into my sister's beautiful caramel eyes, glistening with tears, I watched that very dream shatter.

She hadn't known what they were capable of.

My sheltered sister hadn't been taught that they were the enemy.

It didn't surprise me that my sister remained on the floor, shocked by the news that her home did not return her sentiment. But my father. Why wasn't my father moving?

"There's not much to pack," I said. "But we shouldn't dawdle. I'm sure there won't be room in between the gates within a few hours."

Neither of them moved.

"Listen, I know this is a shock—" I began to say, before my father interrupted me.

"We're staying here."

The shawl I had been forcing into a raggedy burlap sack sunk to the floor.

"What? Did you hear..." I fumbled, my outrage having gotten the better of my tone. My father wasn't stupid, and I wouldn't yell at him. Not after all he had sacrificed for me and Dinah. "Father, Dinah is going to make that list."

My father swallowed, the lines under his eyes streaked with fear.

"My child. There is nowhere to go."

"Nowhere to go?" I asked, the words catching on the back of my tongue. "What do you mean there's nowhere to go? There's Avelea. And Charshon. And Mystral. I know we're not used to the snow, but it's not like we're used to a life of glamour. We'd learn to be cold."

We'd learn to be cold. We'd have to. The fae soldiers would make their rounds tomorrow. It would take one look at Dinah for her name to be put on that list—most likely at the very top, if beauty was to be used not only as a qualification, but as a ranking.

"What are you expecting, my child?" Grief welled up in the lids of his eyes. "To be welcomed as refugees in the other kingdoms? You know of their history with humans. Our young king is not creative in his rulings. Calias, king of Charshon, is no stranger to taking young women into his courts. My heart aches for the women here who are to be taken and slaughtered. But Asha, one night with our king to meet the sword the next morning... It's civil compared to the others. What those girls endure day after day, year after year..." My father shuddered.

"Well, what about Laei or Avelea?" I asked. Surely there was some province in this entire continent where we could at least mind our own business. That was all father had ever wanted from life, anyway.

My father buried his forehead in his palm. "Those kingdoms are saturated with traffickers. Dinah's just as likely to be taken there."

"Well… We can't just stay," I said, though the words sounded less confident than they had in my head.

"I am afraid we don't have another choice. Even if we had anywhere to go, there's no making it across the Sahli, not anymore. Not without a pass."

A pass. A court-issued card that granted its owner royal protection to cross the horrid desert. There was no way a human could survive the journey without one, without the king's resources.

"But—"

"No," my father said, his face stricken but unmoving, all the same.

My next words caught in my throat. I turned toward Dinah, whose eyes had glazed over in the midst of our argument. After a moment, she caught me looking at her and straightened.

"Jealousy is a cruel and horrible thing. It's driven our fair king mad," she said, and the words seemed to clear the mist from her eyes. "But Asha, Father is right. I'd rather be here than anywhere else. Naenden is a haven compared to the rest of the world. My heart aches for the girls who will suffer at his hands, but… But this will not last forever."

My stomach churned. *The girls who will suffer.* How my sister could use that phrase, as if it were going to happen to someone else, and not to her, I didn't understand. I couldn't understand.

"Dinah, they're going to choose you," I said, my voice breaking.

"Asha!" my father warned, but Dinah smiled with that same look of adoration she always showed toward me.

My sister touched a hand to my collarbone. "You don't know that, Asha. It's just your fear. It speaks loud, but that doesn't give it any power. Or any truth."

I gently removed her hand, even as her well-intentioned words sent a pang through my chest. It wasn't my *fear* that whispered to me of my sister's demise. It was my magic, though it never bothered to make itself clear with words. No, overtaking my mouth was only worth its time when it had a good story to tell. Never mind warning my father and sister of the danger that lurked just beyond today's grasp. An otherworldly dread soaked my heart and fringed the edges of my sister. My magic knew Dinah was in danger. And, if it knew, I knew.

CHAPTER 4

ASHA

*A*z brushed his dark hair out of his sage-green eyes, as he often did when we sat atop his family's rooftop, which overlooked the goings on of the busy town below us. Business in the market was just getting started for the evening, the sun just beginning to set behind the clay-stone wall that surrounded the city. Light buzzed along its edge, and I figured it was as good of a distraction as any from my companion's exposed forearms. Why he insisted on rolling up his sleeves at night, when the West wind fluxed over the walls and danced atop the rooftops, I had no idea. Regardless, it was best I look away.

I wondered what was out there, past the streak of searing orange and pink that outlined that barrier between me and the rest of the world. I had not always dwelt within the capital's borders, but my parents had relocated from a small town on the outskirts of Naenden before my mind had developed enough to form memories, back before my father was crippled and his pass taken away, so the little I knew of the world came from stories he told, as well as the occasional book I managed to get my hands on.

"They're saying he strangled her. With his bare hands, just like he did his brother's wife." Az rose to his feet and paced on the edge of the roof. The sight clenched my chest, and I went dizzy for a moment. I hated when he did that. Hated what it reminded me of.

"Those are just rumors. That's not what I heard," I said, wondering how much of my magic's version of the story was any better than the whispering of our neighbors. It at least matched up with what the heralds had proclaimed, that the king had destroyed his wife so completely that there was no body left to display. "I heard his Flame consumed her before he could even touch her. That he was so heartbroken over her betrayal, it sort of just erupted out of him."

Az stood, his back to the edge of the roof, which he would surely topple off of soon. "How would you know that? Actually, you know what, never mind. I don't want to know. I don't—I can't understand. Our lives mean nothing to him, do they?" He must have caught the blood flowing from my face as I traced his footsteps with my gaze, panic rising in my chest, because he frowned. "Sorry, I forget that freaks you out."

That was an understatement. Watching Az balance on the edge of the rooftop sent me into a cold sweat, clamming my hands as I tried to unsee the flash of hot, blue light that haunted my sleeping hours. It had taken years after the incident for Az to cajole me back onto a roof at all. And even though this particular rooftop had become *our* place over the years, and I could sit on the edge without spilling my gut of its meager rations for the day, it still made me dizzy to see him in any position other than planted on his butt. Az found his place next to me, allowing his feet to dangle from the roof, and relief flooded over me.

"Can you believe it? One girl every mooncycle? Twelve a year," Az said, shaking his head. He cringed, and one might have wondered if it was because of his words or the frigid burst of wind that swept his hair back into his face. I didn't wonder, though. When you've known someone your whole life, the difference between a shiver at the cold and a shiver of dread were as evident as the difference between the stars and a piece of coal. There was no mistaking one for the other.

Az had been different lately, ever since the proclamation. Shaky, jittery.

Moody.

Not at all how he'd been the last several months, ever since returning from his adventures as a merchant's apprentice last year.

He'd come back from his trip to Avelea with a glimmer in his pale eyes. The merchant Tijan had seen a business opportunity and had carried Az with him.

It had been Az's first time to cross the Sahli desert.

He'd come back a new man.

No, he'd come back a *man*.

"Next time, you're coming with me," he'd said, a line I'd replayed in my mind more times than I dared admit to myself. "There's a whole world out there, Asha. A world where water runs faster than the fae, a world where humans don't have to hide from the sun." His eyes had gone determined, fierce then, and he'd glanced north, toward where the curve of the palace dome could be seen scraping the sky. "A world where *they* can't oppress us any longer."

I'd simply laughed and pretended my heart wasn't racing faster than an oncoming sandstorm at the way he spoke of the future as belonging to the two of us. "Right. A world where, instead of *them* ruling us, we can just be ruled by some other fae."

There wasn't a single kingdom left where humans remained in power. Hadn't been for centuries. Maybe longer than that. They hadn't exactly had time to cover a millenia worth of history in the few years of school human children were allotted.

He had just wrapped an arm around my shoulder and squeezed, a horrible gesture that my mind so often interpreted as being more than it was. "I don't know," he'd said, all those months ago. "Apparently, anything's possible. Haven't you heard about our new queen?"

I had frowned. I'd known that the king and prince of Naenden had traveled to Avelea to attend a ball, a ball in which the prince was to pick a bride to carry back with him. But the royal envoy hadn't returned yet, and so no, I had not heard.

He'd scooted in close then, his words laced with thrill. "I was there, Asha. I watched as he chose her."

"And?" I couldn't say I cared which spoiled fae princess had gotten a boost in an already noble rank.

"Asha. He chose a human."

I'd almost fallen off the roof from the shock. He'd then gone on to explain how, when it came time for the prince to choose his bride, he'd eyed the daughter of the rich human host. She'd been pouring drinks, and he'd picked her.

Wonder had filled Az's green eyes as he watched me drink it in. What that meant for us.

That there was someone close to the king, within his court, who might actually have our best interests in mind.

He'd grinned as a matching expression overtook my face. "What would you do," he'd asked, "ff you ever became Queen?"

I had snorted, and because news of the king's assassination had not yet made it back to Meranthi, I'd said, "Even the prince's new wife barely has a chance of that. You do realize her father-in-law is immortal."

"Oh, come on. Dream a little. What would you do, Queen Asha?"

Not that any of that mattered now. Because only a short year later, our human queen was dead.

"You fear for Sharina," I said. He nodded, his sharp jaw tightening as he clenched his teeth. I frowned. It wasn't every day that my friend showed signs of anxiety, even with the host of family responsibilities that had been laid on his shoulders when his mother had died, almost two years ago now. Az was the oldest of his mother's children. He had never known his father, and despite his attempts to wrangle a name from his mother his entire childhood, that secret had died with her. Az's step-father, the father of Az's five younger siblings, had died from the same plague, leaving Az the position of head of his house.

It had killed him to leave for Avelea on that merchant's endeavor. But the pay had been enough to support his siblings for the year, and Sharina, Az's sixteen-year-old sister, had proved her ability to keep the children in line while he was away.

"They won't take her...not any time soon," I said. He cut his gaze to me, and his green eyes widened.

Something tugged at my stomach—hard.

"How can you know?" he asked.

25

"You know."

"Yes, but...the...your *gift*... It gives you stories, right? The future? You've never been able to see the future before."

Gift. I smiled weakly. Az had inherited a superstition that dated back generations, back to before the fae and the humans had integrated. Back when even invoking the term *magic* was believed to summon a curse. I didn't quite share his paranoia, though I had no good argument to back up my stance. For Az, the contrast between how my face looked before the accident, and the one working eye that gazed up at him now... Well, that had been enough to reinforce his beliefs.

"I'm not saying I can see the future. All I know is that there's a presence I feel when my ma—my gift—takes over. It's almost like my gift is mischievous, in a way I've never been. And those feelings are so completely unlike mine, I can tell there's a difference between me and it. Even when I'm not telling a story, there are times I can still feel it within me. But this mischief... It's scared. It's terrified for Dinah. I think it must have gotten attached to her."

"How could it not?" Az smiled. Dinah's infectious kindness was known throughout the entire community. "I wish Sharina would take a few lessons from her about graciousness."

I chuckled, despite that pit of sinking sand in my stomach. No matter how hard I tried, I couldn't shake the way the Magic stirred within me as it heard the proclamation.

"My sister could take a lesson from yours in seeing reality for the ugly creature it is," I said. "I take it Sharina didn't act like everything was fine when she heard the news."

"Not exactly." Az sighed, running both hands through his hair this time, tugging at his dark strands until his ears peeked through.

Something pinched stomach again.

Az had kept his hair long for as long as I could remember. When we were children, I convinced myself that Az was fae, because how else could he have been so beautiful compared to the other children our age? Compared to me? There was no telling how many times I had forced him to show me his ears, to prove they were rounded, just in case pointed tips had burst through them overnight.

They never had.

"If they try to take her, I'll…" He gritted his teeth again. I placed a hand on his forearm, the warmth of his exposed skin flushing my chest with heat, even in the sharp wind.

"They won't. I'm telling you. My gift isn't worried for her." I tried to keep my voice steady, even as the heat rose to my face from the slight touch. There was never any reason to wear my veil around Az. He had long gotten over being distracted by the scars that lined the left side of my face. But part of me wished I had worn it tonight, if only to conceal my flushing cheeks.

"Well, that's got to be because your gift actually knows her," he said, and I let out a surprised laugh. Sharina possessed a *personality* all of her own, to put it the way the elderly women of Meranthi did.

I brought my hand back down to my lap, fearing the touch had already lasted too long for Az's comfort. He turned his sage-green eyes on me again as I pulled away. His arm fumbled a bit in the air, but then he brushed it against mine, his warm fingers wrapping around the hand in my lap. Pins and needles coursed up my arm, and I cut my eye away from his gaze.

How many nights had I dreamt of Az taking my hand in his? Only to wake up and remember that, in all those dreams, I had possessed two eyes. Not to mention a face that matched on both sides.

"At least I know they'll never take you away from me," Az said. My heart leapt in my chest, but only high enough to trip and stumble and come crashing down. I ripped my hand out of his. He stared at me, his eyes widening as his words finally circled back around into his ears and, more importantly, his brain. "I didn't mean it like that, Asha. You know I didn't."

"Doesn't matter." I busied myself gathering my skirts so I could stand without tumbling headfirst off the rooftop. Az clambered to his feet next to me. He might have extended a hand to help me up, but I pretended not to notice. He was standing on my blind side, after all.

As I shuffled away, I couldn't seem to distract myself from the way my tears streamed onto only one cheek.

CHAPTER 5

ASHA

"You've got to stop pining after that boy like a poor street dog begging for scraps," Bezzie said. She fixed her beady eyes on mine, even as she scrubbed dishes behind the counter. Something on the stove bubbled over and hissed, but it didn't seem to faze her.

My plate clattered on the counter as I jolted, nearly sending me toppling off my stool. I caught myself on the edge of the counter just in time, and the airborne leg of my stool landed with a thud on the ground, steadying me.

Heat flooded my cheeks, as I realized exactly which daydream Bezzie had so gently ripped me from.

Az and I had stood underneath a blanket, this one woven by Dinah just for us. We'd each held our own mirrors, dusty, lackluster things handed down to us from the last couple from our neighborhood to get married.

Because that's what we'd been doing, getting married.

And when we'd turned our mirrors upon each other, to witness our spouses for the first time, I'd made sure only the right side of my face was showing, grinning back at my best friend, my husband.

"I don't *pine*," I said, rolling a ball of lamb fried in cheap imported oil over my plate as I avoided her judgmental gaze.

"Mmm," Bezzie said. I sighed. There was no arguing with Bezzie, an elderly woman who had enough gumption to be the only woman in Meranthi to own her own storefront. Her homemade hummus had made her somewhat famous in the area, and she had spent her youth practically bullying innocent market-goers into purchasing it, regardless of the fact she didn't own her own stall.

Eventually, disgruntled stall-renters had driven her out, but by then, it was too late. The community knew of Bezzie's cooking, her ability to make even the smallest portion sizes feel satisfying to the hungry belly. They sought her out at her father's home until she could afford this place, a small apartment on the corner of Twin Alleys. She had extended the counter around the stove and had scavenged the streets of the wealthy district for perfectly useful thrown-out cushions.

And the people of Meranthi had come. In fact, so many of them had come that Bezzie now owned the apartment upstairs as well, and no longer had to sleep on the floor of her own restaurant.

So, in the end, there was no use in arguing with a woman who, if she decided something to be the case, usually made it so, even if it had not been true in the beginning.

"He held my hand last night," I said, deciding it wasn't worth trying to convince Bezzie I wasn't a pining fool.

Bezzie hissed so loudly, her voice drowned out the sizzling stew as it hit the stovetop counter.

"Do you think I'm an idiot for believing, somewhere down in him, he feels what I feel?" Heat surged to my cheeks as I lowered my voice. The man sitting on the opposite end of the counter leaned in closer. I turned my full face upon him. He startled and went back to inhaling his stew.

My face might not have been useful in attracting men. But, in my experience, I found there were more men out there worth repelling than attracting, so I tried to consider myself lucky.

"I don't call you a fool for believing what's true," Bezzie said, to which my heart lightened a bit. That is, before she sent it plunging back into the quicksand. "But I'll not put up with your blind spot when it—"

The man at the end of the counter sputtered on his stew.

Bezzie tapped her ladle against the counter, sending bubbling liquid spewing in the man's direction. "It's a figure of speech. Your bill's due. Ten coppers."

He drew back, aghast. "That's double the price on your menu!"

I swallowed, a meager attempt to stifle a laugh, because I knew what was coming next.

"I don't believe you read the menu. Or that you read at all. Because if you had," she whipped her ladle at a crusty sign on the wall next to the man, "then you would have expected the up-charge."

The man turned to read the sign, and his outrage turned to bewilderment.

For the sign read, *"Any customer who allows themselves to comment, laugh, chortle, spit, glare, stare, or otherwise act like a child with reference to the girl with one eye, will be up-charged double their original bill."*

In the end, he shook his head, slammed his coppers on the counter, and left.

Bezzie grinned. "I must admit, you're good for business."

I laughed. "I've got to start collecting a percent of the profit."

"Consider the free meal you get almost every day as your cut."

"Don't you worry you'll lose customers?" I asked.

"Oh, he'll be back. Hunger is a forgiving friend."

I laughed again, glad the topic had departed from my feelings for Az.

Bezzie cleared her throat. "Anyway, what I was saying was—" I groaned. "—that no one's saying the boy isn't fond of you in that way. All I'm saying is that Azrael is vain, too handsome for his own good. I've seen him gawking at the fae in the marketplace."

"Az hates the fae," I snapped.

"Yes, but does he hate them for who they are, or because they have what he does not?"

"If you're talking about the fae's *attractiveness*..." The word was bitter in my mouth, because I didn't like admitting it. Not when they all treated us so foully. "Az has no reason to be jealous. He's handsome enough that the fae females mistake him for fae all the time until they see his ears."

In fact, the fae females had a tendency to fall all over Az any time we were out in public. They never quite knew what to do with me, though. I could see it burning in their eyes, eating them alive. A question: What is *she* doing with *him*?

My stomach couldn't ever decide whether to deem that look worthy of annoyance or deep satisfaction.

"And is he flattered by their assumptions?" Bezzie asked.

"I—well, who wouldn't be?"

Beezie humphed. "All I'm saying is, while such a thing as appearances might not matter to you, they matter to him."

I didn't answer. Not because I didn't have thoughts on the topic, but because my heart cracked at the words. Leave it to Bezzie to be honest. I tried to stifle the anger welling within me. As candid as Bezzie was, she never said anything that didn't come from a place of loyalty.

It was true, as much as Az despised the fae, his hatred for them had become a bit of an obsession lately, especially after his mother died. But that was only because he had to have somewhere to direct his anger, so it didn't eat him up inside. Sure, it made me uncomfortable sometimes, when I'd catch Az staring at the fae in the marketplace, or when he'd try to get me to come up with theories about how the fae had come to dwell in Alondria in the first place, how they accessed their *gifts*.

But his mother had died. When my mother died, I went and got my face burned half off, so I didn't quite feel it was my place to judge.

Still, I did sometimes wish he spent more of his time staring at me.

Apparently, Bezzie could sense that she'd pushed me, because she graciously decided to change the topic. Not that the new topic lifted my spirits all that much.

"Our young king seems to be following in his father's footsteps, doesn't he?" Bezzie asked, a bit too loudly for my comfort. I turned to examine the rest of the restaurant before I breathed a sigh of relief. No fae here today. Only humans who would spit on gold if it meant tipping off the Royal Guard on one of their fellows.

"I wish you wouldn't speak of it so loudly in public," I said.

"You forget I have better peripheral vision than you," Bezzie said. The other man on the opposite end of the counter buried his head in his bowl of stew. Apparently, he didn't feel like paying double for his meal today.

"You're right, though. Bezzie, I'm nauseous over it," I said. A flood of shame washed over me. I'd allowed my own petty problems, my disappointment over Az, to distract me from the gravity of the proclamation.

"Why's that, child?" She scanned me with those beady eyes of hers. I figured she would normally make a joke about how neither of us had to worry about being chosen, but I must have looked like a trampled street puppy after our conversation about Az, because her voice betrayed more tenderness than I had heard in a long time.

"It's… I've just got this…" I paused. No one knew about my Magic other than my immediate family. And Az. It wasn't exactly *legal* for a human to possess magic in Naenden, never mind that the fae could use it as much as they wanted. It wasn't that I didn't trust Bezzie, but the fewer people who knew, the better. "I've got this horrible feeling they're going to pick Dinah."

I looked down at my plate, the one I hadn't been able to finish with all my emotions swimming around in my belly, taking up space.

Something soft landed on the back of my right hand. I looked, only to find Bezzie's hand on mine. It was cold, refreshing in midst of the heat leaking through the windows and off the hissing stove. It always surprised me how soft her wrinkles were, as if I expected her skin to be as rugged as her personality.

"I worry for her too," Bezzie said. I met her gaze, and those dark, beady eyes trembled a bit. I remembered that Dinah stopped by Bezzie's every evening, just before closing, to pick up a bag full of leftovers and distribute them amongst the beggars. Human and fae alike.

Bezzie let out a rattly exhale. "I know it's cruel of me. But I keep hoping there's some sad, suicidal soul out there who will answer the king's challenge. I know I shouldn't think thoughts like this. That I'll likely be punished for them. But maybe a girl betrothed to a cruel man against her will... Or one with a terminal illness..." Bezzie's voice wandered off, smothered in guilt at her admission.

I stared at her. "What are you talking about?"

"Did you not hear the entire proclamation, child?" Bezzie asked.

I shook my head. I had been too quick to run home. The thought that I could get my family out before the crowd scattered and clogged the streets had consumed my attention, and I hadn't bothered to listen to the rest.

As it turned out, the gates hadn't been clogged anyway. Apparently, none of us had anywhere to go. And even if we did, we had no way of surviving the journey.

"Oh, it's dreadfully cruel. I suppose the young king's heart must have gone terribly bitter. He's decreed that, should a young human virgin offer herself as the first bride, he will reverse the decree. That, once she is executed the next morning, not a single woman will perish at his hands, or be required to marry him."

Something twisted hard on my stomach as the meaning of Bezzie's words sunk in. Guilt.

Guilt because I had the power to stop the killings.

Guilt because I wasn't going to.

CHAPTER 6

ASHA

he king's scouts arrived on the doorstep of our hovel the next morning. The knock on the door was so brutal, my father thought someone was breaking in to rob us. Anyone who knew us would also know that the cripple and his two daughters couldn't defend themselves anyway, so why not just be direct about it and knock first?

After commanding Dinah and me to hide in the shadows obscuring the farthest corner of the hovel, he answered the door.

Relief flooded his face before the dread set in.

"Is this the residence of Arun?" the elderly fae male said. His voice sounded as worn as his face, and I wondered how old this fae must be to have patches of wrinkles on his forehead and at the corners of his mouth. No one really knew how long a fae could live. Just that none of them in recorded history had died of old age.

"Yes," my father replied curtly, staring down the two guards on either side of the older male. Both of them were high fae, human in appearance, except for their unnatural beauty. They returned his glare, though they didn't address it otherwise, for which I was grateful.

"I am the king's vizier. You are required by law to register any daughters you might have on the king's list of potential brides. I am here to…assess the candidates." The vizier shuffled on that word.

Assess.

My father paused just long enough for me to pinch Dinah's arm, a silent command for her to remain hidden within the shadows. Then I stepped into the light of the doorway.

"I am the daughter of Arun," I said. The two guards flinched.

The vizier did not. Instead, his dazzling eyes rested upon my scars. "I see." His gaze flickered to the corner for a moment, and my chest tightened. But then he nodded at my father. "I apologize for disturbing you in the early morning."

He turned and beckoned for the guards to leave, and the knot around my chest released. I glanced at my father. His jaw slackened, though his legs still trembled.

"Wait," one of the guards said. My heart plummeted. "There's one hiding in the corner."

The vizier paused, his back outlined in the blazing sunrise. He straightened his shoulders and turned. I made the split-second decision and stepped between him and Father. They wouldn't harm my sister. She was too beautiful, too valuable.

But the same couldn't be said of our father.

The vizier's eyes traced my path. The small step between where I had been standing and where I now stood, a fragile wall between my father and an elderly being who could take my life with a single swipe of his hand.

"I apologize for my oversight. My vision is not what it once was," the vizier said. I craned my neck at him. Remembered how his eyes had flickered to the corner, where he had surely sensed my sister moments before. Thanks to an ancient curse, fae lacked the ability to lie, but, rather than preventing their deceits, it had only made them experts at diction. I had a hard time believing the vizier hadn't seen my sister in the corner, but I supposed he'd never actually denied seeing her, had he? "Please step into the light, young one."

Dinah did as she was told, emerging like a star over the horizon as she stepped from the shadows. My gut twisted at the sight of her.

Never before had I felt the need to be jealous of my sister, to wish her beauty away, as if it detracted from mine. I had always thought she deserved every bit of smooth skin on her teardrop face, every one of her perfect teeth. My sister was simply the embodiment of her spirit. And for this, I could only find her lovely.

But today.

Had I thought ahead, had I known the guards would come here. At this hour. So soon after the decree...

I shuddered at the thought of what I might have done to my sister's face in the middle of the night.

One of the fae guards whistled. I sensed my father flinching at the sound.

Dinah's delicate body trembled, but she clenched her teeth and held her chin high. She didn't dare cower, even as the guards no doubt undressed her in their minds. I thought I might be sick.

"What does your assessment involve?" I asked, rounding on the vizier. I couldn't help but notice, as much as I didn't want to, that both guards' eyes flickered with lust.

The vizier locked his twinkling blue eyes upon mine. The corners of them drooped.

"It is already done, child," he said.

"Already done," I repeated, soaking in the words, their meaning— that the vizier would not allow my sister to be humiliated in front of these guards.

And then another realization.

"What is your name, child?" the vizier asked my sister.

Her voice shook, even as she raised her chin. "Dinah."

Dinah. A name for their list.

* * *

I DIDN'T SLEEP that night, though Dinah did, somehow. She lay beside me in our cot, her breaths shallow, few and far between. I couldn't understand it. My sister was no fool, no matter how hard she tried to pretend she was oblivious to pain. To fear. How could she sleep, knowing what had happened today, knowing her name was sure to go to the top of their lists? But, then again, I didn't think Dinah had ever experienced a nightmare in her life. So, perhaps, for her, sleep was a respite from the same dread that knocked upon my limbs, try as I might to steady them lest I wake her.

The nightmares had started long before I met my magic, cursed thing, useless thing. If only some worthwhile magic, keen on deception or fighting or changing minds, had decided to inhabit me. At least then I would have some way of protecting her.

The terrorizing dreams had occurred soon after our mother died. For months, I witnessed the death of my father and sister every time I closed my eyes. Starvation, thieves, bucked from a mule, lost in the desert. My little eyes had seen it all, without anyone to witness the horrors with me. I used to wake to Dinah blotting the tears from my face, holding me through the night until she managed to convince me she hadn't left forever.

Az had told me that similar nightmares oppressed him from time to time, though not nearly as often as they did me.

So Dinah lay next to me, enjoying a pause from whatever fears must be swirling inside her, despite her refusal to acknowledge them aloud. I didn't attempt to pursue sleep. If I was going to have to live out a nightmare anyway, I had no desire to allow my mind to indulge in putting a creative spin on our situation.

As it turned out, I didn't need my subconscious to spin the tale of my sister's demise. I was doing quite a stand up job of that myself.

I tried to force my eyes open, but every so often my lids would meld with the darkness of our hovel, and Dinah's death would flash before my eyes. Beautiful, stunning in her scarlet wedding robes and painted face. Death cooling her warm eyes as blood stained her dress a deeper shade of crimson. Sometimes, a knife in her chest. Mostly, the king's brutish hands around her neck, crushing the breath from her throat and the life from her eyes until there was nothing left. Nothing except the shell of my sister.

My legs trembled. My torso and arms quaked until I could not fathom how my sister continued to sleep.

There's a much higher chance they won't choose her than a chance they will, I attempted to reason with myself. Except, myself reasoned back. *The first mooncycle maybe. But how many young virgins do you think live in Naenden? And how many mooncycles before she is no longer considered beautiful?*

Too many.

Perhaps we could marry her off. We would have to wait until the next mooncycle, after the king had slaughtered his first bride. As Dinah's name had already been placed on the list, she was not permitted to become betrothed until after the king's wedding.

But my sister was only sixteen. And even if my father would allow it, which I doubted considerably, I didn't know I could stomach such a thing. Marrying my vibrant sister off to an old bachelor to live out the rest of her days in an existence she never would have picked for herself.

No, that would not do.

But then, there was another option.

My stomach twisted into a knot, and I gulped down the bile rising in my throat. I wouldn't wake Dinah if I could help it.

My muscles spasmed and trembled all night, to the point that I wondered whether it was possible to become feverish from fear alone.

Because by the time the sun crept over the horizon, its rays slipping through the uneven cracks between the door and its frame, I had discovered a way to keep from imagining Dinah's lifeless eyes at the hands of the king.

I simply imagined my own.

CHAPTER 7

ASHA

I left before either Dinah or my father woke. It wasn't Dinah's gaze I feared. No, one look into those innocent eyes, and courage would have filled my bones, as well as resolve.

It was my father's gaze I couldn't bear. The look of a man who loved me so desperately, he had given up his gait to keep his ugly daughter safe from a set of bored fae males. Like the ones from the market. Father hadn't walked straight since.

He would never agree with my decision. As much as he loved Dinah, I knew exactly what he would say if I tried to convince him why I must do this dreadful thing.

Why would I sentence one daughter to a certain death over the possibility of losing the other? Better to lose neither of you, my child. That's what he would have said, had I told him.

But as much as my father and sister reassured themselves that Dinah's life was not nearly as endangered as I thought, I would not be convinced.

It took me the better half of the morning to walk to the palace. This was only natural, because what king would wish to position themselves adjacent to the slums of Meranthi? My neighborhood was full of destitute humans who might just be desperate enough to attempt an assassination, if only because they had become bored enough with the pointlessness of their lives to resort to such a glamorous suicide. Not that a poor villager would ever succeed in murdering the king. But I was sure he would consider it an inconvenience, nonetheless.

By the time I reached the palace gates, my trek had provided me plenty of time to consider my plan. Not reconsider. Just admit to myself that I had absolutely no plan at all. As I had left the proclamation early, I had no idea how a human woman was supposed to go about contacting the king to inform him she had accepted his sick proposal. It seemed just as possible that the proclamation had allotted no guidelines. I had a sneaking suspicion the king didn't expect a human woman to be virtuous enough to take him up on his offer.

Well, I'd show him.

Right before he turned me to ash.

The sight of the palace never failed to boil my blood. Which was saying something on a day like today, when the sun radiated against its pinnacles, glaring down on me, as if in judgment for even approaching such a gluttonous place.

The entire facade was made of white-washed marble that reflected sunlight. It was the only light-colored thing in this city that didn't burn to a crisp in the excessive heat. Instead, it projected the heat onto the section of the city surrounding it. As if its inhabitants needed any more of that particular commodity. Not that I cared too much, for the apartments that surrounded the palace were at least half as glamorous. Each one of them could have housed and fed all the beggar children of Meranthi. So no, I supposed it didn't bother me all that much that it might be difficult for them to step outside on a regular basis. Especially since they had no need to.

The rest of the palace etched the skyline in pointed domes, each as sharp as they looked, in case the Fates ever decided to descend upon us.

And the gate. I couldn't tell if it was actually encrusted with gold leaf or an alloy that would hold strong against an oncoming threat.

As I approached the gate, I pulled my thickest veil over my face. I was fairly certain the exception to the decree hadn't specified that the sacrificial virgin had to be beautiful, but I didn't trust the guards to have been listening that carefully, and I surely didn't care to have them ruin my chances of speaking to someone better informed.

"We don't give handouts to beggars, woman," one of the guards said as I approached them, my head bowed low in feigned reverence. Perhaps they would be vain enough to believe the act and never bother to check my face.

"I request no handout. Nor am I a beggar. I have come to offer something of value to the king."

The guards broke into laughter. One of them shoved me hard enough to knock me a few steps backward. "Get away, leech. What could a beggar woman give to the king that he doesn't already have in plenty?"

"I wish to offer myself as a bride to the king. In return for the king's mercy on my fellow kinsmen."

A pause, one that made me wish I could risk looking up at them. Then, one of them grabbed me by the shoulder and ripped the dark scarf from my face. It yanked at my hair as he uncovered me, and I bit back a gasp.

"The girl's a witch," one of them sneered.

"Think you could get close to the king, did you?" the other guard asked, not bothering to withhold his spit as he growled at me. He clenched my hair, sending a jolt of pain through my scalp. His breath soured in my nostrils, and I thought I might gag. I hadn't realized the soldiers were Scriel. Scriel were lesser fae, though they didn't consider themselves as such. Their almost-bald heads and scaly skin gave them an ogreish quality. It was said that the least civilized of them feasted on human flesh.

Surely, as cruel as the young fae king might be... Surely he had enough propriety not to keep flesh-eating lesser fae around.

"If I were a witch..." I said, holding my head high. Now that my secret was out, there was no use in cowering. "I'd conjure myself a different face. Especially if I intended any harm to the king. How else would he consider me amidst all the fae princesses longing for his hand?"

This seemed to startle the guards, and they turned to one another in consideration.

"Get," one of them said as he waved me aside.

"The king won't be accepting the likes of you," the guard holding me said as he thrust me away. I had to steady myself so not to hit the ground face-first.

Pushing myself off the ground, I batted the dust from my robes and stood. "Do you presume to make decisions for the king?" The sun glared down on my exposed face, and I wrapped myself again with my scarf, daring myself not to cough as dust entered my nostrils.

"It doesn't take presumption to know he won't be interested in marrying you," the guard still standing by the gate said.

"Perhaps one might have said that of Queen Gwenyth," I said. The guards exchanged a measured glance. I wondered what was going through their minds. Perhaps they wondered about their young king's preferences and thought there might actually be a chance he would fancy me.

I tried to bite down a laugh.

"I won't take you to the king. But I'll take you to someone who'll know what to do with you. Since you're insistent on bothering us and I don't feel like murdering today," the guard added, lest I assume he allowed me into the gates out of pity.

"I understand." It was the closest phrase I could find to a *thank you* without telling a complete lie.

The guard took me by the nape of my neck and beckoned to his friend. The other guard retreated behind a large stone wheel with a handle, which he started to spin until the doors creaked and whistled open. And then we were through.

As soon as we entered the gates, a rush of cool air settled over me. Rumors had spread to the streets of Meranthi that the fae king employed wind faeries to regulate the temperature surrounding his home. I had mostly thought it to be a superstition of the hopeful and destitute, and of those who groped for a reason to be angry. Well, angrier than they already were. But as the cool air hit my skin, I found myself breathing it in, allowing it to invigorate my lungs and fill me with life, though guilt instantly plagued my chest for indulging in it. Who was I to enjoy the breeze when my people suffered in the heat of the day?

But then I remembered what had led me here. A surge of anger boiled through me. I sucked in the cool air, as if I could steal a little of the pleasant weather from the king himself as revenge.

Well, it made me feel better, at least.

"It's not yours to enjoy," the guard growled at me.

I wanted to say, *Oh yeah, and isn't this half the reason you're allowing my counsel? So that you'll have a few moments in the shade?*

But I thought better of it and walked beside him without response.

I became keenly aware of my own filth, my own odor, as we walked into the main foyer. I had never set foot in a foyer before, I realized. In fact, the only living quarters with more than one room that I had visited was Bezzie's apartment.

Every bit of this room, one certainly meant for first impressions, seemed to blanch at me. The dust from my skirts had already left a film of the outside world on the otherwise pristine marble tiles. A great chandelier hung from the ceiling, casting prisms of light about the white-washed walls of the room. The glass figurines perched around the room on cedar pedestals looked as though they might shatter if a rogue gnat were accidentally let in.

Untouchable. That was clearly the intended message from whomever had decorated this place. And here I was, muddying the foyer.

In my defense, there was no welcome mat as far as I could see.

"Rand," the guard called.

A moment later, a thin, prudish looking fae in robes a bit too pale for royalty and a bit too indigo for servitude shuffled up and eyed me with disgust.

"She'll need to be swept after. On the way out, too. If she lives through her council, that is," the guard told him.

I swallowed and tried to enjoy the scene as we walked down the hallway. The patters and grunts of Rand, who I assumed to be the chief of servants, echoed down the maze of hallways as he dusted the floor behind me. Truth be told, I found my cheeks flushing at the whole ordeal. People staring at my scars—that, I was used to. But no one had ever noticed my filth before. Not when it coated even the folds of our fingerprints back in my neighborhood.

Finally, we arrived at a small cedar door, ornately carved with a lion's crest.

"Word of advice," the guard said.

Why did I get the feeling that whatever he said next would be immensely unhelpful?

CHAPTER 8

ASHA

"*I*'d get your words out before the vizier gets a chance to look at you."

"The viz—?" I started to ask, but then the guard opened the door. And there I was. In the office of the man who had tried to ignore my sister but, in the end, had etched her name into his list all the same.

Books upon books upon books lined the cedar shelves of the vizier's office. Even with my poor depth perception, I could still make out the names of titles gilding the leather spines. They shone so brightly of golden paint. My heart gave a tiny wrench as I imagined my father sitting at home on his tattered pillow, reading with squinted eyes his lone book that no longer clung to its spine. I decided then and there that I had one question for the vizier to determine whether I hated him or could tolerate him. Not that it would matter much to him, being a high fae as well as a noble official. But, at this point, I was relishing the small things.

He beat me to the questioning.

"Why are you disturbing me, Roe?" the vizier asked, not bothering to peer up from behind his half-rimmed spectacles. That was what I would do if I had more time to live. I would save up and buy my father spectacles. "Are you not aware the king has decided to limit plea hearings to once every other mooncycle?"

I might have allowed my eyebrows to raise a hair. Was that disapproval I sensed in the vizier's voice? Not directed at Roe, but toward the king himself?

"She's not here for a plea. I assure you, she'll be whipped if this turns out to be a waste of your time." Roe tightened his grip on my neck. I winced, and the vizier's gaze shifted at the pitiful sound. His eyes rested on my face, and he blinked once. I wondered if he recognized me, until I remembered that, of course, he did.

How could he not?

The vizier pursed his lips. "Now, I don't see why that would ever be necessary. Is it this woman's occupation to filter who and who does not enter my presence and receive my council?"

The grip on the back of my neck loosened.

"Well, no sir. I just—"

"Remind me, Roe. Whose responsibility would that be?"

"But the girl—"

"A one-word answer will do just fine," the vizier said, smiling pleasantly, though his wrinkles delved no deeper behind his spectacles.

"Mine," Roe finally conceded.

I swallowed hard, hoping to stifle the giggle that was trying to escape my lungs at the moment. Why, in Alondria, I was giggling right before I was about to sign my death sentence, I had no clue. But at least I wasn't bawling my eye out.

"Why exactly have you brought this woman to me Roe?" the vizier asked.

"She's capable of speech, believe it or not," Roe sneered. The laughter in my chest turned to molten brimstone. How easy it would have been for Roe to relay my request himself. But no, he was going to make me say it again. Make me force the words out of my reluctant, swollen throat.

Just get the first word out. The first word and then the rest will follow.

The vizier widened his eyes expectantly.

The first word, Asha.

"I... I am here to offer myself as a wife for the king in exchange for the guaranteed safety of my fellow human women." The words rushed out of my mouth, just as I had hoped they would. Just as I had practiced.

The vizier scowled.

Roe scoffed. "You see. I told you she wasn't worth the effort. But I couldn't not bring her down here because of the decree, even though she doesn't fit the mold with that—"

"Out." The vizier's voice was even and quiet as he jolted from his seat and pierced me with those cool blue eyes. They reminded me of two small pools on the rugged desert of his wrinkled skin. From where did this fae come, with eyes too light to brace our ruthless sun?

"But, sir—"

"Out."

I didn't turn as I heard Roe shuffle out and slam the creaky wooden door behind him.

"Why?" the vizier asked, his voice shrill before it was muffled by the plethora of books and scrolls that soundproofed his walls.

"My sister," I said, surprised at how easily the words came. Because I had a sister. Of course, what an obvious answer. So obvious, I wondered why the vizier had asked in the first place.

"I see." The vizier sighed. Almost as if he were crumbling, he fell back into his plush scarlet chair. "Your sister is a beautiful girl. Does her face reflect her character?"

So he did recognize me. "That would be an understatement," I said.

The vizier bowed his head and pinched the bridge of his nose between his weathered fingers.

"If you're concerned with my appearance, there is nothing in the proclamation stating that the woman who offers herself must be beautiful." *I think*, I didn't add.

He simply stared at me. Unsure of what to do with my trembling hands, I balled them into fists at my side, hoping to cover the evidence of my fear between the folds of my skirts.

48

The vizier sighed, and he frowned again, though not unkindly. "Your appearance has little to do with my concern."

Figuring I was dead as a human who wandered too far from an oasis, I decided engaging in a dialog was not going to hurt my survival chances all that much.

"What concerns you, then?" I asked, my heart hammering in my chest, as if it were begging to be let out. As if to say, *This one's defective. This one's suicidal. I demand a new one.* Shameful as it was, there was a part of me—a significant part of me—that hoped the vizier would turn me away. That he'd declare me too ugly to accept.

But then I thought of Dinah.

My magic's fear, my fear, for her swelled up within my chest, overcoming my primal need for survival.

"I'm not sure how many good ones of you are out there, but it doesn't sit too well with me to kill you off," he said. "You are aware that the mooncycle renews in six days?"

"Yes."

"You are aware you are volunteering to marry the grieving king?"

The word lodged itself in my throat like a jagged rock. "Yes."

"You are aware of what marriage entails?"

I cringed. "Yes."

"And you are aware you will be slaughtered the next morning?"

Silence.

And then.

"Yes."

The vizier's chest appeared to deflate. "Very well." He flourished a scroll from behind him and spread it open on his desk. "You can write?"

I nodded. Not well, but I doubted that mattered.

"Then sign here." He pointed to a line at the bottom of the scroll.

I scanned the tiny scrawl of the contract, just to make sure nothing I signed would cause any trouble for my family. When nothing seemed amiss, well, other than the part about my public execution, I grabbed the quill from the vizier's outstretched hand and printed my full name.

The vizier raised his eyebrow.

"If you want your citizens to sign your documents in script, perhaps you should invest more in our education," I snapped.

"Hm," he said, peering at me curiously before he rolled up the scroll. "You are to be married in six days. I'll send a pair of guards to retrieve you at dawn the day of the ceremony. No need to bring any of your possessions, unless you would like to, of course. You are free to go."

I gulped. "That's it?"

"Were you expecting otherwise?"

I shook my head, feeling silly. My mind still spinning, I turned to let myself out. As the door creaked open, I remembered I still had one question.

"Sir?"

The vizier looked up from his parchment, which he had not seemed to be reading at all, rather just glancing over quickly with glazed eyes.

"Yes?"

"Have you read all these books?"

The vizier turned back to his parchment without a word. Assuming he had considered my question unworthy of an answer, I pushed the door open. But, as I nudged the door back into place, I thought I heard a quiet voice.

"Thrice."

CHAPTER 9

ASHA

*E*ach day that passed, each moment leading up to my execution, I intended to tell my father and sister what I had done. But every time I summoned the courage to open my mouth, Dinah would ask for a story about us. One where the three of us escaped the slums of Meranthi after trekking across the desert, only to find a colony of humans thriving in some evergreen land untouched by fae rule. My magic would give in to her begging. I would tell myself that it stole my voice, but I gave it freely, so it could tell us legends of a colony of human assassins who lived in the hills of Avelea. Humans who would someday overthrow the fae. I held the stories close to my heart, telling myself they were true, though reason told me otherwise.

I sometimes worried that my magic wouldn't have enough time to finish this last tale.

When Dinah wasn't asking me for stories, my father would mention something to the effect of how much I reminded him of my mother. He didn't have to say he missed her dearly, or that I provided some amount of solace for her loss. We both knew it to be the case.

And so, every time I opened my mouth, and I nudged the truth forward, driving it up my dry throat and to the cusp of my tongue, guilt snapped my jaw shut into a forced smile.

I'd tell them tonight. I would. After I finished the story Dinah had fallen asleep to last night.

My father sat reading by the light of the lamp one evening as I prepared dinner. I had wanted lamb for dinner, my last meal in this home, possibly in this life, depending on how generous those at the palace were feeling tomorrow. But the wretched fae meat vendor had sold the last bit of lamb to the faerie standing in line behind me. I had been too weary to even argue. Now that I prepared our rice and vegetable broth, I wondered if my stomach would have even processed the meat. If I could keep any food down tonight. The odor of the boiling broth snaked into my stomach and twisted, threatening to spill its contents. Not that there was much in my stomach these days.

An angry creak alerted me that Dinah was home. I jumped at the sudden noise, spilling onto the floor a handful of rice that I had just been about to put into the stew.

"My child," my father scolded mildly, mostly for the break in Dinah's character rather than the noise itself. He hardly bothered to chastise me for my innate loudness in moving from place to place anymore.

"Father, Asha," Dinah gasped, out of breath. I turned to look. Her scarf slipped down the back of her wind-tossed hair. Her cheeks flushed red.

My father stood from his seat, his knees causing almost as much of a ruckus as the hinges of the door had. "What is it, child?"

My stomach melted. Dinah had just gone to the market.

"We're saved!" Dinah flung her arms around me, burying her face into my hair. Oh, Dinah. She wasn't even feigning kindness when she implied I was also at risk of being taken by the king. She truly believed it. "Oh, I feel terrible for even finding joy in it. It's so dreadful. I'm sick for the poor girl... But I suppose a soul so brave would want us to rejoice in our freedom..." she said, her voice solemn now.

"What nonsense are you speaking?" my father asked, though not unkindly. He hobbled toward her, concern stretched across his face. And the slightest bit of hope, that dreadful feeling I wished he would not entertain.

I gulped.

"They declared it today. The king is to be married tomorrow. And it's to a human girl who offered herself. Tomorrow will end it. The rest of us are safe."

My father burst into sobs, as I had never seen him do before. He wept and tears fell from his cheeks into our hair.

A waft of broth hit my nose, and I vomited.

My father lurched back, but Dinah, after a single startled moment, ignored the rank mess on her clothes and wrapped my hair around her left hand, placing the right on my shoulder as I emptied the contents of my stomach.

"Oh, Asha. I know. There are so many emotions at once. You're better than I am, to feel that girl's pain so deeply..." Dinah kept on like that, until I wasn't hearing her words anymore. But my father.

My father.

My gaze found him as Dinah wiped my mouth with the edges of her robes.

Tears still stained his cheeks, but they no longer flowed freely. The relief that had been in his eyes just a moment ago had been replaced by darkness. By cold itself.

"What did you do?" he asked.

I dry heaved.

* * *

WHEN I STUMBLED into Bezzie's place, my hair still reeking of vomit, the echo of Dinah's sobs still ringing in my ears, the last customer was just leaving.

"Bezzie, I'm afraid I've done something foolish."

Bezzie looked up at me from behind the counter, her grey wisps of hair curling out from underneath her kitchen scarf in wild, untamed knots.

A glint of suspicion sparked in those cold grey eyes of hers. "Is it to do with young Azrael?"

I pondered her question for a moment, and not for the first time, either. Since my meeting with the vizier, I had tumbled my motivations over in my mind. Had I truly offered myself up with pure intentions? To save Dinah from even the fear, the possibility of such a fate?

The answer had been a resounding yes. Of course I was doing this for Dinah.

But then there was that nagging thought. That perhaps Bezzie's assessment of Az's feelings for me, that they would never outweigh his vanity, had made it a tad bit easier, had contributed to my willingness.

But, even if there was some glimmer of truth in the thought, I decided I wouldn't give it any weight. If I was going to die at the hands of the fae king, I was going to die brave in my own mind. My own judgment. Not a silly girl who counted her own life worthless after being rejected by a silly boy.

"No," I finally settled upon.

"Well, that's a relief to hear," Bezzie sighed with a bit more enthusiasm than was necessary. "I know you're fond of him, Asha. And I won't deny he's a decent kid. But decent is all he is. Especially the way he drags you on."

I fought back a wince. Brave, brave. I was going to die brave.

"I don't want to talk about Az right now," I said, so hastily that Bezzie shut her mouth. The wrinkles on her worn face softened, and her beady eyes widened in concern.

"What's troubling you, child?" She reached behind her and plucked a stew from the hot coal stove and placed it on the wooden counter in front of me.

"I'm not hungry." I attempted to push the bowl away from me as politely as possible. "Maybe we could give it to one of the beggars?"

Bezzi fixed her coal eyes on me.

"When was the last time you've eaten, child?"

I didn't answer.

"Has your father fallen upon hard times?"

I shook my head. What a strange question. I imagined that

someone looking in on Meranthi from the outside would have assumed we were all living through hard times.

But Bezzie and I both knew the difference between portioning out our rations and stewing cactus needles just to trick our stomachs into feeling full for an hour or so.

"No, we're doing fine. I've been giving my rations to the beggar on the corner of Twin Alleys." Never mind it was because I couldn't hold down the food.

Bezzie's eyes narrowed in judgment. "You are aware that you also need to eat, aren't you?"

"Yes," I said, though there was no truth in it. Why did it matter if I did or didn't eat? It wasn't like my body would need the sustenance for much longer.

"Well, then. Explain yourself," Bezzie said. Just then, a customer walked in from the streets. Before a word could escape his mouth, Bezzie held a palm out to silence him. The man stormed away, furiously rambling about how he'd never frequent this business again. The whole time, Bezzie didn't take her eyes off me. As intimidating as her stare was, I couldn't help but be grateful. Bezzie would scrape the truth out of me if she had to use her ladle to do it.

"The king's decree—"

Bezzie laughed. "Good thing the two of us don't qualify!"

I offered up a weak smile, rather than my usual laugh. Bezzie was the only one who felt comfortable enough to tease me about my scars. Truth be told, she was the only one who actually acknowledged them. At least, of the people who cared for me. Those on the street always had a way of reminding me how unsettling my face must look.

"Tell me what's wrong this instant, child," Bezzie said, registering danger when I didn't join her in laughter. "Is it Dinah? Are they taking Dinah?" Her eyes went bleak with terror for my sister. Warmth bellowed up within me and filled my chest.

"No, it's not Dinah," I said. The air seemed to leave my lungs, as if my whole body was protesting my confession with all its might, as if saying the words aloud would speak them into existence. Make them real.

"It's me," I said.

For a moment, Bezzie looked me up and down, her jaw unhinged slightly. I could see the cogs in her mind spinning, searching for any plausible reason the king would have picked me. Her eyes scanned the air around my edges, searching for a way in which she must have misheard me, misinterpreted my words.

"I don't understand, girl." Just then, I knew then I had committed a great injustice against Bezzie, for making her feel simple, when she most certainly was not.

"The clause. The exception."

Bezzie's eyes widened in realization.

"I offered myself. And it's happening tomorrow."

I couldn't bring myself to say I'd be married. Something about that dream my magic had squashed long ago seemed agonizing now that it was happening.

Bezzie gasped. The ladle she'd just been holding clattered on the floor.

"You foolish girl," she said.

I prepared for the full flood of her anger, but her hard eyes flickered past me and landed on the entrance.

My empty stomach hit the dusty floor.

I knew who'd overheard me, even before I turned to find him slipping his hood over his head and slinking out the door into the crowded streets.

Az.

CHAPTER 10

ASHA

"*Az*, Az, please wait up," I called to him. I tracked his grey robe as it wove through the street crowd, bustling with urgency as the market would be closing within the half hour.

A faerie in a woven green hood bumped into my side. "Watch where you're going," he grumbled, but I ignored him and pushed on.

My heart raced to the pace of my feet as I ran after Az, bumping into and off of market shoppers on the way. Grey wasn't an easy color to spot, especially in the dim market lamp light, but at least he wasn't wearing scarlet and indigo like all the faeries who inhabited the streets.

"Az!" I called again, but no one in the crowd turned their head.

Once I reached the edge of the marketplace, I ducked into the few alleys that I figured he could have escaped into. They were all empty. Perhaps he went home? My heart rose into my chest at the thought, and my cheeks flushed. I couldn't bear to have this argument in front of his family, not with what it might imply existed between us. Well, for me, at least.

So I searched for him in the one place I knew we could have this conversation in private.

* * *

As soon as my head peeked over the edge of the roof, I saw him. His back slumped like a wilting plant in the sand as his feet dangled carelessly off the overhang.

"You weren't going to tell me, were you?"

I bit my lips and swung myself onto the roof before coming to sit next to him. He didn't stir as I sat, didn't bother to look at me as his gaze traced the path of his feet as if they were twin pendulums. So this was how it was going to be.

"I was saving telling you for last," I said.

He gritted his teeth. "That's a pretty clever way to admit you've been avoiding it."

"Alright. So I've been avoiding it," I said, mirroring his posture and staring at the stars rather than continuing to try to get him to look me in the face. I wasn't even sure I wanted him to look at me.

"You should have told me what you were planning to do before you went off and did something so stupid."

Tears sprung up in my eye as that word punctured my chest. *Stupid.* He was just angry, afraid, upset, I had to remind myself. "It's not stupid if it saves Dinah's life."

Az buried his face into his hands and groaned. "We didn't even know if she would be chosen. Do you know what the chances of that were? Do you know how many women live in Meranthi?"

"Not enough to outnumber the mooncycles in an immortal fae's life."

"She would have aged out before they got around to her."

"You don't know that. You weren't there when they assessed her. For all we know, they had a ranking system. Dinah would have been at the top of the list."

"So you just forced yourself to the top of the list instead," he said, his words acid as he stared at the streets below.

The lump in my throat swelled. "I am the list."

"Yeah, you just had to go and make yourself a martyr."

My throat burned, and I wanted to shake him, to scream he didn't have any right to speak to me that way. That he should be holding me, keeping me warm on one of my last nights to live. But I swallowed the anger before it could ferment and reminded myself that I had hurt him, not the other way around. "You would have done the same for your sisters, if you could have."

Az shook his head. His dark, wavy hair fluttered in the evening wind, giving him this dazzling, unkempt beauty that made my heart flutter, even in my frustration. "I have a responsibility to Sharina. But you know who I also have a responsibility to? My other siblings. I would never be so foolish to go and get myself killed. Not when I have so many people who depend on me."

"Well," I said, my throat going dry. "Then it's a good thing it was me and not you. Because no one's depending on me." I forced a smile in a weak attempt to communicate that I wasn't angry. That I was just stating the truth.

Az turned his dark glare on me. Finally. The fire melted out of them when he glimpsed the tears running down my face. His hand slid across the rough roof and over mine, sending a buzzing warmth up my arm and a flush to my cheeks that I hoped he couldn't see in the darkness.

Not that there was any use in hiding my feelings now. Not when I'd be dead in less than two days.

"That's not what I meant," he whispered.

"I know."

"What about your responsibility to me?" he asked, his sage-green eyes going wide, vulnerable as he brought his hand to my cheek and wiped away the tears. His body leaned in, and I couldn't help but notice how close his face was to mine. My chest tightened, and I could feel his warmth drawing me in. Closer.

What about your responsibility to him?

The thought almost made me jump, it was so unwelcome. So uncomfortable.

Uncomfortable enough to cause me pause. I forced myself to pull away for just a moment.

"What exactly is my responsibility to you?" I asked, my words soft, fearful. So weakly spoken, I was surprised the wind hadn't whisked them away.

"Asha, we've been friends since before we could walk."

My heart slumped from its bed in the stars, the one it had been presumptuous enough to assume when he'd leaned in, just a breath away from kissing me. "Last I checked, friends didn't owe each other their choices. Last I checked, I didn't owe my friend my sister's life."

Az's face tense and he squinted. "That's not what I meant, and you know it."

"Then what did you mean?"

Az let out an agitated sigh. "Just that you should have told me first. That we're... Crap, Asha. You know what we have is more than just friendship."

"You've never said anything."

"Yes, and I guess now I'll never have to," he said, pushing himself to his feet and pacing to the other side of the roof. He stopped there, crossing his arms as the stars provided a backdrop for his dark silhouette.

Rage boiled up inside me. The years of pining, the aching, all bubbling to the surface. The thousands of occasions he could have told me how he felt, any of which could have changed the one moment that was going to kill me. The thousands of conversations that could have led to us being married, to a moment where I learned of the exception, but wouldn't have been forced to make the decision, because I wouldn't have qualified anyway. And for him to suggest that I *owed* him something, some consideration in my decisions that went beyond friendship...

"You never said anything," I said, with greater force this time. "I could have married someone else, and you never would have had the right to complain about it, because you—"

"Yeah, well we both knew that wasn't going to happen," he said.

The wind seemed to halt in place, as if to turn its head to confirm it had just heard what it thought it heard. A blade in the form of his voice shattered my ribs, and by the time he turned to me, by the time his face went pale and his jaw dropped in stunned regret for the words that had just come spearheading out of him, out of his heart, it was too late.

He'd already crushed me.

I'd allowed him to.

"Asha, I didn't mean that," he said, rushing to me, clutching my hands. "Please, Asha. I didn't mean it. I'm just so afraid..." His voice trembled, and the tears began to flow. "I'm just so afraid of losing you."

He buried his face into my shoulder, and I found my hands making their way to his hair, to stroke it, as they might have stroked Dinah's hair when she'd busted her knee as a little girl.

Az wept for a long while, and trembled in the cold wind for longer than that. I held my friend all night, let him mumble his frantic apologies, all the while wondering what it would have been like to have him comfort me about my own death.

CHAPTER 11

ASHA

A servant girl painted my lips red. Why? I had no idea. Perhaps to match my scarlet veil, which would reach from the top of my head to my restless bare toes. Not that anyone could see my paint under my veil. But that was beside the point.

I hated the way the substance gummed between my lips. Whoever had invented this paint must not have had ease of communication among their top priorities, which I now realized, *was* probably the point. I wished my father and Dinah could be here with me. The guards issued with escorting me to the palace arrived before dawn, earlier than the vizier had said they would, and I'd barely gotten the chance to say goodbye.

"You look stunning," said the fae female applying my makeup. I smiled weakly back at her. There was something familiar about her eyes. They were kind, despite their paleness and their lack of contrast to her milkweed skin. They reminded me of eggshells—the green ones I always picked in the market for their odd color. When she spoke to me, she looked at my whole face, not just the cavern where my eye should've been. She must have meant the compliment.

Or perhaps she just felt sorry for me. I was going to be slaughtered tomorrow morning, after all.

I crumpled the silky fabric of my wedding gown in my hand. It was smooth to the touch and could've fallen from my fingertips had I not gripped it so tightly. Red. That was the color of birth, of weddings, of a bride.

And the color of something else.

I bit my newly painted lips to hold back the tears. I must've ruined the paint, for the girl reapplied it as quickly as I had smudged her artwork.

"Thank you," the girl whispered, not daring to look me in the eyes this time.

"For what?" I asked.

"For saving the rest of us." Her gaze fixated on my lips instead of my stare as she touched up my paint.

"But you're fae," I said, her strange comment breaking me out of my pity party for a moment. "The proclamation applied only to human women."

The female's greenish cheeks flushed red. "Only half-fae, my lady. The rest of me's human."

Once she finished with my paint, she reached for an ornate, gold leafed box to store the brush she'd been using. When she did, her sleeve slipped, revealing raised silvery stripes across her wrist.

My chest clenched, and mouth moved faster than its reins. "Who did that to you?"

She flinched, wrenching at the sleeve to cover her mangled wrist. "No one, my lady."

I frowned, my heart beating wildly, and though I knew it was silly, that I was allowing my imagination to run away from me… Once I'd thought it, I couldn't purge the idea.

Because what was easier to believe than that the being who had drawn this female's blood was the same being who would spill mine?

A knock on the door broke the silence between us, and a muffled voice sounded through the cedar.

"Is she decent?" the voice asked.

"Yes. Come in," the servant girl said, rushing over to the door and opening it.

I turned to face the vizier as he strode into the room. He was not dressed for a wedding, at least not a wedding at the palace. His fine robes would have attracted attention at the type of wedding I might have been invited to back in the slums. But here? I was pretty sure he was wearing the same robes he adorned the day I had surrendered myself.

Six days ago.

It had only been six days.

He looked me up and down, and then he bowed.

"You don't have to do that," I said, noticing the gravel in my voice. The conventions of the palace were ridiculous. Why bow to someone who was going to be slaughtered the next day?

"On my account, you've earned it," the vizier said.

I didn't know how to respond to that, so I didn't say anything at all.

He turned to the servant girl and reached into the purse tied around his waist. Then he drew out five golden coins and placed them in her palm. "Thank you," he said, before dismissing her.

"Wait," I asked, as the girl reached the door. "What's your name?"

"Tavi," she said, blushing before she left in haste.

Alone now, with the vizier, I tried not to slump so much. Over my short life, I hadn't paid much attention to my father's complaints about my poor posture, but if I was going to face death, I might as well do it without slouching.

"You look lovely," the vizier said.

"You don't have to lie. I'm years past needing to be told I'm beautiful."

The vizier looked me up and down and sighed. "Then let me rephrase my compliment. You look fierce."

Something tugged at the corners of my lips, even as his comment burned my eye and the tip of my nose.

"Does the king know?" Dread nipped at my belly. Sure, I already knew I might as well be the mutton at the tip of a skewer, but I was sure the king had ways of making my death less pleasant than the typical execution. Especially if I humiliated him by, well, by being me.

I shuddered.

"No, he doesn't. And I would prefer to keep it that way until you make your public appearance," the vizier said.

I shot him a questioning look with my one eye. "Do you despise the king?"

"Absolutely not. However, the king has always gotten his own way. His parents made sure of that his entire life. I believe it would do him some good to…to learn the consequences of his actions for a change."

"I never took him as one to be easily humiliated," I said. A stupid thing to say, as it wasn't as if I knew the king personally.

"Perhaps you can change that for the better, then," the vizier said, either a smirk or a grimace spreading across his face—I wasn't sure which.

"Will he punish me more? Because of the embarrassment I'll have caused him?" I asked. I rubbed the smooth fabric of my wedding dress between my fingers, the friction causing the pads of my fingertips to chafe.

The vizier didn't answer as he turned and left me alone in a room too big for me and my thoughts.

* * *

THROUGH THE SCARLET veil that covered my face, I could barely make out the details of the crowd. Just that there were many. Whether the throng of beings lining the edges of the massive banqueting hall were human or fae, I could not discern. Only shadows leaked through my face covering, its fabric sucking up against my nostrils as I inhaled, making each breath more difficult than the last.

Muffled whispers filled my ears, which were much less limited under my wedding veil than my lone eye. Some of the sounds had a high-pitched quality, as if not originally from this world.

Fae. The crowd was definitely fae. How many mortals had been allowed inside the confines of this white-washed palace? Never mind that the bride was human.

I searched the shadows for the outlines of my father and sister.

Surely they had been allowed to attend, though I figured that was a fool's hope given how the guards had treated them this morning. Even if they were in attendance, it was no use looking for them. Beyond my veil, they could have been any number of the forms in my periphery.

Or standing to my left.

Then again, I could have been anyone, anything, to the fae crowd. Even as my stomach churned, a smile tugged at my lips at the thought. What they were imagining, the beautiful human girl with heavy-lidded eyes and a perfectly symmetrical face... Well, they would be in for a surprise, that was for sure.

Lights shone in the form of little bulbs on the floor, marking my path down the aisle. At least they had been considerate enough to know there was no way I was going to be able to make it to the altar without some assistance.

I lifted my head. At the end of the banqueting hall, I glimpsed a looming shadow.

Massive.

The king was massive.

CHAPTER 12

ASHA

I shuddered underneath my veil and hoped no one could tell.

The music started. Music that I might have danced to, had this been any other occasion. Someone plucked at a lyre, and the humming of the strings filled me with courage. I knew in my heart the minstrels weren't playing for me. They either played for the promise of coin or the threat of death if they didn't. They played for them-selves, for survival. But I silently thanked them, nonetheless. If this was going to be a party celebrating my ultimate demise, at least the music was decent.

I took a step, careful to kick the flowing scarlet silk out of my way before I did. As prone as I was to tripping, with my lone eye and my poor depth perception working against me, that was not going to happen today. I might have offered my life up like it meant nothing, but I intended to retain some pittance of dignity.

The procession slithered along, as if time itself could not be hurried, even for a royal wedding. The shadows to my right side leaned forward as I passed, hoping to get a glimpse of the doomed bride's face. As if my profile, jutting out from underneath my veil, would tell them more about me than the fact I had forfeited my life.

Fae. Such vain creatures.

I tried not to look at him, the king, my bridegroom, as I approached. Yet, each time I prodded my skirts out of my way with my bare feet, I couldn't help but notice him. His form grew larger with every step. Now that I was close, I could make out the pointed lines of his shoulders, the acute angle of his jaw.

Lines.

Sharp, jagged lines.

My mind spiraled into a flurry of violent images. The proclamation had not specified in what manner I was to be executed. Now that I stood before him, this massive, unearthly creature, I thought for sure it would be at his fingertips. He would strangle me, then allow his Flame to consume my last breath, just as he had his brother's traitorous wife. Just how my predecessor had met her fate. Why bother with a weapon when his body practically was one?

I gulped, savoring the ability, as I imagined the air leaving me for dead, fleeing my throat to avoid his grasp.

And then, before I knew it, I was before him. My legs trembled beneath me, and not for the first time today, I found myself thankful to Tavi for her choice in my attire. The faeries could lean across the aisle and peer as much as they pleased, but they would never see me tremble thanks to the seven layers of silk concealing my legs and waist.

I stepped to my left side, just as Tavi had told me to do, bringing myself in line with my murderer. A shadowy figure stood before me, and when he spoke, I almost gave a lurch of surprise.

"Today, we are gathered to witness the union held so sacred…"

The vizier. He hadn't told me he'd be performing the ceremony. Not that he owed me such information. But my shaking heart steadied a bit at his weathered voice. I was not alone up here.

"…the bond made eternal through the Fates that pilgrimage within us all…"

I tried to focus on his words, to find them interesting. I had never attended a fae wedding before, so I had no knowledge of what they held sacred, under what pretense they viewed a marriage union. Still, my mind wandered far from the vizier's words as the dread, which had made its home in my stomach these past few days, seemed to swim up my esophagus and take hold of my throat, conspiring with the heat under my veil to stifle my breathing.

Instead, I honed in on the cadence of the vizier's voice. I clung to the depth of his tone, the way it ebbed and flowed. Why it brought me so much comfort, I had no idea. But the vizier had betrayed himself to me this morning. He was kind, not to mention that a sense of justice teemed from his presence. He saw what the fae in attendance did not. He saw me for who I was. A girl trembling beneath a veil of rash bravery. A girl who, perhaps, found it a bit too easy to give herself up for others.

It wasn't that I regretted my decision. How could I ever regret guaranteeing my sister's life, her freedom? But now, facing the being who intended to cut off my life from under the sun after a night of... I distracted myself from the thought of what was inevitably coming this evening. Part of me clung to the hope that my butchered face would be enough to stave off the king's lust. But I knew enough about the fae males to know that lust wasn't the only reason they took human girls to bed, and if this one had a temper... I couldn't think of that now. Not without vomiting under my veil. That threat alone forced my back to stiffen, my spine a column of iron.

A question nagged at me. Why had it been so easy to give myself away? Sure, it had felt difficult in the moment. But not impossible. And something within me wondered if maybe it *should* have felt impossible. If my inherent urge to survive should have fought back a little harder.

"Do you, Your Majesty, King Kiran Shahrayr, son of Rajeen, accept the burden of a husband and father in taking Asha Shahrazad, daughter of Arun, for your own?"

My attention jolted back to the ceremony. Burden. Husband. Father. On a typical day, the statement would have had me fuming. Today? Today, the dread inside me bubbled up to the point it almost tickled. I might have laughed, had the thought of tomorrow, tonight, not paralyzed my voice.

Such a vague, meaningless vow. That was probably intentional. The fae had been cursed long ago with the inability to lie. That made taking vows tricky business, as breaking a vow could stop a fae's heart. So, the vaguer the terms, the better.

Well, for him, at least. Not at all for me.

"I accept," the king said, his voice low and deep and…empty. Only two words had I heard my bridegroom utter, but those two words… the flatness of them. This was not a man who stood before me. This was not even a fae. This was a hull, a husk of a soul, if he had ever possessed one in the first place. My arms trembled now, and I grasped onto my thighs, digging my fingernails into the silken material, hoping to steady them before anyone noticed.

I waited for the part in which I was to make my vows.

They did not come.

"Then you are pronounced husband and wife. May your spirits unite as one, in both this world and the one beyond."

Let's hope not.

A tingling sensation crawled across the back of my left hand, leaving behind an inky tattoo of flames and smoke.

The mark of marital union.

The mark of the king.

The brand that marked me as *his*.

And then, someone turned me and pushed something cold and heavy into my hand. The room went dark. Except, I realized, it wasn't the room's lights that had gone out. No, someone had thrown a shawl over me. I hadn't noticed, so they must have stood on my left side or behind me. And then I remembered. The shawl.

The first time I had witnessed this tradition was at a wedding I attended in my childhood. Someone had thrown the shawl over the bride and bridegroom. My father had explained to me that the bride-groom had a mirror and would see his bride's face for the first time. A tear had flecked my father's cheek as he recounted the custom, as he remembered another mirror, another shawl, another face.

How many times had I envisioned this moment over the years? How many times had my fingers tingled and my heart levitated with the thought of Az's face in that mirror, seeing me as his bride for the very first time? His face lighting up. His eyes gleaming. A tear staining his cheek.

I missed the weight of my dreams as they fled my imagination for good. That had always been the downside of pleasant dreams. They had a tendency to be erased by the real thing.

No, no, no.

Rage boiled inside me. This wasn't even a fae custom, I was sure of it. They had taken this from us, from me.

Sure, I had known they would take my life. But this? This dream I held so sacred? No. It wasn't theirs to take. It wasn't his to take.

Shadows flickered on the edges of the shawl as the king lit a lamp. Someone had turned me around, and now the king was at my back. If the ceremony was going the way it did in the human realm, his back was to me as well. My mind raced. This wasn't right. I wanted to lash at him, throw my fists into his chin, break that straight-cut line into jagged pieces.

But Dinah. What would happen to Dinah if I made such a public assault?

The cold metal of the mirror handle chilled my fingertips. I'd just have to power through this part, I figured. For Dinah. For all the other human girls in the kingdom, I'd play my part in this show.

I slipped the veil off my face and, out of instinct, held the mirror up to my right side. The handle almost slipped from my shock at the person who stared back at me. With only the right side of my face visible, the part left unmarred by my magic, my face teetered dangerously close to attractive. I hadn't thanked Tavi enough, apparently, for the wonders she had worked with the paint. A full-lipped girl stared back at me with one hazel iris, shimmering in the pool of my warm tears, highlighted by the crimson veins coursing through the white of my eye.

Bright as molten gold, my eye could have been forged in Draidon itself.

The king stirred behind me, and I realized he hadn't lifted his mirror yet. I caught one last glimpse of myself—myself, as I might have been without my magic.

And I switched the mirror to my other hand.

The face staring back at me this time? One of nightmares. There was a reason my family didn't own any mirrors.

Alright, the reason was that we were poor. But even if we had all the coin in the kingdom, I was sure my father never would have allowed me to see myself this clearly.

My dead eye socket recoiled into my skull. Blotches of pink and white crept down my cheek, giving the impression that my face had been stitched together by an amateur.

It had.

Fates, bless my father.

As hard as Tavi had tried, as talented as she was with the brush, she had not managed to apply paint to the gnarled edge of my lip.

The king lifted his mirror to meet the reflection of mine.

I glimpsed his face for the first time, cringing with horror as he let out the beginnings of a squeal. As he stumbled away from me, catching himself just in time to keep from falling to the floor, but not in time to escape the crowd's notice…

I thought I caught the edge of my twisted lip curl into a smirk.

CHAPTER 13

KIRAN

*H*umans lie.

This is the line in the sand that distinguishes the border of one nation from the next. The blotch of ink that crafts the difference between two letters, two words, two meanings. The rise in pitch that notates the difference between a statement and a question.

It's not the way the elements berate against their flesh, weathering their skin and carving wrinkles into their foreheads as easily as a butter knife to fresh clay. It's not the ease with which they reproduce, their uncanny ability of even the least of them to pass on a portion of themselves to a new generation. Nor does it lie in their inability to master the Old Magic, their tendency to be possessed rather than to possess.

Humans lie.

We do not.

In this lies the difference.

This line, this canyon between us and them, is clear enough. What is unclear, what is as blurred as the desert horizon as the sun cusps the sky, is which of these beliefs are mine, and which are my father's.

Were my father's.

There was a time when the two were distinct as the sun and the moon. But now they've eclipsed, and I can no longer tell the difference.

Humans lie.

That's what he'd told me regarding my first marriage. The one that counted. I'd been so eager for him to be wrong. Wanted nothing more, in fact. Nothing more but the truths my father declared to wither to dust, not as lies, but as the fabrications of his own truth, his twisted perception.

I'm not sure who I hate more. Gwenyth, for lying. Or my father, for making it so. For speaking it into existence.

Her treachery wasn't the only thing he spoke into existence.

I was born to be a monster—no, conceived to be a monster. Decades of preparation, years of obsession and planning, went into molding me into his image. Lydia complains about her treatment, the torture Father put her through as punishment for her first of many sins—robbing my father of having a son for his firstborn.

She was his shame.

But I was his obsession.

I don't know who I hate more. My father, for claiming my soul as his own, or Lydia, for not being an eligible heir. For leaving it to me to take her place.

There was a time I thought I'd gotten the best of him—that I'd wrecked his plans, screwed a hole in his carefully constructed dam, spoiled the water at the bottom of his favorite well. Through it all, Gwenyth had been my partner. I just hadn't been hers.

Humans lie.

He's been dead for over a year now, but his voice still drips at the edges of my consciousness, incessant, dull, constant.

I don't know who I hate more, my father for ruining me, or the assassin who stole what was rightfully mine. The faceless, nameless being who got to relish in the life fleeing my father's eyes. If they even cared enough to watch, to truly understand what a precious moment they witnessed.

Humans lie, and that's why the one standing before me must die.

The veil contracts around her mouth and nose as she breathes, revealing little evidence of the shape of her face. The thrumming of her heart taps against the callous that cocoons my conscience, the one my father solidified on the occasion he forced me to drink the blood of his cook's wife after a maggot was found in the dinner bread.

I was twelve.

As the copper twang of her blood mingled with the salt of my tears, my mind tucked that part of me away, the part I'd fought to preserve for so long. It was tuck it away, or allow my father to scorch it to cinders.

Practically speaking, I'm not sure there's much of a difference.

But it's still there alright, because this human's shallow breaths—the ones that remind me just how delicate her human body is, how easily I could crush the organs causing that noise—they're grating, not against my nerves, but that protective layering of soot and ilk and scab that keeps my conscience safe and sound.

I wonder for the first time who she is, this woman standing before me. I wonder how many lies have passed between those lips, the lips whose outline I can barely trace under that scarlet veil caking her open mouth.

If the count was zero, would I let her go, allow her to leave this place unscathed? Or would I play Fates and put her out of her miserable existence before this life under the sun could taint her?

Her breaths scrape, notching into the curve of my ears and slithering into my skull, flooding me with dizziness, threatening to scrape away the sludge coating my heart.

How long does it take wind to erode rock, water to carve mountains?

Surely more mooncyles than a human woman could hope to endure.

She offered herself. I remember the vizier saying as much when he came to inform me a bride had come forth.

Those words had acted as a chisel, tapping away at me in the nights leading up to our wedding. I hadn't expected as much from a human. Hadn't expected as much from any being.

Fae might be cursed with the inability to lie, but that doesn't make us noble. As for bravery, can the predator at the top of the food chain ever claim such a title?

Perhaps that was yet another thing that separated us—humans and fae.

Humans lie.

Fae do not. We can't. The Fates made sure of that.

But we can't be brave, either. Not really. Not in the sense this human showed when she apparently marched up to the palace doorsteps and traded her life for her kinsmen as if it were nothing.

I suppose I could soothe that blister developing on my callous if I convinced myself of that. That her human life truly is nothing. It's so fleeting, after all. Even if I allowed her to live, her existence would pass from under the sun before a wrinkle marred my brow.

Taking her life now is like plucking fruit when it's ripe, putting it to good use rather than allowing it to wither, rot.

Yet.

Yet.

Perhaps it's the other way around. Perhaps it's the brevity of her life that makes it precious.

Like Gwenyth. Brief. Fleeting.

I have to clutch my fists to bury the swell of anguish threatening to spill over, reveal itself.

The vizier is speaking, but I haven't processed a word. All I can hear is her breathing, the wild frenzy of her heart as we turn to face away from one another, as someone pushes mirrors into our hands and throws the wedding shroud over our heads, enveloping us in darkness.

Trapping me in here with her, with the heat of her breath that clouds my senses and threatens to dampen my resolve.

She has to die. I decreed it so.

It doesn't matter why I decreed it. That in my anguish, in discovering what *she* had done, what my love, my everything had done, that the Flame had threatened to consume me, to swallow me from the inside out. It doesn't matter that after Gwenyth was...

After she was dealt with, there was nowhere left to pour the flames, no father left to dissolve to ashes.

That was just it. Gwenyth had left me with nothing. It hadn't been enough to take another male into her bed. It hadn't been enough to plot against my life.

She had to go and make me love her.

She had to break my heart and crack it wide open for the entirety of Alondria to see.

And now this girl, this nameless, faceless girl, had to die. Because someone had to be punished. And what I did to Gwenyth would never be enough.

When I married a human, my father warned me of the dangers. He'd said it would be my downfall, my humiliation.

He'd said the kingdoms would see me as weak.

I hadn't cared at the time.

I suppose my father got what he wanted in the end, because love left me stranded, and now power is the only branch I've left to cling to before I plummet.

Power is my everything.

It's all I have left.

Now that I think of it, it's all I've ever had.

I think I might be sorry that this girl has to die. I think I can afford her that much, little value as it may contain.

Maybe she wants to die, and that's why she offered herself. Maybe I'll be doing her a service.

Sometimes I wish someone would grant me the same mercy.

I sense her shift behind me and realize she's actually going through with the wedding tradition, so I follow suit, raising the mirror, dreading the delicate, kind face it's sure to reveal.

What I glimpse is far worse.

What I glimpse is not a delicate lamb, a beautiful martyr.

What I glimpse is my undoing.

CHAPTER 14

ASHA

*S*weat beaded on my forehead, causing my veil to stick to my skin as I paced around the king's room. I chuckled to myself, if only to force the breathing. They really were going to pretend the marriage was real, even though I'd be checking out in the morning, never to return.

The room itself could have packaged three of my family's hovel. Thick, bloodred curtains obscured the bed, which stretched across a good third of the room. Just the thought of how the king's mattress was hidden, obscured, made me want to puke. The curtains were stiff. They didn't even flutter in the breeze, the draft allowed in through the open white-washed doors that revealed a marble balcony overlooking the city.

The gentle draft drew me to the overlook, and I tossed my head-dress on the ornate rug, welcoming the fresh air into my lungs. The icy wind, which I might have detested under any other circumstance, now provided a release from the suffocation of my wedding garb—the suffocation of my decision.

I felt silly for it, but I wasn't sure which part I was dreading the most. Dying, or the how the night's activities would unfold before I ever got around to the dying part. My ears prickled with every shuffle in the hallway, bile stinging my throat as I waited. And waited.

Perhaps the king was taking his time on purpose. Perhaps the torture had already begun. I clung to the sensation of chill bumps forming on my exposed arms. This last bit of life, freckling my skin. I would no longer feel the bristle of a chilled wind, the shudder of an ominous thought. Not after tomorrow.

My mind raced to Dinah, to my father. Had they attended the ceremony today? I hadn't been able to find them in the crowd. Someone had reapplied my veil, shortly after a servant had ripped the shawl off of mine and the king's heads. A horrified, disgusted gasp had rippled through the crowd at my face. Then, silence. Perhaps out of a realization that their uncomely reaction had betrayed them. What would the king do to the guests who had dared gawk at his bride?

That didn't bother me much. The fae deserved it. My father and sister? No, the king wouldn't hurt them. The vizier would make sure of it.

That is, if the vizier didn't beat me to the gallows for neglecting to mention the details of my appearance.

A knock on the door thudded against my nerves.

He didn't wait for my answer before he strode in.

This time, he was prepared.

His stern mouth didn't as much as twitch as he beheld my face. His firm cheekbone didn't flinch. Those brilliant, golden eyes didn't widen in shock. His pupils didn't dilate.

The king, my king, was more handsome than I could have imagined him. High fae were all like that, as if each of them got to be their own individual color never before beheld by the eye. A portrait of angles never before conceived by the human mind.

Irritating was what it was.

Blank. This being's face had been emptied of any emotion, any flaw that might have drawn me to him, piqued my interest.

I ignored the voice in the back of my mind reminding me that Az's features were almost perfectly symmetrical, so much so that he was often mistaken as fae, yet I never found myself irritated with his appearance.

If the King of Naenden could judge me unfairly based on my humanity and sex, then surely there was a little room for me to hate him based on his annoyingly symmetrical face.

The bile soured in my throat. I might have spat it at him, had I not feared for Dinah's life. For her I would hold my tongue, bite back the insults whirring through my head.

Or, rather, I'd try.

Now, faced with my one and only audience with the king, I wasn't sure I could bring myself to go silently.

"Have you come to strip away my dignity?" I noted the tremor in my voice as I asked, and hated myself for it. It was supposed to have come out even, laced with cool hatred. But my voice quavered at the same frequency as my legs.

When he spoke, the words flowed out, even and smooth as his tan skin.

"I have no intention of engaging you in such activities." His voice could have challenged the fae females who balanced fine dishes upon their heads, for as little as it wavered.

An insult regarding my appearance? A subtle apology? A statement of self-righteousness? I couldn't differentiate between them. All I knew was that the throttling grip around my neck loosened a bit, though my limbs shook all the more in relief. Like the trembling of prey having just come down from the rush of flight from its predator.

But I had only escaped one of my two undesirable fates.

"Why are you here, then?" It took a conscious effort to lift my chin when I wanted nothing more than to curl up into a ball in the luscious bed. At least I'd be able to savor the plush sheets, now that I knew the king wouldn't be crawling into them.

"You are to be granted one request this evening, within reason, of course."

So no asking to be spared tomorrow. Got it.

"Is that a custom of the fae? To grant their innocents a wish before they slaughter them?" I couldn't be sure—my eyesight wasn't exactly spectacular even in my remaining eye, but I thought I saw his right eyebrow raise just a hair.

"It depends on the crime," he said.

"And what exactly was my crime?"

He paused. "On your certificate of execution? It will say suicide."

"Sounds like I should have jumped off the balcony when I had the chance," I said, squinting, hoping to glimpse the slightest twinge in his face. The most minuscule amount of pain I could administer to the cruel king, that alone would have been enough revenge.

He wouldn't even give me that.

"You made the decision to die. You signed your own certificate of expiration when you approached my vizier. Do not for a moment be deceived into thinking a choice was taken away from you."

"Then why place the exception for a sacrifice in your proclamation? Why allow the option, if you don't believe what I did was noble? If it wasn't going to change your mind about the possibility a human woman might be a decent person?"

This time, the king shuffled, ever so slightly. He hadn't expected an interrogation.

"You didn't think anyone would actually take you up on your offer, did you?" I said, relishing the last bit of satisfaction I would have the privilege to taste in this life. Being right. Being right, over this fae being I hated. I would take that to my grave as a parting gift, lousy as it was. "What? It didn't align with your expectations of human women, that one would dare offer herself in place of the others?"

The molten gold in the king's eyes flickered hot and wild, and twisted into the deepest of cerulean blues. It was then I remembered the king's fae-born gift.

Fire was pretty high on my list of ways I *did not* want to go. Well, at least if he burnt me to cinders right here and now, Dinah and my father wouldn't have to witness my execution.

But then, as quickly as they had appeared, the blue flames died out, settling into that warm, golden hue.

"Tell me your request," the king commanded.

I didn't have to think about it.

"I'd like my sister's company tonight," I said. "We're in the middle of a story I'd like to finish."

* * *

THE KING ESCORTED Dinah to his rooms himself, a gesture of faux kindness and mercy that made me want to grab one of the ornate brands nesting beside the fireplace and shove it down his throat.

I didn't though. Great restraint on my part, I know.

"My lady, your sister." He nodded toward me and left, locking the door behind us as Dinah flung herself into the room.

She swept me up in her embrace, and I might have fallen over had the king's fae-sized bed not been directly behind me. Her tears wet my garments, her sobs echoing in my ears.

I clutched her back, trying not to dig my ridiculously long, fake fingernails into her skin. But it was a feat. I wanted nothing more than to cling to her so tightly that the guards would have to pry my dead body off of her in the morning. I might have caused them such inconvenience on purpose, had I not thought it would make the experience even more traumatic for my little sister.

She withdrew from the embrace, her hands still gripping the soft silk of my garment. Then she gargled a bit and wiped her eyes. "I'm sorry. I'm sorry. You're the one who's had the awful day. I should be letting you cry, not the other way around."

My heart crumbled at her generosity. "It's alright. The more you cry, the more I can distract myself by pretending I'm comforting you."

She didn't laugh; she only hiccuped, and guilt panged in my chest. Here I was, on my last night alive, and all I wanted to do was joke about it.

I gestured for her to sit on the bed, but the look of disgust that displayed on her face was enough to have me scrambling to make a pallet of pillows on the floor.

After a moment of quiet nesting, Dinah whispered, her voice trembling, "He didn't... Did he? All I mean to say is that, if he did, you can tell me."

I shook my head. "He didn't."

She let out a gust of relief. "Well, at least our *gracious* king has the decency not to defile the women he slaughters."

I dropped the pillow I was carrying, so disarmed by the bitterness in sweet Dinah's voice.

In fact, I hadn't been sure that Dinah even knew what the word *defile* meant. At least, not when it came to a man and a woman. I certainly hadn't explained it to her. And there was no way in Alondria our father had.

Sure, she was plenty old enough to know. I just couldn't imagine the conversation, or a creature daring enough to broach the topic.

In the end, I fought the curiosity, figuring that whoever informed my innocent little sister of the ways of the world would be a mystery I would gladly take to my ever-nearing grave.

"Yes, how thoughtful of him." I rolled my eyes.

Dinah stomped on one of the cushions, soiling it with her muddied slippers. When my eye caught hers, she blushed, but I let out a roaring laugh.

Before long, we were both on the floor, rolling in the pillows, the sounds coming out of our mouths a mixture between howls of laughter and wails of grief.

"I'm sorry... I'm just... I'm just so, so angry," my sister coughed out between bouts of hysteria.

When I'd finally caught enough breath to answer, we were both on our backs, sucking in the cold air. "I'm... I'm just glad...I get to see... this side of you. How did you like my wedding, by the way?"

Heat rose in her face, and her glare could have pierced an armadillo's shell. "They weren't going to let me in. I banged on the gates for hours, screamed at all the guests they let through."

My jaw dropped. "How are you still alive, then?"

She shrugged. "They tried to take me to the dungeons, but that elderly fae who came by our home to record my name recognized me and told the guards he'd take care of me. Instead, he found some fae wedding attire for me and snuck me in the back before the wedding started, but he made me promise I wouldn't go anywhere until he came back from the ceremony to get me. He'd just taken me back to his office when the king sauntered in, demanding that his bride's sister be fetched."

"And Father?" I asked.

"He tried to come, he really did."

"You didn't let him, did you? He would have stroked from the heat of that walk."

She shook her head, then frowned.

"How'd you convince him to stay home?"

"I sort of got Az to force him."

One look from my sister told me not to ask whether Az would have come to see me one last time otherwise.

Dinah smiled, a deep aching in her brown eyes. "I already miss you terribly."

I swallowed and closed my eye, unable to bear the look in hers.

"Why did you do this?"

Her question hung in the air between us.

When I opened my eye, hers were raining tears, streaking her usually smooth face with red blotches. "Because I adore you too much to let anything happen to you."

She frowned, a pained wince that looked as though I might as well have stabbed her in the gut. "But you could have waited it out, Asha. They might have never picked me. And, even if they had…" She jolted up and gripped her stomach, wincing as she fought for breath. Her pretty smile soured as she gritted her teeth. Agony stretched across my sister's dainty features, contorting them and molding them until she finally managed to get the words out. "I would have rather died than… I can't get through this, Asha. I won't. The pain, it's like it's filling my lungs with water. I can't. I can't breathe."

I lifted myself onto my elbow and stroked her sweating brow with my fingertips, wiping the strands of dark hair from where they'd fallen into her eyes. "Father and I wouldn't have managed in the house together without you. You know that."

She gagged on her words. "You two are just alike. You'd be fine."

I shook my head. "That's exactly why we wouldn't have survived.

So much cynicism under one roof. We would have withered. It had to be me, Dinah. You don't remember, but when Mother died, Father and I almost drowned in grief. But then there was you, our ray of sunshine worth living for. We wouldn't have laughed again, if not for your smile. It had to be me. Because you have to live. For Father, you have to live."

She winced again, then swallowed. "That's entirely unfair. And since it's unfair, I don't care that it's your last night to live. We're doing what I want to do, and you're going to tell me a story."

I didn't think I could have smiled wider.

But when I opened my mouth to speak, it was not the story I had intended to tell.

CHAPTER 15

*T*horns rustled in Farin's hair as the northern wind blew, scratching the boy's scalp and causing him to grit his teeth. He knew better than to wince, though. The Others could tune into the sound of a fae's voice from three miles away, and though his family camped well out of their range of hearing, Farin wasn't one to heed the tribe boundaries his father had solidified.

Not that Farin meant to be trouble.

He just happened to be drawn to the same places Trouble was. He and Trouble had strikingly similar interests.

For instance, the grass in the Netherworlds, the blades that grew so high even Farin's father could have disappeared in their wake, without even having to kneel or lean over—why did it grow so tall, when the rest of the vegetation was consumed by the Others before they even bore fruit? Was the tall grass just that unpleasant to eat? Farin didn't think so. He'd tried it before, chewed it up about sixty times before he could get it slobbery enough to swallow, but that wasn't so different from the foods Mother grew in her sanctuary. Every living being in the Netherworlds was used to having to chew their food at least thirty times if they didn't want to spend hours huddled in the reservoir in pain. Mother sometimes told stories, her grandmother's stories—stories of plants that were left in peace long enough that they would eventually sprout colorful bulbs that could be eaten. Bulbs that had filled the eater with energy. Mother said they had tasted sweet and tangy and juicy.

Farin didn't know what it meant—to be sweet, or tangy, or juicy, but he'd tried to imagine it many times. Juicy, he thought he had a grip on, as his mother had explained that the colorful bulbs had mostly been full of water, but a harder, crunchier version. But to imagine sweet and tangy without ever having tasted it—Farin's imagination didn't quite stretch that far. And that was saying something, because Farin believed he was the only fae left in the Nether who possessed such a thing as an imagination. Sometimes, he wished he could meet an old fae with an imagination. Perhaps they would have had more practice at it and could help him learn how to discover what sweet and tangy meant. Mother had said that sweet was the opposite of bitter, a taste Farin knew all too well from the roots she grew in her sanctuary. But imagining sweet from bitter was about like trying to describe the color blue as the opposite of brown.

Mother had scrolls that she said were full of imagination. She said the scrolls contained stories inked with the blood of an Omigron, and that, if he ever learned to read, he could enjoy them too.

Farin hoped that one day he could read them, once Father was content enough with Farin's hunting skills to allow him to learn something he actually wanted to learn.

After much pondering, the breeze blew against Farin's back, and, without gasping—his father had trained him never, ever to do so— Farin dropped to the earth and huddled as still as he could manage.

Breeze was the enemy, as Farin's father often reminded him. It carried their scents to the Others. Farin couldn't help but think that perhaps the Others were the true enemies, and that the Breeze was just doing the only job it knew how to do, but he was familiar enough with the taste of the back of his father's knuckles—bitter, of course— not to mention so.

After what seemed like an eternity, Farin lifted his head, figuring that if a monster had picked up his scent, he would be dead by now.

He even found himself grateful for the breeze, because it reminded him why he had ventured out to the Grassplace to begin with.

He had seen something here, just the other day when his father had taken him hunting for the first time. Only hunters were allowed outside the borders of the tribe, and only full-grown fae males were allowed to be hunters, but his father had trained Farin early. Farin had no desire to be a hunter, at least not by trade. He figured if he ever wanted to be a cartographer, he'd have to learn to kill food for himself. One could only carry so many pounds' worth of root, after all. He would have preferred if Father had cast the burden of training him on one of the other hunters, though. At least the other males of the tribe wouldn't have had the guts to admit that he was a burden aloud.

"There are many, more useful things I could do with my time," his father had told him just the other day, while they were in the confines of the Tribe, out of earshot of the Others, of course.

Farin had thought to answer, *"like what?"* But then he remembered that his father often mistook his honest questions for disrespect, and Farin's teeth still hurt from his last inquiry.

It had taken them the better half of the morning to reach this place, the place Farin had named "The Grassplace," in his head, never aloud, obviously. Then another half of the morning to sit and wait. And sit and wait. And sit and wait.

Farin had about decided that was all there was to hunting—sitting and waiting—when the grass had shivered.

At least, Farin thought it had shivered. He'd patted on his father's back, noiselessly, of course, and pointed toward where he'd thought he'd seen movement. But when he looked again, there was nothing there. His father had scowled at him, and his teeth had throbbed in anticipation.

Only minutes later, it had caught his attention again, but this time, he'd known he wasn't making things up. Light had shifted in the corner of his vision, and when he turned his head toward it and cocked it in just the right direction, he saw it again. A ray of sunlight shimmering above the blades of tall grass, except it wasn't a ray of sunlight at all. It couldn't have been, because the sun was in the middle of the sky, and the ray of light seemed to emerge from the air itself. Farin had gone to tap his father on the shoulder again, but before he did, he checked over his own shoulder once more and was distraught to find that the ray of sunlight had disappeared.

When they'd arrived home, Farin had received five lashes on the back for wasting his father's time and had been denied dinner for his failure to bring any meat home for them to eat. Farin couldn't help but think that his father hadn't brought any meat home either, yet he was still eating, but he decided instead to be grateful that his teeth had stopped hurting. Or, at least, the lashes on his back hurt enough to distract him from them.

But today? Today was different. Father had gone off to hunt in the West with a pack of tribe hunters, and Mother had been tending her sanctuary all morning, so it had been the perfect day to slip away.

Farin was going to find that ray of light.

He didn't know why, but something—perhaps it was just his own silly imagination—told him that, if he could find that strange ray of light, if he could touch it, then he'd be *that* much closer to finding sweet or tangy.

The only problem was that the ray of light had been situated on the hill. The hill surrounded by the tall, reasonably bland and bitter grass. Grass that made noise when it shook.

It was trouble. Again. Farin knew that.

But.

He'd overheard Mother and Father talking last night. Mother was worried. The soil in the tribe's current settling spot was growing old; the community had used up all the nutrients in the three years they'd lived there.

So they'd do what they always did.

They would leave soon. Walk through the plains in fuzzy moccasins, the hunters surrounding the females and children, the few of them who existed in the Nether. Most tried not to have children, if they could help it. Fae babies' cries were louder than the average fae adult voice. The borders weren't wide enough to keep the Others from hearing them scream. The tribe's people didn't like babies, would cast out the families who had them until their children were old enough to know when to keep quiet.

The tribe would leave, and then there would be no finding this place, the origin of the strange ray of light. There would be no tracking his way back, even when he was an adult, for he knew his cartography skills were still immature.

He'd never find his way back.

So through the noisy grass, it had to be.

Farin held his breath, then stepped into the long blades. They scraped against his cheeks as he passed through them. Father would ask about the scrapes later, and Farin's imagination wasn't trained enough yet to come up with a lie that would satisfy him. It seemed no one could grow an imagination mature enough to satisfy his father, though. Sometimes, Farin considered feeling sorry for him, for he figured a male who could never be satisfied must feel quite sad on the inside. But then Farin would remember that his father leaked sadness onto his mother, that he beat it into her on occasion, when her crops didn't grow enough roots for a sufficient dinner. Farin didn't know why that made his father so angry, especially since Farin would always give up his portion so Father could eat plenty. So Farin supposed he didn't feel sorry for his father, not today at least.

The grass didn't rattle nearly as loudly as Farin had expected it to. It wasn't silent, sure, but he'd always been trained to think of brush and tall grass like he'd been trained to think of babies. Now he figured he'd been exaggerated to.

Farin made it to the hill in what felt like almost no time at all. In fact, he was proud of his accomplishment. Now that he was here, he felt he could breathe, slowly, so he didn't make any noise. Then he tiptoed up the short-grassed hill and toward where he thought he had remembered the light.

It took him a while to scan the area. The hill was tall, and Farin wasn't used to climbing inclines, as the borders were all on flat land, less likely to cause someone to trip. By the time he made it to the top, Farin found it was difficult not to pant, but if anyone had been trained not to be loud, it was Farin. After all, he wasn't allowed to make a sound when Father was punishing him. Father said it was good practice.

Farin wasn't sure what the practice was for. He figured if he got mauled by an Other, screaming and alerting all the other Others wouldn't put him in a much worse situation.

Then Farin saw it, right in the middle of his pondering. He whipped around on his tiptoes, for the flash had come from the corner of his eye. There it was, a ray of sunshine coming out of the air, right at the top of the hill. Farin had to make a mental note not to gasp, which was unusual for him, as it was usually so engrained.

He reached out to touch it and wondered whether touching a ray of sunlight, or airlight, as it appeared to be, would simply feel warm, or if it would contain an entirely novel sensation altogether. Like how plants could contain bitter and sweet.

Farin braced himself and bit his lip, lest the ray of light be hot to the touch. He certainly didn't want to cry out in pain here. Especially when he'd already risked trouble by wading through the tall grass.

But when his fingers grazed the ray of light, Farin had no choice but to let out the quietest of gasps. For his hand, upon reaching the ray of light, disappeared into thin air. And that was not at all what Farin had been expecting.

His elbow recoiled, bringing his hand back with it, and it instantly reappeared on his wrist. This was an oddity, to be sure, and something Farin's father had never mentioned. Farin wondered if it was dangerous and what would happen if he put his whole body into the ray of light. Would he turn invisible? Farin thought he would quite enjoy being invisible, except that he'd still have to eat at some point, and he doubted his father would let something as inconsequential as invisibility get in the way of punishing him.

Or perhaps the ray of light hadn't made his hand invisible at all. Maybe it had made it not exist, and the only reason it had reappeared was because it was still connected to Farin's wrist. Perhaps if he stepped through it, he would no longer exist. And if he no longer existed, then he wouldn't be attached to anything, and he might not be able to pull himself back.

Farin narrowed his brows at the light, concentrating. That idea sounded dangerous, but Farin was sure that his father had already warned him of everything that could be dangerous in the Nether, even babies. And if his father hadn't mentioned rays of light, then surely they couldn't be dangerous at all.

With that thought to comfort him, Farin took another step, allowing the suspended light to wash over his tiny frame.

CHAPTER 16

ASHA

Speckles of sunlight flecked across Dinah's face, having seeped in through the artistically warped windows, which the wind must have closed sometime in the evening.

I woke with a start.

I hadn't finished the story.

During the night, my magic had curled up inside my chest, releasing my voice.

And I had fallen asleep.

In the light of the sunrise, the seal on my death sentence, Dinah's eyes opened, and a tear glistened as it rolled down my sister's sun-kissed cheek.

My stomach sank. That was the last story I would ever tell. And I hadn't even had enough time to finish it. I pleaded with the magic inside me to continue, to take hold of my voice once more. Surely we had enough time to weave an ending. I couldn't—no—I wouldn't pass from underneath the sun without knowing the ending.

Please, I begged the magic inside me.

It didn't as much as stir. Perhaps it didn't know we were about to die.

Please. I am going to die today. Please let me finish the story. We are going to die.

My stomach was the only thing that rumbled in response. Tears welled in my eyes. Why I cared so much, I didn't know. It felt silly, foolish, worth scolding to be crying over an unfinished story when I would be dead in a few hours.

But that was just it.

My story wasn't finished. It couldn't be. I hadn't… Well, there was too much I hadn't done to even bother keeping count.

But then Dinah stirred, and upon waking, she shot straight up. Her eyes darted from my face to the window, which now flooded the room with light.

Her cheeks drained of color. "I fell asleep. I don't know how I feel asleep." She grasped onto my robes. "Asha, I'm so, so sorry. How—" Horror gripped her voice, and I tried to soothe her.

"It's okay. I fell asleep too." My words didn't seem to bring her any comfort, so I added, "That's just how we always do it. I wouldn't have wanted it any different."

Lie. That was a lie. But what else was I supposed to say?

She brushed her hair from her face in panic, her eyes settling into focus. "Well, maybe we can still finish it. We still have time, right?"

The knock on the door informed us otherwise.

* * *

I wondered then if they would allow Dinah to attend my execution.

I hoped not. She would want to be there, of course. But the thought of my death staining her memory for the rest of her life, which, given her glowing health, would probably be a relatively long one for a human… I couldn't bear it.

I wouldn't.

Surely someone here in the palace would grant me the favor of barring Dinah to my parting from under the sun. If I could find the vizier before the ceremony… Something told me he would understand.

The angry screech of the door ripped me out of my scheming. When I stood to face my Fates, Dinah jumped and spun around, slinging her slight frame between me and whoever had disturbed us. Her tear-stained hood blocked my view of the intruder, and fear seized me as I imagined what a high fae soldier might do to her for such an act of defiance.

I went to shove her out from in front of me, but as soon as I laid my hands on her shoulders, a familiar voice whispered, "Lady Queen."

Dinah's protective stance faltered at the gentle voice, and I nudged her away.

Tavi, the servant girl who had dressed me for my wedding, trembled at the doorway. Her pale, eggshell eyes drooped, and she winced at the sight of me.

Not the same wince I was so used to, the one when people tried to pretend my gnarled face hadn't shocked them.

No, Tavi's wince had less to do with my scar than it did my imminent demise.

"I've been sent to dress you, Lady Queen." Indeed, a garment bag sprawled across her outstretched hands. An offering for a queen.

Dinah's trembling hand gripped mine. "No. You're not going to take her."

Tavi frowned. "No. I'm not. I'm only to dress her."

Something guttural spilled from my sister's mouth, and she buried her face in my hair, sobbing. Instinctively, my hands found the nape of her neck, and I curled my fingers through her tresses. "It's alright, Dinah. It's alright. I'm going to be alright."

She pulled back, her eyes wide. For half a moment, I could see her every thought spread across her face like an open scroll. As if to say, *No you won't, you'll be dead.*

But the horror was gone so quickly, I wondered if I had imagined it. Dinah swallowed and straightened. My sister, ever the picture of duty. "Of course you will." She smiled weakly.

My sister, my kind, innocent sister, was going to comfort me to the end. Even if it meant forcing her own pain deep, deep down. Shoving it into a box and stuffing it into the quiet corners of her heart until the moment of my death, when I no longer needed her to be strong for me.

It wasn't fair, but I asked it of her anyway. "Will you stay with me?"

She nodded, her breaths uneven as she forced them into submission. "Until the end."

Only then did Tavi approach. The girl was gentle and found ways for Dinah to help by asking her to pin a piece of fabric at my shoulders or tie my silk sash around my waist.

The garment wasn't as I'd expected. Not that I'd known what to expect. What did a king force his bride to wear during her execution? What colors and fit were appropriate for such an unprecedented occasion?

Whatever it was, I hadn't expected it to be the color of snow. Or, rather, what I'd imagined snow to look like. Not that I'd ever seen such a thing, but Father had told me about it. Well, he had read to me about snow from that tattered book of his, in which the characters traversed the Plyny mountains. They had seen snow, touched snow.

As I'd never do.

Strange that this was the thought that strangled me, not the idea of the king's fingers cutting off my longstanding relationship with the air.

Snow.

I'd never gotten to see snow.

What an insignificant life I'd led.

When Dinah and the servant girl finished, I couldn't bring myself to look into the gilded mirror that scaled the height of the room.

"You're stunning," Dinah whispered, wiping a section of matted hair from my face. The servant girl started on that jungle of a project next, pulling and tugging on my long hair until she'd arranged it in what I imagined was an intricate braid worthy of a basket weaving prize at the market.

Though I couldn't bring myself to look, the expression of wonder and painful delight on Dinah's face was enough to prove that Tavi had given a dying girl the only gift she could.

A crumb of dignity.

It was then that I realized why Tavi had looked so familiar. She was in charge of dressing me. That made her the queen's lady's maid.

She had been the servant holding the branch over Queen Gwenyth the day of the coronation, the girl with the trembling hands as she struggled to ensure her mistress's delicate skin remained shaded from the unforgiving sun.

"Thank you," I said to Tavi, the girl who'd been so kind to me.

She blinked, startled. "My pleasure, Lady Queen."

That brought a weak smile to my lips. "You don't have to call me that."

Her pale eyes met mine with a fervor, a rage I hadn't yet seen in her delicate face. "Yes, Lady Queen, I do."

Someone knocked on the door, loud enough to be clear about one thing—this wasn't an attempt to be polite, but a threat.

"Is she decent?" a brute voice called.

I might have laughed, had I not been sure it would have sent Dinah to the floor. Was I decent? What a ridiculous question. As if they cared about my dignity, my honor, when I was about to be executed in front of a crowd? Was there anything more intimate, more personal, than standing by and watching as someone's soul was severed from their body?

As if to prove my point, a guard shoved the door open and sauntered in. "It's time."

I expected Dinah to lose it.

Instead, she hurtled herself right at the guard.

To her credit, she managed to get a hand around the hilt of his sword before he realized what had happened.

Before I had the chance to scream.

But the guard was fae, and even the element of surprise was not enough. With an effortless wave of his hand, he plucked my sister by the back of her robes and sent her flying across the room. Her body slammed against the mirror. Glass rained down upon her as she slumped to the floor, unconscious.

I screamed and lunged for her, but the guard was faster. Faster than my limbs, faster than my voice. He had a hand clamped to my mouth before as much as a noise could escape my lips.

Dinah, no.

Tavi's gaze met mine, and I pleaded with her.

In understanding, she nodded, and tiptoed to my sister's side, wiping the shards of glass off her bloodied face with a gentleness I wouldn't soon forget, as long as there existed consciousness after this life.

The guard swept me out of the room. As soon as Dinah was out of sight, he pinned me against the wall. "You can walk like a big girl, or I can help you." His hot breath wet my face as he snarled and bared his teeth.

I nodded, understanding.

There was no way I was going to give him the satisfaction of carrying me kicking and screaming to my death.

Maybe if I cooperated, they wouldn't feel the need to punish Dinah for her outburst. Maybe they'd leave her alone. Tavi was going to take care of her. She'd all but promised such with that look she'd given me.

I had to will each footstep, each turn as the guard led me through the palace. Down, down, down flights of stairs, until we reached the dungeons.

We came to a cell that differed from the others. Instead of a dirt floor, this one was wooden and had ropes hanging from the ceiling to the floor on all four corners. The guard shoved me inside, and I tripped over the raised floor as he slammed the metal gate behind me.

Was this where I was about to die? In the dark?

If so, at least something had gone right.

I hadn't exactly been thrilled about the whole public execution thing.

The guard seemed to have other ideas about how much humiliation I deserved, for he sneered at me, his handsome fae face warping with a special hatred only fitting for complete strangers. "It surprised me when they said a human girl had offered herself."

I pushed myself up on my hands and stood. As much as I would have liked to curl up on the floor and cry now that Dinah couldn't see me like this, I'd have rather done it alone. If it was between getting some much needed catharsis and leaving this fae guard wholly unsatisfied for the day... Well, I was apparently about to find out just how petty I really was.

He went on prodding as I stood to my feet. "I just couldn't come up with a reason a human woman," he spat on the term as if it were a vile curse, "would act against her own nature. After all, it's unnatural for a woman to act in a way that would sever her ability to procreate. But then I saw you, and, I have to say, I was a bit relieved. Of course, you jumped at the chance of ending your meaningless existence. How else were you supposed to leave your mark on this world?"

Ah, good. At least the Fates had been kind enough to see to it that the guard entrusted with overseeing me wouldn't have anything new to say.

At least this, of all things, was something life had prepared me for.

Familiar, that's what this was. Just another day of strangers hurling insults at me. Somehow, it grounded me.

"It must be thrilling, being one of the king's guards," I said. The guard tugged at his uniform, straightening smugly.

"Just doing my duty. Ridding the world of scum like yourself."

I approached the bars and could have laughed at the way the guard tensed, how the muscles in his jaw twitched. It didn't matter how harmless I was, no one ever seemed to get over the fact that I looked born to kill. Never mind the only information one could infer from my scars with any accuracy was that someone or something had harmed *me*. "Tell me," I said, "how did you manage to get the assignment where the absolute least is expected of you? The job of guarding helpless women who have no chance of escape, when the rest of your cohort is out gaining intel, or guarding the king, or fighting in his battles?"

Just because the guard was fae, just because he was quick, didn't mean he could catch me, not when I'd seen it coming from a mile away.

He lunged at me, but I'd already stepped backward before my insult had time to process.

"Hm." I made my voice as high-pitched, as feminine as I could muster. "Not all that quick, are you? I guess that answers my question."

The guard's face went scarlet, and a wave of fear coursed through me. Why was I doing this? Taunting him? The guard was going to throttle me before I even made it to my execution.

But perhaps that was what I wanted after all. How better to humiliate the king than to be dead already by the time this platform I was standing on raised to meet the crowd?

Because that's what this was, this panel of wood and rope. The crowd had already gathered outside, and I could hear their murmurings through the stone walls. Because this wasn't the actual dungeons. This was just a waiting room.

I watched the guard as his hands clasped around the keys at his belt. Fumbling. Contemplating.

Hunger for blood and submission pulsed in his dark eyes. A shudder coursed up my spine as I realized what I'd done, the act of violence a fae so insecure might choose to use against me. To humiliate me.

Despite myself, I stepped backward, but this only fanned the hunger in his eyes. His fingers grasped the keys, more sure of himself now. "Oh, don't be scared, now. Don't you want the one thing you could never have? One last experience before His Majesty cuts your brief life even shorter? I'm sure His Majesty didn't give it to you."

Panic coursed through me as the key scraped against the inside of the lock, rattling in the excited guard's hand.

The lock clicked.

CHAPTER 17

ASHA

I opened my mouth to scream, but he cut me off. "Make a noise, and it will only be worse for you. You're right, you know, about my friends and I having nothing to do. Alert them, and they might want to join in on the fun."

No, no, no.

But then something caught my eye. A shadow moving independently from the shadows. Behind the guard, a pair of narrowed eyes flashed in the darkness. I backed against the far wall of the cell as the dark figure, wrapped from head to toe in black fabric, stalked the guard.

"What is it, dearie? Reconsidering? Thinking it might not be so bad of a deal, after all?" the guard crooned, his voice sickeningly sweet.

The hooded figure, his face obscured by a dark shroud that covered everything but his midnight eyes, emerged from the shadows and pressed one finger against his lips.

I nodded, which might have tipped the guard off, had the shadow not already consumed him.

The figure curled its arm around the guard's neck and yanked him back into the shadows.

Under cover of the darkness, I didn't see him die.

I only heard a gurgle before a faint thud and the sound of a body hitting the floor graced my ears.

When the figure emerged again, his eyes were black as soot. He reached for the key, still dangling in the lock, but then his head jerked, and he stared at the ceiling for a moment. Then he put a finger to his lips again, grabbed the key out of the door, hung it on the nail in the wall, and disappeared into the shadows.

A moment later, voices filled the staircase that led down to my holding cell.

Unfamiliar voices, but one standing out from the rest, a voice I recognized.

The vizier rounded the corner, huffing, his blue eyes wild, followed by four fae guards.

My heart pounded, as a mix of conflicting thoughts swarmed through my head. Should I warn them of the figure lurking in the shadows? The being that would surely slaughter them in a few seconds' time?

But, whoever it was, they had saved me just now.

And as much as I did not believe the vizier to be as wicked as his king, that was more than I could say for him.

The vizier ripped the keys from the wall.

"Where's your guard?" he demanded.

I shook my head, fumbling for a lie. "Took a break. Wasn't worried about me getting out, I guess."

The vizier sighed, but apparently did not have time to address it, because he shoved the key into the lock and opened the door. "Come with me."

I frowned and shook my head. "Dinah. She's still here. If I try to escape, they'll kill her."

His blue eyes pierced mine. "You're not saved yet, my dear. But if you play your cards right, you might have a chance."

Despite myself, I gambled a glance into the shadows. Nothing moved.

It appeared my rescuer was just as confused as I was.

I stepped from the cell, and the vizier clasped my arm. "Listen to me carefully, child. There's a crowd out there waiting for blood. It's of the utmost importance that you become more interesting than your execution." He pulled me up the stairs, two guards behind us, two in front of us. Every step, we slipped further from my savior in the shadows.

"What are you talking about?" I stopped, if only to give the hooded figure a moment to act, to lash out against the two soldiers separating us.

My savior didn't come.

"The king has granted you pardon for the day. To postpone your execution."

"Postpone?" I almost spat the words. "Why?"

The vizier's eyes blazed. "Will you question his mercy?"

"Is it really all that merciful to force me to live another day dreading my demise?"

His expression softened at that, his cheeks sinking into his wrinkled face. "No. No, it isn't. But listen to me very carefully. Somehow, you've managed to win the king's favor. But if you want to live, and live a long life, his is not the only favor you'll need. Whatever you do, you must make the crowd hope that you'll live."

"The crowd? I thought you said—"

But we weren't in the dungeons any longer. We'd reached a set of cedar doors, and in front of the doors was the king, and behind the doors was the rumbling of a bloodthirsty crowd.

* * *

THE KING TOOK my arm in his, his eyes dark as coal, as if the blaze of blue flame from last night had been snuffed out.

"I assume the vizier has already briefed you on what you must do if you wish to live."

I choked. "Ask you nicely?"

He bristled, then turned a pointed stare on the vizier, who shrugged and said, "You didn't exactly provide us with ample time, Your Majesty. Perhaps if you sought my council *before* making your decisions—"

The doors opened, and the sun blinded me as it slinked across the heavens. The lesser moon hovered in the distance, a white shadow against the backdrop of the blue sky, as if it too had made a special appearance to witness my death.

And then we were walking, arm in arm, the king and I, to face an angry, restless crowd.

They roared at us from below. My eye adjusted, and I realized we were standing on a balcony.

The same balcony I'd stared up at just a short year ago, when the king had presented Queen Gwenyth.

He'd smiled then.

He wasn't smiling now.

The king raised a warning hand, and the buzzing crowd quieted. "People of Naenden, fae and human alike..."

This little comment sent a swell of jeers through the crowd, but the king squelched it with a surge of flames that engulfed the previously unlit torches surrounding the crowd. They calmed, and the oppressive heat dwindled, until the scorching temperature was only the sun's doing.

"As you well know, the sins of human women have dripped thick as blood from the beginning. Treachery. That is the word that comes to mind when their kind is mentioned."

The crowd roared, and I tensed, which he must have felt, my arm still clasped tightly between his forearm and elbow.

"You came here for justice. For an execution. For spilled blood."

The cries of the people heightened, bloodthirsty and cruel. Because of course they were hungry for spilled blood. Queen Gwenyth hadn't exactly tried to make herself a friend of the people, and I was sure there were plenty in the crowd who regretted that her execution had occurred in private. How much unnecessary suffering had occurred since, on this same balcony, Queen Gwenyth had announced an increase in our already hefty taxes? Since she had demanded the crowd bow before her?

I supposed my blood was better than nothing.

Even the humans, my people, craned their necks to watch the bloody scene unfold, to see the ugly creature die like she deserved.

I wondered if they might have averted their gaze if such a fate were to fall on someone who looked like Dinah, someone whose features were undefiled.

"But—" The king raised his hand, subduing the crowd. "What sort of ruler would I be if I had not the capacity for mercy?"

The crowd murmured, only loud enough so that they could still hear his words.

"You see, within my decree was an embedded exception. A clause. An opportunity to display my mercy. But mercy only befalls the brave, the honorable. And you—I am speaking to you humans, now—one of your own stepped forward to save the rest. One girl," he flourished to me, "exchanged herself for the majority.

"And for that act of bravery, one so unexpected, so unnatural for your kind, whose only prospect, only purpose, is survival, I, the merciful ruler that I am, have deemed to grant her yet another day."

Understanding enveloped me, suffocated me like a sandstorm carried on the Western wind.

One more day.

He was the power that granted me my life, my breath.

Each day I lived was a mercy, a gift from him.

In this moment, I was not me.

I was the people, the humans, under his rule.

It was at his mercy they lived to see another day.

He held my life, their lives, in his calloused hand.

And I was to remind them of such.

He went on, and my stomach twisted on its empty self. "Each morning your queen will come before me, before you. And I shall deem her worthy or unworthy of another day under the sun. Each day, each *night*," I winced at the implication of the word, what the crowd would assume, "she must prove herself worthy. And if she does, she will find me most merciful."

He turned to me and took my hand, bringing it to his lips. The kiss was cold, despite the fire that roared within him, the flame that lay dormant at his fingertips, the flicker of blue I'd witnessed last night.

When his eyes met mine, I returned his stare with equal coldness.

The sound of disgruntled peasants, disappointed that the king had robbed them of the day's entertainment, coursed through the crowd.

What had the vizier said? That if I wanted to live, the crowd must want me to live too?

Power, that's what this was about. By assessing me each morning, the king showcased his power over my mortal life. Over my kinsmen's mortal life.

But this could go wrong for him. The decree had stated I must die the morning after our wedding.

Honestly, I was shocked that sparing me was even an option. I would have thought reneging on a decree would have been akin to lying, something my fae husband should not have been able to do. Perhaps the loophole dwelled within the lips of the human heralds who the king had assigned to proclaim the decree. Perhaps that was his intention in hiring them—so that he'd never find himself trapped by his own words.

Either way, the late king, this king's father, had possessed a reputation for never relenting on a decree, not once.

Some would perceive this as weakness.

And one look in the king's eyes told me that was a perception he would not tolerate.

That if my blood needed to flow to drown such a notion, so be it.

The crowd needed to want me alive.

I needed the crowd to want me alive.

So I dropped the king's hands and walked to the edge of the balcony.

And there, in the same place my predecessor had declared a tax increase to fund her pet's sanctuary, I bowed before my people, knees trembling and all.

Their servant in a position of power.

One of them.

Their silence, their shock, told me it had been enough.

At least for today.

CHAPTER 18

ASHA

*D*inah flung her arms around me as soon as the vizier led me
through the doors of the king's room.

Out of instinct or habit—I wasn't sure which—I pushed her away,
grazing my fingers over her cheeks to search for the cuts, for the
evidence of where glass had pierced her delicate skin earlier that
morning.

Red welts, marking the various paths of her tears, swelled on her
face, but nothing more. Blood still coated her robes, but where was it
coming from?

"You're alive, you're alive," she choked, almost sounding like she
was drowning.

"Your cuts, how—"

She shook her head, salty droplets losing their grip and falling
from her round cheeks. "Tavi took me to the palace healer. She gave
me a salve that healed them right away."

Her words turned to stone in my belly. The palace had a salve that
could heal a human's cut within a few hours; meanwhile, just outside
the palace walls, humans died every day from infection.

"But you're alive. How did you do it?" Amazement mingled with
elation, lighting up her face as she whispered.

Leave it to Dinah, my constant over-estimator, to assume I had had anything to do with it. "The king's found a way to use me to dangle his power over the humans' heads."

If this news upset my sister, it certainly didn't show on her face. She simply flung her arms around me again, clenching her fingers into my robes, as if to make sure I was real.

She pulled away, her face paling.

"What's wrong?" I asked.

"Father," she whispered. "I must tell Father you're alright."

Father. Had he attended my would-be execution? Would he have even been able to travel all that way on his bad leg? Was he somewhere mourning me, wondering what had happened to Dinah as well?

My stomach twisted into knots at the thought.

"Go."

She nodded and kissed my forehead before heading to the door, her blood speckled robes fluttering behind her.

The vizier, who I hadn't realized had stayed for our reunion, stood silently by the door, his gaze fixed on my sister, on the streaks of blood staining her clothes. On her way out, Dinah grabbed his worn hands. "Might I bring my father to see her? He won't believe me unless he lays eyes on her himself."

The truth of that ached. She was right. He'd assume I was dead, that Dinah simply couldn't bear to tell him the truth, until he saw me breathing himself.

The vizier frowned, deepening the already cavernous lines between his brows, but there was no denying Dinah. "Of course. Come by the West gate. I'll inform the guard there ahead of time."

She pushed herself on her tiptoes and kissed the vizier on the cheek, causing his face to blush crimson, before grabbing one of the guard's hands and making him hurry down the hall with her.

Once we were alone, the vizier bowed his head. "I'm to send for Tavi. She's to dress you for breakfast."

"What?"

The vizier raised his eyebrow. "Did you expect to remain among the living with no food?"

"No. I just figured they'd send me back to the dungeons and have my food delivered. Probably in butterfly portions."

"On the contrary, the king wishes you to breakfast with him."

I balked, but the vizier only grimaced, his thin lips carving sharp edges into his cheeks. "Do not think your confusion goes unshared. I understand the king's motivations about as well as you do, and I've known him his entire life."

With that, he left me alone in the king's room, blood spattered shards of mirror still littering the floor. Only then, with a moment left to myself, did I remember the figure from the shadows this morning. The being that had saved me from the hungry guard.

Who had lurked within the shadows, hidden behind the dark mask? Friend or foe? Had his intentions been pure, to save me from an awful fate? Or had he had something else in mind, some other purpose for me? And why hadn't he followed through on his plan? Perhaps four guards had been too much for his strength.

But, then again, something told me he'd done this before.

Before I had a chance to come up with any theories, Tavi entered my room, her tiny, pale hands shaking with delight as she grinned at me, obviously stunned that I was alive.

"Your Majesty?" Tavi asked. I jolted, preparing myself to meet the igneous eyes of the fae king glaring at me in the doorway.

"Your Majesty?" Tavis's pale eyes glittered with concern as she asked again.

As she asked *me*.

* * *

THE KING DIDN'T BOTHER to spare a glance at me as one of his guards led me to the breakfast room.

Porridge, cheesy from the smell of it, sat steaming in front of the king, as well as in front of the seat directly across from him at the far end of the table.

Well, good. At least they'd picked out the seat I would have picked for myself.

The room was well lit, painted an eggshell color that reminded me of Tavi's eyes. A windowed alcove protruded from the wall behind my chair, showering the room with natural light.

As the guard showed me to my seat, a decorative piece with edges more ideal for admiring and less ideal for sitting, I tried to ignore the hulking beast of a male across from me and instead focus on my breakfast.

The porridge practically scoured my mouth, but once it touched my tongue, I found I couldn't stop. I devoured it before the guard had returned to his station by the door, and then I moved on to the fruit, the likes of which I'd never laid eye on in Naenden. Most of them, I didn't even know the names of. While there was plenty of desert fruit sold in the marketplace, my family usually saved fruit for special occasions, as it was more expensive and spoiled quickly. The green one with the fuzzy exterior and tiny black seeds was my favorite, with its tangy but sweet flavor.

My plate was empty far too soon, leaving a hole in my belly that outmatched the large bowl in front of me.

"Would you care for some more?"

Now that the food was no longer before me, I remembered the savage ruler that sat across the table. He peered at me with curiosity in those molten eyes of his, and only then did I notice the bits of porridge that had found their home on the edges of my lips.

I scooped up a napkin and wiped myself off, my face going hot.

My stomach pounded. There were few times in my life when I'd denied it food, this past week being the exception. Nerves had kept my appetite abated since my meeting with the vizier, but that didn't mean my stomach wasn't keeping score.

I wasn't keen on taking anything from the king.

In the end, my stomach won. "Yes, Your Majesty."

He snapped, and another plate of porridge appeared before me at the hands of a bustling servant.

I inhaled it before its contents finished sloshing from the impact.

"You like our chef's cooking, then?" the king asked.

He wasn't serious. Surely he wasn't serious.

"I can't really say I tasted it."

He frowned, and I explained it to the spoiled idiot. "When meals aren't a guarantee, it's the feeling in your stomach that's most noticeable. Not the taste."

Great. Our marriage was already off to a terrible start, all because I couldn't keep my mouth shut.

Or maybe we were off to a terrible start because my husband defined kindness as refraining from slaughtering me publicly on the morning after our wedding.

As if to solidify my concern, the king turned to his guard. "Leave us."

The guard nodded and disappeared out the door. My fork clanked against the table, leaving bits of porridge on the pale blue tablecloth as my hand shook, my knuckles white with trepidation.

He examined me for a while, and I wondered if he was already scheming a creative way to execute me tomorrow morning, when he finally spoke. "You spark my curiosity, you know."

"I don't know, actually."

His lips curled, and he nodded. "Why did you offer yourself as my bride?"

"Because I wish to keep my sister alive."

He cocked his head, examining me with such intensity I had to fight the urge to look away. "There was no guarantee that your sister would be chosen."

"There was no guarantee she wouldn't."

"And that was enough? That chance was enough for you to throw your life away?"

"Yes. You should understand taking chances, though."

He frowned.

"You decreed that you'd murder innocent women every mooncycle on the chance we were all evil, plotting adulteresses."

To my surprise, he smiled, a sly, knowing grin that only highlighted the sharpness of his features. As if I'd just given away a bit of information he'd been fishing for. It made me want to squirm. "I'd be honored to hear the rest of your story this evening."

My throat went dry, and I stumbled over my words. "Why, when you missed the first part?"

"Oh, but I didn't miss it."

The porridge was coming back up now, creeping its way up my esophagus, preparing to flee my body and secure a home anywhere other than my soon-to-be corpse. If he had heard... That meant he knew. He knew about my magic. Magic that was more than a little illegal for me to possess. "Do you make a habit of lurking outside of women's rooms?"

"Technically, it's my room."

I clutched the folds of the flowing, pale pink housedress Tavi had dressed me in this morning after my not-execution, trying my utmost to keep a hold on his eyes. Not to show him how terrified of him I truly was.

"Tell me, Asha. How did you acquire such a gift for storytelling?"

So that was why he spared my life this morning. Not so he could flex his power over his people, though that was probably an added benefit.

He had heard. He knew about my magic, and he wanted to know how in Alondria a human could access it.

Because he was fae. And the fae were the only ones who were supposed to be able to wield magic.

His molten eyes went cold as he leaned forward. "Tell me. Who did you steal it from?" My collar went taut against my neck as the heat in the room rose, suffocating me. "Did you have to kill a fae to get it?"

I shook my head, but I couldn't breathe, not when the very air scorched my lungs.

The glass in the windows behind me shattered, stray fragments nicking my back as a wall of heat erupted behind me. To my surprise, the king's face went pale and lingered on something behind me.

I ducked underneath the table before I had a chance to find out what it was.

A female voice shook the room, and the dishes clattered on the table above me. "What did you do, brother?"

The king shot to his feet on the other side of the table, and on my

T.A. LAWRENCE

side, all I saw was the hem of a flaming red dress and stiletto shoes to match. "Do what?" he yelled.

"Oh, I don't know. Murder our precious brother Fin's wife, then your own? Then declare that you're going to kill an innocent girl every month if one doesn't offer herself for the rest? Let's see, did I miss anything?"

"You trounce all about the kingdoms doing whatever you please, soiling our father's name, and then you think it right to hurry home to pass judgment on me?"

The stilettos stalked across the room, apparently unconcerned by the king's accusations.

"I changed your soiled sheets when you peed yourself in the night out of fear of our father. I'd think again before you use his name to defend yourself."

Silence, sticky, sweltering silence, filled the room. The blazing fire licked at the ornate rug.

The rug that ran under the table.

No matter that the king had granted me mercy, or his version of it, this morning. His sister was going to kill us both.

But then the fire dissipated, as if at the snap of a finger. "That's what I thought," the female said.

The table sheltering me went flying, plates and goblets shattering against the wall across from us, leaving me cowering and exposed to the king and his sister.

Princess Lydia was everything they'd gossiped about and more. Her blazing red dress smoked at the hems, an effect I imagined her magic foddered. Her face was staggeringly beautiful, and her violet eyes blazed to the point I would have believed in purple fire even though I'd never heard of it existing.

She pranced over to me, offering a hand. I wasn't stupid enough not to take it, and when I did, it didn't burn as I expected, but radiated with warmth. Without a hint of effort, she lifted me to my feet amid the wreckage.

"Well hello darling," she grinned. "I always wanted a sister."

CHAPTER 19

ASHA

I might not have been raised in a palace, but my father had at least raised me with enough propriety that I knew better than to ask the princess what that particular comment implied about her feelings regarding her dead sister-in-law.

If anyone in Naenden had a dishonorable reputation, it was Princess Lydia, the eldest child of the late King Rajeen. What Lydia lacked in inheritance, she had made up for in, well, *experience*.

At least, that was the word the gossiping women of Meranthi liked to use when they spoke of her.

Princess Lydia wasn't one to stay at home, tending to parties and gatherings, or—the most important of her tasks as a princess—finding a husband that would solidify an alliance with one of the other kingdoms.

Instead, Princess Lydia "trounced" about the Kingdom, doing "Fates know what." Which I had learned was simply code for, "we don't know what she's up to, so it must be scandalous."

Apparently, that list included vandalizing her childhood home and directly insulting her brother, the fire-wielding king whose curiosity was the only thing keeping me tethered to this side of the sun.

"Lydia," the king warned, his voice quavering with rage. But all she did was flit her hand, dismissing him.

I recoiled in case the blaze devoured me with her.

But it never came. Instead, Princess Lydia led me across the wreckage and out what used to be the windowed alcove.

Despite my better instincts, I chanced one last glance at the king, who stood, quite literally fuming, in what used to be the breakfast area.

"Will he punish you for that later?" I asked. As grateful as I was for the princess's rescue, the thought of witnessing her hanging from a noose tomorrow wasn't appealing, even if it was in my place.

Her laugh danced through the cool air, probably making the birds jealous.

We were in the palace gardens, I realized, which would have been astounding anyway, what with the fact that succulents were about the only thing that grew in Meranthi, and this opening was lush with greenery.

What was more, a gentle breeze pattered against my cheeks as we strode, yet the garden was still bright with sunlight.

The princess must have interpreted the confused look on my face, because she gestured toward the sky. "There's a protective bubble, of sorts. Magicked by some wind faeries. It controls the climate, so our lovely garden can flourish. And so we get to enjoy the sunlight without burning to a crisp."

"I thought fae couldn't die of heatstroke."

She tsked. "Just because we can't die of it doesn't mean it doesn't make us want to."

Something writhed in my stomach, an unpleasantness I had no desire to attribute to the female who had just saved me from the king's questions—accusations—but I couldn't help it.

"You can speak your mind, you know," she said. Heat rushed to my cheeks as I realized how easily she'd read my expression. I'd always had the advantage of others refusing to look at my face. I supposed I'd gotten spoiled, never having to mask my feelings. Dinah and my father and Az would have interpreted them anyway, so there was no use trying to hide them from them.

But the princess seemed unfazed by my scarring, something that unnerved me more than I would have expected.

"It's just—" I cleared my throat. "If such magic exists, why not offer it to the rest of Meranthi, the rest of Naenden even."

Amusement flickered in the princess's violet eyes. "And already, I'm much preferring you to my late sister-in-law."

My stomach twisted as I remembered the late Queen Gwenyth's fate. "I thought you were upset with the king for mur—for killing her."

She picked at her bloodred nails, the length and cut of which brought up an unwelcome image of an alleycat sharpening its claws. "If it had just been Gwenyth, I might not have had to cut my excursion short."

"I take it the two of you weren't friends," I said, not sure what else to say.

Her teeth flashed, white as snow. "Kiran said we should have gotten along better than we did. That we were *just alike.*" She rolled her eyes and carried on, and I struggled to keep up with her as we strode through the gardens. Even in her impractical shoes, her stride was almost double mine, the difference between our athleticism even more drastic.

I stopped in my tracks, wondering what I was even doing out here. "He's going to kill me."

She stopped and turned, slowly, lethally. "If it's any consolation, I'll kill him if he does. And I'll hang his body from the fingertips of that abhorrent statue of Tionis my father built over my mother's tulips. Have you seen it yet? It's on the West corner of the garden, and it's massive and gaudy. He bullied the King of Charshon into sending it here from his own royal gardens, just because he could."

I cleared my throat, unsure how to tread on the clearly sensitive topic of the princess's parents. My mind whirred, searching for something to fill the uncomfortable silence between us, but the only thing I could come up with was how I had learned during my fleeting time in school that

Tionis was an ancient fae known for washing his feet in the blood of his victims. For some reason, that didn't seem to be an appropriate conversational topic at the moment, so I settled on, "I can't say I've seen it."

A wry smile curved on her lips, a smile that indicated just about every emotion except happiness. "Right. I forgot my brother kept you in that dungeon this morning."

The tiny pebbles beneath my feet flitted about as I shuffled. "Why are you being kind to me?"

The edges of her perfectly symmetrical face twitched. Terrifying, that's what Princess Lydia was. Anyone who spoke against her must have never stood in her presence, must have never known what it was to fear her. Her braid started at the top of her skull, her hair stretched tight against her head, and coursed down the better half of her back.

I wondered if she'd ever strangled someone with that braid.

Thankfully, I was at least well enough in my right mind not to say such wonderings out loud.

"Thank you?" I said, when I could no longer bear the discomfort of her silence.

She laughed, that elegant chime that befitted a princess, though perhaps not one so terrifying.

As I followed her though the garden, we found ourselves amongst a patch of shy looking flowers that reminded me of Dinah. Soft, and stunning, yet closed up in on themselves.

"What are they called?" I asked, before I realized what an embarrassing question that was. How uneducated did one have to be not to know the names of most flowers?

"Tulips," the princess said, and if there was any judgment in that statement, she hid it well. "I replanted them in honor of my mother."

I reached out to touch the pretty flowers, then thought better of it.

"Why did you do it?" the princesses asked.

I straightened, tucking my hand behind my back. "Why did I do what?"

She rolled her eyes. "You know what."

"To save my sister."

"Was your sister summoned to marry my brother?"

118

"No."

"Then why'd you really do it?"

I groaned, wishing the fae of this palace would stop asking me that. "Why is it so hard to believe I did this for Dinah?"

Her violet eyes flickered, and she didn't break her stare. "As you witnessed in our poor breakfast nook, not all families are so close."

I sighed and plopped on a nearby bench, hoping, but not really caring all that much, that it wouldn't offend the princess to sit in her presence. Apparently, she wasn't one for propriety either, because she perched herself next to me.

"I've always had horrible nightmares. Nightmares where something terrible happens to my sister. That she's been kidnapped or sold to the merchants or...mauled..." My throat caught on that one. "I can hardly sleep some nights. The worry that today might be my last day with her, the last day before my world is ripped apart... It's too much." I turned to face Lydia and was grateful when she didn't flinch from my gnarled stare. Instead, her violet eyes deepened into a bright, gleaming purple. "Just knowing each mooncycle that it could have been her this time. It would have been too much. It would have ruined my life anyway, just the possibility."

A shadow clouded Princess Lydia's beautiful face. "I might not understand it with Kiran. But our youngest brother... I would do a great many difficult things for him."

Something about the way she said it made me think she already had.

"Why is the king doing this?" I asked.

The princess gritted her teeth. "He's his father's son. He always has been. I thought maybe he would turn out differently, especially when he brought Gwenyth home. But my hope was short-lived, it seems."

She went to leave, and I reached for her arm. She turned slowly. "Yes?"

"I'm terrified of him. Of what he might do."

Princess Lydia frowned. "So am I."

CHAPTER 20

ASHA

I wasn't sure what to do with my free time on my second, second-to-last day alive.

That's what I decided to call it in my head. Why I found an unnecessarily lengthy term referring to my imminent peril so gratifying, I wasn't sure. But, as today was indeed my second, second-to-last day alive, I felt I deserved to be a tad amused.

Yesterday had been full of so much pomp and anticipation, with all the preparations for the wedding, that the day itself had rushed by, as if time had accelerated, impatient to witness my death.

Except I wasn't dead.

And now, on my second, second-to-last day alive, all I had done was eat breakfast and go for a walk.

Oh, and woo the favor of my kingdom.

And watch in horror as my mystery savior strangled my would-be assailant in the shadows.

So perhaps I'd done more than I'd given myself credit for.

If only Dinah and my father could arrive soon, but I wasn't sure how long it would take my father to walk all the way from our hovel to the palace with his limp, especially in today's heat, which was oppressive even for a desert's summer.

Dinah would be smart about it. She'd probably wait for darkness to fall before allowing him to set foot out the door. And if he protested, Az would help her.

Az. My heart lurched at the thought of him. How would he feel when Dinah told him I'd survived the king's wrath, at least for the day? Or did he already know? Had he attended my execution this morning? Had he bowed in return when I offered my not-so-subtle message that I was on the humans' side?

I could only speculate. After all, I would have thought that the boy I'd loved for over a decade now would have come with Dinah to see me off yesterday, would have tried to force his way inside, like she had.

Perhaps the boy I knew, whose mischievous eyes and boyish smile I could trace as well as the scars on the back of my left hand, was the boy I'd scaffolded within my imagination, the boy I'd superimposed over the shape of my friend.

All I knew was that I couldn't bear to stand still. So, after Lydia left me in the garden, I waited just long enough to be sure I wouldn't cross paths with her.

Because I intended to snoop.

Not for any malicious reason. It was just that, on my second, second-to-last day alive, I was bored.

And that would not do.

I would not die bored.

Besides, boredom provided ample opportunity for my mind to experiment with all conceivable execution techniques. Burnt to cinders at the king's hand. Strangled, my legs dangling off the ground at the king's hand. Decapitated at someone's hand, probably not the king's. I wasn't sure where I had gotten the idea, but I was pretty sure kings had other people do the decapitating for them. Just like a king wouldn't strangle his own lamb for dinner.

Just a theory.

As I paced through the hallways of the palace, I made a point of marking every turn. When Dinah and my father arrived, I wouldn't want to be lost somewhere in this behemoth.

I was not going to be bored on my second, second-to-last day alive, and I was not going to embarrass myself either.

Thankfully, I didn't have to wander far before I discovered just the room I hadn't even known I was looking for.

The library.

Perfect. My other quest, the one that probably should have been more important than avoiding boredom, would be well served here. What better place to avoid the king who knew I was possessed by magic—very, very illegal magic? Because there was no way under the sun that the person who thought monthly murder holidays were a good idea could be an avid reader. Because, to read—that would require getting into someone else's head, something that would probably be a less than comfortable experience for someone who reveled in the torture of others. Besides, a room packed full of books was my dream, and if the Fates were kind at all, they would not allow the king to pollute this dream too.

Not like he had my daydream about a mirror ceremony with Az.

Ugh.

The doors were taller than twin elephants and made of ivory. I pushed them open and walked in, a stuffy heat warming my face. A fireplace stood at the far end of the room. It looked normal enough, except that there was a suspicious absence of wood on which a regular fire might have perched. I wondered if it burned eternally on its own, or if some poor fae around here constantly had to summon it in their mind to keep it from going out. As far as I knew, the royal family possessed the exclusive right to wield such power, but the royal siblings had to have distant cousins or something. Maybe they enslaved them and forced them into eternal fireplace keeping.

Sounded like a cushy job to me.

But then there were the books. Stuffed shelves fanned outward from the fireplace, so that the fire was the focal point of the room. I poked my head in first, craning my neck to examine the left side of the library. When I determined it was sufficiently empty—and by that, I mean completely empty—I walked into the room and shut the doors behind me as quietly as I could manage.

The books lining the walls twinkled in the glow of the woodless fire. I was pretty sure that not a single book in this library was brown or black, or any neutral color, for that matter. Instead, they all boasted vibrant teals, oranges, fuchsias, and ceruleans, as well as a host of other colors I had never learned the fancy names for.

If today was my second, second-to-last day to live, at least the Fates had felt sorry for me and thrown me their scraps. Perhaps my father and sister would be content to spend their last evening with me sitting quietly, my father reading a book other than the one he had mangled with overuse over the course of my life. Dinah could sit in one of the velvet chairs delicately arranged over the intricately woven woolen rug. And I could lose myself in one of these stories. One that would take me far, far away from the Fates I'd surely not be lucky enough to escape tomorrow.

Yes, this would do.

But which book to pick?

I started toward the sliding ladder closest to me, but I wrenched my hand back as soon as my fingertips touched the wood. A burning odor that had nothing to do with the fireplace singed the insides of my nostrils, charring the edges of my memory. I shoved the thought down, down, down and ignored the phantom pain on the left side of my face.

No climbing for me on my second, second-last day alive, I thought as I winced. Perhaps some scars never healed, even when one knew they were going to die anyway.

So I reached for the largest book I could find within arm's length. It was a fool's gesture. I knew that. Anyone with the tiniest bit of sense would have told me to pick a book I could read cover to cover in a day. But as I lazed on a pile of cushions, sprawled out on my belly before the fire, something about holding such a gargantuan book in my hands made me feel…

As if I would live to read it.

It was a history book, which sparked my interest. Whether it was actually illegal for me, a human, to read history books was a bit of a grey area. We received some education on history in the local school that graced us with—wait for it—three whole years of education. But the lessons didn't date as far back as the origin of the fae in our realm. Humans weren't supposed to bother themselves with that information, and I'd known of black market merchants being arrested for trafficking such books.

But, other than sharing my body with my magic, I'd been a law-abiding citizen up to this point, and look where that had gotten me.

And so I started *A History of Earth: Prefaeistic Era.*

THOUGH THE HISTORY of humans on Earth is extensive, in my studies, I find its story more compelling when told backward. Perhaps this is my fae nature taking precedence over my scholarly pride, but I hope the reader too will find that events unfolded in such a way that it was as though the Fates desired the fae to inherit Alondria from its inception. Therefore, I believe our arrival to this world to be both the beginning and the end of the human narrative.

I rolled my eyes. Typical fae, to think their part in history was so important it outranked Time itself. But despite my instant dislike of the author, I continued.

It is common knowledge that the fae who first discovered the tear in the threads of the universe was but a child. Now, at the time, the fae resided solely in the land of the Nether, a dangerous realm, full of wicked sorts of creatures, of which the fae, try as they might, could not tame. In fact, though this might be surprising to a human audience...

Oh, the condescension... *the fae were not themselves masters of nature in the Nether. In fact, they found themselves prey to other creatures, beings, elements, of which I do not dare name or describe here lest I call to them and the vile beasts hear me through the Rip in the Fabric and follow us here.*

The Rip? Was that what they called it? My memory fled backward to last night's story. There had been a boy from what seemed to be another world, and he had found a ray of light that made his hand invisible. The boy had stepped through the light in the end. At least, that was the last part of the story I could remember, whether it was the end...

"Doing some light reading, are we?"

I slammed the book shut and hopped to my feet to face the vizier. My face flushed. I hadn't anticipated anyone finding me lounging, making myself comfortable in this palace that was not my own.

Except it was my own, technically. I was the queen, after all.

Then I remembered I had made a commitment to myself not to let myself become embarrassed on my second, second-to-last day alive, so I tried to swallow the heat in my cheeks.

"It's very interesting. I had never heard the story of how the fae came to dwell among humans," I said.

"I assume you weren't searching for the history of the fae, though, were you, child?" The vizier's wrinkled eyes were soft and kind, though I supposed he couldn't help the tinge of rebuke in his tone. It probably came with the territory—being the sole elderly influence in the life of a king whose decision-making skills I considered rash at best.

"If today is to be my last day, I'd like to know a bit about where I came from. I know it's not allowed, but surely it wouldn't hurt anything. You know, since I have to prove my worth and such. We both know come tomorrow, I'll be..." I grimaced and mimicked slitting my throat, to which the vizier responded with a look of uncomfortable distaste. I again wondered how old this fae must be, if he had lived long enough for Time to carve its mark into his face.

"If that's the case, you won't get what you're looking for from that waste of parchment." The vizier gestured down toward the enormous book. "Written with all the fae bias one could imagine. You'd be better off reading from one of these." He beckoned me to follow him, and I did, to a dark corner of the library where I discovered brown books did indeed exist.

"Were these written by humans of old?" I asked, my heart fluttering with excitement as the vizier handed me a pile. That the ancient humans had recorded our past, so that all these centuries later, a woman like me could extend the writers' lives by just a few moments by hearing their stories... A well of anguish opened up within me. Regret swallowed any excitement I had mustered.

"What's bothering you, my young queen?" the vizier asked. I wiped the tears flowing from my right eye away, embarrassed.

"It's silly," I said. "But part of me wishes I had kept a journal or something. I always thought I wouldn't have much to say. That there was no use chronicling my life. It's not like I went off on adventures. But..." I couldn't bring myself to say it. It sounded too ridiculous. Not that I could stoop further in this fae's sight, weeping before him without a drop of dignity. Fae probably didn't weep before they died. They probably faced it with some sort of dignified one-liner that would end up engraved into a bust to match their decapitated head.

"But what, child?" the vizier said. His vibrant blue eyes did not shy away from my face, wretched as it must look as my tears soaked my scars and the mismatched patches of skin on my cheek.

"But I wish I could leave something behind," I said.

He peered at me for a moment. His eyes wrinkled and his mouth opened as if he might tell me something, but then he shut it again. I met his gaze, and something about my pitiful state must have made him reconsider, for he said, "Surely there is a way you could leave something behind, young *queen*." He nodded his head forward expectantly at that word.

Queen.

"I don't have any time left to make the title useful," I said.

"No, not time," he said, and I gathered we were playing some sort of game. That perhaps the vizier might find himself in trouble if he were the one to give me the idea, and that, if it came down to it, he would not want to admit to be the first to come up with the notion.

"What else is there?" I asked.

The vizier chuckled.

"It would do you well to think outside your own limited experiences."

Anger flared in my chest. "It's not as if I've had many *experiences* to draw from. You remember, I am poor," I said.

"Are you?" the vizier asked, one wiry eyebrow raised.

"Aren't I?" I asked.

The vizier shrugged.

"But *Queen* is just a title. He's going to murder me tomorrow. It means nothing except to humiliate me and my people."

"Do you think the marriage laws know that?" he asked.

I gaped. "Will you help me draw up a will?"

"Is that a request from a poor human?" the vizier asked, a flicker in the blue of his eyes.

"No," I said, as I held my chin high and grinned. "It's an order from your queen."

CHAPTER 21

ASHA

One would have thought that for a poor human girl with only two living family members, writing a will would have been easy.

The vizier had probably assumed as much when he planted the idea in my head.

Turns out, we had both been wrong.

"My dear child! Are you going to give every pauper in Meranthi a piece of your inheritance?" he had asked when I remembered the beggar on the corner of Twin Alleys and inquired if there was any way we could find his name in the records. "It would be faster to walk to Twin Alleys ourselves and just ask him."

"Can we do that?" I'd said.

I might have exasperated the vizier with my ever-growing list of people who might benefit from a portion of a queen's inheritance should I meet an unfortunate end. Perhaps that was why he'd offered me a pile of books to borrow and encouraged me to return to the library as soon as we'd finished the will.

Later, after the sun had set, Tavi brought my father and sister to the library to meet me. After a reunion marked with tears and hugs and my family's insistence that I had somehow finagled my way out of my execution by being clever, I couldn't seem to assuage the pit in my stomach, the dread that I'd gotten their hopes up by surviving one more day. But when I witnessed the sheer joy of seeing my father's face light up at the collection of books, something tugged at my heart. I should have added a section to my will that allowed him to borrow books from this library. That would have kept him occupied, transported him from his grief, if only for a little while.

"Have these even been touched?" my father asked, running his fingertips close to the spines of the books, as if he were trying to feel their essence without tainting them with a smudge of oil from his fingertips.

"I wondered the same thing. They're all pristine. But I believe they're made of saber hide. Fae prefer it because it doesn't wear with age."

My father humphed. "The fae must be ignorant of the love a book feels when its owner has taken the trouble to sew its spine back together thrice."

I smiled and watched him pick out a book. It took him nearly an hour, as if we had time to spare. But I didn't mind so much.

He finally settled on an adventure novel, one set in the frigid kingdom of Mystral. Dinah and I lounged on the cots near the fire as he read it aloud to us, the warmth of the fire tickling the hairs on my arms and blanketing my face. I had never experienced warmth like this before, the type that could touch my skin without scalding it. Wrap its arms around me without consuming me.

I considered that a life next to a warm fire might be a nice one. And if today was to be my second, second-to-last day alive, lying next to the dancing flames, listening to the familiar cadence of my father's low rumble telling of a hero surviving in a frigid wilderness, might not be the worst way to spend it.

Sleep tempted my heavy eyelids, weary from having their usual slumber stolen from them, not just last night, but for the previous week. But then, just as my mind drifted off into a serene oblivion, the book snapped shut and I jolted from the floor.

"That's not the end is it?" Dinah asked. I assumed that whatever my father had read just now had not been a satisfactory conclusion to the story.

"Not the end," he said, smiling with a hint of smugness. "We shall finish it tomorrow. And perhaps begin another."

I didn't even fight him on it. Because, for a moment, I let myself enjoy a fraction of Dinah's and my father's hope, even if it wasn't my own.

* * *

THAT NIGHT, Dinah accompanied me to the king's chambers. She had convinced me to let her stay the night again, contending that she didn't want to leave me by myself with, "your own...forgive me for saying this...morbid thoughts."

Tavi brought us dinner, two steaming plates of roasted chickpeas and tomatoes, and a savory sauce that made my mouth water.

The king strode in, his scarlet robes billowing behind him, his jaw set underneath his well-trimmed beard. Tavi scampered to the corner of the room, and I worried perhaps I had been presumptuous in allowing Dinah into his room without asking.

Instinctively, I pushed Dinah behind me, though it was a bit of a struggle, because apparently she had the same idea.

The king cleared his throat. "I find sleep to be fleeting. Would you mind if I stayed to listen to your tale?"

When I spoke, my words spat like acid from my gritted teeth, which I had forced into a less-than-genuine smile. "But you missed the beginning, Your Majesty."

His eyes slanted into an amused smirk, but he didn't address the fact I had just called him out for eavesdropping on us the previous evening.

Dinah whipped around to face the king. His golden eyes darted back and forth between us, searching for the tells that would give away how a girl so beautiful could be any relation of mine. My stomach clenched. When I stepped in front of Dinah, it had been out of instinct, not rational thought.

"Yes, please, Your Majesty," Dinah said, shocking me with how little her tiny voice trembled in his presence. "You must stay. You'll have never heard a tale like it."

I refrained from shooting my sister a disapproving look, mostly because, if this was to be her last memory of me, which it probably would be, now that I'd been sarcastic with the king, I didn't want it to be soured. But why my sister insisted on encouraging my murderer to share this last moment with us, I could not comprehend.

The king hesitated for a moment before lowering himself to the floor and sitting cross-legged. I stifled my sneer under a cough. His massive form, curled up like a child might sit, looked ridiculous.

"No, please, Your Majesty. Take the bed," I said, trying and failing to mask the poison in my tone.

"The ladies should take the bed." He nodded toward the source of contention.

Well, at least I was going to be murdered by a gentleman. What a comfort.

"The *ladies* are accustomed to sleeping on the floor," I said. Blood rushed to my cheeks. How dare he give himself the pleasure of thinking he was gracious to his victims?

"Would that be more comfortable for you?" he asked.

I had to clench my teeth together to keep my jaw from dropping. Were all fae rulers like this? Completely oblivious to their own cruelty? Just this morning, he'd not only had me taken to the dungeons where one of his guards attempted to assault me, but he'd had the audacity to corner me at breakfast and accuse me of stealing my magic.

He was a fool if he thought I'd interpret his chivalry as anything other than a change in approaches aimed at getting information about my magic out of me.

"I'd be pleased to make the ladies a pallet, if you wished it, Your Majesty," Tavi said from the corner, bowing as she addressed her master.

"Very well," he said, sounding a bit defeated. He stood and moved toward the bed before sitting on the edge, as if the bed might swallow him whole if he lay in it. What a peculiar king, I thought. One who would decree the demise of his innocent citizens on a whim, yet seem so unsettled by their discomfort.

Before she left, Tavi dragged a pile of pillows from around the fireplace and arranged them so that our sleeping surface was mostly even. Not that we'd be getting any sleep tonight.

We all sat in silence for a moment.

And then, my magic spoke.

CHAPTER 22

*W*hen the boy Farin reappeared into the Grassplace, it was with a new skip in his step. A skip that had been squashed sometime between the moment his first screams were muffled with an Otherskin rag and the moment he'd learned that running was not allowed in the Nether. Unless one was being chased by an Other. Farin had always thought this rule silly and didn't think running would do anyone much good at that point, if they'd never practiced before.

But Farin didn't make the rules.

At least, not in the Nether.

But Farin had found a new Nether, one he didn't think he'd name Nether at all. He wasn't sure exactly what he would name it, but he figured he had better call it something in his mind in the meantime, so he would know what he was talking about when he thought of it.

For now, it would be called Mine.

Because that's what this place was. The only Mine Farin had ever truly possessed.

In fact, Farin had spent so many hours running and frolicking and rolling in the grass of Mine, which was green and not brown, like the grass in Nether—though it still tasted bitter, much to Farin's disappointment—that, upon reappearing in the Nether, he set off for home in a fully fledged sprint. After all, Farin had lost himself in the joys of being able to run and scream as he willed, and, in doing so, had lost track of time.

The sun in Mine was positioned differently than the sun in the Nether, and Farin's heart sank when he realized the Nether sun was slipping behind the horizon, taunting him by moving so much faster than it did in the middle of the day.

Farin was halfway through the Grassplace, stoked by the sense of panic in his chest, the memories of lashes on his back and aching teeth, before the true dread hit him.

He had sprinted through the Grassplace.

His heart pounded, *thu-thum, th-thum,* and he shushed it, lest it alert the monsters.

But his heart only beat faster, as if to taunt him, to remind him it couldn't possibly be any louder than his feet pounding against the ground, his shoulders shaking the dry, rickety grass.

Father had always said that the scent of blood grew stronger the faster it pulsed.

The thought didn't help to slow the throbbing.

Farin stopped, his legs sutured to the ground. The grass still quavered and battered against itself in his wake. Loud. He'd been so loud.

Farin's nose tickled and his eyes stung and his throat grew a heavy lump that hurt to swallow.

It didn't hurt as bad as seven lashes. And it probably didn't hurt as bad as being ripped to shreds by the Others, but Farin couldn't be sure, because he had never been ripped to shreds by an Other. He'd only used his imagination to feel such a thing, but his imagination couldn't even imagine up sweet and tangy, so he figured it couldn't be trusted.

Still, he wished his imagination would turn itself off at the moment.

Even if it wasn't mature enough to imagine exactly what it felt like to be ground into meat between a monster's razor-sharp teeth, it was still doing a pretty good job of frightening Farin.

And fear was against the rules. The Others could smell it.

The Others.

Farin remembered that most of them hunted at night, though Father had always reminded him that, if a fae woke one, an Other wouldn't hesitate to punish them by ripping their head off. But the sun had slipped even further past the horizon, and the night chill had already set in, whispering through the Grassplace and raising the bumps on Farin's arms.

He had to get home before it was dark.

The Others hunted at night.

So Farin took another step, fighting the urge to bolt straight through the grass and all the way back home. The thought was tempting, as Farin had already sprinted and was still in one piece.

But he knew the chances of running all the way back to the tribe at this hour unscathed was unlikely, especially when the Others were probably already stirring, stretching out their long, muscular limbs and flexing their claws into the dry dirt.

By the time Farin reached the last row of tall grass, he thought his stomach had scooted its way to his throat. His imagination had decided that, as soon as Farin brushed away the last blade of grass, a monster would jump out and swallow him whole.

This was another reason Farin did not trust his imagination to give him an accurate idea of how painful it would be to be eaten by an Other. Because he was fairly certain Others were too mean to swallow fae whole.

He thought of the stray cat that sometimes begged outside their tent. The one who was so used to Father kicking it, it jumped at the sight of Farin too, even when he was only trying to sneak it a few tidbits he'd saved throughout the day.

But when Farin brushed the grass away, there was nothing there. Nothing there to pounce on him.

In fact, Farin was so relieved, he let out a sigh. A long, loud sigh.

Farin's heart clenched up again.

Everyone knew that pumping blood had a potent scent, that the Others could track pounding footsteps from miles away, that monsters hunted at night...

And that a fae's voice was the loudest, most salient of all.

Tears bulged from Farin's eyes as his legs seemed to move for themselves, so close to a run that Farin was sure his boots would make less sound if he gave into his primal urges and sprinted.

But he couldn't help himself. He couldn't stay out here any longer, not when all he could see was the edge of the sun skirting down below the horizon.

Soon it would be too dark to see his way. He'd have to just set himself toward home and keep walking and hope he didn't trip over a loose rock or root.

Perhaps he should crawl, he thought to himself. With that, he kneeled and dug his shaking palms into the dirt. With every inch forward, he felt the earth before him, checking for anything that might trip him.

What he didn't think to check for was sleeping Others.

So it was that when Farin's hand brushed against something that felt like a pelt coat, against something that moved outward and inward against his palm...

When Farin's hand brushed against an Other, he screamed.

FARIN'S SCREAM—A sound he had never heard, at least not since he'd been a baby, a time which he could not remember—sliced through the air. The sound was so unfamiliar that Farin jumped a second time, sure the horrid noise had come from the Other's jaws, that it was some call to the Other's family, alerting them that dinner was ready.

Run, Farin told himself. You're allowed to run.

But Farin's legs did not budge. It was as if they were furious at him for making them run when they weren't supposed to, and now they were standing their ground, refusing to move on the principle of the matter.

Dry earth shuffled in the wake of something heavy, and though Farin could barely see in the dark, he now saw its shape, long and massive, stirring. Legs extended into the night, and the dark mass moved to its feet. In the distance, Farin noticed the crest of the moon rising above the horizon.

Only a few seconds later, the moonlight bounced off the monster's bared teeth. They were long and jagged, as if most of them had been broken against the bones of the Other's prey. The effect of which only made them sharper, more adept at ripping.

Another scream boiled up inside Farin, but it clung to his throat, as if even his voice would rather not come out and face the monster. As if it would rather take its chances inside of him, even though he was about to be ripped to pieces, and not just in his imagination.

Farin's heart sunk, and he said the gentlest of goodbyes to his imagination. He felt he should apologize for foiling its chances of ever developing into a fully grown, mature imagination.

But wasn't it his imagination's fault he was in this situation to begin with?

Paws thudded in the dirt, and the glinting white teeth, the milky white eyes, circled Farin, until he could see them no longer. His back seized up as he prepared for the monster to strike from behind, but then its eyes came into focus once again, and he realized the creature was stalking him. Taunting its dinner.

Well, technically its breakfast, since it had just woken up.

Move, feet, move, Farin thought at his legs, but they didn't listen. They were punishing him for all his disobedience, since Father's lashes wouldn't do any good once Farin was dead as the dirt below his feet.

The monster halted in front of Farin. Its heavy exhales filled the otherwise quiet night with noise, and its hot, rank breath wet his cheeks.

Farin closed his eyes. Even his imagination did not care to witness his death.

The monster roared, a shriek that somehow reached the heavens and rumbled the earth at the same time.

Then Farin heard the scraping. The creature must have launched itself toward him. He clenched his fists, preparing for death, and tried to be thankful.

At least he'd be dead before his father got to him.

CHAPTER 23

ASHA

The three of us awoke the next morning with clear heads, certain of exactly which point in the story we had fallen asleep, and equally uncertain of how such a coincidence might occur.

Though I had my suspicions.

Dinah stretched her limbs like a cat after a bath in the sun. Or, at least, that was a comparison used in the adventure book my father had read yesterday. Not a single stray cat in Meranthi had ever stepped out of the alley shadows as far as I had witnessed.

Cats didn't tend to be suicidal.

Even as Dinah emerged from slumber, her face remained relaxed, as if we were simply on holiday. As if we were the type of people who went on holiday. As much as I found my sister's eternal optimism endearing most of the time, I couldn't bring myself to share her hope that the king's heart had changed overnight.

Well, over two nights now.

"How do you think the story ends?" the king asked as he perched himself on the edge of the bed.

"I don't know. It's not my story. And, even if it was, wouldn't my telling you ruin the ending?" I asked, tucking my knees into my chest as I sat up and stared at mine and Dinah's makeshift pallet. It reminded me of a patchwork quilt, with all its colors and jagged lines, except it was much fluffier and nicer to sleep on, though I hated to admit it. Either way, I much preferred looking at it than the king, whose perfect features refused to be masked even under that dark beard of his, which rather annoyed me.

"But isn't that half the fun?" he asked, more genuinely than I had expected. "Guessing the end and then being able to celebrate yourself if you're right, or celebrate the storyteller if you're wrong?"

So that was why the king of Naenden had kept me alive? Because he was bored and couldn't stand a cliffhanger?

As if murdering both his brother's wife and his own a few weeks ago hadn't flavored his life with enough drama.

The king wasn't interested in my magic's story. He just wanted to know about my magic, how I'd obtained it, and probably, how he could keep other humans from doing the same.

Still, I couldn't exactly confront him about that, could I?

"I believe your circumstances allow you to find more levity in this story than I do." I traced the ribbons tying together the corner of a lumpy sage-colored pillow. He didn't respond, and I felt the pillow deflate beneath me as Dinah shifted with unease. I shouldn't have said that, allowed him to bait me. What was entertainment for the king was life and death to me, sure, but that also meant the king could easily find his bit of fun elsewhere.

"I would like to hear the rest this evening," he said, his voice devoid of anything resembling intrigue. "I have my guesses how the story will unfold, and I would like to know if I'm correct." The bed creaked as he stood to leave. I didn't look up until I heard him close the door behind him.

"Maybe you could come up with a guess to tell him tonight," Dinah offered, her voice as gentle as the breeze in Lydia's garden.

I sighed. "It's a good thing you have the demeanor of a lamb, you know. Because I think you could be quite the manipulator if you tried."

* * *

140

WHY HIGH FAE insisted on living in quarters with so many mirrors, I couldn't fathom. Sure, most of the high fae were beautiful—if you had an affinity for faces that lacked the slightest evidence that the owner had lived an actual life, that is. But if one's reflection hadn't changed in centuries, why bother checking it? It wasn't as if they had to work to make themselves presentable. No, mirrors should be reserved for the beings unfortunate enough to straddle the line between attractive and ugly. The ones enslaved to the paints and rouges, lest they glimpse an accurate reflection of themselves in the mirror.

There were very few of those beings in this palace.

There were the high fae who made up the ruling family. There were the servants, most of them lesser fae or half-fae like Tavi, but clearly selected in part for their exotic beauty. And then there was me, a being whose only mirror for years had been the well from which I had drawn my family's water every day.

Well, and the balking of passersby. The disgust in their eyes had painted a fairly accurate picture of what I must look like.

I flinched, actually flinched, every time I passed one of these horrible, gilded objects.

And they were everywhere. *Everywhere.*

Two in the king's bedroom—which remained my chambers as well since apparently whoever was in charge of preparing mine didn't want to go to all the trouble on the chance I might die the next day— one above the mahogany dresser, mounted on the eggshell colored wall. One free-standing in the northwest corner. Each of them gilded on the edges, the gold setting whirling with beautiful shapes and figures. Well, I thought they were beautiful, until I realized what the figures actually represented.

Apparently, fae artisans enjoyed carving severed heads into just about any piece of furniture one could imagine. Only a few of them had pointed ears, if the smith had left them their ears at all.

That was just the bedroom. The king's bath, which I only dared use once he'd left his chambers for the day, was practically a mirror all in itself. Why anyone would want to watch themselves bathing was yet another peculiarity I couldn't make sense of. Having been unused to mirrors—or bathing regularly, if I was to be honest with myself—I kept finding myself finally relaxing in the hot bath, only to jolt in terror any time I opened my eye to find a horrifying face watching me.

It was the stuff of nightmares.

Between my bedroom, my bathroom, the many halls of the palace, the dining area, and the library, I had counted one hundred and fifty-nine mirrors.

One hundred and fifty-nine.

I was pretty sure there were not that many beings living in the palace. And that was counting the lizards. Which were everywhere.

Everywhere.

And who could blame them, when this was the only building in the entire city that didn't turn into a clay oven in the middle of the day?

The second, second-to-last day of my life turned into the third, second-to-last day of my life, and so on, until a week had passed since the wedding. Every night, the three of us all fell asleep at a convenient moment in the story that opened up more questions than answers. And every morning, the king would present me before his people. My people.

And every morning I would bow.

Some of them had started to bow back.

Dinah told me there had been whispers in the marketplace of the human queen who'd saved herself.

Except I knew I wasn't the one saving myself. It was my magic, plotting away at a story I was no longer certain would ever have an ending, not as long as the king remained intrigued. The past few nights, my magic's story hadn't even focused on Farin. The last Dinah, the king, and I had heard of the little boy, he had stumbled across an Other in the dark. My magic had since taken the creative liberty of sending Farin's mind into a flashback of a story his mother had told him when he was young. And within that story, a character had told another story. And so on.

I figured it was quite obvious to all involved that my magic was drawing this out as long as possible.

Not that I didn't appreciate the fact that my magic saved my life every evening.

But that didn't make me a fool.

My magic's motives were based in self-preservation. I figured, with as hard as it worked to keep me alive, that if I died, it would die as well. Or at least be forced to find another unwilling host, which I assumed would be a bit of a chore. So I didn't have to be *too* grateful. Besides, I squirmed at the thought that whatever dwelled within my bones had the power to lull, not just me to sleep, but a high fae as well. Not only did I feel uncomfortable admitting that this level of power existed at all, I especially wasn't fond of the fact that it dwelled inside *me*. And that I had no control over it.

Besides, it wasn't really my magic's story that saved me anyway. It was the fact that the magic dwelled in me at all, something I was sure the king spent every evening trying to dissect as he pretended to be interested in poor little Farin's tale.

My magic had better not kill off that child.

I spent most of my days in the library with my father and Dinah, though, as each day passed and the king declared me worthy—whatever that meant—their visits shortened. After all, the scarves weren't going to make themselves, and I wasn't dead yet, so they didn't exactly have a queen's inheritance to live off of. Not that I had told them about the inheritance. They both went hushed and sullen any time I even hinted that the king might one day tire of my magic's story, so I figured telling them I had already planned out how to take care of them in the case of my demise might not go over so well.

So they would go back to the stall to work, and I would stay in the library, the vizier checking on me more often than I thought was good for his productivity and bringing me books he considered accurate versions of history.

The one I found most intriguing was a diary, a human woman's account of the fall of the last known human kingdom. I cried as she described the battle, the one the humans knew they could not win but fought anyway. She didn't understand why the men chose to fight. If it had been up to her, she would have had the city surrender, if only to keep her husband safe from the perils of war, the perils of the fae.

The entries ceased before the war did.

* * *

AFTER BAWLING my eyes out at the end of the woman's diary, I decided I had better find something lighter to read. Like, baby hummingbird feather kind of light.

Part of me felt guilty about it, that I was purposefully ignoring the pain and suffering of my ancestors. But the fact still stood that, if my story didn't hit exactly the right tone tonight, I'd be adding plenty of my own pain and suffering to that brimming chalice of misery. And if today was going to be yet another chance at my second-to-last day alive, I wanted to feel happy, if only through someone else's words.

During my conundrum, Tavi slipped into the library, carrying a worn book with a cloth cover. She set it back in its place with such attention, such delicacy, that she didn't seem to notice anyone else was in the room. When I greeted her, she jumped, then giggled nervously.

"My apologies, Lady Queen. I didn't notice you standing there," she said.

I bit back the urge to tell her she didn't have to be so cordial with me. Again. "How was it?"

Tavi frowned. "I'm not sure what you mean."

"The book," I said, gesturing toward the poor, worn copy that looked like it should have resided in my father's hovel rather than among its ornate neighbors.

"Oh, I didn't read it." She blushed and picked at the sash of her servant's dress. "I... I borrowed it for my brother. He's quite the avid reader. Goes through at least one a day. I grabbed this one for him from his list, but then I realized he's already read this one."

I wondered what kind of job, or lack thereof, Tavi's brother could have that allowed him so much reading time.

Not that I was the one to judge, I supposed.

Though, she was acting strange for a girl who claimed to be up to nothing other than borrowing a book. Tavi was rocking back and forth from her toes to the heels of her feet, glancing sideways across the library, as if to make sure we were alone.

It took me a moment to realize what she was waiting for. "Oh, you're dismissed, Tavi." Stupid custom. I was always forgetting about the fact I was technically royalty.

She curtsied and practically fled from the library.

After debating for a good twenty minutes over a pile of ornately adorned books and scrolls, I found my attention fleeting back to the worn book, which was bulging like a hernia from the shelves.

Clearly, Tavi hadn't meant for me to see her return the book. Everything in my upbringing told me I should leave it alone, not pry.

I almost picked what looked to be a lighthearted faerietale to distract myself, but from what I knew about human faerietales of old —that they always ended with children turning to cannibalism, or step-sisters cutting off their own feet—I figured fae-rendered tales couldn't end much better.

Tavi's tattered book it was.

If Tavi's behavior surrounding the book was strange, then her taste, or rather, her brother's taste in books, was even more so.

Instead of a novel, or even a history book, as I'd expected, the first page revealed it to be a record of ordinances.

The pages felt as though they might turn to dust between my fingertips as I rifled through them, hoping to find something that would convince me that Tavi's brother wasn't the most boring person in existence.

Or if he existed at all.

A chuckle escaped my lips. What an odd thing to think. Why on earth would Tavi lie about having a brother over a book? Boredom must have truly taken hold, if I thought someone would make up having a sibling just so I wouldn't catch them returning—returning, not stealing—a library book.

Just as I was about to give up and continue my hunt for something interesting to read elsewhere, I noticed a tiny scrawl in the margins of one of the pages.

I can't stop thinking about you.

Now, that was interesting.

Maybe Tavi really had made up the part about her brother.

Tavi had a suitor. A secret one, by the looks of it. Was this how they communicated, leaving notes for each other, sneaking kisses after hours?

My heart gave a lurch, and I remembered Az's hand in mine, that night on the roof. Before I'd left him. Before I'd let my hand slip from his.

Would it have changed my decision, if Az hadn't been so...so... well, so much like Bezzie assumed him to be? I re-imagined that last conversation with him, morphed the scene until those words in the margins of this book were coming out of his mouth, until he leaned his face into mine.

Pain squirmed in my belly, and I washed the thought from my aching mind. No use, there was no use thinking about such things. Not when I'd made my decision. Not when, if I had it to do over again, I'd still make the same decision. Repeatedly. I'd leave him to save Dinah. Every time.

I slammed the book, suddenly not in the mood. Whoever Tavi was courting, I wished them well, but I had no desire to witness anymore of their happiness.

Not when my happiness was out of reach.

* * *

I WAS SITTING, or, to be more honest, sprawling in the floor, reading a lighthearted faerietale, when the doors flew open and crashed against the nearest bookshelf, breaking from their hinges as they squealed.

I jolted at the noise, and before I could even steady myself, the king's fingers wrapped around my shoulders and hauled me to my feet.

He growled, pinning me with his gaze. Eyes on fire, he pulled me close enough to feel the blaze of his smoky breath on my cheeks.

"What treason are you planning?"

CHAPTER 24

ASHA

$\mathcal{W}$hat treason was I planning? Seriously? I could barely decide which book to read next.

My voice shook, and the mere closeness of this massive being fogged my head, scrambled my thoughts. "I don't know what you're talking about." My mind raced about, clawing every corner of my memory for something I could have done that even would have resembled treason.

But I'd mostly been reading.

"I don't believe you," he said, his breath stinging my forehead, the grip of his calloused fingers holding me in place. Despite my shaking, I couldn't help but notice that he took care not to dig his fingernails into my flesh.

"Do you mean the books?" I asked, and though the rage in his scowl didn't clear, something like confusion joined it. "The books on human history. I knew they were illegal for me to read, but I thought there would be no harm in it. I haven't lent them out or told anyone what I've read."

At this, the king's grip lightened, though his hands remained planted on my shoulders. As if running away would do me any good.

"If you've been planning treason this entire time…" He released his grip, apparently coming to the same conclusion I had, that he didn't need to have a hold on me to detain me.

At least I could inhale something other than his dizzying breath again.

His feet pounded against the vibrant rug as he paced, kicking it up in places, though I couldn't tell if he meant to or not. "I have to say, I'm impressed. You took a risk, assuming I'd spare your life while you spun that story of yours… That story…" He approached me again, this time the rage in his demeanor shaking me to my core. A quiet rage. A contemplative one. I wondered what atrocities one could come up with when given such intense focus. "It's enchanted, isn't it? Not just created by magic, but spoken with it? To enchant the mind to pity you…"

He turned from me again, pacing more vigorously around the room. Out of my peripheral—I didn't dare take my eyes off him lest he think it suspicious—I thought I glanced scorch marks tracing his path along the thick rug.

"Perhaps you even marred your own face to make your story more believable…to intensify my guilt…" he muttered to himself, more than addressing me. "No, human women are too vain for that… That means someone else is behind this… Calias, perhaps…"

My limbs, which had, just seconds ago, shaken in fear, now trembled in outrage. Sure, the king could be angry with me for making him look like a fool for not following through with his decrees. But he was not… He could not…

"You won't strip me of my dignity." Though I had intended the words to come out fierce, they shook almost as much as my legs.

But they still stopped the king in his tracks, and he turned toward me, his eyes blazing with mingled bewilderment and offense. How dare a human girl speak to him that way?

Well, it seemed I was going to die. He had already decided I was a traitor with who knew what kind of evidence. Might as well speak my mind.

"You dare address me in that tone?"

I stepped toward him.

I am bound to an idiot.

My limbs froze in place, not from fear of the king, but at the voice. The voice that had just spoken to me in my head.

A voice that was not my own.

If I'm going to be honest with you, the voice you use for your internal thoughts is a generous rendition of the real thing. I don't believe you're aware of how grating you actually sound.

As much as I wanted to snap back at my subconscious, the fragment of my mind which the stress of the past week had clearly chiseled off, I had a bigger problem to deal with.

A king who thought I'd committed treason.

Even better, one who was extra sensitive to that particular crime.

I took great pains to keep my voice as level as possible. Not that I cared about being respectful to the king who would have slaughtered dozens of human women had I not stepped in.

But I would be heard.

And he wasn't going to hear me if I was screaming.

"First of all," I said, marveling at the way my almost-whisper carried through the library. "There are many causes for which any decent human woman would trade her looks without hesitation. Family, being one of them. Or perhaps you aren't aware of the changes that occur to a woman's body after bearing children."

The king's face actually recoiled at that comment. His neck flushed red, and though it could have been from anger, I hoped very much it was not.

"Second, I didn't self-inflict my wounds. Power isn't exactly among the list of assets I would wound myself over."

I drew myself up for my last point. "Third, if your heart has been so neglected that you can't imagine a person might put the needs of their siblings above their own, then perhaps this might do you some good. Why don't you try putting aside your paranoia that a human might try to plot against you, and instead, take a look at your siblings, who actually have the power to destroy you? And, as far as I can tell, have every motive to?"

At this, the king clenched his teeth.

You've done it now.

I don't even care, I thought back, just accepting the fact I was hearing voices in my head.

He paced toward me, moving with the grace of a lion stalking its prey.

"Explain to me this," he hissed. "If you truly offered yourself for your sister, then how did you have the presence of mind to alter your will the very day you should have been savoring your existence?"

It was my turn to recoil. "Is that what this is about?"

"You've been caught in the act. Now tell me who sent you to plunder me."

My jaw dropped, and although it would probably be the death of me, I laughed. It seemed I was becoming numb to things that might have been my undoing. Death had been making a lot of empty threats these days.

"Oh, yes. Because Dinah, my father, and the beggar on the corner of Twin Alleys are all masterminds plotting against you."

At this, the king paused, and his eyes flickered. "What beggar?"

"You know, the man who sits on the corner of Twin Alleys and sings while he plays that broken lyre. I thought he could buy a new one. As well as some crutches to beat you to death when he stages an uprising." I cackled, unable to control the spasms in my throat any longer. My belly ached with laughter, and I wondered if this would be the last sound I ever made.

Fool.

I laughed even harder.

The king took a step back. "You left your inheritance to the beggar."

"Not...all...of it," I said, between wheezes. "There's enough to keep my family well-fed. And then enough so my friend...Bezzie...can pay the quarter...ly taxes on her shop..." I couldn't go on, couldn't breathe. I keeled over.

The king blinked, and though my gaze dropped to the floor as my stomach cramps forced my abdomen to bend, I could feel his stare boring into me.

But then a thought landed like a block of iron in my chest, and I inclined my neck toward the king. The laughter died in my throat. "Please don't hurt any of them. They didn't ask me to," I said.

He just stared me without moving. Without blinking.

"I was mistaken," he said, before turning away and departing the library. Since the unhinged library doors could no longer close, I watched as he charged down the long hallway.

I supposed that was the closest thing to an apology I was going to get.

* * *

NOW THAT IT seemed I would be keeping my head, at least for the rest of the day, I turned inward.

Why in Alondria was I hearing voices?

A voice, the voice promptly corrected.

"Well, that was nearly a disaster, wasn't it?"

Fairly certain I wasn't imagining it this time, I whirled around, but found no one behind me.

"Great, now I'm hearing two voices."

"That's probably something you should mention to our healer. Though I have to say, she can be impatient with maladies of the mind." A handsome face peered out from behind an ivy suede chair that, oddly enough, faced the bookcase instead of the fire. He had that same olive skin and thick, dark hair that linked the king and Princess Lydia, but his face was round rather than angular, giving him a boyish look. His messy tangle of curls might have led me to believe he was some poor, illegitimate child of the late king, except that a hint of his scarlet robe poked out from behind the chair.

"You're Prince Phinehas." I realized as I said it what a tactless thing it was to blurt out someone's name without even a polite introduction. But, then again, I wasn't exactly curtsying either.

"Oh, please don't call me that. Call me Fin," he said, standing from his chair. At his full height, I figured he was even taller than the king, though it might have been an illusion, since the prince had a much leaner build.

"How long have you been sitting there, Your Highness?" I asked, suddenly wondering how oblivious I had to be to miss a fae prince occupying the same room as me for hours.

"I arrived shortly before you did this morning," he said. Ah well, the chair was positioned to the left of the fireplace. At least I could blame it on my lack of eye. "I apologize for not greeting you when you entered, but I was so immersed in my book, I forgot my manners. Besides, I didn't realize who it was I was sharing a reading space with until my brother stormed in here and accused you of treason. If I had realized you were my sister-in-law, I certainly would have introduced myself." I examined his eyes, searching for any sign of mockery, but I found none. His eyes glowed of molten gold, though his were paler than his brother's, softer.

"I'm Asha." But surely he already knew that. Or maybe he didn't, since the plan hadn't originally been to keep me around.

"I apologize for my brother's behavior," said Prince Fin. "Not that he deserves your forgiveness at the moment. It seems he could find treachery in a starving puppy these days."

I nodded, remembering the original source of the king's paranoia. Not knowing what to say, but also having no idea how to avoid addressing the fact that Prince Fin's wife had just died at the hands of his brother, I said, "Thank you. You have my sympathies for your recent loss, as well."

A shadow clouded the prince's eyes, and it took him a moment to respond, as if there was a memory standing between us. But then he blinked, and the shadow dissipated. "Thank you, Your Majesty."

"You've come on business?" I asked, unable to resist my curiosity. Why had Prince Fin come to Naenden, to the home of the person who had murdered his bride only weeks ago?

"That was the excuse I used," he said, grimacing sheepishly. "But I might as well be honest with you, my queen. There's not a single room in my house that doesn't ring with Ophelia's laughter. I just wanted some quiet. And to... Well, I wish to numb my hatred for my brother if at all possible, and I figured that would not happen if I continued to waste away in that house dwelling on my last memory of him. I figured if I took some time to get used to him, perhaps I could under-stand...come to sympathize..."

"Well then," I said, lifting my chin. "If that's your strategy, I wouldn't waste time getting to know me. What if you end up liking me? I can't imagine it would strengthen your sibling relationship if your brother invites you to my hanging."

The prince's warm eyes flickered with curiosity as he examined me. Shame washed over me in waves. Leave it to me, to find someway to make a joke about the fact the prince's brother had a tendency to murder people he cared for.

But then the prince shook his head and laughed. "And just to think, every time I try to make a new friend..."

CHAPTER 25

ASHA

*D*inner that evening was awkward.

No, that was an understatement.

Dinner was painful.

Dinner was having a camel step on your sunburnt toe.

It shocked me when Tavi scurried up to the king's room later that evening and informed me I had been invited to dine with my husband.

That is, until I entered the dining hall and remembered that both of the king's siblings were now in town.

A dining table made of ivory and painted with peppered gold cut the room in half. It might have sat two dozen, had the king had any friends.

Instead, there were four seats the servants had prepared with golden-leafed table settings.

Lydia and Fin had taken two of the seats on the far end of the table, and the king sat across from them.

None of them spoke.

That arrogant weasel was using me as a buffer.

Do try to dodge when the silverware goes flying. The fae forget that even butter knives can be lethal to humans when flung at an unmannerly velocity.

Oh, now you're going to talk to me?

I am not a dog. I do not speak on command.

This afternoon, I'd rushed from my chance meeting with Fin, up to the king's rooms, since I still didn't have my own chambers. Thankfully, he hadn't been taking a nap or bathing or doing whatever kings do in their chambers during the day. The room had been empty, which was for the best, because anyone who might have observed me would have thought me mad, with the way I had been screaming at myself to say something.

At one point, I'd threatened to gulp down some ipecacuanha leaves, just to make myself throw up and force whomever resided in my head to share the experience.

Clearly your threats were empty.

It was right, whatever it was.

I hated throwing up.

But it probably already knew that, depending on how long it had been living in my head.

Oh, stop pretending you don't know exactly how long I've been up here.

It took all my effort not to wince as a flash of blue light berated my memory.

A servant, this one dressed in a cream-colored uniform with gold buttons, led me to the seat next to the king. He pulled out my chair, and I sat next to my husband, trying my utmost not to touch him. It turned out to be an impossible feat, because the king's arms were practically boulders, and I would have had to scoot my seat over to keep our arms from grazing.

Something told me I couldn't get away with that without drawing unwanted attention to myself.

As if my burn marks and missing eye didn't already do that for me.

"So, my lady," Lydia said, her chin held high, her eyebrows arched as if readying to loose a set of twin arrows. "How are you enjoying begging for your life each evening while our omniscient judge here determines the value of your existence?"

Fin snorted from behind his raised goblet.

The king's arm twitched.

My mouth went dry. A servant immediately filled my goblet with water, and my mind posed the uncomfortable question of whether the fae could sense such subtle changes in my saliva.

They can.

That didn't exactly make me feel any better.

"I—well, I—"

Apparently Fin felt the need to be my prince in shining armor, because once he'd stopped choking, he turned to Lydia. "Oh, it seems our brother has forced her to defend her existence in the daylight hours as well. Just this afternoon, he came in accusing her of treason, of all things. Though I wouldn't call her delightful response begging."

I blushed, and Fin offered an encouraging nod.

It was nice to have friends. Never mind that when the king erupted in a blaze of fury and flames, they'd most likely survive.

"Treason? Really, Kiran?" Lydia's violet eyes lulled.

The king cleared his throat, but where I expected a dull response, fueled by rage rather than intellect, I found myself mildly impressed. "Queen Asha defended herself with notable skill. I was wrong to accuse her." He turned to me, his eyes molten gold, rather than the dark pits I expected. I promptly returned to examining the intricate designs etched into my empty dinner plate.

This time, I thought Lydia might be the one to spit out her drink. "An apology, from *His Majesty?*"

"It might be difficult for you to believe, Lydia, but I am generous with my apologies to those who deserve them."

She snarled, and I felt the blades in her words before the king did. Apparently Fin did too, because he winced in preparation. "And have you apologized to Fin for snuffing his wife before he had a say in the matter?"

Silence, silence that should have been frigid as the Western wind, settled over the room. Heat swelled around us, radiating from not one, but three focal points around the table.

I would not die in public, executed for being nothing more than a human woman with a sister to lose.

I was going to die in the literal crossfires of a sibling feud.

Great.

When the smell of oyster soup filled my nostrils and the servants strode in, placing bowls of piping hot liquid before us, I might have kissed them in gratitude.

The air cooled, though not completely, not back to its original temperature.

How had these siblings not killed each other yet?

The fae are quite difficult to kill, my dear. One must sever their heads, or rip out their hearts. There are, of course, rare venoms, like what the late queen attempted to use, but—

I wasn't talking to you, I chided.

Man, was it annoying to have another person in my head. I couldn't even think rhetorical questions without having some idiot trying to answer.

I can't say I'm fond of your tone.

When the king spoke, I was actually glad to have something to distract me from the fact that my subconscious had been body-snatched.

That relief was short-lived.

"Lydia, tell us of your travels." A double-ended question, meant to cut.

Even I knew Lydia's travels were doused in an air of shame. Impropriety.

I wondered then if she had a male who whisked her away from here. Made her forget about her horrible, dysfunctional family for a while.

"Oh, there's nothing much to tell, really," she said, dabbing her blood-red lips on her napkin.

"I'm sure that's not the case. Your trips are the constant talk of the people," said Kiran.

"Because you speak with your subjects so often," she said, and that was the end of that.

Fin cleared his throat. "My Lady Queen, you could tell us about your family. Your home." He grinned. "I'm sure they're much more amiable than ours."

"Yes, do tell," Lydia said. "We'd love to hear about how a functional family goes about their day."

The servants pushed two carts through the side doors, each one bearing its own load of covered dishes. When they pulled off the tops, I thought I might lurch for the potatoes, chickpeas, roasted carrots, the fish. So much fish. How in Alondria were these people so rich that they could afford so much fish in the middle of a desert?

But all eyes were on me, even the servants', so food was going to have to wait.

"Well, it's just my father, my sister, and me. My mother passed when Dinah and I were young. We run a stall in the market selling scarves. My parents set it up, but it's me and—well, I guess Dinah mostly runs it now because my father has difficulty moving around. And, well, my father likes to read. He reads to us pretty often, actually."

Fin's face lit up at this. "What are some of his favorites?"

I swallowed and chanced a glance at Kiran, who was eying me from the side, though pretending not to. "He just has the one. It's so old, none of us know the name. The script on the cover's worn off, and the first few pages are missing. Dinah and I used to always make up a different beginning." I blushed a bit as Fin's eyes widened, though politely.

At least Lydia didn't at all appear shocked by the depths of my poverty.

Kiran shifted in his chair, his coat scratching my bare arm.

For the rest of dinner, we sat in silence.

No one asked about my scar, mercifully.

CHAPTER 26

$\mathcal{F}$arin braced himself for death, but it never came. At least, not from the direction he was expecting. As soon as the Other launched itself toward him from the front, something punched Farin's ribcage, slinging him to the right.

The earth hit his face and pushed its way into his mouth and nostrils and in between his teeth. He rolled onto his back and blinked the dirt out of his eyes. A howl, not a taunting one like the one before, but a scream of rage, broke from the monster's jaws. Moonlight bounced between the Other's teeth and a white, criss-crossed mass that shone between the monster and another tall figure.

Father.

Farin would have recognized that shield—the one made of Other femurs, carefully woven and glued together by crawsap—anywhere.

While the monster howled, Father grunted quietly, and only because he had to breathe to continue fighting. Farin's jaw gaped as he watched his father spar with the Other. As the moon rose behind the sparring figures, the Other's full shape cleared before Farin's eyes.

A mere. Farin had woken a mere. Father had told Farin about them, and what Farin could not see in the dim lighting, his imagination filled in with the help of Father's stories.

The mere was a cat-like monster, except Farin only wished it was simply an oversized version of a stray cat. No, the mere's coat was a deep shiny silver that now glistened in the moonlight, from which it received its magic. The mere would only grow stronger as the moon, full tonight, came into view.

Farin could only pray Ein, the lesser moon, wouldn't make an appearance tonight.

As if the sky could hear him and despised him for being disobedient, a second pale crest scaled the horizon.

It seemed Farin was in trouble, by all accounts.

The mere lunged for his father, and Farin bit back a scream, but Father was fast and lifted his bone shield just in time. The mere's paw collided with the shield, its claws scraping into the bone, leaving streaks of yellow venom in its wake. Venom that would paralyze its prey if it nipped even a scrape of flesh. Even a drop of blood.

But the mere wouldn't get to Father.

Only one Other had ever made it as far as Father's skin.

And that Other's skin now hung from the beams of Father's tent.

The mere stumbled, surprised by Father's attack, likely not used to its prey fighting back.

Taking advantage of the Other's stumble, Father unsheathed his saber, a jagged elafan femur into which Father had carved serrations. He swung, and though the mere was quick and lashed out with a defending paw, Father's saber made contact with the creature's outstretched leg. The sound of slicing flesh cut through the air, and when Father withdrew his saber, part of the mere's bone came with it.

A snarl rippled into the night as the Mere bared its teeth once more, but there was a newfound hobble in its stalk, and Farin noticed the creature spent little time on its front right paw as it circled Father.

Unlike Farin, who had frozen in place at the monster's intimidation tactic, Father spun with it, keeping his gaze locked on the mere, even when it jolted and changed direction.

Frustrated at its prey speed, the mere's eyes darted, and, for a moment, Farin thought it might run away. Though he was sure no one wanted that. Meres liked to keep meals for themselves and set off a warning call that threatened to gut the throat of any fellow monster who tried to claim ownership of the prey. But if a mere thought it might lose a fight, it would run off and find friends whom it'd bring back to finish the job. Father always said that, once an Other had a fae's scent, they never forgot it.

That was why a fae could never let an Other escape.

Farin's heart raced, for though he was confident in Father's ability to survive the mere's attacks, there was no way a fae could outrun an Other. Especially not a mere.

But Farin's fears were both short-lived and misplaced, for as soon as the mere's eyes darted toward him, toward the boy shivering on the ground, Farin realized the monster's plans were not to run after all.

The beast lunged, and Farin turned his head. He clamped his mouth shut, determined not to shame his father by branding his last memory of his son as that of a screaming fool.

But the blow never came. The beginnings of a guttural wail filled the air, one that would surely alert neighboring monsters to come to its aid, but the shriek was cut short, and when Farin opened his eyes, all he could see was that there was no longer one glittering monster, but two shining halves, separated by a blade dripping of silvery, moonlit blood.

Farin swallowed the vomit before it could hurl itself from his mouth, a skill taught to children quite early, since retching tended to attract monsters and children tended to have stomachs made of daffodils.

Not that Farin had ever seen a daffodil, but the way Father talked about them, Farin thought they must be quite delicate indeed.

Father's gripped Farin's shoulder and lifted him to his feet, landing him gently on the solid earth, tempting Farin's heart to interpret this as a tender, fatherly gesture, but he knew better than that. Father would not be gentle once they were out of earshot of the Others.

Farin trembled at the thought.

Indeed, Father's eyes glistened in the moonlight, boring into Farin. Father didn't have to speak to convey how ashamed he was. How it had been foolish to allow Mother to have a child, as she'd wished.

How he'd thought that at least he would get a proven hunter, a warrior out of the deal.

He hadn't. Farin and his father both knew that.

Father nodded toward the silvery mass on the ground. Farin swallowed his bile in advance before he looked. There, on the ground, lay the head of the Mere, its silvery blood trickling out onto the ground, its fangs still bared, a few of them dripping yellow venom. Its body lay, just as dead, a leaping distance away.

Farin's heart sank. Even though mere venom was precious to the tribe, even though they'd be able to use it to dip their arrows, to paralyze at least a few dozen monsters, despite the fact that mere blood had magical properties, and Father would probably feast on it this very evening and be back in the wilderness to hunt before both the moons could escape over the horizon, Father would still be displeased.

He preferred to bring in Others with their heads attached.

It looked better hanging from the tent poles. It looked better under their feet, covering them at night. It looked better as a hood for their heads.

Farin knew that Father didn't leave the heads on his blankets because it looked better, but because Farin had always been afraid of the dark, and Father believed that, if he woke to an Other, its teeth bared, every evening, he might be dissuaded from waking up in the middle of the night.

It hadn't worked. In fact, it had always made Farin's sleep less sound, less sweet. But Father didn't know that. Farin had stopped climbing into bed with him and Mother, and that was all that mattered.

Never mind that Farin had finally realized the Other head could not hurt him. That his father still could.

Father nodded toward the severed head again, and Farin obeyed. The head was still warm to the touch, fueled by moonlight, and Farin lifted it from behind before turning it face up and wrapping his arms around its jaw as he rested its skull against his chest. Not that he preferred looking right at the mere's still dripping teeth, but he didn't want to risk scraping his finger against one of its fangs.

Sure, it would only paralyze him temporarily, but as Father was lifting the rest of the mere's body onto his shoulders, he was fairly certain Father would not abandon the valuable pelt in order to carry his son home. He'd probably come back later for him, but Farin didn't quite like the idea of being unable to move when the Others were out hunting.

Not that it really mattered, since he hadn't been able to make himself move anyway, even without venom in his blood, but that was beside the point.

As they turned to go, Farin chanced one last look at the top of the hill, the crest of which he could barely distinguish in the dark.

He thought he glimpsed the slightest sliver of moonlight protruding from where it shouldn't have.

CHAPTER 27

ASHA

*I*t was summer in Naenden, not that one could tell. Nor had I ever heard anyone from Meranthi acknowledge a difference between this season and the rest. In my mind, there was no such thing as spring, summer, autumn, and most especially winter, but in the climate-controlled area of the palace, the fae celebrated seasons with changing of decor, differing plates of food, and a host of other details I found ridiculous.

I wondered, if the king delighted so much in changing seasons, why he didn't go to war with Avelea and take their land.

Apparently, with "summer" came the Summer Solstice, the longest day of the year, which someone—probably someone who lived in a region that actually experienced winter and feared it—had decided was worthy of celebration.

So Naenden observed the Solstice, even though, to the city dwellers in Meranthi, the longest day of the year also coincided with the highest mortality rate.

But I figured the king pored little time over those numbers. Or, if he did, he probably just made assumptions at first glance, without delving into the truth of the matter.

Perhaps I was still feeling bitter about his accusations.

"You remind me of the sun in its glory," Tavi said, grinning at me as I stood in the shimmering golden gown she had picked out for me. I couldn't bring myself to remind Tavi that, where I came from, the sun wrought death and not life. But, then again, as someone daily condemned to die, perhaps the look was appropriate after all.

"You seem to have found the king's favor, Your Majesty." Tavi averted her eyes as she buttoned the silky golden cape around my neck.

"I don't know about that." I couldn't tell if Tavi had heard about our row and was trying to ease my concerns, or if she sincerely believed the king was beginning to like me and would have held a different opinion had she overheard his accusations.

"He gave the command this morning to keep you alive. That's eight days in a row," she said. As if keeping someone alive for an extra eight days was an immense kindness. Though I supposed it was, coming from someone who had choked then burned his brother's bride to death without trial.

Tavi was right, in a way. I had thought for sure yesterday, after my pride had settled down and left me feeling exposed, that I would die come morning. Even if for nothing more than daring to be right in the face of the king being wrong. But last night after dinner, he had returned to his quarters just as he always did, sat on the bed, and listened as my magic spoke its wretched tale.

He had left without addressing me or Dinah this morning. I had pretended to be asleep, wishing to avoid his gaze at all costs, my chest gripping my heart with a chokehold as the door closed behind him.

An hour had passed before Tavi had come to prepare me for what had become our morning ritual. Except, this morning, she had surprised me with a new gown to wear to my maybe-execution.

As it turned out, the king hadn't bothered to commission me many clothes, thinking I'd only be staying in the palace for one night.

It had still been white, the dress for the morning ceremony. The part where the king decided whether I lived or died.

But this morning, just like all the others, the king had declared me worthy.

Something about the glimmer in his eyes had tried to convince me he meant it, too.

Perhaps he enjoyed having me around as a buffer between him and his siblings, after all.

"Are you excited about the parade, Your Majesty?" Tavi asked.

"You don't have to keep calling me that," I said. Partially because the title was ridiculous, given my status with the king. Partially because I was not looking forward to the parade and didn't wish to poop on something Tavi found exciting.

"Of course... Your Majesty," Tavi said, her pale greenish skin blushing red at the edges of her cheeks.

* * *

THE PARADE WAS different than I remembered it, but only because I had only ever witnessed it from the streets, not from within the procession itself.

The king and I rode in a carriage pulled by two camels. Purple linens cascaded over the edges of the carriage, protecting us, protecting *me*, from the blast of the sun, which loomed over us at full height. Peasants lining the streets peered at their feet, choosing to shield their eyes from the bright sun rather than gaze at their king as he passed.

"They have no shade," I said, unable to help myself and finding comfort in that I had managed to swallow the thousands of other accusations screaming in my head. All of which were directed at the king.

The king did not turn to me. In fact, he hadn't looked at me the entire hour since we'd been caravanning down the streets, the sounds of tambourines and horns and lyres and the stomping feet of soldiers filling the space another couple might have used for conversation.

"They're used to the heat, are they not?" he asked. My tongue riled, ready to lash out. But then his words replayed in my head, and I noted his tone.

No sarcasm.

A genuine question.

"They work around the heat. No one in Meranthi leaves the shade at midday. Most sleep to conserve their energy."

"Oh," the king said.

My jaw dropped. "Someone dies of heat exhaustion almost every week in Meranthi."

He clenched his teeth.

I couldn't believe it. He had no idea what went on in his own capital, what they did…what *I* did to survive from day to day.

"Today, there will be elderly men and women who will die from dehydration. Or choose to risk being found out by the Palace Guard for refusing to attend the parade. I guarantee it," I said.

Silence.

Oh, I was definitely going to die tomorrow.

We sat like that for a while, and I returned my gaze to the crowd outside our carriage. Still, most of the humans kept their eyes to the ground, while the fae residents searched with initially reverent eyes, hoping to get a glimpse of their king. Their eyes turned to slits as soon as they realized they had chosen the wrong side of the street, and that they not only had to look at the human woman they despised, but that they had caught her on her invalid side.

Well, at least they could revel in having seen the beast up close.

As we passed through the market, I glimpsed a girl. She looked to be about six years in age and was sitting atop her father's shoulders to get a better view. She cupped her hands on her forehead, shielding herself from the sun.

Until she saw me, that was.

I prepared for the scream. The recoiling that children did so often in my presence, the pain in my chest they didn't mean to cause. Not like the adults anyway. Of all the burdens that came with the wounds on my face, the children were the worst of it. They didn't mean to hurt me, I knew that well enough, and I never held it against them. But it left a void, an emptiness in my life where a child's laugh might have been. I'd seen them playing with adults in the marketplace, how their mothers and fathers all seemed to have tricks tucked away, silly games that always brought a smile to their children's faces.

I'd never been able to do that. Children never allowed me close enough, at least not the young ones.

Sometimes I'd used that fact to comfort myself, on nights when the realization that I would grow old alone had plagued me and kept me tossing. I'd remind myself that it was for the best, that it wouldn't be fair to bring a child into the world anyway, not when the face of their mother would inspire nightmares, horror.

I almost turned away, thinking to spare the little girl of haunting dreams, but then the girl waved, a smile overtaking her tiny face, and I thought she might lose her balance for how vigorously she shook her hands about. I offered her a somewhat shocked smile and a shy wave, for now more of the humans had lifted their heads get a glimpse of their moral queen. The girl's father grinned at me too.

I didn't understand.

The carriage passed them too soon, and I lost them among the crowd in our wake. But then there was another little girl, this one only a toddler, small enough for her mother to lift her up. The child smiled, but her mother smiled more, her teeth too few to match her youthful face.

I waved back.

And then there were more of them. Some little boys too, but mostly little girls, waving. And not all of them little. There were girls close to my age too, but instead of waving, they offered me solemn nods, silent gestures of gratitude as we passed.

Some of their fathers cried.

That was the part that broke me, so that I could no longer bear to gaze out the window. It reminded me of my father, how I knew he shed tears for me every night, despite Dinah refusing to admit it.

It was then that I felt the king's heavy gaze upon me.

I turned to face him. He stared at me, tracing all the lines on my face, scars and all. "They owe you their hearts for saving their daughters."

Fear gripped my chest at the words, for this king's folly was in his suspicious mind. And, if he believed the humans of Meranthi to be loyal to me rather than him… I could not bear to think what he might do to me.

"I did it for Dinah. That doesn't mean I deserve their reverence," I said. "Had I been born an only child, I wouldn't have condemned myself for strangers. It's shameful, but it's the truth."

He examined me again, the curve of my lone eye before tracing the bad, the patchwork skin that made up my left cheek before it crossed the bridge of my nose and smoothened out.

"That might be the case. But you've earned their respect, regardless."

"Such was not my intention."

"I know," he said. "I only mean that, in such a short time, you have won the hearts of a people I strove for years to entice."

Ah, when he was happily married to my predecessor. I was pretty sure he meant *year*, not the plural.

"I have the distinct advantage of being human. They'll never love a fae," I said.

He shook his head. "I disagree. They hate me because I'm not like them. But you're not like them, either."

My heart clenched, defending itself from whatever insult hid beneath his words. But there was none to be found, nothing but truth and observation in them.

As we passed Twin Alleys, I heard my name. Over and over, I heard my name. I turned to look. The beggar stood on the corner, his holey cloak barely protecting his chest from the heat of the day. But he didn't seem to notice.

"Asha! My queen! My queen!" he cried out, waving at me from his spot on the ground, his three crooked teeth beaming at me. He swatted at the people surrounding him, blocking his view, and they lurched away, gripping their robes to themselves lest he touch them. "Asha, you brave girl!"

I waved and gulped down the stinging bulge in my throat. When he found me waving at him, he grinned even brighter. I couldn't distinguish what else he yelled as we rolled past.

"I'm assuming that's the beggar to whom you left a portion of your inheritance," the king said.

I nodded.

The king sighed. "Well then, Your Majesty. I am at least comforted that the master plotter who finagled her way into being queen is quite bad at scheming."

I didn't smile. Though I almost did.

CHAPTER 28

ASHA

*A*fter Tavi helped me out of my parade attire and into soft, billowing trousers and a simple white tunic, I headed to the library. The huge ivory doors, which someone must have repaired since yesterday, opened, and I grinned as I found Dinah and my father already waiting for me in our spot by the fireplace.

Dinah's braid whipped to the side as she heard me approach, and she jumped from her velvet seat and threw herself at me. "You were lovely," she whispered.

"I kind of just sat there," I said. When she cast a chastising look in my direction, I added, "And waved. I guess I did that too."

"You're their hero, you know," she said, leading me by the hand back to our cozy little corner.

I frowned. "I shouldn't be. The only reason I did what I did was to save you. I wasn't thinking of them."

"Still," my father said, his voice gruff and low, as if he'd been settled into a deep nap in that blue velvet chair of his before I arrived. "You showed all those little girls that someone who looked like them could be brave. Those girls are going to interpret that as permission to be brave themselves."

"I don't really look like them," I said, pointing to the socket where my eye used to be.

"The children don't realize that," my father said, then he squirmed in the chair a bit, making himself comfortable, and began snoring.

"Let's find another book to read," Dinah said, nodding toward the one Father had picked out yesterday. He'd only made it halfway through before we'd all nodded off by the warm fire. "He seemed to really like that one. I wouldn't want to finish it without him."

I grinned. "Ah, so you'd rather finish it tomorrow without me then?"

Dinah's face contorted in confusion at first, but then a wave of hurt crashed over her beautiful features and she reached for the book on the table next to Father.

Guilt twisted at my stomach, and I reached for her hand. "I'm only joking, Dinah. I didn't mean it."

Tears welled in her delicate eyes, and I thought she might bite back for once, but she simply wiped the tears with the back of her hand and smiled weakly. "I know. It's how you cope. Humor is a healthy way to deal with pain for some people."

Some people, not including Dinah.

"Let's find something happy to read," I offered, still tasting the bitterness of having caused my sister pain, even if I hadn't meant to.

We searched the bookshelves for a while, and I found something more mild to tease Dinah about. "You know that the last three books you've chosen all have had lavender binding, don't you?"

She smiled and stroked the spine of the book she'd just pulled from the shelves. It was a romance about a fae princess falling in love with a lesser fae merchant who had crossed the desert on the pretense of trade, but had actually come because he'd heard tales of the princess's humor. "How about this one?"

I nodded, and we settled in next to the fire. Between the heat from the flames bristling my cheeks and the rhythmic rumble of my father snoring, I almost fell asleep.

"Aww!" Dinah squealed, and in my half-conscious stupor, I jolted upright, heart pounding.

Dinah giggled. "I didn't mean to scare you! It's just, well…look!" She handed the book to me, and along the margins, I recognized that same scrawl I'd seen in the book I'd read the other day.

I'd wait a millennium if I thought I had the slightest chance with you.

"Isn't this adorable?" she asked, her eyes glowing with tears. My heart warmed at the sight. Dinah transferred every emotion—elation, sorrow, guilt, joy, mild amusement—into a feeling worthy of tears. I wondered sometimes what it would be like to feel so deeply, to allow my heart to be so raw and open to the world.

I certainly wasn't brave enough to try it.

Desiring nothing more than to bring more of those joyful tears to my sister's eyes, I took the book from her and waltzed over to the bookshelf. "Just wait. It gets even better." I traced my fingers over the soft leather spines of the colorful assortment of books until I found Tavi's book. Once I'd found what I was looking for, I walked back over to Dinah and opened the book for her to see.

Her hands shot to her mouth as she gasped in delight. Then she ran her fingers over the scribbled, one-line love letter.

I can't stop thinking about you.

"Want to help me find the others?" I could feel the mischief course through my face, even the left side, even through my scars.

So, for an hour or two, Dinah and I were children again, and I was the one dragging her into trouble, and she was delighted to be along for the ride.

We must have already pulled a hundred books off the shelves by the time the vizier walked in with a pile of scrolls. They almost toppled out of his hands when he found us.

"Stars above! What are you two doing?" he asked, glancing back and forth between Dinah and me, and our father, who was still steadily snoring in his chair. Dinah and I exchanged a wide-eyed look of panic before bursting into giggles.

"Don't worry, we've kept them all organized, I promise," I said. The vizier swept his eyes over the piles and piles of books stacked across the woven rugs, exhaling loudly enough to betray his lack of belief in my claim.

"Oh, truly!" Dinah said, hopping to her feet, "They'll all be back in their rightful homes by the time we leave. You have my word." Earnestness poured out of her, any giggling now buried by the extreme anxiety of having displeased an authority figure.

The wrinkles on the vizier's face relaxed, and though a smile didn't quite break the corners of his lips, they quavered a bit. "Very well, just have them put back by the time you leave."

"Of course, sir." Dinah curtsied. I rolled my eyes and smiled, just so the vizier could see. He sighed again and shook his head. Then he found the homes for his armful of scrolls and left.

"Do you think he's upset?" Dinah asked.

"No, no one could be upset with you."

"Are you sure? Because if he's upset, then he might tell the king, and you might—"

"Dinah. He's not upset," I said, placing a soft hand on her shoulder. "Now, let's get back to work."

She nodded, and within a few minutes, she was back to our mission.

After another half hour of rifling through pages, my enthusiasm waned. The edges of the pages had dried out my fingertips, the feeling of which made me want to grit my teeth in outrage.

"Found it!" Dinah screamed, jumping up from her prison of books. She handed the book to me and pointed to the bottom margin of the page. Sure enough, someone had scrawled the words in tiny, almost illegible letters.

Three more days.

"Three more days until what?" I asked.

"Oh, don't you see?" Dinah said, taking the book back much more gently than I ever could manage. "They must have been in love. And they only had three more days left until they were getting married!"

My heart sank again, but I tried not to let it show on my face. "Pretty bold of them, to scribble in the palace manuscripts just to be cute, don't you think?"

"I think it's sweet," Dinah said. "Besides, people in love do silly things."

I could almost feel my hand slipping from Az's. I swallowed. "Who do you think they were?" I asked, though I had a sneaking suspicion I already knew the answer. I just wasn't sure that I wanted to gossip about Tavi's love life before I even knew if the notes were really for her.

Dinah shrugged and held the book to her chest. "Probably servants who met here, don't you think?"

My thoughts exactly. "I guess that's likely. There are more servants here than anyone else."

Dinah frowned. "You okay?"

I straightened, realizing I'd slumped. "Yeah, let's see if we can find some more," I said, happy to drown myself in a mission if it somehow numbed the aching in my belly.

We searched for another hour, and I had about given up, when Dinah squealed again. I prepared myself for another note that would intrude its way into my memories. But then Dinah's jaw went slack and her face drained of color.

"What is it?" I asked, sitting up from where I'd been lounging on my belly as I poured over the books.

She handed the book to me, but this time, the handwriting was different. A mixture of the common hand and script, the handwriting children learned in schools, never to use again. It had gone out of style in the last decade, and I hardly ever saw it.

But the change in handwriting wasn't what caught my attention, and it certainly wasn't what had made Dinah's face turn the shade of the full moon on a cool desert night.

Your name will die with me. Know that I loved you to the end.

CHAPTER 29

ASHA

I didn't want to know what had happened to the lovers.

Especially if I was right, that the author of the notes had been someone Tavi loved.

Neither did Dinah, apparently, for she joined me in silence as we embarked on the near-impossible task of returning the books to their rightful places.

Any other time in my life, I would have been dying to solve the little mystery Dinah and I had uncovered.

But something about the fact I had to wait to be told every morning whether I was allowed to live through the day had stifled that morbid curiosity.

Dinah and my father left to tend to the shop just before dinner, and I meandered to the dining hall rather than taking a straight course.

Sure, I had survived last night's dinner, although I had been certain one of the three siblings would blow the entire room to smithereens before the servants brandished the pudding.

But perhaps the king wasn't so much of an idiot as I thought. Any time the conversation became, literally, heated—and by that, I meant the entire room morphed into the outskirts of a furnace—someone would ask me a question, and I would tell them about my very ordinary life, and the temperature would cool.

That didn't mean I was looking forward to making dinner with the royal family a regular occurrence.

Perhaps that was why I didn't wait for Tavi to come fetch me from the library and escort me to the dining hall.

Perhaps that was why I found myself in a corner of the palace I'd yet to explore.

The growl, earthy and feral, was what initially yanked me from my thoughts, causing me to realize I'd wandered far from any hallway I recognized.

This corridor was darker than the rest, bare, and at the end, two catlike green eyes gleamed out of the darkness.

While every corner of my consciousness begged for me to run, my legs seemed to have other ideas. My feet cemented to the floor as the creature with glittering eyes approached.

No, stalked.

My stomach lurched into my ribcage, and I thought I might vomit.

Perhaps that would be enough to turn the beast off of eating me.

And a beast, she was.

When the saber emerged from the shadows, it was as though she'd materialized from beyond the reaches of the sun.

Her eyes gleamed with hunger, with pride. The shimmer of her black coat glistened in the candlelight. Her teeth, chiseled and sharp, snapped.

The noise echoed through the hall.

I ran.

It took less than three steps for her to pounce.

A scream, guttural and frantic, escaped my lips as her huge paws, the size of saucers, forced me to the ground.

I barely had time to flip on my back, to face the wielder of my fate —not the king, after all—when she let out a roar that made the hallway rumble and...

And licked me.

And licked me?

Her tongue, dry and scratchy, lapped up my cheek.

Then the enormous beast flopped down, half of her weight thudding against my chest. She sprawled her legs, allowing her razor-sharp claws to flash, and purred.

It seems she wants you to pet her. I would comply if I were you.

I didn't need to be told twice. Heart still pounding, I reached out and scratched her belly, her fur warm and soft against my trembling hands. When that didn't seem to be enough, she nestled her huge forehead into my arm. I stroked her slick head, the bridge between her angled eyes, and her massive body hummed.

Footsteps sounded in the hall. The saber and I both craned our heads to watch as Kiran and Fin sprinted down the corridor They caught sight of us—me, probably looking as frazzled as I felt, the saber, as content as could be to serve as my living blanket.

The brothers halted, their inertia sending them sliding down the marble floor.

Fin was the first to crack a smile. "I see you've met Nagivv."

His eyes scanned the beast with fondness, though he didn't take a step toward her.

Kiran scowled. "She's not supposed to be out."

Fin patted his brother on the back. "Would you like me to check which of her wranglers she ate this time?"

My hand flinched in horror, at which point Nagivv's predatory eyes darted toward me.

I promptly resumed petting.

"Is she yours?" I asked Kiran.

As if to answer, Nagivv snapped her fangs in Kiran's direction. He took a step back.

Fin swallowed a nervous laugh.

So two high fae were afraid of the animal whose teeth were less than an arm's length from my face. And my good side, at that. Great.

Fin's nervous laughter was contagious.

"So, if she's not yours, whose is she?" I asked.

Fin shook his head behind Kiran, and Kiran only pursed his lips and turned to his brother. "Go get Lydia."

"I don't know if that's the best idea."

Kiran glared at Fin, as if to command him without words to please have a good explanation for why he was disobeying his king's orders.

Fin just shrugged. "You know she hates you."

Kiran and I spoke at once. "Which one?"

The only sound that followed was the purring coming from Nagivv, who was now cleaning her paws.

Fin bit back laughter. "I meant Nagivv. Lydia hates you too, but she'll come to help if she knows Asha is in danger."

Again, my shoulders tensed, but this time I knew better not to cease my petting.

Kiran must have silently agreed, because he backed down the hallway, his molten eyes fixated on Nagivv until he rounded the corner.

"What's Lydia going to do to her?" I whispered, as if the saber understood the human tongue.

Fin eyed the purring beast. "If I were you, I'd be asking what Nagivv will do to you."

I shot him a glare, and he held his hands up. "I'm kidding. Really, she much prefers fellow females. That's why Kiran went to get Lydia."

"Has she really eaten some of the guards?"

Fin grimaced. "Let's just say she's been antsy of late. She keeps finding ways out of her sanctuary, and ends up stalking the shadows down here in the South Wing. Speaking of which, what were you doing down here?"

"Just trying to take the long way to dinner."

"What, you don't enjoy our company?" Fin's white teeth flashed, the smirk as playful as the saber whose fur I scratched.

I turned back to the beast. "Why do you think she keeps trying to escape?"

Nagivv turned her eyes on me, and the corners drooped.

Fin grimaced, and for a moment, he looked ill. "Because she belonged to Gwenyth."

Sympathy twisted my heart at the thought that this beast fought her way out of her pen, no, her sanctuary, and wandered the halls searching for her owner.

Her dead owner.

"Or maybe she just likes paying homage to the great Tionis," Fin said, clearing his throat of any discomfort as he masked his pain with that carefree facade. He nodded toward a statue engraved into the marble wall. A high fae in battle attire. "They say Tionis liked to wash his feet in the blood of his captives. I could see Nagivv appreciating that about him."

Fin cast a macabre grin in my direction, and before I could decide whether I even wanted to address the fact that my education hadn't been *that* lacking, Lydia and Kiran turned the corner.

"Up," Lydia commanded, and the animal craned her neck lazily in the princess's direction. As if to assess what sort of threat lay behind the sharp tone.

Apparently, Nagivv deemed Lydia capable of backing up her word, because the saber slipped out from under my hand and lazily pawed her way to her feet. She turned in the opposite direction and strode off, apparently knowing where she was going.

Lydia followed Nagivv, and Fin disappeared around the corner, clearly eager to get as far away as he could from the beast now that I wasn't in any sort of mortal peril.

It warmed my heart a bit that he'd stayed with me despite his apparent fear of Nagivv.

That left me and the king, alone in the dark hallway, with only scraps as fodder for our conversation, to make the silence any less unbearable.

I pushed my palms against the cold marble floor, readying to stand, but the king offered his hand instead. Figuring I had better not spurn his attempts at kindness lest he stop extending them altogether, I slipped my hand into his.

A sharp pain jolted through me, and I gasped as he lifted me to my feet. As soon as I gained my balance, I dropped his hand.

"What's wrong? Are you hurt?" he asked, reaching out and nudging my sleeve up my arm, as if to check for bruises where Nagivv might have stepped too hard.

His fingers blazed a trail of ice up my forearm, explaining my initial shock. I slunk away from his touch, tucking my shoulders in and interlocking my fingers, to which he frowned.

"You're just really cold," I half-laughed.

He bunched his shoulders, tucking his frigid hands into the pockets of his trousers. "Is that so?"

"Ridiculously cold. You'd think your skin would feel like a furnace or something."

His throat bobbed and he cracked a partial smile. "When exactly were you thinking about that?"

Heat that had nothing to do with my husband's Fates-blessed abilities flushed my cheeks, my bare neck. Desiring nothing else besides my embarrassment to dissolve, I snapped, "Oh, I dunno. Maybe all the times I've imagined you strangling me with your bare hands in front of that bloodthirsty crowd."

The king's jaw ticked, his shoulders going rigid as his golden eyes dulled to the color of soot. My heart raced in panic, but he took a step back all the same, gesturing toward the long, dark hall. "If you'd allow it, I'd prefer to escort you to the dining hall, lest you attract any more trouble."

Grateful I still had a neck to nod after my outburst, I agreed, though he didn't extend his hand again.

His eyes didn't melt back to their usual golden that evening at dinner, or when he returned to his room for my magic's tale.

CHAPTER 30

*M*other watched as Farin scarfed down his grimroot for breakfast. She hadn't touched her food. In fact, she hadn't come near her food in days. Not since Farin hadn't come home that evening, the night she'd spent curled up into a ball, weeping, sure her son had been ripped to shreds by an Other.

Sure that her husband would finish the job if he found Farin alive.

When Farin and Father had come home—Farin, tiny, quiet, sweet little Farin, holding that mere head at arm's length, his hands trembling as he stared at its fangs rather than where he was going—Mother had thrown off all pretense.

She'd run to him, despite knowing there would be consequences. She'd wrapped her precious little boy in her arms, though he'd tried to pull away from her, fearful that a mere fang would nip her skin and paralyze her weary muscles.

She hadn't cared. In that moment, she'd have sliced off her own hand with a mere fang to embrace Farin. To ruffle his hair, to breathe in the scent of dirt and grimroot, just to be sure he was real, that her grief hadn't forced her into a coma, that he wasn't a dream.

He'd been just a dream for so long. For years, she'd wanted a child.

For years, she'd been told it wouldn't happen. That the tribe was the last of the fae. That her race would die with her generation. That all they could do was try to evade their extinction as long as possible by sticking together, protecting one another.

And protecting one another had meant no babies.

So she'd married the only male above the rules.

She'd been so young, she hadn't imagined what a mistake that would be.

A mistake. Her heart ached with guilt every time that unwelcome word popped into her mind, slipped through the carefully cemented walls she'd built around such a bitter idea. That the decisions that brought a child as wild and beautiful as Farin into the world had all been mistakes.

That Farin was a mistake.

But every time she cleaned Farin's lashes, every time she salved the cuts delivered by his father's belt, every time he bit back a scream at the agony that came with salting a wound, that dreadful word would pound against her head, knocking at her skull until her headache lasted long after she'd managed to suppress the thought.

Mistake, mistake, mistake.

Her mother, her father, the tribe elders. They'd all been right. It had been cruel, selfish to bring a child into this world. Into a world that had once borne flowers, fruit, before the Others had grown too many.

Before they'd killed off everyone else. Before the tribe were the only ones left.

It would have been cruel if Mother had married another male. Would have been cruel to expect a baby not to scream, to expect a child not to frolic.

But to bear a child to Father. That had been her unforgivable crime.

Of course, she hadn't known that. She had been young, beautiful even, according to the rest of the tribe. Not that there had ever been enough water for Mother to glimpse her reflection. Not that she'd ever had a way of confirming their praises.

But Father, the newly instated chief, only ten years her senior—which seemed like a bargain, considering most females were married off to males forty years their senior, after their first few wives had died of starvation or age had hindered them from escaping an Other attack—he had thought Mother had been beautiful too. Had wooed her with his descriptions of her teardrop face, her sparkling eyes, her honeyed hair.

He had seemed kind then. Although Mother had come to realize that flattering and kind were two distinct qualities indeed, and that they rarely described the same being.

If he had beaten her at all, before she'd become pregnant, she never would have asked him, never would have begged him for a child.

But that was the thing about predators.

They knew how to wait before the strike.

Now, as she held Farin in her arms, she knew the beating would come. She might have avoided it tonight, as Father would surely be occupied with Farin for hours. But she thought that, perhaps, if she angered him by embracing the child he believed had sinned badly enough to be deprived of love for at least a few days, perhaps she could bear a portion of Farin's beatings. After all, she knew Father would be itching to drink the mere's blood. Tonight was a double moon. Another wouldn't come around for another two mooncycles. He only had tonight, and though this was the longest night for the next two months, he wouldn't want to waste too much time disciplining his family.

If she could just take the beating tonight, perhaps he'd be too high on the reaping of his hunt to bother with punishing Farin at all.

She had born the beating in the end. And she'd been right. He'd returned the next morning with four mere pelts he'd dragged through the settlement on a blanket. Apparently, he'd killed seven more on the way, creatures who'd been drawn to him by the scraping of their fellows' corpses against the brittle ground.

He'd been too rushed to gather the bodies to remember to punish Farin.

He'd been too drunk on the mere's blood to ask how she was feeling, as he used to do after every beating. Every *discipline*, as he liked to call them. He'd been so sweet, so gentle, after that first time. The first time Farin had cried. The first time he'd blamed her for it, told her she should have anticipated that he would be hungry.

He'd stroked her hair and whispered apologies, or rather, what she'd thought were apologies. She'd grown wiser with age. Grown to understand that, *I only did it because I love you. I just don't want any harm to come to this family. I had to make sure it didn't happen again, because I couldn't bear to lose you, to lose our son*, had not been apologies at all, but tactics to erase her anger while maintaining her fear.

She'd been glad when he hadn't bothered with the charade that morning. That she hadn't had to lie by saying she forgave him.

She's stopped forgiving him long ago.

About the time she'd realized he'd never asked her to.

But now, as Farin hurried through his breakfast, she scrutinized his every twitch. He'd scarfed down his grimroot, the taste and texture of which he despised, every morning since the incident. Then he'd watched for Father to leave. She'd seen him checking outside for the placement of the sun, calculating how long ago his father had set out. Then he'd kissed her on the cheek and whispered that he had to meet the tanner for lessons, that they were part of Father's discipline.

Farin, even with that wild imagination of his, had never been capable of conjuring a believable lie.

She had longed to trail him that first day, to keep him from wandering off again. She'd forced down the fearful sobs when he'd left, sure he'd never make it home again. Sure, that if she followed him, if anyone from the tribe saw her outside the tent unaccompanied by her husband, that Father would assume the worst. That she had a lover in the tribe.

Not that Mother wouldn't gladly die to keep Farin safe, alive.

It was just that she was certain her being alive was the only thing sustaining his. The only bit that kept Father's beatings from going too far.

But, when Farin had come back that night, when she'd wrapped him up in her arms, kissed his forehead and cupped his cheeks in her palms, he had grinned at her.

Smiled. Actually smiled.

Something she hadn't seen on the child's face since the first time he'd attempted a laugh.

And she knew it wasn't right, knew that she wasn't doing her job as a mother to protect him by allowing him to lie to her every morning, to wander off somewhere she knew was not within the tribe limits.

She'd resolved every day to put an end to it, whatever it was.

But every day he'd come home well before dark, well before his father made it home from his hunts, and he'd smiled.

And he was sleeping. Her child had never slept. She'd stayed awake for years listening to him breathing, the panicked, shallow exhales that contrasted with the quiet, unbothered breaths of the husband at her side.

But, in the past few nights, Farin had fallen asleep and slept through the night. She'd known, because she couldn't fall asleep, hadn't wanted to. Not when the sound of her child sleeping, spending the night hours in some peaceful oblivion or pleasant dream, was the happiest thing that had happened to her since before that first day her precious baby had screamed.

But she couldn't go on like this forever. She couldn't allow him to become food for the Others. But, perhaps, just perhaps, Farin wasn't doing what her mind, primed to assume the worst from years shackled to Father, had assumed. Perhaps he'd found something innocent, something harmless. Something in which his father would undoubtedly find betrayal or immaturity or false danger. If that was the case, she could keep his secret. For as long as it brought a smile to his face, kept him sleeping at night.

But she had to know for sure.

So that morning, when Farin kissed her softly on the forehead and shuffled out of the tent, she donned the heaviest coat she could find, one with the face of a Tigren that covered her own, and she followed him.

* * *

MOTHER SHOULD HAVE STOPPED Farin as soon as he reached the border. She was much too far behind to assist if something were to attack him, and the dread caused her heart to scale the length of her dry throat. She'd had to trail him from a distance. Not that Farin had spent any time looking behind his back. Children were like that. He'd done this four or five times without being caught, so now he assumed there was no chance of his illegal treks turning out otherwise.

She wondered how long that would last. How long he'd remain under the illusion that he could somehow escape his father?

Mother shuddered and swallowed the urge to call out to her son. It was too late for that anyway. She'd allowed him to come this far, which had been foolish. A sign that Father's poor parenting had finally rubbed off on her.

But there was no use in wasting time regretting it now. If she called out to him, commanded him to come home, she'd risk waking one of the Others. Mother would just have to punish herself later. But not now.

Now she would identify the source of her child's smile.

* * *

BY THE TIME Farin disappeared into the tall grass, Mother was confident she'd made a dreadful mistake. Surely this wasn't what he'd been doing every day, not if he'd made it home alive every time. She wanted to scream at him, to beg him not to wander into the tumultuous blades, but all she could do was quicken her pace, try to land as softly as she could on the hard, caked dirt beneath her feet.

When she reached the grass, there was no questioning what she had to do. She waved the towering stalks out of her way as she weaved through it. Frantic panic pulsed in her chest, and she had to force herself not to allow it to infect her breathing. She made it through the grass in no time, but when she pushed the last sharp blade away, all she found was a hill.

An empty hill.

Where was Farin? She turned and waded through the grass once more, sure that he must have taken a turn somewhere in the swaying blades, but after wading and wading, he was nowhere to be found. Panicking now, she returned to the entrance of the grass, where she had entered, and scanned the plains.

There was no sign of her son.

Although the plains were silent, she pushed herself back through the grass, but after circling the hill twice, she found herself at the base of it once more.

He wasn't there.

Until he was.

Mother, who'd been trained her entire life to do so, swallowed her scream as her son appeared from nothing. Instinctively, she hid herself in the towering stalks, lest he see her and be startled and cry out. He tiptoed down the hill as Mother tried to reason through what she had seen. Perhaps she hadn't seen it at all. Perhaps, in her panic, she had overlooked him when she'd stumbled upon the base of the hill, and he'd been there the entire time. Or maybe he'd wandered to the other side of the hill and simply appeared on its crest as he'd walked back.

But then a startled look overcame Farin's face, as if he'd realized he'd forgotten something. He spun on his feet and began pacing back up the hill. Mother stepped to follow him, but then he was gone. Disappeared, not over the top of the hill, but into the air.

Mother sped up now, her heart pounding in panic. Why had her child vanished, and how could she hope to find him now? She paced up the path, trying her utmost not to make a sound, and completely unable to determine whether she was being successful for the pounding in her ears, when she saw it.

A ray of light, flaring from where it shouldn't. Mother reached her hand out to touch it. When her fingers disappeared into the air, she wasted no time following her child into the Nothing.

And then she was there, on a hill, full and lush rather than barren.

And there was Farin, running and giggling in the wildflowers at the bottom of the slope.

And there was an Other, teeth bared as it stalked her blissfully ignorant son.

CHAPTER 31

ASHA

*D*ays passed and fleeted and melded together, until, most days, I didn't know what day of the week it was. Each morning was the same, except, these days, the king snuck out before Dinah and I awoke. Neither of us stirred until Tavi arrived to dress me for mine and the king's daily ritual.

I guess I was getting brave, sleeping so soundly in the king's presence.

Because every morning he presented me to his people, and every morning he found me worthy.

Worthy for what, though?

To sit around and read all day, apparently.

Oh, and to keep Nagivv company. Though, the guards would have probably admitted this was a prudent use of my time, because the more time I spent in the sanctuary with the saber, the less often she attempted to escape.

The less often she ripped one of them apart.

It was probably foolish of me to visit her, but Fin had been right. She much preferred the company of women.

I wondered sometimes as she lounged there, cleaning her silky coat, sharpening her claws with her fangs, if she suspected what had happened to her owner. Why Gwenyth had never come back for her.

If she did, she was either in utter denial, or bent on finding her master's body, because I still found her roaming the South Wing at least twice a week.

Kiran had caught me down there, once or twice, looking for her after a guard had burst into the library and requested my help.

The first time he had turned those cold eyes on me again. Apparently he still wasn't over my outburst.

I had asked if he'd rather me not help, and risk another of his guard's life, which had only reminded me of the guard from my first morning here, the one my mystery savior had slaughtered in the shadows. I hadn't seen or heard from my savior since. Perhaps there had been a reason for that, and that reason listened to my magic's story every evening. I imagined the penalty for killing one of the king's men was fairly high.

Though apparently the king turned a blind eye to a human possessing magic.

Unless, of course, he was just trying to study me before deeming me unworthy.

Or he preferred having at least one person at the dinner table who wouldn't constantly insult him.

Not that I wasn't doing that in my head, which he was clever enough to know.

As I strode through the garden one evening after a blissfully silent dinner with the royal family, the cool breeze lapped at my face and my mind wandered to Tavi. To her lost love, and the notes in the library to which she clung. How had her lover died? She hadn't gone into detail, and by the way she had been sneaking in the library, uncomfortable to be noticeable, I couldn't help but wonder whether their relationship had been forbidden. She was half-fae, the only half-fae person I'd ever known. Perhaps there were laws about marriages between the half-fae and others. Perhaps their being together had been against the law.

Had the king had something to do with the death of Tavi's lover? I doubted he would stoop so low to mingle in servant affairs, but if there had been such laws, and one of his servants had been executed, surely he would have known about it.

Then again, maybe the male had died of natural causes.

Aren't we assuming this male was fae, given most of the king's servants are?

Right, I thought back, engaging the voice in conversation, as if I'd accepted the fact something was living in my head. *Fae are strange beings. When they die, it's actually more likely foul play was involved.*

A rustling in the bushes shook me out of my thoughts.

I debated whether to call out, whether to greet the intruder or call for the guards.

Either way, I was not alone.

The rustling stopped as soon as I did. Someone had seen me. They knew I was here. And they knew I knew they were here.

My heart raced. Back home, rustling, someone hiding in the shadows, that would've been danger for sure. Probably a thief. But I was not in the streets of Meranthi. The mark on my eye no longer betrayed my poverty, that no one would be there to save me. Now, it was the mark of the queen.

It occurred to me that was infinitely more dangerous.

I broke into a run.

The rustling behind me started up again, and I ran faster, tripping over my skirts. My bare knee scraped against the pavement.

"Wait," a familiar voice called out, huffing.

I turned to look at my assailant, and I started.

It was Az.

He'd grown his hair out since I'd last seen him, but it still fell carelessly across his forehead and into his eyes, covering those rounded ears that remained the only evidence of his humanity, the grounding point to his dazzling grin. He put his hands on his knees, recovering his breath as he stared at me.

I had no words for him.

"You never could outrun me," he said, that beautiful grin spreading across his face. My heart gave a lurch. Then it twisted in my stomach.

He could only be here for one reason.

And I couldn't lie to myself. Elation welled within my heart at the thought.

He had come for me.

"How…how did you get past the guards?" I asked.

Az beamed. "When I was in Avelea, I met a Charshonian advisor who told me there was a secret passageway into the palace. I blew it off as another crazy story, but then they took you, and I got desperate. And, well, apparently the guy wasn't exaggerating."

"You can't be here. It's trespassing," I said, despite the fact I wanted to say the opposite. Despite the fact I wanted to wrap my arms around him and hold him close. But it was not safe. If anyone caught us here, even just talking in the garden, at night, alone… The king would jump to conclusions. I knew enough about my husband to be sure of that.

Az's eyes narrowed, my words wiping that beautiful smile off his face. "You're the one who shouldn't be here." His voice possessed that steely quality, one that was now shining in his usually warm eyes. "You don't belong here."

As if I didn't know that already.

"Az, if they find you here…with me, at night… They will not ask questions first."

"Well then, it's a good thing they won't find us here. You're coming with me. I'm taking you home." Az offered a hand to me, that same hand that had held mine all those nights ago. The night I had stormed off in tears. What had I been thinking? He hadn't meant to hurt me with his words. How could I have expected my best friend since child-hood to reveal his feelings to me? In perfect prose? I could've laughed at myself, had the dread not been seeping through my stomach.

I took his hand, and he pulled me from the ground into his chest. The warmth from his body ran deep into mine, filling the marrow of my bones, shaking alive something inside me that must've been asleep all these days in the palace. Then, as if to remind me where I belonged, he took my hand and brought it to his face. My fingers curled through his tousled hair instinctively, grazing the curve of his rounded ears.

Rounded.

Human.

Like me.

My heart stirred, as if to tell me, Yes, yes, this is right. This is where we belong. Safe. Safe with Az.

But I was not my heart, just as I was not my magic. Just as my magic and I inhabited the same body, my heart and I, we were not the same. We never had been.

I pulled away.

"We can't do this," I said, though the words cut at the inside of my throat.

Az drew away from me, staring into my eyes with those wide, sage-green irises of his. How long had I wanted him to look at me like this? How many nights in the palace had I dreamed of him taking me away?

Perhaps this was just a dream.

Or perhaps this was a nightmare.

"I know you're afraid," Az said. "But you don't have to be. I'll protect you, Asha, I promise. I already have a plan, for you, for Dinah, for your father. We'll run away, all of us. I know a smuggler who can get us out of town. We'll get out of here, just like we always talked about."

My breath faltered.

My character did too.

But only for the slightest moment as I drew into his chest once more. As soon as my face made contact with the beating of his heart, I pulled away again. For a moment, he and I were the two ends of the globe, being propelled together by that magnetic force that kept the world spinning.

But I had learned a long time ago that I was not the one who kept the world spinning. Nor did it revolve around me. The force between us drew me to him, so much so that it physically hurt to resist, to withdraw from his touch. As if I were ripping my body in two, no, as if I were ripping my soul in two. This soul, Az's beautiful, adventurous soul. How long had it been one with mine?

How I longed to go with him, to be safe in his arms, far, far away from this wretched marble prison.

Safe. When was the last time I thought I would live with that luxury?

In a moment's time, I saw that life, *our life*, folding out before us. The magic inside me might as well have spoken by the way each scene rolled out before my mind as if it were the next stone in a pathway through a garden. Az's hand upon mine. The laughter of my sister as we exchanged our vows. Not like the vows I had exchanged with the king. *My* future. The one I'd dreamed up all throughout my childhood.

Our first child wrapped in cheap burlap rather than fine silk.

Poor, we would be poor.

Elation filled my heart with that thought. Being poor with him, with Az. Our child, swaddled in nothing but love and adoration, screaming for me. It was hungry, mine and Az's baby. Az's face flashed before my eyes as my dreams unveiled our future. That grin, that sideways grin, melted me. And I could see in his eyes what he was thinking, even as a baby screamed.

I trust you. I love you. Our life is my world.

And just for one fleeting moment, I truly believed I would go with him. That I would forsake the king. My horrible, horrible husband, who had practically forced me into our marriage. Who allowed the threat of my death to linger over my head every single day. Who refused to give me the mercy of a swift execution. I hated my husband, I now realized. Despite our occasionally civil conversations, despite his curiosity and the way he looked at my entire face rather than just my scar. Neither of which half made up for the future he had stolen from me. Yes, I hated the king.

And I loved Az.

But then a thought crossed my mind.

That life, the one I'd imagined, it wasn't complete.

And as I examined it, that picture of Az and me and a child, I noticed the shadows surrounding us. Not an actual substance, not a true environment. Not a true home.

Not a true kingdom.

That world was just me and Az. But we would bring a child into a world much more complicated than the bubble I'd constructed for the three of us.

My heart sank. Even if this future between Az and me and our child and children to be, even if it could exist, in what world would we be living?

Being exiled from this place? No, I wouldn't mind that. Meranthi had stopped being my home the day the queen died, not that it was much of a home before that.

Another face crossed my mind. The little girl from the day of the parade, the one in the market who had waved. Her brown eyes, so innocent and young, full of so much hope as she admired me. They twinkled in my memory.

Hope. I had given the girl hope.

As long as I was alive and here in the palace, that girl's hope would not be in vain.

Even if the time came when the king decided to kill me, even if my magic's story ran out, or the king lost interest in it, I would not die the way Queen Gwenyth had died.

I would not die a traitor.

No, if I was going to die, I was going to die innocent, and I was going to haunt my husband to his grave.

There would be no others.

None to come after me.

"I can't go. I can't go. Please, you have to leave," I said. Tears puddled in my eye, running down and spilling over my right cheek. Az grazed his hand over the salty tears and dried my face.

"You don't owe him anything," he said.

I replayed the statement over in my mind, allowing it to wash over the crevices of my brain. What he said, it sounded true. How could I owe this evil, broken male any part of me? I didn't deserve what he had put me through. But. Then again, what did I owe that little girl? The one who would suffer oppression if yet another human queen betrayed the king.

"I chose this, Az," I said, though the words sliced at my throat.

"You don't seriously think that you owe this to him? All because of a ridiculous marriage bond he practically forced you into?"

"No one forced me to do anything," I said, rage boiling beneath my already hot skin. "I made this decision on my own." It felt strange, claiming my agency, when all this time, I had blamed the king for my choice. But it *had* been my choice, and I understood now that my spirit would be the one to pay the price if I allowed anyone to convince me otherwise.

"Which is how you ended up in this mess to begin with. I can't believe you didn't even tell me. I could've... I could've told what a stupid—"

"Stupid? Do you think sacrificing myself for my sister was stupid?"

Az glared at me, his sage-green eyes glowing in the moonlight.

"You didn't just sacrifice yourself. You put me up on that altar of your self-righteousness too."

The icy breeze caught in my throat. Why was he saying these things? "I didn't... No, you can't make this about you," I said. "You had years, Az. Years. For ages, you've known how I feel about you," I said, the word spilling out of me now. "You knew all along. You could've... At any moment, you could've asked me to marry you, and I would've been yours within the hour."

"You act like this is easy for me. Like confessing my love to you would be just like proposing to any other girl. But there are stakes, Asha. There are things I had to work through. And you just up and left without giving me time."

The aching in my heart turned to steel.

"Things you had to work through?"

"Asha, you know I didn't mean it that way," he said, running his fingers through his hair. It didn't even make my stomach tighten this time.

"Get out," I said.

"Asha..."

"Get. Out. That's an order."

His pleading eyes hardened. "Fine. Enjoy your life of luxury," he said.

I opened my mouth to fight him, to scream he wasn't being fair, that I had never wanted this. But he turned to go the way he had come, through the bushes. I watched him, my heart aching with every one of his footsteps. He didn't bother to look at me one last time before disappearing into the shadows.

That place in my heart that I'd reserved for Az, for my childhood friend and the simple life we might have together, shattered. Nothing took its place. Not even tears.

The sunflowers mocked me as I made my way back to the palace. They swayed in the wind as if dancing was the appropriate response to my heart caving in on itself.

That was when I saw him.

A looming shadow, edges lit by the backdrop of the moon.

The king.

Our eyes met, and even in the darkness I could see those molten eyes gleaming hot. Dangerous. He had seen. The wind seemed to clutch my neck, refusing to allow me to take it into my lungs.

"If you hurt him, I'll—" I stopped. Because my threat was as empty as my chest.

I fled to my room, praying that the king had enough decency to leave me alone for the night.

The Fates didn't grant my request.

CHAPTER 32

*M*other lunged down the hill, hand upon the hilt of Father's dagger, the one she'd stolen from Father's collection that morning for such an incident as this. She cried out to warn Farin, who didn't see the Other coming, and he twirled around to face her.

Shock overcame his small face, and panic pulsed through Mother, for she hadn't intended to draw his attention to herself, but to the Other who was only feet from her child, its maw open wide, jagged teeth glinting in the sunlight, its tongue hanging from its mouth, surely tasting its meal in the air before it dug into him.

"Run!" she screamed, and Farin turned around this time. But Farin didn't run. He froze, just like he had the night his father had slaughtered the mere.

Except Mother wasn't Father. She wasn't used to running, but fear for her child propelled her legs, forcing them to extend further, faster than they should have been capable.

She ran faster than she ever could have imagined, but not fast enough.

The monster barreled into Farin's chest, knocking him to his back.

She couldn't even bear to close her eyes, couldn't bear to leave him alone in death as the creature lunged at his face.

And licked him.

Mother's heart stopped, though in her haze, she couldn't tell if it was due to confusion or relief.

Farin giggled and tickled the Other, which quickly rolled off him and onto its back as he scratched its belly.

"Mother!" he called, grinning up at her as she ran to him, and though his hair was disheveled, she could see even from a distance that the marks on his face were old, that the beast hadn't as much as scratched him.

Something odd snagged her mind. Why could she see the marks on his face when she was only halfway down the hill? She kept running, her speed only barely diminished in her relief. When she reached him, she practically tackled him in her arms.

"Mother!" he called out, and even though the intensity, the loud abandon of his voice frightened her, she recognized it was only out of a deeply ingrained habit. That there was no reason to fear the sound of her child's laughter.

She drank it in, allowed its timbre to fill her withered belly as she clutched him closer.

The Other seemed to feel left out, because it placed its paws upon her and halfway climbed up her back, as if to join in on the embrace. Water beaded on Mother's forehead, and it took her a moment to realize it wasn't sweat, as she'd assumed. It was drizzling from the sky.

What kind of world was this?

"It's okay, Mother," Farin said, stroking her back as the skywater peppered his sandy hair. "You don't have to be scared. The Others here are nice."

Kind. Mother corrected him in her head, though she didn't have the words for it. There was a difference between kind and nice, a subtlety that meant the difference between a smooth back and one dappled with welts. Her whole body trembled, and she realized why Farin had felt the need to comfort her. Why he'd thought she was trembling in fear, when, really, it was relief.

Relief that Farin was safe, most of all, but also, that he'd discovered this place, this wonderful world that Others hadn't yet destroyed, hadn't yet consumed. A world where Others played with children and water fell from the sky.

"Are you angry?" Farin asked, his voice serious now as he turned those wide, brown eyes on Mother. Her heart sank. No matter how many times she'd told him she would never, ever relay his misbehaving to his father, he had never quite believed her. And why should he, when she was the one who'd chosen to put him in his father's way to begin with?

"Of course not," she said, trying to blink away the tears, though they streamed down her face.

"I've made you sad, haven't I?" Farin asked, his face sinking.

"No, child," Mother said, kissing his moisture-speckled forehead. "You've made me the happiest female alive."

His face lit up at that, and he piped up, "Do you think it'll make Father happy too?" he said, gesturing, as if to this entire new world.

The skywater stopped, as if the heavens held their breath for her answer.

Mother's heart plummeted. Father. They'd have to tell Father. They'd have to tell everyone. Of course. Father would lead the entire tribe here. They'd settle into a new life, one where they wouldn't go hungry, and females could bear babies, and babies could cry.

That should have been enough to answer Farin's question. A new life, a life free of fear and hunger, should have made his Father happy.

She might have thought so too, only a few years ago.

But Mother was no longer a child.

She knew better.

And in that moment, every beating, every whimper that had escaped Farin's mouth, every female Father had not bothered to hide when he'd grown tired of Mother's love, every apology that wasn't an apology at all, flashed before her eyes, burned in her memory, brought itself forward as a witness.

"No, Farin," she said. Tears welled in his eyes, because to him it must have made little sense. Yet it didn't quite surprise him, either. "We're not telling your Father."

Farin cocked his head toward her. "But Mother. We have to! Father will make the tribe move soon. The land doesn't have food in it for the roots anymore. You said so yourself. If Father makes us move, we'll never get to come back here!" Tears poured from his dark eyes, replacing the skywater and carving streaks into the dirt on his face. The dirt that had caked itself to him the day he'd been born. The filth she'd never been able to wash off, lest she waste drinking water.

Just then, her ears tuned into something. A rushing sound that was unfamiliar. She turned her head to the right, but couldn't see the source through the trees.

"It's more water, Mother," Farin said, tears still spilling from his face. "There's so much water, it moves. I haven't even found the end of it yet. Please, if we don't tell Father..." He collapsed in his mother's arms.

Water falling from the sky. Water roaring as if it was an Other itself.

What sort of world was this? What magic pulsed through the air?

"Farin, listen to me," she said, cupping his face in her hands and lifting his chin. "We're not telling your father, because we're not going back."

Farin blinked twice, as if to aid him in absorbing the words. They seemed to sink in all at once, because his forehead, his cheeks, the corners of his lips, his eyes, they all softened.

And Mother realized, for the first time in his life, her son was experiencing the feeling of relief.

That she was as well.

CHAPTER 33

KIRAN

*H*umans lie.

Asha is human.

Therefore, Asha lies.

So why does this logic stir doubt in my soul? Why does this conclusion taint my tongue with the bitter taste of metal?

Asha lies, yet she stays. She honors our marriage covenant, despite knowing there is no substance to it. She bargained for a night with me, but I've overdelivered, denied her the escape from our bond.

Of course, if we had struck a true bargain, I would have no choice but to slaughter her. When I chose to appoint humans as my heralds, as the ones to proclaim my intentions to execute a human woman every mooncycle after taking her as my bride, it had not been with the intention of reneging on my threat. No, it had been the other lie, the most nefarious of all, that had influenced me to use the mortals as my mouth.

Humans lie.

But it's fae who feed them the words.

Regardless, there's an attachment worming its way into my soul that is grateful for the loophole. Grateful that my fae curse won't force me to murder my wife without cause.

Because that's where I stand with her. Without cause.

When the frantic pleadings of her childhood friend reached my ears from across the garden, it wasn't the pang of jealousy that shocked me. My father had taught me from an early age that jealousy was a king's right over what was his. And after the events of these past dreadful months, after Gwenyth...

Jealousy was no stranger; therefore, it was no surprise.

I stalked them in the shadows, like the feral predator I suppose I've become. Like the monster I was born to be, I laid in wait, ready, no, eager to pounce upon the lovers and rip them to shreds for what they were about to do.

For what Gwenyth had done to me.

That was the sickest part of all of this. I had *wanted* Asha to betray me, as if that would have somehow justified what I'd done in condemning her for sharing a distant ancestor with the woman I loved. The woman I hated. The woman I adored and loathed and cherished and despised.

The woman I could no longer punish.

I'd made sure of that.

Only a few hours have passed, and though Asha and her sister are fast asleep on the floor, the sound of their even breaths taunt me as I lie awake, wondering.

Wondering.

Wondering when my steadfast heart, so devoted to my wife, newly freed from the snare my father had set around it before I was old enough to understand a lie from reality—when that heart had rotted.

When I had let it.

I replay this evening, the way my muscles tensed and my Flame curled within me, readied to lash out, to relieve me of a portion of the agony that's coiled itself around my ribs, pushing at the walls of my chest for any way out. I replay the way the couple's exchange caused me to salivate, as I tasted their blood in the air before I had ever spilled it.

I *wanted* her to do it. To take him into her arms and kiss him and make a run for it.

I wanted her to do it, because I wanted her to make me right. To absolve me of the wretched aching in my soul, the incessant pinching sensation that never seems to gives my sternum a rest.

I wanted her to justify me.

All I got was the sharp needle of conviction.

It took the breath from me, stifled my Flame, when she spoke.

When she told him *no*. It hadn't taken my fae senses to catch the longing in the air, the desire she fosters for this human male.

Yet, in the face of immediate temptation, she had stood firm.

My wife—the one I despised, the one I had threatened and humiliated every morning since our wedding day by assessing her before her very people—she had remained faithful to me, when the wife I loved, the woman to whom I'd poured out my soul in reverent sacrifice, had found refuge in another's arms, in the poison by which she intended to end my existence.

I had *wanted* Asha to betray me, to give me a reason to end this miserable marriage that's had me thrashing in an ocean of guilt, seeking for a way to justify myself, since the day she grinned at me in that mirror, showing off her scars like the Fates had sent her to foreshadow my punishment when I faded from under the sun.

Instead, she had stayed.

She had stayed, and the armor safeguarding my soul had cracked.

I should have gone after him—after the human who'd attempted to steal my wife. It was a fool's decision to let him flee, and even now I'm kicking myself for the security threat I've left wide open by not following him. Even after sweeping the gardens, my guards have no clue how he got in.

But I'd known that if I caught him, I would have killed him.

For some reason, I couldn't bring myself to do that to her.

I know she didn't do it for me. I'm not so much of a fool to believe she's developed an ounce of affection for me. She made that clear enough when she reminded me how out of touch I'd become to the needs of my people. When I hadn't considered that hosting a mandatory parade to celebrate the longest day of the year—the day with the highest mortality rate—might not have been the best way to win over my subjects.

I'm pretty sure it's a reflection of my twisted childhood that something about her so blatantly pointing out my shortcomings had sparked a curiosity within me about what it would be like to know her.

Not that I dwell on such things. In fact, I try to shove such fantasies from my mind as soon as they slither through my mental barriers. I figure there are plenty of fae who would shun such thoughts with disgust, particularly because of the scars that mar the left portion of her face.

Me? I know better than to convince myself that, of the two of us, Asha is the disgusting one. She might be my wife by law, but any woman brave enough to put her neck to the blade for her sibling deserves more than to have her would-be murderer fantasizing about taking her to his bed.

So I try to distract myself, try to ponder her Old Magic's story, try to decipher the history lost to the ancient, the power over the other kingdoms that the ancient tale might reveal, the repercussions of humans who could possess the Old Magic, what that means for the fae, for our power.

How I might use my wife to expand the reach of our sand-locked kingdom.

I try to dwell on anything other than what it would be like to join myself to her, to become one, to knit my soul with a being who had kept hers pure.

I'd probably just soil it anyway.

CHAPTER 34

ASHA

"*I*'m sorry for your pain, Asha," the king said. I looked up from my untouched breakfast plate, the one I'd been fixating on the past half hour. His eyes settled upon me, warm as the first rays of sunrise in the windy months.

I tried not to gape at the not-so-subtle reference to last night. The king had followed me to my quarters, just far enough behind not to disturb me in my grief, just close enough that I could be sure he wasn't strangling Az. Then he had sat without a word and listened as my magic continued our nightly ritual. He had left as soon as we woke this morning, and though Dinah had pestered me to tell her why I seemed so sullen, I had brushed her off, unable to formulate words for my shame. When she left to join Father at the shop, I had wept.

"I don't want to talk about it," I said, returning to conducting the train I had made with potato fritters, nudging them with my silver fork. I felt Lydia hasten to rise from her seat and scurry from the room. Fin quickly followed. Why they left me alone in his presence, I had no idea. Perhaps, as much as they seemed to like me, they still couldn't tolerate their brother's voice.

I couldn't blame them.

"Well, I would. It's my business too, you know," he said with an urgency that secured my full attention, the not-so-subtle reminder of the king's paranoia shoveling a heaping pile of thick, sticky dread into my empty stomach.

"There's no reason to lay a hand on Az, Your Majesty." Panic fluttered inside my chest. Just because he hadn't hunted down Az last night didn't mean he hadn't been brewing some sinister revenge plan all evening.

Something flashed in the king's ember eyes. For a moment, I thought it was jealousy, the byproduct of a challenged pride. How dare a peasant boy attempt to seduce the wife of a king? But then, as I looked closer, watched as the lower lids of his eyes narrowed slightly, I wondered if I might have been mistaken.

Was the male sitting before me even capable of pain? I had been under the impression that Gwenyth had seared that callous shut.

"You can call me Kiran, you know."

I didn't respond, unwilling to change the subject at hand.

"I have no intention of harming a lifelong friend of yours, Asha," he said, his deep, thrumming voice echoing off the walls of the recently repaired breakfast alcove, despite his attempt at speaking quietly.

"Because I turned him down?" I dared him to deny it with my stare. There was at least one advantage to having a missing eye. I never had to try to look intimidating. Even if we both knew I had no weapons for wounding my fae husband. "Forgive me if I have a hard time believing you would have sent us a wedding gift."

A flicker of a smile tugged at the corner of the king's lips.

"There's no use in kicking a male when he's down," he said, his voice lighter than before, and I glared at him as his lips twitched, trying their uttermost to suppress a cocky grin.

Rage boiled my blood. How dare he mock Az? Mock me for turning him down? Surely he could see my eye, how my weeping had left a crease in my lid that no amount of makeup could have concealed, the blood soaking the veins where my eye should have been white as milk.

I opened my mouth to whirl an insult at him, spear him with any bit of cruelty I thought might pierce his soul—or, rather, the desolate cavern that once held one. But the words fled my lips, packed up and emigrated from my mind.

That cursed magic. What was it good for if it couldn't toss me a good insult every now and again?

Oh, I don't know. Keeping you alive every evening, perhaps?

So now you decide to talk to me, I spat back.

No sense in letting your temper get us both killed.

I mentally huffed. *Maybe you should have spoken up before I volunteered to be personally executed by the king.*

A noble death I could live with. If you give me a fool's death, I will personally haunt your spirit in the next life.

Great.

"Is something wrong, Asha?" Kiran asked, his eyebrows narrowing the only creases on his ancient face.

"I'm not hungry." I slid the plate of untouched food toward him and jolted to my feet. "Would you please excuse me?"

"Of course. You don't have to ask."

I cocked my head at him, wondering why in Alondria he thought I should know not to excuse myself from the table, when he still expected me to beg for my life every dawn. Just because almost half the crowd had bowed in return to me this morning didn't make it any less humiliating.

Especially when my eye was all puffy.

I rose and headed toward the door.

"Asha," Kiran called out from behind me, his voice actually sounding earnest for once. I halted, though I wasn't sure why. Probably because if I peeved this king off I'd end up burned to a crisp, and after living my entire life in a kingdom where I was more likely to die of heat stroke than old age, that wasn't the way I wanted to go.

My fists clenched. "Yes."

"From where I'm standing, there was nothing for that boy to work through."

His words lodged a rock inside my throat, then twisted. I opened my mouth, but nothing but garbled mumbles came out. Habit scanned the inflection behind his words, searching for mocking, but it found none. I didn't dare look at him as I excused myself from the breakfast room.

I managed to find the kitchen doors and hide myself in the pantry before I broke into a disgusting mess of snotty sobs.

By the time I'd gotten a hold on myself, convinced myself that it was imperative that I force my magic to reveal exactly who it was and why it had chosen to take up residence with me, no amount of pestering I attempted could force my magic to speak again.

Not that I was focusing all that well.

For some reason, another voice infiltrated my head. *From where I'm standing, there was nothing for that boy to work through.*

* * *

I FELL asleep in the cupboard and dreamed of Az.

He was kissing me when one of the kitchen servant's screams ripped me from his arms.

I imagined it was mildly traumatic on her part.

Taking advantage of the chaos in the kitchen, as everyone assumed the servant had found a mouse, I'd slipped away and back to the king's chambers, with every intention of taking a nap that could rival a python in length.

Tavi had met me there, prepared to get me out of my breakfasting clothes and into my daily wear.

Decades could have passed like this, and I wouldn't ever get used to changing so many times a day.

"Are you alright, Your Majesty?"

The words jolted me from a fog, the blur of Az's face in the garden, his smirk as a child, his fingers on mine on the rooftop. My hand slipping...

"Yes, I'm fine," I said, straightening.

Tavi peered up at me with those pale, eggshell eyes. The dark lines that traced her milky green irises jolted back and forth as she examined my face. Not my scars. Not my missing eye. But the pain that hid behind them. Her gaze unsettled me, so I broke eye contact and stared at my silk slippers. Tavi was wrapping the laces up around my ankles before tying them off right under my knees.

"There's pain in your eyes," she said. Then her spine stiffened, and I recognized the look. The look of someone who'd accidentally used the plural word to describe what was only one.

"It's fine, Tavi. I'm not offended," I said, honestly grateful for a distraction from Tavi's questioning.

"You're too gracious, Your Majesty," she said, starting the work on my left slipper now.

We sat in silence for a moment, and I felt my mind slipping back into that fog, that fog that seemed to appear out of thin air. It wrapped its tendrils around my chest, and I coughed, foolishly thinking a loud noise could rip me out of it. It didn't work, of course, and I sank, sank, sank, until...

"Tavi," I said, unable to bear being alone in my head with myself any longer. "Have you ever been in love?"

Tavi's eyes flashed with such shock, my cheeks went hot with embarrassment. "I'm sorry. That was inappropriate of me to ask."

"No," Tavi shook her head, as if to shake water out of her ears. "It's alright, Lady Queen. I don't mind. It's just...the question surprised me, is all."

"You don't have to answer."

"It's nice to be asked, though." Tavi's hands froze in the middle of tying the knot on my left calf. "No one mentions him anymore. Not my family, even. I think they worry that, if they bring him up, I'll..." She trailed off, and I watched as tears brimmed on her pale lids.

"Did something happen to him?" My heart thrummed as I witnessed the pain manifest itself in the tension in her neck, the furrow in her brow. Guilt rapped against my chest for even asking such a question, especially after the notes I'd found in the library.

She blinked and swallowed, and it was as if she'd banished the pain altogether, caused it to disintegrate into thin air. I wondered how long it had taken her to master such a skill, to learn to swallow the grief.

"He passed from under the sun," Tavi said, her voice trembling slightly, though so faintly I might not have noticed if we'd been talking about anything moderately less sensitive.

"I'm so sorry," I said, and she began lacing up my shoes again.

"That means a lot, Lady Queen," she said. She smiled, and even her eyes joined in, and I realized she meant it, the gratitude. Something swayed in my heart, and I wondered if, in a different life, Tavi and I might have been friends.

Perhaps we could be friends in this life too.

"What was he like?" I asked, looking to fill the bleak silence between us, unnerved by the lack of manners I'd utilized by asking what had happened to him.

"Very romantic. He used to write me letters every chance he could yet. He was a servant here too. That's how we met." Tavi choked on a giggle, her face lighting up, something about the way her eyes crinkled reminding me of Az's smile. Because, of course it reminded me of Az. Everything was reminding me of Az, even Tavi's story...the story I should be invested in instead of making it all about me, instead of allowing my mind to wander to my own problems, my own hurt.

"I didn't notice him for the longest time," she said. "I wish I'd seen him sooner. But one day, while I was cleaning the library, he waltzed right up to me and introduced himself. I thought it was quite odd, but he kept finding reasons to come run errands in the same room I was cleaning—" She stopped when she noticed my hesitant expression. "He wasn't creepy, though, really. He'd always talk to me and tell jokes to make me laugh. And we got to be friends, and then..." She trailed off again.

My mind whirred back to the notes scribbled in the margins of the library books. If the library was where Tavi's suitor had first introduced himself, and where they'd spent their time getting to know one another, it made even more sense that the notes would be theirs. Sure, Tavi had told me she'd been borrowing the books for her brother, who devoured at least one a day, but I found it unlikely that a half-fae would have time for that amount of reading. Especially with the long hours her brother must work in the city to scrape by. No wonder Tavi had lied to me. It must have been too painful to admit she was finding comfort in the notes of someone who had passed from under the sun.

But something nudged at my mind. That last note, in which it seemed her suitor had known he was about to die and had vowed to keep her identity a secret. Who was he, that Tavi would be endangered if their relationship ever came to light? And what had he been involved in that had caused him to know his demise was nearing?

I opened my mouth to pry, but then I glimpsed how the glossy, wet film had returned to Tavi's eyes. Felt how her pain mirrored my heavy heart, and I wondered—if my heart felt like someone had doused it in water and left it to mildew, just because I couldn't be with Az—how I would feel if he was dead, how that pain would amplify.

My jaw seemed to clamp shut on its own.

"What is it, my lady?" Tavi asked, her pale irises still shining from the tears she'd attempted to banish.

"Nothing, Tavi," I said, and I meant it. If those scribbles were Tavi's connection to a male she'd loved, who was I to pry?

I decided I'd have to find an excuse to keep Dinah from searching for the rest of the notes.

* * *

I ASKED Tavi to walk me down to the library that day, mostly because I wanted her to have a reason to visit it, rather than having to bother with the mental energy of making up an excuse. She grinned when I asked her, and her mood seemed to lift as she escorted me down the stairs and through the long hallway toward those grand cedar doors.

When we arrived, she shuffled off to a dim corner of the massive room, muttering something about how her brother hadn't asked for another book lately, and how she was worried he was depressed, and that she thought she could find something to his liking that might cheer him up.

I tried not to notice which book she pulled from the shelves. Instead, I searched for a new read. By the time Tavi left, I still had found nothing that fit today's mood—weepy. Some titles I tried seemed too whimsical, and I worried I might throw the book across the room in an act of bitterness if the couple ended up happy and together in the end. Some seemed so dark the concern was that, if I buried myself in them, I might never come out.

Disgruntled with my lack of choices in this vast library, I trudged over to the fireplace, hoping if I got close enough, the heat might sear the memory of rejecting Az right out of my mind.

I didn't think I'd mind if it left a callous behind, either.

As I reveled in the heat and wondered what Dinah and my father were up to today, I traced my fingers on the mantle. There wasn't a trace of grime left on my fingertips, and I wondered how often Tavi snuck in here to "dust."

On the mantelpiece was an inscription I'd never noticed before, perhaps because, whatever language the symbols were written in, I didn't recognize.

I can read them, you know.

I startled, knocking a vase off the mantle in the process. The blue crystal shattered as soon as it hit the floor. Tiny crystalline flecks coated the rug and wedged themselves into the spaces between the stitching.

You've got to stop doing that. It's unsettling, I hissed at my magic. *Too bad you're not the one who's going to have to clean this up.*

A shame, really, it said.

You know it'll only take me messing up once for us both to be hanged tomorrow morning, right?

The base of my ribcage contracted, and I was pretty sure my magic had actually yawned at me.

Pieces of the shattered blue crystal bit at my fingertips as I tried and failed to pick them out of the likely equally expensive rug. Fairly certain there was no way I was getting it out all by myself, I stood up and tried to figure out who best to help me. But my magic had other plans, it seemed.

I'd be interested in reading those symbols, if you don't mind.

I rolled my eyes. *I was under the impression you don't really care if I mind or not. I minded that you took one of my eyes, for example.*

A misunderstanding, indeed, was apparently the closest thing to an apology I was going to get.

I groaned and faced the inscription. *Fine.*

My voice rendered its loyalty over to my magic, and it began.

What must have been a terribly ancient language poured forth from my mouth, in that deep, resonant voice that didn't belong to me. My tongue moved in strange ways, clicked against my teeth, hissed, and even inhaled on the sounds that didn't even exist in my language.

The flame in the fireplace smoldered. Smoke billowed in its place, and I jolted back. Now, how was I going to explain to the vizier why all his precious books reeked of smoke?

But then the smoke vanished.

And so did the wall that made up the back of the fireplace.

Only darkness remained in its place.

CHAPTER 35

ASHA

"Alright, that's enough of that," I said aloud because I was too freaked out by the fact that my voice had just opened a secret passageway within the fireplace to care if I sounded like a crazy person. I looked around the room, thankful no one was in the library to hear me. Or see what I'd just done.

"What was that? If anyone sees this, they're going to think I'm a witch, and they'll disconnect my head from my body within the hour," I hissed.

A double standard I find lamentable. Fae do magic, and they're called fae. A human does magic, and suddenly, they're a witch.

"I'm not really interested in your social commentary at the moment," I said. "Just fix it."

I will. After we go exploring.

I groaned. "You want me to dive into a dark hole in the back of a fireplace that we opened with some, probably illegal, creepy Old Magic?"

Exactly.

I really wished my magic had a face so I wouldn't feel so ridiculous glaring at him.

You didn't used to be so afraid of exploring. From what I've heard, you used to rather enjoy it.

Yeah, and look where that got me, I thought, pointing at my eye, or the little that was left of it. My magic didn't respond, and I examined the dark hole where shadows oozed from behind the fireplace. This was going to look really, really bad if someone found it. Found me.

"Fine. We take a peek, and then we come right back out, and you fix this mess."

By mess, you must mean the fireplace, because I'm afraid there's nothing I can do about the vase.

I grunted and ducked my head into the shadows.

* * *

THE DARK ROOM WAS COOL, much cooler than the palace, and I found myself shivering. The light from the library seeped into the stone floor and illuminated a lamp that sat alone on the cold stone.

"Well, that's too convenient," I said.

Pick it up.

"You do remember what happened last time I messed with a magical lamp, don't you?"

Pick it up. This one only contains a remnant of the Old Magic. I would be able to feel it if one of my kind still dwelled within it. It's more likely this one has been blessed with magic, and no one ever dwelled in it to begin with.

I didn't even want to ask what the difference was between Old Magic and plain old regular magic, so I squinted my lone eye as I leaned down and nudged the lamp with my knuckle. Unlike the room it inhabited, the lamp was warm to the touch, and it sent a pleasant wave of heat up my arm that stilled my shivering.

See? Not so bad.

As I lifted the lamp closer, I noticed that etched into its metal frame were similar markings to the ones on the mantle.

Before I had the chance to stop it, my magic had taken over my voice and boomed that creepy ancient language into the dark space. A few short words, and a blue flame appeared at the tip of the lamp, licking the dusty atmosphere as if it were alive and parched for air. I shuddered despite its warmth.

The room lit up—much too bright for the size of the flame coming out of the lamp—but I was too emotionally drained to bother being surprised. What did surprise me was what lined the walls of the room.

I didn't know what I was expecting. Probably for this to end up being some strange, unholy tomb where a witch or an ancient fae had been laid to rest. I supposed I'd half-expected a decaying body to be mounted on some ancient relic in the middle of the room.

But there was nothing in the middle of the room.

In fact, the only items in this room seemed to be a pedestal at the far end of the room, the lamp, the bookshelves that lined the walls, and the scrolls not so neatly piled on the bookshelves.

The sigh escaped my mouth before I'd even realized it.

There, I thought. It's just another library. Happy now?

Oh, immensely, my magic cooed in a way that made me want to rinse my throat out with saltwater.

Tell you what, it said, *I'll let you pick out what we read today.*

"I'm just so grateful. Really, you have no idea."

I thought I could feel my magic's chuckle rattling my ribcage. My shoulders shook almost involuntarily, as if they could somehow shimmy it out of me.

When it became clear that my magic had no intention of speaking another word until I did as it asked, or rather, coerced, I stomped over to one of the shelves and plucked out the first scroll that my fingers came across.

Then I waltzed over to a podium on the far wall of the room and unrolled the scroll atop it. The paper, so dry it seemed it might disintegrate at any moment, crinkled against my fingertips as I opened it. I glanced over the writing, all of it in that strange ancient language I was beginning to recognize despite being unable to read it. The ink hadn't faded a bit, at least not at the rate the parchment had weathered.

I traced the bold letters with my fingertip. What sort of ink didn't fade with time?

The blood of an Omigron.

My fingers recoiled back into my palm. "I wasn't asking you."

But then my throat surrendered itself again, and my jaw and lips contorted. My voice morphed as it bounced off the stone floors, as it dissolved in the softness of the room full of parchment. The cadence started off slow, telling, and I was familiar enough with storytelling to know the tale was just beginning, even if I couldn't recognize the language. My magic read for a while, pausing occasionally, at which point I would ask if the story was over.

It didn't bother to grace me with a response.

I'd unroll the next portion of the scroll, annoyed that my magic had taken even my ability to groan away from me.

I supposed I was grateful that my magic's story didn't carry me away with it. Typically when it spoke, I found myself *within* the story, a sensation similar to dreaming. Perhaps it was because this story was told in a language I didn't understand, or perhaps my magic had decided it didn't want me knowing the words' interpretation, but, either way, I wasn't complaining.

I did find it a tad boring, though.

Eventually, the cadence of the words picked up, became more choppy, excited, and I realized we must have reached the climax of the tale. My heart galloped with every lingering moment we remained in this odd room, completely exposed to anyone who might walk through the library doors—friend, or most likely, foe. It didn't help that my magic had wrenched my throat from my control, causing a tension that made me shiver with terror even though I had no idea what the words flowing from my mouth meant.

But then, something cold and hard landed in my right palm. Unable to yelp in terror, I dropped the object, and it clanked and rattled on the stone floor.

My magic ceased, and my voice returned to me, though the urge to scream had passed. I glanced at the floor, and my blood went cold.

"Lady Queen?" a quavering voice asked behind me. I spun around, only to find Tavi, shivering in the cold, gaping at the object on the ground.

I fumbled for words, trying to find the right ones to explain why a sword dripping in silver blood had fallen from my hand and onto the floor.

* * *

"I—I came to check on you, Lady Queen. Lady Lydia sent me, since you didn't arrive for lunch. She was worried, and I told her you were probably lost in some book, and when I got here, I saw the shattered glass and worried, and then I heard a voice." Tavi shuddered. "It was coming from the fireplace, and I thought...well, I don't know what I thought..." she said, her eyes still glued on the bloodied sword.

"Right..." I said, stumbling over my words. *Any help?*

Not really. Someway, somehow, I felt it shrug.

Rage boiled within me that my magic, my little parasite who possessed a bottomless well of perfectly-crafted words, had decided to sit this one out.

"Tavi, I'm so glad you found me," I said, swallowing my reservations and deciding in that moment to entrench myself in my half-thought out plan. I ran to her, and she tensed up, but thankfully my position in the kingdom seemed to keep her feet glued to the ground, although her knees were bent to run. Tossing my lamp to the side in my haste, I threw my arms around her and trembled, which took little acting. "The words on the mantle... My magic took my voice and read them. And then the wall opened up and...and it made me come in here and read one of the scrolls... I promise I didn't know... I didn't know what would happen. It made me..." I shook in her arms, which she tightened around me. The breath she'd been holding in her chest loosened, and she patted me on the back.

"It's alright, Lady Queen. I know you didn't mean any harm."

I pulled away from her, keeping my hands on her shoulders. "You believe me?"

Tavi smiled, and relief washed over me, as I couldn't detect a hint of dishonesty in her eyes. "Of course, Lady Queen. You sacrificed yourself for your sister. You gave us all hope. I don't know what happened to you," she said, averting her eyes from my scars. "But I know it can't have been easy. And it really can't be easy living with that...that..." her words stumbled off. "With *it* living inside of you."

I can't say I'm fond of her tone.

Shut up, I hissed at it.

With pleasure.

Tavi's face warmed despite her pale, cool features. "Don't worry, Your Majesty. Your secret is safe with me."

I sighed. "Thank you, Tavi. I can't tell you what that means to me." I pulled my hands back to my side, and Tavi curtsied.

"If you don't mind, Lady Queen, I think I had better hurry off to get the broom," she said.

"Of course," I nodded, and she scurried away.

"Don't forget some gloves!" I called after her, and she turned and grinned before sneaking out of the cedar doors.

"Alright, now help me put this back," I said, stepping through the hole and back into the library.

With your permission, of course.

As if you need it.

Just trying to be more sensitive. I wouldn't want to make you do anything.

Oh, shut up.

That was some fine acting.

I didn't say anything that wasn't true.

Even better. The best liars are the ones who do it with their actions, rather than their words.

I gritted my teeth, but I didn't have a retort. The only words I spoke for the rest of the afternoon were the ones that closed the fireplace wall.

CHAPTER 36

*I*t took several days for Mother to soothe the feeling that Father was at her back, that he'd tracked them here, that he'd found them and was going to kill the both of them for defying him—Mother for leaving him, Farin for existing, for the unforgivable sin of giving Mother something to hope in. To hope for.

And though the dread was substantial, though she knew there was no escaping it, that it would cling to the marrow in her bones for the remainder of her living days, she hoped better for Farin. That he still had enough childhood left in him to warp the memory of Father into the same category as childhood nightmares.

Besides, the fruit here was good.

She'd almost cried when Farin had climbed a tree, insisting that those from the top tasted better than the ones that had fallen to the ground, and that he wanted to find the best tasting fruit for his mother.

"This one is sweet and tangy," he said, after sliding down the immense trunk and flourishing a fuzzy orange orb. "There are others that are just sweet. And others that are just tangy. But this one is the best, because it has both."

Mother had taken it, though only after scaling a difficult mental hurdle. She'd never taken food from Farin before. At least, not of her own will. Father had forced her to from time to time, when he'd thought Farin had sinned badly enough to deserve to go without dinner. She'd never eaten the portions she'd taken, though.

"Mother?" Farin asked, his face stricken with concern. "I promise it's not poison."

Mother forced her lips into submission, strained until her mouth bent like a blade of dry grass in the wind. "Of course it's not. I'm just... savoring the look of it."

Farin cackled, something he'd been trying out in almost every situation, just because he could. "Why would you savor the look of it when you could savor the taste of it?"

Mother couldn't argue with that, so she took a bite. Her stomach rumbled in greed as her teeth sank into the soft, juicy flesh. Flavor, sweet and tangy, as Farin had described, exploded in her mouth, and she consumed it so quickly that the juice ran out the side of her lips and onto her cheeks and fingertips.

"You're making a mess!" Farin said proudly, already scrambling up the tree to find her another. They feasted on the lovely fruit until their bellies had expanded three sizes and all they could do was lie on the soft, cold soil, giggling.

They spent the next week like that, and each day, Mother would convince Farin to go exploring with her. Each day, they'd find themselves a little farther from the hill with the ray of strange sunlight. A little farther away from the world of hungry Others.

A little farther away from Father.

She'd never admit to Farin this was intentional. The fact she still feared that, any minute now, he'd track them down. Snatch their beautiful world from them.

But not Farin. Farin feared nothing here. And she'd never let him. Not when this world was so safe. Not when he could laugh and cry as he willed.

Not when he'd taken up singing, a sport he'd only ever heard described in stories.

Words were good for a great many things, but there were no

words that could take the place of a melody, no words to adequately describe a song.

Mother could listen to Farin sing all day. Sometimes he even convinced her to join in, though the lyrics she created often slipped into something cold, something dire and mournful. So she never joined in for long. Not when Farin was so much better at it anyway.

The friendly Other, whom Farin had named Teeth, returned often, most of the time bringing them some strangely morbid gift, usually a dead flying Other, or a tiny, furry Other with a long, wormlike tail. It disturbed Mother that Teeth seemed capable of Other-like things, and she sometimes couldn't fall asleep if it stayed the evening with them, sure it was just waiting to attack Farin in the night. But it never did. And the way it curved its black lips when it saw him almost looked like a smile, and Mother felt her heart falling for the creature despite herself.

Besides, the small creatures it brought them were useful. Though Mother and Farin both agreed that they would happily live off fruit for the rest of their lives, their stomachs did not agree, and they both suffered a bout of intestinal illness after splurging on the sweet, fleshy orbs.

Once they had recovered, Mother had used the backside of a knife she'd borrowed from Father, the side that was made of flint, just for this purpose, and some fallen sticks and leaves to build a fire. Then she'd skinned the little creatures and cooked them. Though they were tough and chewy, Farin acted like they were the most delicious food he'd ever eaten, and Mother remembered that, on the rare occasion Father and the hunters had supplied meat for the tribe, Father had never allowed Farin to sample any of it.

The image of Father wrapped around her mind, sneaking in unwanted, and she found herself pushing Farin farther up the river, farther away.

They never strayed far from the moving water, of course. Mother knew it was unreasonable, but the fear clung to her anyway—that they would wander away, too far to hear the water rushing, and they wouldn't be able to find their way back.

It was too risky, even if her hearing had mysteriously improved since inhabiting this new land.

Farin liked to call this new realm Mine, which Mother could not quite bring herself to make him to give up, even though it was probably breeding selfishness in him. But what did that matter, when it was just her and Farin?

Her heart sank when she remembered that one day, she would die and Farin would be alone in a world with Others that, despite being kind, could not talk back.

But this was still better. For it wasn't as if Farin's voice was heard in the tribe anyway.

But he would have had a better life than you, that tiny voice in Mother's head nagged. *He would have been chief one day.*

Only after his father had beaten every fragment of kindness and compassion out of him, determined it was the manifestation of weakness, she reminded herself. It still bothered her she'd deprived her child of any relationship beyond her own.

But she couldn't think of that now.

All she could do was get Farin as deep into Mine as possible, so far that, by the time Father discovered where they'd gone, time itself would have smeared away their scent and tracks.

That night, Mother and Farin curled up next to the campfire, Teeth asleep at their feet.

"Mother?" Farin asked, his voice quiet and muffled underneath the rush of the moving water.

"Yes, child?" she asked.

"I don't miss Father," he said, before hiding his face in her tigren-pelt coat.

Mother's heart faltered, not at her son's words, but at the guilt in his voice, the immense responsibility in his face when he peered up to discern her reaction. She wondered where he'd gotten that from, shouldering the burden of other beings' actions on his own shoulders, as if he had caused this, not Father.

"I know. I don't either," she said.

Farin went quiet for a while, then sighed. "Mother?"

"Yes, child?" she asked, trying her best to keep the trepidation out of her voice. Back home, neither of them had ever known the freedom of speaking their mind, which had been especially difficult for Farin, but he had learned eventually. Now, Mother had no idea what would come out of her son's mouth at any given moment. No idea what kind of wild thoughts had been swarming in his mind, locked away all those years.

It hit her that she did not know her own son very well at all. The realization gnawed a hole in her stomach, a hole representing all the lost time, the lost conversations, the lost childish questions that had slipped through, misplaced and scattered in time. Hate boiled within her, fury toward her husband who had stolen those moments from her.

The heat in her chest did nothing to suture the hole.

Farin spoke, snapping Mother back into the Now. The Now she wouldn't waste. "Was Father always mean?"

Mean. A child's word, the best he could muster to describe the void that infected his father's heart. She thought back, resisting the urge to confirm his question, that his father had come out of the womb as a parasite, that he'd always feasted on displeasure.

But, even if that were true, it wouldn't help Farin. Lies never did, even when children were the ones on the receiving end. Besides, Mother remembered Father's father. And though it was perhaps difficult to accept, she knew her husband had been born into a world that intended to obliterate his soul.

"No. He was a child once, too," was all she could say.

"But when did he start being mean?" he asked.

"I don't know," she said, truthfully. "But your grandfather was a harsh man. It must have been difficult for your father to grow up to be anything different."

Farin went quiet for a moment, and when Mother looked down, a tear dropped from his cheek to the back of her hand. "What's wrong, child?"

She hated Father for even having to ask that question. They had finally found safety, peace, and nothing should have been wrong at all.

"Will I grow up to be mean, too?"

Mother frowned and squeezed Farin tighter. "No, child."

"How do you know?"

"Because you are stronger than your father."

Farin looked up at her, his eyebrows scrunched in confusion. "But I'm small. I can't even lift a saber off the ground. It drags."

"Not your muscles or your bones. Your heart, Farin. You are kind, and you are curious, and you've taken—" She choked on the memories the words brought to her mind. "—you've endured so much pain, so much hate, and yet, it's never once broken you. It's never caused you to lash out or become cruel. That is strength, Farin. To endure cruelty and remain tender in heart. It takes strong skin not to develop a callous."

Farin bit his lip, chewing on this new bit of insight about himself. "Then you're strong too," he said.

And though Mother disagreed, knew deep down that Father's hatred had leaked into her soul, sowed a resentment she knew she'd never be brave enough to dig up and burn, she couldn't bring herself to disagree. Not aloud, at least. Not when it would undermine all the things she'd said about Farin, at least in his mind.

Besides, it was nice to have kind words said about oneself. And it didn't make a bit of difference that the compliment came from a child, a child who didn't know any better.

In fact, that might have made it all the more significant.

* * *

When Mother awoke to Farin's screams, she thought she must be having a nightmare. A horrible dream that had transported her from their haven, back to the camp, back to the world where beasts tore fae apart, rather than snuggling up to them at night.

But then Farin screamed again, and Mother realized the nightmare was occurring in the new world.

And that it was very much real.

CHAPTER 37

ASHA

I returned to the garden a week later, despite myself, despite knowing I was only doing it to torture myself, to reimagine the encounter with Az. In this alternate version of recent history, this tale of desperate romance I weaved in my mind on a nightly basis, I ran away with him. I surrendered my heavy heart to the boy I'd loved so long I couldn't remember when that first little ember of feeling had flickered. He took my hand in his and led me from this garden through the shadows, far, far away from this place. But the more I tried to reconstruct the events of that night into something more palatable, the more my daydreams turned nasty.

Fighting. Az resenting me for forcing him into exile. Cold dinners eaten in a colder atmosphere as our decisions cut us off from our families and from one another, until they all reached the same conclusion—it would have ruined us to run.

I'd already ruined us the second I'd given myself up to the king.

But Az and Asha, separately. Could those two entities still function? Would my choice to sever the bond between us somehow preserve us?

As I strode through the garden, lost in my thoughts, I tried my best to keep this beautiful place, just that, beautiful. Not the place Az had declared his so-called love for me. Not the place I had pulled rank on my best friend and commanded him to leave. Not the place my heart that had shattered as I'd discovered something about myself, something I couldn't have known for sure before.

That I would rather be honorable than happy.

I wasn't so sure about that anymore. There were nights when I would wake from my few hours of sleep in a cold sweat, after my magic had lulled Kiran and Dinah to sleep. Nights when Az had come for me, and I had agreed to run away with him rather than tell him to leave. In those dreams, the little girl's face, the one from the market, never haunted me. Never even crossed my mind. Sometimes, I would feel myself waking from those dreams, and my eye would squeeze closed, hoping that, if I didn't open it, I could cling to that version of my story for just a few moments longer.

Ugh, I was doing it again.

I shook my head, hoping that might clear it of these useless thoughts, even if my willpower didn't have a shot at doing so.

A lone clematis sprouted on the dangling limb of a tree next to me. Probably the only sign in hundreds of miles that we had entered the autumn months. I wondered how far I would have to travel to experience a true autumn, the type spoken about in that book on which Father perseverated. The budding flower glowed in the moonlight. I reached out and grazed its fuchsia petals, savoring the softness of it. A softness I could not have dreamed up as a child, not until I had felt it for myself.

That was the thing about desert plants.

They were all so prickly.

I guessed the same could be said about the people.

Except for Dinah, of course. Her spindles were more fuzzy than anything.

I wasn't sure how my mind had managed to wander to comparing my loved ones to succulents, but I supposed it was about as productive as trying to rewrite my decision to reject Az.

A muffled sob sounded from the west corner of the garden, wrenching me from my thoughts.

Deep and low, someone wept here. I recoiled my outstretched hand and tucked it into my robes, immediately recognizing the ridiculousness in doing so. Obviously, my companion in the garden had other things to worry about than the fact I was touching the audaciously expensive flowers.

I figured I should leave them alone. But then I wondered if they wanted to be left alone.

In my opinion, there existed no greater moment of inner conflict than stumbling across someone crying. I'd take rejecting Az over this. Any day.

What would I want? Certainly not for a stranger to comfort me. But then again, there was nothing as divisive as what crying people might want from others, so what I would have preferred might not have applied.

So maybe I couldn't do much harm by approaching the weeping being, after all.

I crept over to where the sound originated. As much as I intended to help the person, I wasn't quite ready to give up my chance at a quick exit. Once we made eye contact, I wouldn't really have a choice, would I?

As it turned out, the weeping person heard me coming.

As it turned out, he possessed that heightened fae hearing I often forgot about.

Kiran's bloodshot eyes met mine as I peeked around the corner.

Crap.

Mortified, my back went rigid as I jumped behind the lush shrubbery.

Agh.

This was not happening to me.

Though the sounds of weeping had quieted, muffled gasps for breath wafted around the corner of the hedge. The effect was such that, if I didn't know better, I might have thought someone was strangling an animal.

I tried to talk myself out of it. Who knew what my husband might do if I approached him during such an undignified moment of vulnerability? He was high fae, after all. They were known for dwelling on the outer banks of emotional extremes. What would the typically stony king do to the one who stumbled upon him showing weakness? Though the threat of dying every morning had waned a bit, it might not keep him from strangling me in a fit of rage.

But then again.

He had tried to comfort me the morning after I'd rejected Az. Sure, it had been in his own, somewhat cynical way. And he had failed miserably. But he had tried.

Besides, given the king's track record for making important decisions under the influence of extreme emotion, I figured the quicker I could calm him, the better.

My foot stepped out from behind the bushes before I could convince it otherwise.

He knelt next to a stone bench carved out of a single rock. That massive body of his trembled, and I wondered at how I hadn't sensed the ground shake as I'd approached. Now, the dirt path beneath me rumbled with the unpleasant reminder that I had yet to glimpse the full extent of my husband's power.

Come to think of it, I had barely scraped the surface.

I willed myself to approach the fae, the beast of a male that cowered before me.

"Get away," he hissed, and I could imagine the bulge of his jaw as he clenched his teeth, although he buried his face in his palms.

I paused. My legs wanted to take the command and run with it... Run away, that is. It would be foolish to approach the powerful high fae in such a vulnerable state when he had expressly commanded me to leave him alone.

For some reason, my feet remained planted. I hesitated to approach him, but I wasn't going anywhere, either.

"It's not safe for you when I'm like this," he said, and he was right. Even as his body quaked, the air in my throat thickened, swelling with unnatural heat.

The words came out before I had the chance to catch them. "Are you ever safe for me to be around?"

His shoulders flinched. Not for the first time, I remembered the gift that had been bestowed upon my husband's lineage, the Flame that devoured whatever was unfortunate enough to enrage the king. I fought the impulse to step back, and it was just as well, because he lifted his face from his hands and turned to face me.

He had shaved sometime between last night and now, and the effect on the sharp edges of his face was startling. In a way, it made him look a thousand years old, his cheekbones and jawline set as if carved by an ancient master sculptor. But, then again, there was a softness about his face too, something hiding between the sharp angles, something that beard of his usually covered.

I remembered something I'd learned in my pitifully few years of schooling.

The King of Naenden was young. Not just in fae terms, but by human standards too.

His father had practically been one of the ancients, and it had taken centuries to sire Lydia. The twins, Kiran and Fin, had come sooner than expected after their sister, only a decade later. The realization shook me, unsettled me, like sitting in a stool positioned lower to the ground than one expected. I should have known, should have remembered that Kiran and Fin were the same age, Kiran just minutes older than his brother. Minutes that made the difference in a kingdom and a province, a palace and a house.

The fae hardly aged after reaching adulthood. So what had made this male, barely five years older than myself if what I remembered from my history lessons was correct, seem centuries-old?

"Come to think of it," I said, though I tried to keep my voice soothing, like how Dinah might have sounded if she had been the one to stumble upon the weeping king. It was an effort. "I'm not sure anyone is safe when you're like this. Not when you've chosen to do this in the garden, of all places." There, I was doing it again, saying the insensitive thing, though I was trying my best to be helpful. Dinah should be doing this, not me. "Really, though. If you burst into flames in here, the palace is done for. The bushes grow all the way up to the doors. And the doors are made of cedar. Not sure if you remember."

Silence.

I had never been good at silence, not when I felt uncomfortable. So I steadied my grip on my proverbial shovel and dug myself a pit, hoping it would at least be deep enough for me to hide in.

What did they say about surviving a fire?

Something tells me that when your father told you to drop, he didn't mean drop dead.

Ah, well.

At least when I spoke, my voice didn't shake.

"Why is it that the Naenden fae were gifted the power of fire anyway? I mean, we live in the middle of a desert. It doesn't get *that* cold at night here. Wouldn't the power of water have been a more useful gift? I guess I'm assuming your ancestors already lived here when the Fates blessed them with magic. Though I don't really know the history. I suppose your ancestors could have immigrated from somewhere cold. Perhaps they got tired of having to use their powers constantly to stay warm—"

"Do all humans talk this much?" the king growled. Good. He was engaging me in conversation. I'd take it, even an insult, if only to keep him from destroying my favorite evening walk.

You mean the place Azrael confessed his untimely love for you?

As usual, I ignored my magic's unwelcome commentary.

"If we did," I countered as I rubbed my thumb and forefinger together in an attempt to calm my nerves. "Would you fault us for it? It's not like we have hundreds of years to live. We only get a handful of decades. Less time to get all our thoughts out."

"You should consider taking up writing. Your thoughts would last longer that way," he said.

"Takes too long," I said. No matter how pitiful the king appeared in this moment, I had no intention of giving up the fact that my hand-writing had never progressed past the oversized letters my mother had taught me before she passed. Oh, I could read, of course. But write? It would have been more efficient to hire a parrot to transcribe my thoughts. "I promise you I can talk a lot quicker than any of your scribes can write," I added, just in case he suspected my embarrassing lack of skill in writing—something he had likely learned within his first decade of life.

"Perhaps it saved your life, that jabbering of yours," he said. My spine went rigid. He had never addressed the fact that he spared my life every morning because of my never-ending story. At least, I hoped it was never-ending. Whether my magic was capable of such a feat, I had no clue. Besides, I had always assumed the king was less interested in the story than my magic itself.

"What do you mean?" I asked. He lowered his hands and turned to me, his usually golden eyes burning into a deep amber, highlighted by the streaks of red across the whites of his eyes. I had never seen him look so…human.

"That magic of *yours*, as you like to claim it. I don't know how you acquired it, but it's no coincidence you survived the initial encounter."

The muscles around my jaw tightened, my throat clenching.

"What do you mean, it's not a coincidence?"

CHAPTER 38

ASHA

Kiran stared at me for a moment. No, many moments. Enough moments to make a girl uncomfortable.

"Well?" I asked, my voice tilting at the end of the word.

For a minute there, I thought he wasn't going to tell me. That he had remembered he wasn't talking to a friend, but a woman he'd put at odds with himself.

An enemy of circumstance.

But then his eyes softened, and he spoke, his voice low and gravelly, and...

And curious.

"The magic inside you is of the old craft. When the fae first discovered magic, they found it unwieldy. As you would say, it had a mind of its own. They subdued most of the magic in this realm long ago, but there are legends that a few old strands escaped the ancient fae. That they still wander about Alondria."

So there it was. I had been right all along. The king had more interest in the magic that dwelled inside me than the story itself. I gulped. "You think my magic..."

"It wouldn't shock me. And, if that is the case, I would assume it might be particular about the type of being within whose soul it took up residence."

"Wait, a minute. Are you saying it might have killed me, had it not realized how much I like to talk?" I said, crossing my arms, though with a fraction of the spite and annoyance I might typically use toward him. I fought the curve of my lip with all my might. Even the left side of my face twitched a bit.

"You said it. Not me," the king said, those embers inside his eyes flickering once more. This time not in a rage. Not even annoyance. No, there was something else there, lingering behind those warm irises. Something soft. Something tender. The effect of it softened the sharpness of his jawline, the intensity of his stare. It shaped his features into those that belonged to a being with a soul, a being who'd *lived*, rather than having been sculpted.

For the first time, I noticed how attractive he was. *Attractive.* Magnetic. Not simply symmetrical. Perfect.

I ripped my gaze away from his, hoping he hadn't noticed how I had examined him. The king had a sizable enough ego of his own for him to discover my curiosity. Not that I could flatter him, even if I wanted to. I was only human, after all. I imagined it would be akin to having a desert jackal sniffing at him.

"I wouldn't complain if I were you. You seem to feel better," I said, keeping my arms crossed, tinging my voice with the slightest bit of acid.

The king chuckled, though the bags under his eyes seemed to weigh them down, keeping them from participating in the smile. Why did those dark circles make his face all that more endearing?

"It is impossible to focus on much of anything when a gnat is buzzing in my ear," he said.

"Agh!" That was all I managed to come up with in response. My lips jerked again.

He smiled, this time with eyes and all. And, all at once, I discovered why I had always found his perfectly symmetrical face, that firm jawline, dark brows, and perfect skin so unappealing. In all the time I had known him, his features had barely moved. I wondered then if it was the dynamics of a face that humans found so alluring. Not the features themselves, but the way they danced with one another, spinning and rippling, putting on a show. How his eyes glinted in the moonlight as his cheeks rose into the corners of his eyes, revealing the slightest wrinkles. Revealing that this being, this male, had lived. If only for a short time.

My stomach twisted at the sight. That wouldn't do.

"You know they say crying is good for the soul," I said, wishing to keep that smile plastered on his face as long as possible.

"So I've heard," he said. "But I'm not crying."

"Oh, you're not?"

He shook his head and sighed. "When I was a child, before I knew how to subdue the Flame, I'd get upset enough to boil my tears. They even left scars on my face a few times," he said, hesitating as his gaze lingered on my burn marks, as if he thought he might have over-stepped. "Anyway, I haven't been able to let the tears out since, though I hear it's quite cathartic. This is as far as they get," he said, pointing to his lower lid.

"That sounds awful."

He shrugged. "I suppose."

"Would you…would you like to talk about whatever's bothering you?" I asked.

"I fear you would not find it pleasant," he said.

"Eh," I shrugged. "I'm used to you by now."

He sighed. "Very well, then. I…I came to the garden to remember the queen."

"Your mother?" I asked, a moment before the realization of who he meant clicked into place. I blushed.

"Gwenyth. This garden was how I convinced her to marry me. When we met, she wanted to get away from her father, but I don't think she would have agreed to forsake Avelea if I hadn't told her about this place."

"I thought the two of you were in love," I said, the words escaping from my mouth before I considered how they might sting.

He cocked his head, examining me with those piercing eyes of his, those molten irises that made my mouth go dry.

I cleared my throat. "I just mean, I figured why else would you have chosen a human bride over the fae princesses?"

He sighed, the heat of his breath fogging in the chill of the garden air. "Not at first, no. It didn't happen the way Naenden believes it did. I thought she was stunning, intriguing when I first saw her. But it was out of rebellion against my father that I proposed to her. And it was her hatred for her own father that drove her to accept. The falling in love part came swiftly after. For me, at least. She was clever, Gwenyth. And so full of life. Not like the fae females my parents had insisted I marry. They were pleasant, I suppose, but they lacked that...that..."

"Urgency?" I asked.

He nodded.

A question teetered on the edge of my mind, threatening to slide onto the tip of my tongue. I bit my lip, trying my uttermost to force it down. To stay put. None of my business. Some questions could get you killed, I reminded myself.

"What? Now you decide to keep what's on your mind to yourself?" the king asked. "And here I thought we were having productive communication."

I gaped at him, at the change that had come over this cruel, horrid male. Not that I thought him any less horrid. Any less cruel. But perhaps...perhaps those qualities weren't quite as permanent, not quite the core to his very existence, as I had once assumed.

"Do you regret what you did to her?" I finally willed the courage to ask. I had never truly gotten the full story. When my magic had showed the tale to my father and Dinah, it had shown Kiran unleash his Flame on Gwenyth. She hadn't even had time to scream.

But I never quite knew when my magic was simply altering details for the story's sake. Or when it was making things up altogether.

His molten eyes narrowed. My heart raced. There was rage in that expression. But then, when he didn't lash out, I realized he was pondering his answer.

"It depends on when you ask me," he said.

239

"I'm asking you now."

He peered up at me, still kneeling by the bench. I was accustomed to him towering over me, not the other way around. It was strange, seeing his eyes strain against his top lids. My mind whirred.

"Yes, I regret it."

"Why?"

He huffed, letting all the air out slowly, as if to make room for the pain.

"Because I miss her. I hate her for what she did, yes. But that doesn't stop me from wishing I hadn't..." He cleared his throat. "Punishing her..." I couldn't help but notice how, even now, he was so unable to admit it—that he had killed her. As if he thought saying it would somehow make it real. Final. "I thought it would cleanse me," he continued, "but it doesn't erase the memories, the ones I wish I could revisit. It doesn't keep me from...from wondering if I drove her into another male's arms. From replaying every touch, every kiss, every word spoken that I can possibly dig from my memories to try and figure out when...the exact moment she stopped loving me."

My heart constricted in my chest. "Maybe falling out of love with someone isn't like that," I offered. "Maybe it's just something that happens when we aren't paying attention to it. Not one pivotal moment. It's just all the little not-moments that add up. The moments we forget to make."

His wide eyes narrowed. Not in anger, no. Contemplation. When he spoke again, his voice was a growl, low and primal and raw. "And how do we miss out on those could-be moments?" he asked, his hot breath fogging the space between us. The space that had somehow shrunk in the past few moments.

I shrugged—an excuse to mask my effort to pull away from his massive frame, a meager attempt to hide the fact my pulse was accelerating with every word exchanged. Surely he could hear it, with those pointed ears of his.

"I don't know. Probably by ruminating in all the have-been moments... Or the could-be moments," I added. Then cleared my throat.

"Surely you aren't saying you don't think I deserve to suffer guilt?" he said, his molten eyes piercing mine, interrogating me. "When I'm the one who sealed her fate?"

Well, there was the answer to the question I had decided not to ask. I expected a shiver to sweep through me, for dread to grasp hold of my throat, suture it closed.

The king had executed the queen he adored.

What would he do to the queen he didn't?

Except that somehow, sitting here with him as he mourned—it should have felt like trying to comfort a starving saber by petting it on the nose—but it didn't feel that way at all.

In fact, here, when it was just the two of us, I found myself less afraid of him than I'd ever been.

"No," I said. "I think what you did...I think it was wretched. But you can sit here and wallow in it, or you can master it. Use it to fuel change. That, I could...well, I could at least respect that."

He winced. "Respect me, you mean."

Dangerous territory. I was flirting with that fire of his, for sure.

"I don't know why it matters to you."

"Because I prefer for feelings to be mutual," he said. His words caught me, bound my voice in a way my magic had never managed.

His wince morphed into a wry, almost pained smile. "I'll give you one thing, Asha, Queen of Naenden. You are a miserable comforter, indeed."

CHAPTER 39

"Farin!" Mother screamed, her eyes snapping open. They adjusted to the darkness, soaking in this strange world's moonlight instantly.

Farin lay on the ground, kicking and writhing, his leg suspended in the mouth of a beast, one that looked like Teeth. Except this monster was larger, its snout longer, its fangs jagged. And it was dragging Farin away.

Mother lunged for her knife just as Teeth lunged for the massive beast. It dropped Farin's leg for a moment, just long enough to swing its snout in Teeth's direction and send him flying. He landed in a slump after hitting a tree.

Farin scrambled away on his hands, his bleeding foot still dragging on the ground, but it was no use. The Other was uninjured. It haunched backward, readying itself to launch.

Mother got there first. She threw herself between the beast and its prey. The sound of flesh ripping hit her a moment before the pain, and she cried out, but she and the beast fell together. It landed atop her, and she scrambled for breath as the beast's fur pinned her to the ground. Warm, wet blood trickled down the hilt of her blade and her arm, and though she felt the pressure of her dagger lodging itself into the animal's neck, she could not tell whether the blood was hers or the Other's.

"Mother!" Farin cried, a mingled whisper and sob. The sound propelled Mother's arms, and she pushed herself from the ground with the beast upon her back. Amazed at her own strength, sure the Fates had doomed her to smother under the animal's thick coat, she arched her back until it rolled splayed onto the ground, a coat of thick red blood staining its coat where her knife had just been.

Red blood.

Mother had never seen an Other bleed a color other than silver.

She jolted toward her son, though he'd already gained a few feet. As she approached him, she realized he'd been dragging himself over the dewy earth by his elbows, gasping for breath as his left foot toppled over the grass, bumping into every rock and pebble in its path with no reaction.

A dark ooze she was all too familiar with traced his path.

She reached for him and pulled him into her lap. He winced, and the sound sent a wave of pain through her too.

"It's okay, child. It's okay. I've got you. The beast is dead. And you are strong, Farin. You survived." She kept whispering into his hair, though her mind was whirring with such panic she couldn't help but drown out the sound of her own voice. She pressed her hand against his chest, and his heartbeat, fast but steady, served as her anchor.

They had not escaped the Others.

They'd only met new ones.

The thought chilled her blood. This was her fault. Her fault they'd become too lax. Her fault she'd allowed her guard to drop, allowed them to sleep out in the open. Her fault Farin was rocking back and forth in her arms, stifling his sobs as his left ankle hung limp.

Mother's mind locked back into place. Farin couldn't even bring himself to scream. Of course he couldn't. He probably feared more like the rogue beast would come. But even if he didn't, she wondered if he'd be able to cry out, anyway. Or if his father—if she—had stifled that natural impulse until it was too weak to break through.

Either way, something had to be done about his foot. As much as

Mother longed to keep rocking him, to bundle him close and lull him to sleep, blood had begun to pool in her lap.

"I'm going to set you down," she whispered to the boy.

His arms tensed, and for a moment, he clung tighter to her coat, but then reason seemed to strike him, and he let go. Mother lowered him and tucked her hand under his head before placing it on the soft grass.

She rolled Farin's trousers up at the ankle to assess the damage. Her heart plummeted at the sight, and she thought she might be sick. She'd seen plenty of monster injuries in her life, mostly because she'd tended to a variety of roots that aided healing, slowed infection.

But Farin's injuries. To see her little boy's flesh hanging from his ankle, to glimpse in the moonlight a sliver of white under his skin, and to know that the beast had punctured bone...

It might as well have punctured her stomach.

She'd had friends die from far less. Not immediately, of course. That wasn't how infection worked. But they'd died all the same. And everyone had made the same comment.

If only they'd gotten to you earlier.

Mother swallowed, but her throat had gone dry, and it only resulted in pain. Pain in the lump in her throat, pain stinging in her eyes, pain slicing through her heart.

Pain.

That was the only constant.

It didn't matter that she'd traversed the bridge between realms.

Pain had no borders.

It didn't know the difference.

Mother swallowed, the saliva sticking to her throat, but the simple motion anchored her, all the same. There was a salve that could fix this, if applied in time. A salve that would keep the infection in the Other's teeth from making it into her son's blood, from poisoning his heart until it slowed to a still.

Vaneroot. That's what she'd used to make it. It always worked if they made it to her within the first few hours of the bite.

There were three bottles of it on her workstation back home.

Mother rocked in the cold air, as if the motion could somehow stop the truth from being the case.

She could always try to find a root here. With all the lush foliage this world contained, there had to be plants she could fashion into salves. The thought sparked her memory of Teeth's body being thrown against a tree. Her eyes darted toward the direction where he'd slumped, and even in the dark, her eyes focused on the little Other's body. His ribs rose and fell, and she wondered at how she could see such a thing from so far away.

Teeth's life, so steady and even, afforded her the smallest comfort. At least he hadn't perished trying to save them.

"Mother?" Farin asked through gritted teeth.

"Yes?" she asked, her heart pounding. She was never sure what this child would ask anymore.

"Am I going to die?" he asked.

She didn't hesitate. "No."

The lie rolled over in her mind, for he would die. She knew that much. Had seen too much to rationalize otherwise.

Pain and death.

Neither knew of boundaries.

At least he would die out here.

To say that Mother's heart sank would be a grave mistelling. For in that moment, when she realized what she had to do, her heart withered. Shrank and coiled and stuffed itself away.

She wondered if it would ever inflate again.

Oh, if only she had bothered to study the roots of this place in the week they'd been here. Perhaps if she hadn't gorged herself on fruit and lounged on the ground every evening as soon as the sun set, perhaps then…

They had traveled at least two days' journey down the moving water, but that had been walking, and at Farin's place, which had been slowed by his curiosity for every foreign bug or beetle.

Mother knew she could run. Here, in this place, it hadn't gone unnoticed that her legs cut through the air like a newly sharpened blade. That her muscles buzzed with a pent up energy. An energy that would explode at will.

She couldn't take him with her. She knew that much, though the idea might have ripped her shriveled heart out of her body. They wouldn't make it in time, not if she had to carry him. Besides, they'd never make it to the tribe with fresh blood flowing from his wound.

Mother had little chance as it was. The blood caked to her clothes, but it would dry by the time she reached the hill. At least, that's what she told herself.

So she bound her child's wound, though it ached her to do so without cleaning it first.

"I'm going to go get medicine for you," she said.

His eyes flickered up at her with understanding. With dread. "What if he kills you?"

"He won't," Mother said. *At least not before I save you*, she didn't add aloud.

* * *

VIAL OF VANEROOT IN HAND, Mother figured her only advantage over Father was that he did not yet know the fascination of Mine, that their eyes were somehow made sharper, and, more importantly, in Mother's case, their feet swifter.

He had caught her sneaking into their tent, snatching the vials from her workstation.

The bruise on her wrist, one of many, was already peeking through her thin flesh.

But he'd relented only when she'd told him of Mine. A world whose Other's had not yet consumed all the food.

He'd made her lead him here.

She figured she could get a head start on him as soon as he inevitably forced her through the ray of light first. It was a slim shot, and her heart sank when she remembered her hearing had also sharpened in the new world. Father's would too.

There was no escaping him. Her shriveled heart decayed with

every quiet step across the Grassplace as the couple retraced her steps. With every saunter, his hand pressed into her shoulder a little harder, with a little more intent.

To remind her. She was his and his alone.

And that she would never run away from him again.

"See what happens?" he had said.

"See that you're incapable of taking care of our son?" he had said.

If he was right, it was his fault. His fault for suppressing her motherly nature all these years. For punishing Farin with whips any time she tried to comfort him after a fall, any time the roots had not settled well within him.

Father tapped on Mother's shoulder as they emerged at the hillside. She turned to face him. He sneered, and she knew him well enough to realize he'd noted the deadness in her eyes and was displeased.

As if that hadn't been his intention these last fifteen years.

He raised his shoulder and right palm, the left one still on her shoulder, digging under the bone. A question.

She cocked her head toward the ray of light. He nodded, gesturing for her to go first.

This was it.

Mother ducked through the light and burst into a run.

* * *

THIS RUN DIFFERED from when she'd left Farin hours ago, when she'd hid him in the underbrush close to the moving water, so he could get water if, for some reason, she didn't make it back.

Some reason being her husband.

Hours ago, her heart had pumped, furiously fueling her legs with energy. She'd gotten faster with each step, fueled by inertia. By fear. Fear that if she didn't run fast enough, she might not save him in time.

Now her legs boasted that same raw power. She cut through the air like mereteeth in the flesh of its prey, faster than would have been possible back home. Though her body moved with more agility than a Tigren on the hunt, she found herself willing her legs to move.

Step, step, step.

Pick your foot up. Step. Now, the next one.

Because as much as she wished to flee her husband, to disappear into the trees before he stepped into this beautiful world—this world he would surely tarnish with his evil—as much as she wished to wrap Farin up in her arms, to smother his wounds in the salve she gripped so tightly in her palm that she had to make a conscious effort not to shatter the clay, her feet did not want to move.

She tried to push out the reason, the reason she knew all too well.

Because, the faster she reached Farin, the sooner she'd know the truth.

The sooner his death would become real.

He could have died an hour ago, and it wouldn't be real to her. Not yet. She still had the steps in between her and her child before it became *her* truth, her reality.

But even though she had nothing but sheer will and the power of her muscles, even though she dreaded reaching her destination, Mother ran faster than she'd ever run in her life.

Leaves turned to green whirs around her. The sounds of the forest —the tiny creatures who scattered along the forest floor, the deer that crept behind trees and in the brush to hide, the birds, their chippers and stuttering, the moving water's fumbling—they all turned to buzzing in her ears as she ran, ran, ran.

She traced the edge of the moving water, grateful for its strange surety. Grateful it would lead her straight to her son. Grateful that she wouldn't have to search the forest for his sound, only to find silence where there should have been his breath.

Then she was there. In a matter of moments, and also in the matter of eternity. She was there, and so was he, her little boy.

But he wasn't curled up under the tree as she expected, dead or trembling from a fever.

"Mother!" Farin called out to her, his childish voice singing to her, singing to the trees, singing to Father, who would surely be upon them any moment now. Her child stopped his running, and Teeth, its tongue hanging out of its mouth, ran into his backside. Farin let out a cackle. That beautiful sound. That beautiful sound her husband would silence soon. "Mother, look! It healed!" Her child pulled up his trouser leg, still soaked in blood.

Where there should have been raw flesh, blood, and bone, there wasn't even a scar.

"Mine healed me!" He giggled. Then he ran for her and wrapped his tiny arms around her waist.

Her mind caught up with her legs. "Farin, we must run. As fast as you can. Run."

He stared up at her, his face full of confusion, "But—"

"Good boy, questioning your mother's foolish commands."

Farin's face went as white as the bone that had been protruding from his ankle only hours ago. The bone now blanketed with fresh, pink skin.

Mother tried not to tense as she awaited the blow.

CHAPTER 40

ASHA

*K*iran left for a meeting with King Declan of Avelea in the late weeks of the summer months. I only found out, because that morning, Tavi greeted me for my daily *dress to empress* session, and had informed me I would be staying in my own quarters while the king was away.

I had not been aware that I had my own quarters.

She didn't lead me to them until after dinner with Lydia, probably assuming I would want to spend my entire day in the library.

Fair enough.

Tavi, along with Dinah, who had just arrived for our nightly ritual, arrived to retrieve me from the dining hall after a mighty helping of potatoes, roasted vegetables, and couscous. I wasn't sure what to expect as we wound through a labyrinth of corridors.

"Oh." That was the only response I could muster as Tavi opened the cedar door and Dinah and I entered my space. It was larger than three of my hovels back home and amply equipped with furniture for sitting, lounging, and sleeping. It even had two separate beds, one decorated in shimmering golden satin, like the material of my dress from the day of the Summer Solstice parade, and one decorated in lavender, Dinah's favorite color. In the corner, a fire buzzed and crackled underneath a stone hearth. Two cedar bookshelves framed the corner, and a red velvet chair perched next to the fire, accompanied by two lounging mats on the floor.

My mouth hung ajar, but my sister managed to find the gracious words my heart was not quite ready to speak.

"Tavi, how much time did it take you to prepare such a gorgeous room?" she asked.

Tavi's pale, sickly face lit with color. "It's been in the works since His Majesty received his invitation to meet with the King of Avelea."

"You've been too kind, Tavi. To think of the books for my father. And the extra bed for my sister," I said, though the words caught in my throat and my nose burned as I spoke them.

Tavi blushed, the rose of her cheeks causing her face, for once, to look more like a thriving plant than a sickly faerie. "Well..." she said, looking down at her bare toes. "My mother'd be ashamed of me if I took credit that wasn't mine to take. The double beds were the king's idea. As well as the fireplace and cushions. But he had nothing to do with the color palate. That was all me!"

If my mouth hadn't already been hanging ajar, my jaw might have fallen off my face.

"The king's idea!" Dinah exclaimed, hugging me and thankfully hiding my dazed expression from Tavi's view. "Asha, surely this means he sees now!"

"Sees what?" I asked.

"Sees that you're innocent. And that you're good in your heart, not at all like his rotten queen before you." She paused and pulled away from my gaze, crimson flushing her cheeks. "Forgive me for saying such a cruel thing of one who's passed from under the sun."

"I won't repeat it. Not that there'd be many around here who'd argue with you," Tavi said, her shoulders going rigid as she stoked the fire with her back toward us. Again, my eyes searched for those scars on her wrists I had seen during the wedding preparations. I had assumed they'd come at Kiran's hands. But the way Tavi's bright tone had frozen at the mention of the late queen, I wondered if I might have been mistaken about their origins.

Tavi left us to ourselves for the evening. The fire was peaceful, and it almost tempted me to fall asleep on the cushions, to catch up on the sleep I had lost to my magic's story last night. It occurred to me that there would be no more storytelling until Kiran had returned from the Avelea. I welcomed the break, but the longer we lounged by the fire, the more Dinah's hands fidgeted, though she continued to deny it when I pointed it out.

"Oh, your busy hands are going to wither soon if you don't put them to use," I said, nudging her in the shoulder after she had let out yet another concerned sigh. I could see it in her eyes. The guilt for having abandoned her nightly stroll around Twin Alleys for me. "I'm sure your friends miss you mightily. And Bezzie's leftover hummus."

"Oh, but I couldn't leave you!" she exclaimed.

"It's only for the evening. Besides, the king is to be gone for weeks, didn't you hear Tavi? I'm not likely to perish between now and next week."

Dinah teared up, hugged me, and left in quite a hurry. How much her hungry beggar friends had weighed on her mind these nights she'd spent listening to my stories, keeping me company, keeping me alive, I couldn't imagine.

I was deciding whether to stroll down to the kitchens and see if I couldn't retrieve a dessert from the servants when the ivy outside my window rustled.

Odd. I thought I had closed the window to keep out the breeze that chilled the hairs on my arms. I supposed even palaces had troublesome windows, so I went to close it again.

Except it wasn't the wind that had opened my window.

My limbs froze and my heart pounded so hard it might have drowned out my scream, had shock not paralyzed my throat.

The faerie stood before me, his body covered in hair that gave him the look of some wolf-like creature. Lychaen. That was the word for what he was. He flashed me a grin full of jagged, blood-stained teeth, hunger rippling in his moon-pale eyes.

I backed away, but the fae flexed his claws, terrible yellowed things, and whispered, "I wouldn't move if I were you. I was told to bring you alive. But my master isn't one to fuss about a few gashes or a missing finger here and there. Not that you have much of a canvas left for my art."

My blood chilled in my veins.

Asha, don't make it easy for him.

Right. The clutches on my throat loosened, and I unleashed the shrillest scream I could muster.

It was a hoarse, weak thing, but I had no time to regret it. The lychaen lunged. My legs reared and pivoted, and I ran for the door.

I'd beat on it if I couldn't make it in time to turn the handle.

I didn't make it in time.

The lychaen pounded into my back and shoved me to the floor. Sharp claws dug into my arms. The sound of ripping flesh echoed through the air.

A moment, and then the pain.

That was the lychaen's mistake.

The scream that escaped my lungs this time was not weak or hoarse, but primal. The wail launched itself from my lips as agony coursed through my blood and fear rattled my bones.

Lychaen talons were laced with venom. My mind raced for how I knew this, whether the venom would paralyze or kill me.

But all I could focus on was the pain.

I screamed louder. He gripped his fingers over my mouth, the tip of his yellowed talons drawing blood on my cheek. Tears soaked my face, and the stinging rippled up to my lone eye. It throbbed, and though the pain intensified my scream, the lychaen's cold palm muffled it.

If no one had heard my second shriek, no one was ever going to hear me again. I pounded my fists onto the floor, hoping the Fates had stacked the rooms in my favor. That of all the empty rooms in this palace, someone had taken the one below mine.

The creature wrapped his other arm around mine, so I kicked. Kicked at him and the floor and anything in the room that might make a sound.

"You're going to wish the king offed you, lady," the creature hissed in my ear.

I bit the hand covering my mouth and twisted my body at the same time. He gasped, and his grip around my arm and torso loosened just enough for me to turn and face him. I went for the only part of him I knew I had any chances of maiming.

I dug my fingernails into his left eye.

And this time, he was the one who screamed.

A wail so shrill, it must have shaken the metal pots in the kitchens.

"You filthy—" I didn't hear the rest of what he said, for he slapped me across the temple so hard my ears rung. I lunged for the door again, but his hands closed around my ankles.

I beat the floor with all my might as he dragged me to the window. My nails screeched against the carpet as I grasped for something, anything, to hold onto. But there was nothing left. He was going to take me. And, even if anyone had heard my screams, they would have to traverse the entire palace to get to me. He only had to get me to the window.

The lychaen lifted me over his shoulder. The harder I kicked, the harder he dug his claws into my back. Pain shot down the backs of my thighs as his talons ripped into me. My muscles seized, and I no longer had control over my legs above the agony.

He slung both of us over the edge, a pair of claws hooking me, the other scraping down the side of the palace, slowing our fall just enough for the creature to land without dropping me.

We thudded to the ground, but there was no use in trying to escape. My legs quavered, and I couldn't get control of them.

The lychaen turned his wild yellow eyes upon me. "Perhaps I'll get a taste of you on the road, La—" His jaw went slack, his eyes wide.

He dropped me.

Or rather, I fell with him. As I looked down, I saw protruding from his chest the bloodied tip of a blade, a hair away from my ribcage.

CHAPTER 41

ASHA

"*A*sha," a female voice gasped, her voice carrying from at least two floors up. I turned toward the window, and bile filled my throat at the realization of how far we had dropped. A dark figure scaled its way down the ivy, her nightgown, the color of the evening sky that framed the moon, fluttering in the evening wind, reminding me of a poison butterfly, if such an anomaly existed.

I would have recognized that unearthly mingling of terror and grace anywhere.

Lydia.

"Asha, are you okay?" Lydia asked, her voice the only sound as she landed silently on her tiptoes. I nodded, just before vomiting all over my dead, would-be captor.

Satisfied that I was at least cognizant enough to communicate, Lydia pushed the lychaen onto his back and withdrew the dagger. Dark blood spattered the moonlit ground. She wiped the blade clean with the hem of her dress before she sheathed it in a concealed pocket within the pleats around her hips.

"Here, you need to stand up," she said, grasping onto my shoulders.

I winced. "I can't. My legs won't move." I gasped for air as the realization flooded me. The venom had paralyzed me. I couldn't move my legs.

I couldn't move my legs.

And then I was back on that alley floor, my tiny, broken body seized up in agony…

No, no, not again…

"They will," Lydia said, her voice grounding me. "Lychaen venom only paralyzes the mind's perception of being able to move. Not the limbs themselves." She pulled me to my feet, without the slightest assistance from me, and without laboring her breath.

My feet hit the ground, and to my immense relief, didn't crumble under my weight.

I leaned against her shoulder as we stumbled through the moonlit grounds back to the palace.

"There you go. Just keep moving them. It'll help your system work the venom out."

I fought back a whimper with every step and lost the battle for my pride every time. My thighs shook. My lungs rattled.

And the pain.

The pain filled my body as if it were not simply venom but shards of glass that coursed through my blood. Fin met us at the door, wielding a crescent saber in his left hand.

"Are you injured?" he asked Lydia, concern brewing on his brow as he examined her robes.

"It's not my blood," she said, and I couldn't help but marvel at Fin's vision, how he had managed to see the inky lychaen blood against Lydia's midnight robes. In the dark. "Wake the healer, if she hasn't already risen from all the commotion. You'll need to dispose of the kidnapper's body afterward. He's directly under Asha's window on the west side of the palace."

Fin nodded and started down the long hallway connected to the foyer.

Lydia turned to me, keeping her hand tucked under my armpit to support my weight as she pulled me into the foyer. She scanned my blood-soaked arms, and I could see the wheels in her mind whirring, assessing the damage. But there was something different about them. While they usually gleamed violet, their color had faded, leaving behind empty irises, void and black as the night.

I'd have to ask her about that later, when my limbs ceased aching so intensely it was a shock not to hear cracking noises echoing through the hall.

"The healer will be here soon," she said, "but in the meantime, I need you to tell me exactly what happened. Here, no, don't sit. It will only prolong the pain."

I nodded and answered through gritted teeth. "He said...he said he wasn't allowed to kill me. But that his master wouldn't care if he...if he hurt me..."

"I'm guessing he wasn't foolish enough to mention his master's name?" Lydia asked. I shook my head and choked on my saliva when pain shot through my neck.

Fin arrived with the healer what felt like hours later. She was fae, thin and human-looking, except that her slender, tall body could not have been supported on a human frame. Her eyes narrowed to match her face when she saw me.

"Take her to the room adjoining mine." Her voice resembled an echo more than the real thing. "There's no need to sully her new bedsheets the servants have been making such a fuss over. Besides, she'll need special care once she sleeps."

Fin and Lydia exchanged a concerned look.

"What happens when I fall asleep?" I asked.

"Terrors," said the healer.

I gulped over the boulder that felt as though it were lodged in my throat.

"I'll carry her," Fin offered, reaching for me.

"No, she needs to walk," Lydia said, swatting his hand away. "I'll help her."

Fin raised an eyebrow at his sister. "Interesting. I would have thought you'd be dying to get back to the lychaen carcass."

She glared at him. "Just save the claws and teeth for me."

He groaned, having clearly received the least pleasurable of the tasks at hand, before pacing out the door.

"The teeth?" I asked, not because I was particularly interested in Lydia's bizarre obsession with my would-be kidnapper's molars, but because I groped for any bit of conversation that might distract me from the horrible insults my legs were yelling at me as I forced them, as Lydia forced them, to bear weight.

"The venom is useful," was all she said before I swayed and vomited all over the freshly mopped marble floors.

* * *

When we reached the infirmary (for that was practically what it was), Lydia refused to help me onto the white washed bed that looked so inviting, with its plush pillows that resembled clouds, a rare sight amid the desert.

Instead, she forced me to hobble around the edges of the room, both of us trying not to knock over tables of bizarre metal instruments, even as my limbs trembled.

"Trust me, you'll be glad I made you do this," Lydia said, supporting my arm on her shoulders as we paced. I groaned.

"Just because you know a hundred ways to kill a fae in one stroke does not make you a medical expert, my lady," the healer said, striding back into the room as if her toes somehow floated above the ground. I cocked my head at Lydia, instantly regretted doing so as a sharp pang etched my spine, and wondered again what exactly the princess did with her spare time.

"If she lies down, her limbs will spasm," Lydia insisted, avoiding my questioning gaze.

"It's going to have to work itself out of her system one way or another, my lady. Might as well let her get it over with," the healer said, her voice fragments of an echo bouncing off the white-washed walls.

I sighed as Lydia lifted me onto the bed and tucked the soft sheets around my arms, which had begun to shiver as a clammy sweat encompassed my body.

Lydia muttered something to the healer, but I couldn't make it out before sleep overtook me.

* * *

NOTHING HURT ANYMORE. I might have rejoiced with a song, had something about my surroundings not seemed a bit off. The clay apartments of Meranthi surrounded me, and though I couldn't quite place this alley, something about it seemed familiar. As if it were supposed to be another place I knew well, but it simply didn't look the same. I followed the shadows of the alley toward the main street, where I could see colored tents hanging from the city walls, providing shade to the vendors. But when I stepped out into the open, the colored canopies turned out to be tattered robes hanging from a clothesline in the next alley. I turned around, but the path behind me was no longer the unfamiliar one from which I had come.

No, I knew this alley.

A frantic chill clasped at my heart.

No, no, no.

I spun around, intending to run in the opposite direction, but the walls surrounding me remained the same, those same shadows consuming the place where there should have been an exit, a road, a dead end, anything but the shadows.

Once, I had been brave. Once, I had allowed the unknown to draw me in. Never again. I clawed at the clay brick of the walls, willing them to stick to the edges of my fingers, to allow me to scale them. By some unnatural force, I made it halfway up the wall before I slipped and crashed to the ground. I turned to check the shadows, to ensure they hadn't moved.

They had.

My breath caught, and I lunged at the wall again, but this time my limbs froze in place, for a scream cut through the shadows, calling my name.

Dinah's scream.

The words were muffled as they waded through the shadows to get to me. I turned toward the gloom, my breath freezing in my chest as a cold wind cut through the darkness. Dinah screamed again, and I ran toward her. Toward the shadows that turned my heart to ice, toward whomever, whatever, was hurting my sister. But my legs turned to lead, and though nothing laid between me and the shadows, I had to will each limb to move. To run.

But I didn't have to run anymore. Because the shadows cleared to make way for me. So I could witness my sister's death.

I saw the life flee Dinah's eyes as Kiran crushed her windpipe.

* * *

Voices, low and uneasy, swirled in the darkness.

"Surely there's something you can do for her."

"What do you mean, it just has to *work itself out of her system?*"

"What are you two keeping from me? I know you have suspicions about who did this to her."

Something warm and calloused touched my drenched forehead, wiping my hair from my face. I didn't open my eyes to see who it was. I didn't care.

I surrendered to sleep once more.

This time, no nightmares assailed me. Utter darkness encompassed me, and I welcomed it with open arms.

* * *

When I awoke the second time, I recognized the voices, though I kept my eyes closed, too exhausted to endure anyone interrogating me.

"I never thanked you for saving her," Kiran said. Kiran? But that didn't make any sense. Wasn't he supposed to be in Avelea?

Lydia scoffed. "And why should you thank me? I would have thought you'd be grateful if she died. It would have been a simple solution to your problem."

"Why must you turn everything I do and say against me? I'm trying to thank you, Lydia," Kiran said, his words strained.

"I believe what you said was, 'I never thanked you.' That's not the same as thanking me."

"Thank you, Lydia."

"You're welcome."

Silence followed, and I feared the two high fae would notice that my breathing had become less shallow, betraying that I was awake. Not that I wished to eavesdrop on their conversation, but I wasn't ready for the attention, the questions that would surely follow once they knew I was alert.

"You got here quickly for someone who was supposed to be traveling to Avelea. That's a five-week journey." Lydia said.

"At a business pace, yes," Kiran said. "Besides, I'd only just left. I hadn't made it through the Sahli when Fin's messenger caught up with me."

"Why rush back?"

"The security of my palace was compromised. My urgency shouldn't come as a surprise."

"But you didn't go straight to the Captain of the Guard when you arrived. I asked Fin. He said you barged through the gates and demanded to be told where they were keeping her," Lydia said.

Robes rustled as Kiran bristled at the accusation.

"Are you sleeping with her?" Lydia asked.

It took all the restraint within me not to jolt out of the bed.

My clammy cheeks burned hot as my fever.

"You're asking if I'm sleeping with my wife?"

"You shouldn't take advantage of her. She didn't get herself into this situation because she wanted your attention. You should know as well as anyone. All of this is for her sister."

Kiran's rage practically boiled the air surrounding us. I clenched the sheets between my fingers, lest my trembling give me away.

"What, are you going to blow me up for trying to protect an innocent girl?" Lydia said. I could have gaped at her audacity, her seemingly incessant need to challenge him.

But, to my surprise, the air cooled at her question.

"I'm not like him, Lydia. It would be nice if you stopped expecting that from me."

"No, you're not. You're cleverer. Which makes you more danger-ous. Our father never could have come up with something as poetic as forcing an innocent human girl to give away her life to save the rest. Just to prove to you they're not all like Gwenyth."

Kiran didn't answer, but this time, there was no unnatural heat wrapping itself around the room. I peeked my eyes open and peered through the slits. Kiran sat next to Lydia on a white-washed bench, jaw clenched under the stubble he'd allowed to grow, elbows on his knees, ruddy face in his palms as he rubbed his temples.

"So you're not sleeping with her?"

"No, of course not," he said. My fingers tensed, and a sharp fire struck my chest, though I doused it immediately. My mind went back to Az on the rooftop, Az in the garden. *There were things I had to work through*, that's what he had said.

Apparently, Lydia's mind followed a similar path as mine.

"What is that supposed to mean?" she asked. I waited for the heat in the room to rise again.

It didn't.

Instead, Kiran just groaned. "It means exactly what you said earlier. She agreed to marry me to save her sister."

"Then why'd you come here and not to the Captain of the Guard?"

"Because she's a good person, Lydia. Is that the answer you're looking for? She's a good person, and being around her is like being in one of those nightmares where you show up to a gala naked. One of those dreams where you think to yourself, *Why in Alondria did I make this decision? I'm not the type of person to show up in public undressed.* And Asha is the person in the dream who's dressed in their finest apparel and gives you that embarrassed look when they see you. She treats me like she feels sorry for me, Lydia. Like she pities me."

What the crap? Was he talking about *me*? The same *me* who kept sticking my foot in my mouth around him? Sure, I had tried to comfort him the evening I'd found him weeping, but…well, he had said it himself, hadn't he? I was a miserable comforter.

Lydia stared at him for a moment, piercing him with those intense violet eyes of hers. Then she rolled them back and laughed. "Aren't good people the worst? Especially good humans."

The muscles around Kiran's forehead and eyes loosened as his expression toward his sister softened. By the way he was looking at her, I might have believed they were close, if I hadn't known better. "Where do they get the idea that they have the right to make the rest of us look bad?"

He chuckled, and a softness brushed the sharp edges of his face.

"I know how you feel," Lydia said. "She surrendered her life on the chance—the *chance*—her sister might perish."

"I know!" Kiran said, and he actually nudged his sister's shoulder. "I'd never do that for you!"

"We agree at last," she said, her painted smile overtaking the fierceness of her features. She stood and made to stride from the room, but when she reached the door, she craned her neck toward me. I slammed my eyes shut, and she humphed.

Then she left me alone with the king.

I snapped my eyes shut.

My cheeks heated at the sheer vulnerability of the situation. I'd been alone with Kiran before, sure. The night of our wedding when I'd thought he'd assault me, and he'd instead offered me a dying wish. The moment in the garden when I'd found him weeping and somehow managed to offend him at least half a dozen times without getting myself killed.

But this was different.

All of the sudden, I was immensely aware of the sweat beading on my forehead, the too-ragged huffs coming from my chest, the *heat* in my bones, in my fingertips, the tops of my ears, that I couldn't figure out whether it was coming from my fever, the king's unnatural presence, or something else…

The something else I'd rather not think about.

For a moment, all I could do was listen to the rhythm of our breaths, mine short and staccato, his long and wearied and deep.

But then the edges of his robes rustled.

Gentle footsteps mimicked the patter of my heart as that warmth, that casual aura that seemed to brush everything in his presence, approached me. It ebbed and flowed in waves, tingling my skin, soothing my aching bones.

Fingers, warm and calloused, grazed my forehead, tucking my soaked hair behind my ear and leaving a stream of flames in their trail.

I had to hold my breath to keep from shuddering.

But then the pads of his fingers, that paradoxically gentle touch, found my scars, traced them down my cheek. Not my burn marks, not the signature of the magic that hitched a ride in my soul.

He traced the lychean's marks, the divots where its talons had clawed into my skin.

I braced for the pain, for the stinging, but it never came.

Only that liquid, soothing warmth, like a salve to my wounds and a balm on my heart, a warmth that flooded my senses and eased my mind.

I think I could have fallen asleep like that.

What a strange thing to think, in the presence of the being who held my life between the crevices in his fingers, my execution over my head.

In fact, perhaps I did drift off to sleep, because the words that rumbled through the steamed air, wrapping me in a cocoon and setting my blood on edge—they couldn't have been real.

I must have dreamed them, because there was no way I heard what I thought I heard.

"The next being to leave as much as a scratch on your skin forfeits their privilege to breathe."

CHAPTER 42

The Old Magic did not like the healer, not one bit. It hated how she poked and prodded and fussed, always with a tone that seemed to imply it was Asha's fault that she was in pain. By the way the Healer spoke of Asha's wounds, one might have gotten it into their head that Asha snuck out to go on a date with that wretched lychaen.

It was the Old Magic's least favorite experience—feeling Asha's pain. Not because he had a low pain tolerance. No, the Old Magic had experienced enough agony over the years to have learned to numb himself to such ephemeral nuisances.

It mostly bothered the Old Magic because it reminded him of a different time Asha had experienced pain. It reminded the Old Magic of her sickening screams as she fell, of the burns that licked at her innocent face, of her eyes that had widened in unison for the last time.

The Old Magic hadn't meant to hurt Asha. He had never hurt a child, not on purpose, not in however many years he had roamed this realm.

The Old Magic couldn't remember how long he had roamed this realm. That was at least half of the problem.

He had been asleep on that fateful day. That day he so wished he could want to take back, but couldn't bring himself to do so. He had hurt her, lashed out, assuming in his paranoia that, after all these years of hiding, the fae had finally found him out. That they would take him, squelch his voice, force him to meld with their bloodline like they had his siblings.

But it hadn't been the fae at all. It had been *her*. And it had taken every last bit of raw strength the Old Magic had possessed to save her life.

It had been a choice between her spine and her eye.

The Old Magic wished he could have chosen both, for her sake.

She was his favorite, though he'd never told her as much. Never spoken to her, not until recently, when he couldn't bear hiding himself any longer. He'd been afraid, all those years. Afraid that if he spoke to her, revealed himself truly, that she'd trick him.

He'd been tricked before, that much he knew, though he couldn't seem to remember the exact circumstances.

It hadn't ended well.

It must not have. Otherwise, why would he have hidden himself all those centuries?

Oh, how he wished he could remember. And oh, how he wished he could forget altogether, forget that something was missing, for at least then, he wouldn't know he was missing it.

Asha was sleeping now. Sleeping was the Old Magic's least favorite time, because although he had slumbered in the time he'd spent hiding from the fae, he couldn't seem to remember how. It was as if he had taken such a lengthy nap, that his consciousness no longer required sleep at all. Perhaps it would be another millennium before the effects of the prolonged nap would wear off and he would get respite from his awareness once again.

At least Asha's nightmares had stopped, though it hadn't been until the fae King of Naenden had stormed in that she'd met any relief.

The Old Magic wasn't sure how to feel about that, about how even Asha's subconscious seemed to bend toward her fae husband, sensing safety in the king's presence.

When the Old Magic chose to allow Asha and Dinah one last tale the night before what they'd all assumed would be Asha's demise, the Old Magic had known trouble would come of it. He hadn't been surprised at all that the King of Naenden had stayed just beyond that closed door, his pointed ears having no need to press against the cedar to hear the words flowing from within.

It had been suicidal, to grant that last request.

But there was no telling Asha, *no*.

There was nothing but being there for her in her last moments.

So he'd spoken.

Spun a tale that he'd draw out forever if he had to, if it meant keeping Asha alive. If it meant the king of Naenden would spare her, if only because he believed a long lost secret to the fae's power lie within the Old Magic's words.

The king wasn't the only one who'd been intrigued.

The Old Magic hadn't known exactly from where the tale had come, but it seemed familiar. Real and not real at the same time. Not as real as a memory. But not as unreal as an imagining.

More like a dream. A dream from which one awakens, and the faces are distorted, not nearly as clear as they were in the midst of the apparition.

The Old Magic wondered how long it would be before Asha was forced to continue the story. He figured he might as well spend his waking time preparing the rest of the tale.

Surprisingly enough, the story came to him smooth and easy, and he allowed himself to drift off between its lilts and edges.

He thought it went something like this:

MOTHER COULDN'T BREATHE.

Physically, she could. At least, if she placed her hand on her chest and willed the bowl-shaped muscle tucked underneath her ribcage to move, she could feel her lungs expand.

But she couldn't feel the air. She could move her chest all she wanted; it could ebb and flow, but it was if her body rejected the air of this place, this world.

She hadn't breathed since the day Father had found them, the day he'd banished her. Banished *her*, within the very world to which she'd led him in an attempt to save their son.

Their son who hadn't needed saving.

Mother trudged through the wooded area that traced the outskirts of Father's castle—stolen from the people of this world, the humans—dragging her feet through the mossy earth, kicking up pebbles and roots just to make an imprint, an impression on the ground proving she still existed. So much had happened in the past eight years. Well, so much had happened to Father, to the poor humans, the fae-like beings unfortunate enough to have lived during the age when the fae discovered Alondria.

Discover was probably a generous term for what they'd done.

Conquer.

Vanquish.

Those were more realistic.

Father had taken the Rip their son had discovered and had found a way to profit from it. First, he'd led his own tribe over. It hadn't taken them long to realize their strength outmatched the humans of this world, and though their numbers had been small, they'd overtaken the nearby villages without any fae casualties.

But shelter and abundant food and protection from this world's Others hadn't been enough for Father. He'd wanted to rule, lusted after the castle tucked within the nearby hills.

So he'd taken a risk.

Mother had watched as a few of his trusted hunters crossed the Rip once more. She'd staked out the hill for weeks, until the hunters returned.

They'd brought the others.

The tribes of fae Father had always said didn't exist. Their distant kinsmen who he'd claimed had been slaughtered by the Others long ago.

He'd lied.

He'd lied, then he'd hunted them down. Found them and offered them safety and food and wealth in exchange for their loyalty.

They'd come in droves, high fae and lesser fae alike.

And with the currency of land that wasn't his, Father had bought himself an army.

While Father had overtaken the new world, almost nothing had happened to Mother, nothing but the agony of days that repeated themselves. Kill, eat, gather, eat, sleep, repeat, repeat, repeat. It was a lonely life, being banished, lonelier than she would have thought possible, having lived with Father for over a decade.

She might have enjoyed her freedom, had it not been for Farin. Had her heart not ached for him, had she not rushed to his rescue every time she heard the cry of a human child, only to find it wasn't him.

Of course it wasn't him.

Her boy was a prince, not a human child dressed in soiled rags, scraping his knee across the pebbled earth.

She'd tried to befriend the humans on a few occasions, in the beginning, when she'd first been sent away to wander. Sent away from her son. She'd been intent to make the most of her aloneness, and though she would trade her freedom for her son without blinking, that decision had yet to be laid before her, and she figured she might as well enjoy the perks of freedom.

Perks, meaning friends.

But Father had taken that from her too.

He'd taken that hope just as he'd taken the humans' homes, their children, their plows, their barns, their palaces.

He'd taken everything.

Because that's what Father did.

He took.

She might have blended in with the humans, had it not been for her ears, the pointed tips that might as well have blasted a horn in front of her warning the humans to stay away. To honor her with a wide berth as she crossed through town. To whisper in their children's rounded ears until they scurried back into their huts, wide eyes peeking in horror through the windows at the monster who'd come to devour their town. The monster there was no use in attacking, as her skin and bones would heal within the hour.

As if she were the Other she'd so longed to escape.

In the end, she'd still spied on the humans anyway, crept behind their bushes and barrels just to sense the way their voices rang without abandon. She'd listened often enough, she thought she might be able to carry on a conversation in their language, if she ever got the chance.

She'd been waiting a long while for a chance.

But the land was plentiful, and it provided for her, supplying berries that were tart and sweet at the same time, the flavor of which left her heart sick and aching and somehow drunk for more. The rivers always rushed loud enough for her to hear, as if calling out to her like a grandmother to her offspring, after she'd prepared a hearty meal.

Yes, the land was her friend.

In fact, it was her only friend.

Sometimes Mother allowed herself to dream that she had possessed the forethought to grab the scrolls from Father's tent before leaving for this new world. Then, she would have had the ancient stories to keep her company. She sometimes wondered if Father had bothered to bring the scrolls over to this new world, or if they lay forgotten in the Nether, destined to rot and meld into the infertile soil.

At least she could tell herself the stories—the parts of them she remembered, at least. Perhaps she would do that tonight.

With that thought, Mother curled up in the makeshift pallet she'd made of straw and told herself a familiar story—one of the fae in their glory, before the Others had overtaken their world and eaten their crops and turned them into nomads. Before long, Mother fell asleep.

I hear you're in the market for a friend.

Mother jolted upright and swatted at the face that had surely leaned over to whisper in her ear, but her hand only slipped through the empty air, throwing her off balance as the object she expected to hit wasn't there.

She jumped to her feet, ready to swing. If it was a human, out for revenge against the fae for devouring their world, she had little to worry about.

If it was another fae...

There's no need for violence. Unless I misheard. Unless you're not in the market for a friend after all.

Mother hesitated and lowered her fists, though she slipped her hand down her waist to her hip, where she kept her...

That makeshift knife of yours won't be of much use, I'm afraid.

"Who are you?" Mother asked to the darkness.

I've already told you. I'm a friend. At least, I'd like to be.

Mother narrowed her eyes, her eyes that adjusted to the dark so much faster here in Alondria than they had in her world. But the voice in the darkness was right. There was nothing there but trees and bramble and the scuttering of leaves as the night-crawlers bustled through the forest.

And a blue light, one that hovered on the edges of her vision, no matter how far she craned her neck.

"And I'm supposed to believe you want nothing in return for your friendship?" Mother asked.

Why do you whisper, when it is only the two of us here?

Mother bristled, but she lifted her chin and raised her voice all the same. "Longstanding habit."

Ah, yes. In your world, you were hunted, were you not?

Mother nodded, though she wasn't sure how well the creature could see her in the dark, or, for that matter, if a bodiless creature could see at all.

As if in answer, the creature spoke again. *I sense that your head has shifted. Is that meant to be an answer?*

"Yes. My people were hunted," Mother said. Perhaps the creature could see, but it had said *sense*, hadn't it? Could it feel her movements and discern information about her based on them?

By your people, I assume you mean the fae. You claim them as yours, yet I sense no others in your presence.

"Is that meant to be a question?" Mother asked.

Only if it is one that would do you good to answer.

Mother sighed and felt her arms go slack at her side. If the creature meant to attack, surely it would have done so as she slept rather than waking her up. Unless it was the type of predator who preferred to play with its food, but if that was the case, she figured she was outmatched anyway.

You have so little fight left in you, mighty one.

Mother's heart sank, and she leaned against the tree to her back, lowering herself to the ground as the bark grated through her tattered clothes and scraped her spine. "What do you know of the fae?"

Only what I can learn from the whispers. I know that you traveled to Alondria through a Rip in the fabric that separates worlds. I know you are a swift people. A strong people. That your injuries heal before any true damage can be inflicted. I know there is one among you who rules the rest, who led his people through the Rip and slaughtered hosts until the original inhabitants of this land submitted to his will. Tell me, how many worlds have your people conquered?

Mother's mouth went dry, and her voice croaked as she said, "Just this one. We might be a mighty people in this world, but this was not always the case."

Ah. That explains it.

"Explains what?"

Why you're so unnatural.

"Thanks."

I only mean that you have no place in the order of nature, not in Alondria, at least. Here, there is no foe, no predator to balance you out, to keep you from devouring life itself.

"And what about you?" Mother asked. "Are you *natural?*" Something told her that, for a creature who spoke telepathically and didn't seem to have a body, the answer was a...

No.

"Then what are you?" she asked.

I am ancient.

Mother's blood chilled, bumps flushing her skin, though the night was warm. "Is this your original world? Or did you come from another also?"

I do not know.

"I thought you said you were ancient. Shouldn't you know a great deal more than everyone else?"

Do you remember your first cries as you escaped your mother's womb and gasped at the air of that cruel world from which you came? Do you remember your first steps? The first time a meaningful word sprang from your lips?

Mother had no choice but to admit that she did not.

Nor do I. And there is no one older who might inform me. Not that I've found in all my wanderings, that is.

Something about the creature's words gripped at Mother's heart.

I wish to make a bargain with you.

Mother tensed. "Is that what friends do? Make bargains?"

What is friendship but a bargain between two beings, that they will mutually provide for one another's needs?

Mother wasn't sure. Mother had never had a friend. "And what needs of mine can you provide for?" she asked, unable to stop herself as her mind whirled to her son, to how he had grown in the years since she'd been allowed anywhere near him.

She'd watched him grow, of course. She'd hidden herself in the crowds during the human holidays which Father had taken for the fae, during the celebrations he'd forced his subjects to attend where he paraded his heir, Prince Farin, in front of the humans.

Farin's jaw had hardened out, his shoulders had bulked, and stubble now peeked from his chin. He was no longer a boy, but a man.

But boy or man, it didn't make a difference. He was still her son, and she longed for his kinship, his wellbeing.

I can provide you with what the people here refer to as magic.

"Magic?" Mother had heard the word whispered among the humans, but it wasn't as if any of them ever let her get close enough to ask them what the word meant.

A force that operates beyond the natural limitations of a particular world.

"Like the way my skin heals quickly without salve?" Mother asked.

Exactly like that. But magic is not limited to healing. It manifests itself in many forms.

"What type of magic would you provide me?" Mother couldn't help her eager tone, try as she might to stifle it. Father was powerful, stronger and faster than she, and with an army at his disposal. But what if she possessed a power he lacked? Could she overpower the man who had cast her aside and stolen her son from her arms?

I cannot know.

Mother narrowed her eyes, sensing a trick. "How could you not know?"

When I bind myself with a living being, the magic manifests itself in different forms. We will not know what sort of power you might acquire until the binding is complete.

"The binding?" Mother didn't like the sound of that.

You lack power, kinship, meaning. I lack a body in which to move, eyes with which to see, skin to anchor me to this stunning world that surrounds us, a voice through which to speak.

"I can hear you just fine," Mother said.

It is not the same. I sense you know how it feels to be silenced. For your voice not to be heard, not truly.

Mother couldn't deny that, especially with the way the creature's voice pierced her weary heart.

"Will I still have control over my body if I allow you in? Or will you banish my consciousness and take my body as if it were your own?"

No, my friend. I only wish to be a passenger. Other than my voice in your mind and the power my dwelling grants you, you will be no different. Though I sense power might allow you the chance to be quite different indeed.

If what the creature said was true, that didn't seem too much to ask. Mother wouldn't mind having someone to talk to, pitiful as it was. "Why me? Why not a human? Or a more powerful fae than myself? There are plenty others of my tribe, the ones my husband led here through the Rip. Mighty warriors, that sort."

I have dwelled within many humans over my long lifespan. They are a delight, and amuse me with their various eccentricities. But they are weak.

Mother's hope cooled into a scowl. "And the weak are worthless to you."

Quite the opposite. Because they are weak, they inevitably die. As I've already told you, I am quite old, and I am tired of outliving those to whom I've grown attached.

Mother's chest hurt. "And when I die?"

That is the point entirely. I expect you won't.

The words sent a jolt of electricity, of pure fear through Mother's veins. What an odd thing, to be afraid of one's immortality, when she'd spent her entire life afraid of being mauled by an Other, having her life stripped from her.

Now, even the possibility seemed like a curse. She'd considered it, of course, when she happened upon a pool of still water, or when she found herself caught off guard by the mirrors in a traveling merchant's inventory. She hadn't aged a day since she had followed Farin into Alondria, into Mine, as he'd called it then.

She had wondered. But she had never allowed herself to believe.

Because belief would have condemned her, locked her into her dreary, lonely Fates.

"You haven't answered my other question. Why not choose another? I might be fae, but I am the least powerful of them all," Mother said.

Exactly.

Well, that wasn't exactly comforting, was it?

The others are cruel. You do not strike me as such.

"And you care about such things as kindness and cruelty?" she asked.

If you had existed as long as I have, you would not ask me such questions. I do not wish to join myself to a monster. That is no way to live. But if you require a more selfish motive in order to convince you, here it is: I fear that if I were to join myself to any of your kinsmen, they might overpower me and force my magic to do things that would be against my will.

"So I won't have full control over the magic?" Mother asked.

Just as I will not exert full control over you.

It must have been instinctual, the grasping on to such a hope, of a companion who would give without force, provide without control-ling. This was an offer no one had extended to Mother in her entire miserable existence.

She took it.

Excellent, the creature said. *Though I have one last requirement.*

Mother's stomach dropped as the blue light in the corners of her vision pulsed.

You must not reveal the source of your power to the fae. I will not be hunted by your kinsmen.

Who did this creature think Mother was going to tell? "You have a bargain."

CHAPTER 43

ASHA

*I*t took an entire week after the lychaen's attack for me to regain sufficient health to be moved back to my quarters. At least, that had been the healer's opinion. It didn't matter how many times I told her I was no longer having nightmares, that the aching in my limbs had been bearable since that first night I'd regained consciousness. She just couldn't believe that a human could recover so quickly from lychaen venom.

I supposed I could have told her that I'd suffered from worse magical maladies, if I'd thought it would have helped. We hadn't exactly gotten along during my recovery, as she insisted I needed rest more than visitors, and had limited the visits from Dinah and my father to once a day for half an hour.

Apparently, the same rules didn't apply to Kiran, who checked on me every evening, and though I pretended to sleep during his visits, he would often stay for over an hour, reading a scroll and peeking up at me every few minutes as I watched him from slitted eyes. I wondered sometimes if he knew I was faking. Surely he did, with his heightened fae senses and the lack of distractions in the quiet, white-washed infirmary. But if he guessed it, he didn't call me on it, for which I was grateful. There was something about overhearing a conversation that had not been intended for my ears that motivated me to avoid communication with the king as long as possible, lest the heat on my cheeks give me away.

Then there was the whole ordeal of him touching me.

The whole ordeal that shouldn't have been an ordeal at all, except my mind seemed bent on *making* it an ordeal.

Sometimes, during spikes of pain as my body washed the venom from its system, I would wince, and Kiran would place his hand on mine, sending a wave of warmth through my body that distracted me from the pain.

There might have been something comforting about it, if the idea of being comforted by the male who had decreed the slaughter of innocents hadn't been so unsettling. Had I not been pretty sure he'd threatened to extinguish the next person who laid a finger on me.

I wasn't sure what was more disturbing, the threat, or the tingly sensation that swarmed in my belly when his words replayed uninvited in my head.

Dinah was visiting when Fin strode in with the healer.

"You're free!" he said, shooting a toothy, boyish grin at me. "Well, that was poor word choice. You're free from the infirmary," he corrected himself with a sheepish, apologetic grin.

"Don't worry, Fin. I know better than to get my hopes up," I laughed. Dinah shuffled in her chair, and I noted the disappointment creasing her brow. My heart sank. Dinah had taken Fin's careless words literally, because Dinah *was* the type to get her hopes up.

Fin's gaze must have followed mine, because when I looked back at him, his neck had flushed with heat. "I apologize, my lady. I chose my words poorly."

Dinah put on a gracious smile. One I doubted Fin would notice was fake. Indeed, he looked relieved when she said, "Don't trouble yourself. I'm just grateful to you for being Asha's friend. But I'm just a girl, not a lady."

"Just a girl?" Fin asked. "Is that what I'm to call you then, *Just-A-Girl*?"

Cleary astounded Fin would wish to call her anything, Dinah blushed. "You can call me Dinah, Your Highness."

"Dinah," he said, his bright, molten irises lighting up at her name. "Call me Fin."

Dinah's eyes went wide, and she nodded. I suppressed a laugh, knowing good and well Dinah would never presume to address a prince by his name.

"Correct me if I am wrong, but did you or did you not agree to help move the Lady Queen?" the healer asked, her voice reverberating annoyance.

Fin shot me a look of mischief, and I wondered how often he had gotten under the healer's skin growing up in the palace.

"Very well," he said, crossing the room to me, though I noted the sidelong glances he sent toward my sister. "Would you prefer to be cradled or tossed over my shoulder?"

I grimaced.

"Yikes. Using me as a cane, it is."

Fin and Dinah supported me on either side as I hobbled up to my quarters. After two winding staircases and three hallways, I was cursing my pride, but at least Fin had the good sense not to tease me about it as my thighs wobbled.

When we reached my quarters, and Dinah bolted inside to arrange all the pillows on my bed for maximum comfort, I whispered to Fin, "Remind me how old you are."

"Only twenty-four, Lady Ash," he said.

Strange to think he and Kiran were the same age, when Kiran always seemed so worn. "In fae years or human years?" I teased. "And don't think coming up with a cute nickname for me is going to influence my reaction to your answer."

"The sun spins around all of us at the same speed."

"That's not exactly an answer," I said.

He grinned. "Why do you ask?"

"I'm in the market for a good reason to tell you to stay away from my sister."

"Don't fret. I'm sure you'll find plenty," he said. "Besides, don't you humans have a habit of giving your young women away in marriage to men twice their age?"

Before I could whirl on him, he gave me an extra firm nudge into my room. I collapsed on the bed and fell asleep shortly thereafter.

* * *

WHEN I AWOKE, it was not Dinah who breathed quietly beside me, but Lydia. Tired of being tired, I pushed myself to the edge of the bed and stood, determining that pacing about the room would somehow clear the fuzz in my brain.

"Kiran, Fin, and I are looking into who sent the lychaen after you," she said, as casually as one might discuss why a shipment of vegetables had rotted before arrival.

"Any leads?" I asked.

She gritted her teeth, an action that somehow only accentuated the severity of her beauty. "Not any that my brother thinks worthy of pursuit."

I found it did not matter that Lydia referred to both of her brothers by the same label; I could always tell which one she was talking about by the level of acid in her tone.

As she boiled, pondering the conversation between her and Kiran in which he must not have taken her suggestions seriously, her eyes went ashy, grey, cold.

I'd seen that look before. In fact, I'd been waiting for it to reemerge, to confirm what I'd suspected since her dagger emerged from the shadows, since she'd slaughtered the lychaen, since she'd gone back to collect its fangs, since her violet eyes had turned to ash.

Because I'd seen those caverns for eyes before.

"It was you in the dungeons that day, wasn't it?" I asked, apparently unequipped with any general social formalities, such as easing into the topic like a normal person. Come to think of it, I probably shouldn't have asked at all. If Lydia possessed this sort of occupation, it could only serve to her disadvantage the more people who knew about it. Now that she knew I suspected her, it might not be the king I had to fear. "You came to break me out. And you killed that guard who was…" I couldn't even bring myself to say it.

Lydia surveyed me, the tips of my pale yellow slippers to the crown of my head. I shifted uncomfortably at her stare. It was unlike Kiran's gaze, which always seemed to examine me with an intense curiosity. No, Lydia's gaze possessed an assessing quality. And there would be a judgment at the end of the assessment.

"How did you know?" she asked.

"Your eyes. They're usually violet, but the night you saved me from the lychaen, they turned black. I couldn't figure out why they looked so familiar, but then I remembered the stranger in the dungeons, and how you showed up the same day."

She cocked her head to the side. "It could have been any fae. Did they even have my build?"

I frowned. "No. They were burly. I thought it was a male, but I…" I stared at my sister-in-law for a moment, trying to get a read on her, attempting to catch her tells.

Lydia's violet eyes shuttered, blackness sweeping over them like blinds to force out the sun. "Have you heard of the Umbra?"

My mouth went dry. "I thought the Umbra was a myth."

She craned her neck. "And what else have you heard?"

"I don't know. That he's a serial killer who dresses in black and goes around Alondria murdering people. You know, pretty violently."

"Serial killer, huh?" she asked, examining her razor sharp nails.

"That's what they say."

"What if it was the Umbra who rescued you that day? Would you still call him a serial killer?"

"Well, no…I wouldn't. I'd call him a vigilante."

"Hm," she said.

Then I remembered that Lydia was fae, meaning she couldn't lie to me.

I probably shouldn't have let them, not alone in the room with a killing machine, but my lips curved into a self-assured smile anyway. "You're not outright denying that it was you."

She stalked toward me, her purple painted nails flashing in the lamp light. "Perhaps that's for your own good."

I stepped back, but she only flitted her hand and laughed. "Yes, it was me. I intended to smuggle you out, then slaughter Kiran before he could try to harm anyone else," she said.

My heart pounded, and the casualty of her tone chilled my veins. I was pretty sure that, if Dinah went mad and slaughtered an entire village, I'd break her out of prison before they sent her to the gallows. Sure, I'd probably keep her locked up myself, but to kill one's own flesh and blood... What had their childhood been like for Lydia to retain such little affection for her sibling? "You would have killed your own brother?"

Lydia's violet eyes went cold, the same onyx they'd been in the dungeons that day when the guard had threatened to abuse me. "I don't take kindly to those in power oppressing the innocent."

"But you didn't kill him."

"He didn't kill you."

I let out a long exhale. "That's what you're doing when everyone thinks you're off..." Another phrase I couldn't quite bring myself to say, this time from embarrassment. I figured it was best for my well-being to pivot. "So you're the Umbra? Or you aren't?"

Lydia laughed. "I am."

"And you're an assassin?"

"Of sorts," Lydia said, once her fiery eyes had finally returned to meet my gaze.

"How can one be sort of an assassin?" I asked.

Lydia snorted, and a mischievous smile overtook her painted lips. "I'm not for hire. I like to think of myself as a volunteer."

It was my turn to size her up. Did I stand before a serial killer who murdered for the thrill of it? That didn't quite fit, not with the female who had felt enough pity for me to invite me to the gardens for a stroll. The woman who had openly chastised the king for his treatment of me. The woman who'd saved me from a power-hungry guard's wandering hands.

"What sort of beings do you kill?" I asked.

"Only the ones who deserve it," she said, as if she were simply relaying her favorite pudding.

"What sort of deed could one commit to warrant a death at your hands?" I asked, though I thought I had a pretty good idea already.

"Abuse of the innocent. Those who cannot defend themselves," she said.

My mind flashed to that morning in the breakfast room. How Lydia had burst through the windows, dress and eyes ablaze. My stomach did a somersault.

As if reading my mind, Lydia chuckled. "I won't murder Kiran. Though I might change my mind if he ever follows through with taking your life."

My mouth hung ajar. It made it difficult to formulate conversation when the other person spoke of my impending death so casually. Another mildly unpleasant thought trickled through my mind, leaving a bitter taste on my tongue. Perhaps this was why Kiran had spared my life all this time. Perhaps it had nothing at all to do with my magic's story, or the fact my magic possessed me, a human, and everything to do with his fear of Lydia.

"Kiran is unaware of this particular hobby of mine," Lydia smiled. "And I would prefer to keep it that way."

I shuffled, stroking the hem of my robes between my forefinger and thumb. "You don't have to threaten me. I have no reason to speak to him." Even as I said it, I wondered if that was entirely true. We had spoken, the king and I, in the garden. And he'd stayed with me when I was recovering, though I hadn't asked him to. Hadn't wanted him to.

Lydia's eyes flickered with warmth. "It's not a threat. Just a request among friends."

She made room for me on the bed and patted the sheets, beckoning me to join her. I did, and when I sat, I figured now was as good a time as any to assuage my curiosity. "Why do you do it? Go about avenging the helpless?"

"It's only natural when one is unfortunate enough to be born to a father as cruel as mine."

"Did he..." My throat constricted at the unfinished question. I had seen the women, the girls who hid not only their bodies but their wrists from the view of the common marketplace shopper, only to reveal a bruise as their sleeves slipped during an exchange.

"Hm." Lydia's eyes wandered, as if her mind was rearranging the furniture in this room, reconstructing a scene I could not see.

I dared another invasive question. "How did you learn to be an assassin? Did you seek training so you could defend yourself from him?"

Lydia's eyes darted back into focus. "Are you always constructing your own narrative of the lives of others?"

I hung my head, abashed. I had taken her story, whatever horrors clung to the shadows of her memories, and I had already made it my own. To feed it to my ravenous magic within me, whose nonexistent ears were already perking at Lydia's trauma.

"He's the one who trained me." And there it was, that bit of information that made my heart both ache for her, and long for the rest of the story.

Because a story was already unfolding in my head, and it would be best to displace it with the truth before it got out of hand.

"Why would he do that?" My only impression of the late king was that he despised fae women almost as much as he despised human women. Why he would equip a daughter he hated with the power and skills to defend herself, to fight back against his abuse, I couldn't comprehend.

"In case he ever developed a grudge. And he was always holding a grudge. A poor merchant who couldn't quite meet the tax that quarter. A foreign ambassador who implied that my father might have been wasteful with his people and resources. My..." Lydia bit her lip, a gesture that seemed too vulnerable to match her every other feature.

In some strange act of having no idea in Alondria what to do when someone was upset, I took Lydia's hand in mine. "Who did he have you kill?"

Lydia turned her sharp eyes on me, and I had half a mind to drop her hand back on the bed. But then she frowned weakly and blinked away the tears that had been trying to escape her eyelids.

Who had the late king forced Lydia to kill? *My.* She had said *my.* And how many *my*'s could a child really have? Even a princess could only have so many living possessions. A favorite animal, maybe? Or...

My heart froze in my chest. The late queen, Lydia's mother, had died suddenly... When had that happened? It was back when I had two eyes; I was fairly sure, or maybe even before I was born.

The sorrow on Lydia's face was enough to answer my question. And to keep me from asking any more, at least ones that related to her past.

"You have power over fire. Are there any others? I really thought you were a male that day in the dungeons. Can you shape-shift or something?" I asked, eager to change the subject.

"The ability to appear as a male comes from a ring glamoured by an associate of mine. When I wear it on my finger, you'd never know it was me. The power over fire I inherited, just like Kiran."

Her words plucked at a memory, one of my father telling me as a child that the young Prince Phinehas had inherited no royal magic of his own. I opened my mouth to ask Lydia about it, but stopped because she was no longer looking at me. Instead, she rose from the bed and strode to the balcony, where she turned her gaze to the moonlit city below.

"Did you have to overpower the Old Magic to be able to wield fire?" I asked, thinking of mine and Kiran's conversation in the garden. He had said that fae suppressed their magic, forced it into submission.

My hands trembled as I followed Lydia to the balcony, though I wrapped the cloth from my skirt around them, gripping at it so hard, I hoped it wouldn't rip.

Lyda pursed her lips. "Do you always ask so many questions?"

I pondered for a moment before responding. "Only if I don't know the answer."

"Well, that would make for a great many questions, I presume," she said, but then she turned and faced me, concern lining her brow. "I don't mean to imply that you're uneducated."

I shrugged. "I am uneducated."

285

"Yes, but even if you had been brought up under the finest tutors of our world, you would still have many questions. Perhaps even more than you have now. Knowledge has a cruel effect like that. I promise I meant no offense," she said, before turning her back to me to examine the city.

I watched her, the high fae adorned in a violet gown that should have accentuated the hue of her eyes, had they not turned to coal. Her delicate-looking skin that matched the texture of her dress. A killer possessed those small hands, those gowns that disguised her as nothing more than a rich, bored female who had missed out on the throne purely by the inconvenience of her sex. How many beings had she slaughtered? Yet, for some reason I could not fathom, it mattered to her whether she had offended me. Me. A mortal girl, barely past childhood. An invalid girl, at that.

"I took no offense, Your Highness," I said. "But if I need to fake it to receive an answer to my question, I would gladly."

Lydia whipped around with such haste I found myself glad to be out of range of her braid, which slung like a whip around her perimeter. Her eyes widened, aghast at my lack of propriety, I supposed. But then she leaned back her head and laughed into the rafters until her cackles filled the room and floated over the city on the breeze.

"I'll tell you one day. It'll be more rewarding if you have to ponder it for a while. Besides, you're an observant human. I would enjoy hearing your theories."

"I can agree to that, I suppose," I said, laughing. But then something cracked outside the window, and I jolted, my limbs freezing into place, the memory of pain stinging my flesh as fresh as if my scabs were open and flowing.

"It's only the wind," Lydia said, placing a soft hand on my shoulder.

"You think you know who tried to kidnap me, don't you?" I asked. *And, perhaps more importantly, why*, my magic added.

I think we both know the reason has more to do with you than me, I argued.

"I have my theories. But none of them are worth frightening you until I have more evidence. I'm leaving in the morning for Avelea. I have connections there, people who make it their purpose to know more than they should."

I nodded, the news that my sister-in-law was leaving dampening my spirits a bit.

"I'll return soon," she said, turning to stride from the room. "Until then, try to stay out of my brother's way. I know you're obligated to join him overnight to string out that story of yours. But I would avoid his company if I were you."

"Why?" I asked. It was a stupid question. I knew as much as soon as it came out of my mouth. Of course, it was best to stay out of his way. Kiran had most likely soured his reputation with the other kingdoms by keeping me alive. Sure, I might be in his good graces at the moment, but he wasn't exactly known for his deep contemplation before making decisions. If I displeased him, he could easily change his mind and have me beheaded. But, as stupid as my question was, her answer surprised me all the more.

She stopped outside of my door, and without turning said, "Because it is a dangerous thing for the prey to captivate its predator."

CHAPTER 44

ASHA

*A*s much as I valued Lydia's advice, staying away from Kiran turned out to be more difficult than I had thought.

That night, Dinah attended our ritual, but only in the basest sense. Her usual glowing skin had sunk into a yellowy tone, reminiscent of a week-old bruise. Her bronze eyes had lost their usual zeal, and though she attempted to hide it underneath a smile, the corners of her eyes refused to take part.

Kiran strode in, took one look at my sister curled up in my lap clenching her belly, and scooped her into his muscular arms.

"No, I'm fine…" she protested, to her credit, for she gagged even as the words spilled from her dry lips.

"You're ill," he said, his lips pursing in disapproval under his well-trimmed beard. He turned those flickering eyes on me. "I'll take her to the healer. She can spend the evening in the infirmary. If she's not better by the morning, I'll send word to your father that she is within the palace's care and will be escorted home upon her recovery."

I nodded. My belly had ached just watching her writhe on the bed. She had walked from the village like this, cold sweat beading on her forehead and soaking her scarf. I wondered how many alleyways she had painted with her vomit on the way.

"But...but Asha's story," Dinah moaned. Tears soaked her pale cheeks.

"Will still be waiting for you when you recover. We vow not to venture another word into Farin's world until you are well enough to listen. Don't we, Asha?"

I lifted myself from the bed and stroked the back of my palm across her wet forehead, shifting a few matted strands of hair out of her face and behind her ear. A memory, one of a warm hand brushing my forehead, swept through my consciousness, sending a surge of all sorts of unwelcome feelings churning in my gut.

I cleared my throat, as one does in these types of situations. "We'll wait, Dinah. Don't worry, I'll come with you. Maybe I can tell you one of our old stories."

The king shifted at my comment, and I peered at him, lifting a questioning brow.

"You should stay here. You've barely recovered from your own injuries," he said.

"I'm fine." I brushed my hand to the side, as if to signal all my pain had been swept away. But my sleeve slipped down my arm, revealing an atrocious purple gash where the lychaen had so kindly used my flesh as an engraving station.

Before I could cover my wound, which still oozed despite the healer's insistence that a human's skin shouldn't be mending so quickly, the king had already traced the gash with his eyes.

The look on Kiran's face was not one of a male easily persuaded.

I swallowed my protest. Kiran seemed to be in a generous mood. There was no need to spoil it. Not when I had the utmost confidence that the healers would take care of my sister.

It took all the effort in the world not to sigh in irritation. "Dinah, I'll come see you in the morning, I promise."

Dinah answered by closing her eyes and allowing herself to drift into what I imagined was that awful place between sleep and wakefulness. That wretched purgatory that numbed the nausea in her belly and chest, but forbade her the peaceful oblivion of rest.

Once Kiran had whisked my sister out of the room, his red robes billowing behind him, I sank into the bed. Guilt knocked on my chest. I was thankful for another night without my magic's story. Thankful for an evening that wouldn't remind me that my life depended on my words. I hated the relief that flooded my chest at Dinah's expense.

But I sank into the soft blankets all the same, relishing the way the mattress fit itself to me, to my every curve.

"Asha."

My body went rigid, and I shot straight up. Dread gripped me at the sound of his voice.

I had *not* just fallen asleep in his bed.

Oh, but you did.

Agh. Why had I not crawled onto the mat on the floor like all the nights before?

"My apologies. I didn't mean to wake you."

Even the sharp edges of Kiran's bearded jaw blurred in my vision, and I blinked again, bringing his face into view. His harsh features had rounded out into an almost bashful expression, the slightest bit of color tinging his cheekbones.

I mumbled something neither of us could interpret. He opened his mouth as if to ask me to repeat myself, but he must have thought better of it, because instead he said, "I thought you might want an update on Dinah."

Dinah. Her name. Not *your sister.*

"Yes, of course." I wiggled myself out from under the covers, trying my utmost to get away from his bed and onto the floor as quickly as possible. It turned out to be quite the ordeal. The several layers of blankets had become twisted around themselves, around my limbs. I must have looked like a beached whale trying to free myself.

He traced his fingers over the edges of the blankets, carefully pulling each woven piece of fabric away until I was free. "Are you a fitful sleeper?"

"Not usually," I said. A coal flickered in his eyes as he met my gaze. I swallowed. Before he could see my face flush hot, I pushed myself out of the bed and onto the floor.

"You don't have to sleep down there, you know."

"No, thank you," I said. The words scraped their way up my throat.

He cocked his head to the side, examining me. I fought the urge to rip my neck to the left, to hide that gaping hole in my face. But he didn't stare at my blemishes. Not in the way most did, at least. Most who were unfortunate enough to catch my eye on the street either gaped at that pink bit of skin on my face where something should have been, or they bolted their gaze away in embarrassment.

Not Kiran. He held my stare as he might any other, taking in my face as a whole, the blemished with the untouched, as if they were equal.

"Would you sleep up here if I promised to take the mat on the floor?" he asked.

I hesitated. As much as my spirit wanted nothing more than to refuse any comfort offered by this dangerous and confusing male, my aching hips and shoulders complained louder than my spirit. And I really didn't feel like traversing the entire palace to get back to my quarters. Not when, according to the healer, my blood had not completely flushed out the Lychaen venom.

Plus, I had the uneasy notion that the king might attempt to carry me back to my quarters.

That wasn't happening.

"Yes."

He stood from his perched position on the edge of the bed and offered an open hand toward me. I took it for about half a second as I stood and scurried into the warm bed. My fingers barely even scraped his palm, the motion was so quick. So avoidant.

My efforts didn't do much to shoo the ghost of his touch, the lingering static that marked where our skin had brushed.

"Your sister is sleeping well. The healer gave her a sedative." His hand lingered in the cold, empty breeze for a moment before he withdrew it to his side.

"Good," I said, settling my legs under the warm blankets. Sheer will resisted the slight upturn of my lips at the relief of sinking into the bed. "Thank you for taking her," I added. It was a delicate balance, never letting him forget how much I despised him, yet also keeping him appeased enough to continue to watch out for my family.

"The way the two of you care for each other reminds me of Lydia and Fin."

I didn't answer, unsure how to address the implications behind his words. The king went silent for a long while, and I closed my eye, hoping both to welcome sleep and encourage Kiran to leave. But, after a few minutes, he spoke up again.

"Blood has always run thick between those two. I found myself jealous of the camaraderie they shared growing up," he said. "I always wondered why they never let me into that secret little world of theirs. It was strange. Other dignitaries always assumed that Fin and I would be thick as thieves, but it didn't seem to matter that we were twins. Those few seconds between our births might as well have been centuries. My father made sure of that. So while our father trained me for the leadership role, Lydia took Fin under her wing. I'd like to think it was the strenuous nature of the training that kept me from bonding with my siblings, and I'm sure that was part of it. But I'd be deceiving myself if I pretended I didn't revel in that special attention. Use it to exalt myself over the other two. Our father was a cruel man and not keen on affection, even with his young children. When I became part of his training process... Well, I suppose even a king can admit that he craved the attention of his father."

I had to dig my teeth into my lip to bite back a frown. Kiran might have admitted that his father was cruel, but did that mean he knew what the late king had done to his sister?

I couldn't decide if I wanted to know the answer to that, if I wanted my perception of him to be swayed by that kind of knowledge.

So I let it go. For now, at least.

The more he spoke, the farther I felt sleep slip away from my eyelids. The word *training* had been the one to do me in. How many daydreams had I entertained as a child of such a thing? A memory flashed before my mind. Az and I executing our best attempts at a parry in the alleyway between our hovels, using canes abandoned by traveling merchants after their treks across the scorching desert.

Az.

Something sour burst in my belly.

"What was your training like?" I asked, eager to distract myself from the bitter taste in my mouth. I opened my eye and rolled over just in time to see him cock his head in surprise as he turned toward my voice. Apparently, he had still been sitting on the edge of the bed, talking to the ornate wallpaper rather than to me.

"I thought for sure you had fallen asleep," he said.

Unable to help myself, I asked, "Isn't falling asleep during a king's monologue punishable by death or something?"

He let out a gust of air, the escapee of a laugh he was doing his best not to free.

A smile burst from the restraints I'd placed on the edges of my lips. Pleased with myself for the startled and amused expression on his face, I sat up in the bed and propped my back on the velvety headboard.

"Training," he said, as if I had not just committed a felony by using snark with the king, "to be honest, it's a whole lot more fun than what it prepares you for. Father brought in as many experts as he could find, gave them and their families lodging and a fine sum too, to teach me all they knew. He actually hired a fighter from each of the Alondrian kingdoms to train me in combat. I suppose he wanted me to be well-versed in all our neighbors' fighting styles if the time ever came for war. That is a well-kept secret, of course," he said, a serious look overcoming his otherwise nostalgic expression.

"That's too bad. I was planning on relaying that information to all my foreign friends," I said. That same baffled expression assaulted his eyes, and they widened as he remembered where I came from. A hovel. In the poorest sector of the city. Again, his lips pressed together as if his training had beaten out the urge to laugh at a sarcastic comment from a human.

He continued on, apparently unable to acknowledge my joke about growing up in poverty. "Then there was the magic. The senior fire mage, a distant cousin of mine, trained me in the Flame. That was quite a bit of fun, pretending I didn't know what I was doing and setting fire to more objects than I should have."

"Was that the best part?" My pitch heightened, betraying my interest. He settled his eyes on me, examining my face in that same way he had before. As a whole, rather than staring at the blank space where there should have been an eye, or avoiding looking at that part of my face altogether.

His voice sank into that low, pulsating growl. "Are you up for another secret that would be detrimental if shared with my enemies?"

The hairs on my arms prickled, and I found myself thankful for the blanket that covered them. Though I flushed when I remembered his fae senses could probably detect such a thing.

At a loss for words, I simply nodded my head, a tad embarrassed I couldn't seem to keep up my snarky streak.

"I actually enjoyed my studies of literature more than anything else." Apparently he caught my eye widen before I had the chance to cast a look of stone over my face, for he continued, "My father only agreed to it because it is the proper thing to do, for a king to be well-versed in literature. But he despised it. Actually, he made it a point to bond with me over our joint hatred for it. My poor literature tutor received the brunt of it, disparaging comments of how he was fortunate to still have a job after the bore he had put my father through. But he took it all in good nature, probably because he could see right through my act, even as I teased him. I believe he knew me better than anyone, could see how I would pore over the books he wrangled for me from all over the kingdoms, throughout the ages..."

I wondered if Kiran was trying to soothe himself for the cruel comments he had engaged in towards the tutor he seemed to care for so dearly.

"...Yes, I believe he understood..."

"I'm sorry," I interrupted, his melodrama grating on my nerves a bit, "but you were trained in foreign combat and how to control fire with your mind, and I'm supposed to believe you found *books* to be the most interesting part of your day?"

Again, that flicker of surprise overtook his face, but maybe he was getting used to me, because he actually allowed himself to laugh. The bellow rattled the breeze, knocking my ribcage off its hinges. His laugh sent my heart through the ceiling of this lavish bed and had me grasping to its edges as its echoes faded.

Not good.

Not good at all.

"I can see you're not impressed," he said, "but if you only knew the joys of being immersed in another world, the way the written word can transport you—"

"I know how to read," I snapped. It took every fiber of my dwindling self-control not to roll my eye at this pompous male, even if his laugh did make my perfectly normal, rounded ears want to sing.

"Oh," he said.

"Oh," I said.

"I apologize for assuming otherwise."

"What did you think I was doing that day in the library when you accused me of committing treason?"

"Trying to look innocent as you committed treason, obviously."

I couldn't help but crack a smile. "Apology accepted," I said. "That being said, I don't understand why reading would be the best part of your day. I always thought of books, the ones we could get our hands on—they were a way for the poor and inexperienced to live a life so much bigger, more substantial than our own. To eat until our bellies were full of all the colors on the spectrum, not just bread. Or to fight in the battles of old. Or to wield fire." I tried unsuccessfully not to let my voice catch on the thought of such a marvelous thing. A gift of Kiran's I craved and admired despite myself. "Why in Alondria would you take a book over the real thing?"

He cocked his head at me again, his eyes scanning every feature of my face. Every crease where my magic had marked me as its own. Every divot of skin it had taken. Every smooth patch left untouched.

When he finally spoke, his voice was raw and gritty. "Perhaps the anticipation of a thing is more fulfilling than its reality."

CHAPTER 45

ASHA

I swallowed, my mouth apparently deciding it wanted to imitate the climate of the Sahli all of the sudden.

The anticipation of a thing is more fulfilling than its reality. What did that even *mean?* And why did it have me noticing the way he propped himself on his hand as he leaned over me from where he perched on the side of the bed, how that very hand seemed to have snuck its way close to the lump in the sheets that marked where my thigh rested.

Not good, not good, very, very not good.

"I'm sorry, but I cannot accept that," I said, my voice coming out hoarser than I meant for it to. Something boiled deep within my stomach.

The way he looked at me, the sorrow that hid behind those molten eyes, was it for himself? His inability to enjoy the riches that his cruel father had left him? Or did he actually pity me? As if he thought, one day I would experience the same things and come to the same conclusion. That life did not live up to its reputation.

"Ah, because if you, Asha, Queen of Naenden, don't accept something, that makes it less true. Less *real,*" Kiran said, his fingertip tracing the pattern woven into the bedsheet, dangerously close to my now trembling thigh.

Okay, I definitely wasn't imagining things. Kiran had most certainly scooted closer to me at some point in this conversation.

How I hadn't noticed earlier, I had no idea.

Perhaps because you were the one who slithered your way up to him.

I changed the subject.

"You say you and Fin aren't close, but why did you react so strongly to his princess's advancements?" I asked, hoping to throw him off with what I imagined was a sensitive topic. Still, it was a subject that piqued my curiosity. My magic had presented the king's story as if the murder of the princess had been an act of an inseparable bond between brothers. But why such rage if he and his brother had never been close? Had my magic been mistaken, or had it doctored the story for entertainment value? I had always thought my magic had possessed some otherworldly knowledge, but I wasn't sure I was comfortable with the idea that it might feed me falsehoods from time to time.

Kiran's eyes narrowed at my question, but he didn't back away as I had hoped. Perhaps he could sense what I was trying to do. Trying to avoid. But he answered me anyway. "Just because the close-knit relationship between my brother and myself has been fabricated by the palace's diplomats, does not mean I do not wish it to be true."

Even my rounded human ears perked at that comment.

"You went to visit Fin to make amends? To bond with him?" I asked.

He nodded, and I expected his eyes to falter in shame, but he kept my gaze. "After all those years of enmity, I decided to act upon that longing to be close to my siblings. It seemed that Fin's heart was more likely to soften towards me than Lydia's. And I must have even hoped that, if I could win him over, he would talk Lydia into tolerating me one of these decades. It was actually Gwenyth who suggested I make the visit." I flinched at the name. At the way his voice grated when he spoke it.

"But then Fin's wife ruined it," I said.

He nodded, pressing his eyelids shut as if to expel the memory.

"I'm a royal. I've been propositioned my entire life, since before I was old enough to even understand what was happening."

My gut twisted at the vile thought of greedy nobles trying to slink their way into an inheritance by seducing a child.

"I should have had my guard up, but I never expected Ophelia of all people. She always appeared so devoted to Fin. I convinced him to marry her, you know. He was smitten, but too nervous about what our father might do to her if he ever went public with their relationship. So when I decided to rebel against our father and marry Gwenyth, and our father was killed shortly after, I thought I could amend our relationship by giving them my blessing. You can imagine my panic when Ophelia approached me. How was I ever to mend that blood-bond when my brother's wife had attempted to seduce me? When she'd asked me to help her plot against my brother, to murder him and take Talens for myself? It only took a moment for all hopes of gaining a friend in my brother to shatter. Just one look at her, and I knew that had been enough. It wouldn't matter that I had refused her. With just a knock on the door, she had ruined something I had been longing for since childhood. Something that would never mend. And so I killed her for taking that away from me, I'm ashamed to admit." Those ember eyes flickered with rage, even now, but something else hovered beneath he surface—the incessant pulse of regret.

"Have you spoken to Fin?" I asked. Those flames swirling in his eyes went dark.

"No," he said. "I'm not sure he wants much to do with me anymore, though we'll have to maintain a professional relationship, at least."

"Then why do you think he's been staying at the palace?" During my conversation with Fin in the library upon our first meeting, he had confessed that he wished to assuage, if not heal, the hate he felt for his brother. Had they not made any strides toward those ends in these past weeks?

"He needs Lydia to comfort him," Kiran said, confirming my suspicion.

"That's not what he told me. He said…" I grasped for the right words, but I couldn't quite figure out how to turn Fin's statement—that he needed to numb himself of Kiran's presence—into the meaning I hoped lay buried somewhere underneath the pain. "I don't think he wants to hate you forever."

"Comforting indeed." Kiran's flickering eyes drooped and went still, empty. My sympathy stirred, if not for Kiran, then for that lonely book-reading fae boy that still lurked underneath the shadows. The one who so desperately craved the affection of his father that he severed ties with his vibrant siblings before he was even old enough to recognize the weight of his mistake.

"How did you get your scar?" His question ripped me from my thoughts. My spine went rigid as his eyes traced the hole where my left eye should have been. Once was.

But there was no unkindness in his question. No judgment or disgust, either. Not at all like I was used to hearing it asked. Only curiosity. And that, as much as I hated to admit it, I could relate to.

And so I told him my story. My story. Not the story my magic would have preferred to tell. My version, not its. Though I was sure it had its own spin on how that wretched day had gone down.

"I was six when it happened. My friend Az and I had a habit of wandering the allies after we'd hurried up and finished our chores. We were always in trouble for it, because it made us miserable at cleaning and laundering. And we barely spent any time at the market picking out our bread or produce, so the food would always spoil. We must have caused a headache for our parents." I smirked, thinking of how my father would scold me, but then how later, when he thought I wasn't looking, he had chuckled to himself.

Kiran leaned in closer, and I realized he had shifted completely on the edge of the bed, turning his entire body toward me. The picture of it was absurd, the King of Naenden's legs crossed on the bed in front of him, like how a child might sit.

"Anyway. We had been on a mission for a while to map out every alley in Meranthi—"

"Are maps that overpriced? Need I subsidize them?" Kiran asked.

"Okay, Mister *I'd-rather-read-a-book-than-summon-fire-from-my-soul*," I said. He smirked, and I shot a look at him that told him not to interrupt me again. One I had inherited from my father. "So we had almost completed it. But there was one section of town that was still blank on our map. No matter how hard we tried, we could never seem to find an entrance to it. As if the actual space of the town wasn't feasibly possible—"

"Could it be your six-year-old measurements were a tad off?"

I glared, which I knew for a fact was particularly intimidating, thanks to the fact it only came from one eye.

He only chortled.

"Anyway. It made little sense at all. There was this space on our map we hadn't discovered yet. Any time we attempted to broach it, we were stopped by a clay brick wall. Just a wall, mind you, not the walls of an apartment building or a marketplace or anything. We even tried to scale the wall once—"

"I imagined that was difficult in a veil and dress..." Kiran mused, resting his cheek against his fist, his elbow on his knee, his knee hovering dangerously close to my waist.

Even I could feel the twinkle in my eye. "You'd be surprised. The ridiculous amount of extra fabric is actually pretty useful for braiding a rope," I said. He chuckled again.

I continued. "Once we made our rope, we tossed it over a bar jutting out from the top of the wall and used it for a pulley. I tied the ends around mine and Az's waists, and he used his side of the robe to pull me up while I used the juts in the brick as foot holes. But when I finally reached the top..." I shuddered. Until the lychaen venom had forced me back to this place, it had been a while since I'd relived the memory. My magic and I—we had learned to tolerate one another. That symbiotic relationship had become easier once I had pushed this particular memory from my mind. But here it was in the timbre of my voice, as real as the day it occurred.

Kiran waited, his eyebrows raised, yet he did not press me for more information.

"When I reached the top, I went to peek over the wall. Our

makeshift rope had spun in the air, so I had to twist myself back to the left and pull myself up with my left hand to catch a glimpse of it. The rope kept pulling back at me. I remember my torso feeling like it was on fire as I tried to twist around to get a good view. I thought it was just because Azrael and I had done a shabby job, but looking back, I wonder if the rope knew. Or if my magic was trying to keep me from discovering it. But I was going to see whatever was behind that wall.

"So when I finally mustered up the strength to twist myself around, I pulled myself to the edge of the wall. I looked over the rim, and it was just sitting there, on the roof of some apartments I had never noticed, because I had never gotten my head to turn in that direction—"

"What was sitting there?"

"A lamp."

"A lamp?"

"Yes, you put oil in them and they burn so you can light your house. I know you don't have much use for them around here, but they're pretty practical."

"I know what a lamp is."

"Anyway, I reached out to touch it. And it…it, well, it lashed out. There was this flash of blue light. It scared Az so badly, he dropped me. Because then I remember plummeting. Except I couldn't even bring myself to fear it, falling to my death. Because that blue light hadn't disappeared, and it was burning. Burning so, so horribly. It was as if I was one of those men who walk over hot coals, except I was using my eye socket instead of my calloused feet.

"I heard someone screaming the entire time I fell. I thought it must have been Az, but later he told me he had been frozen still. Too scared to breathe. And then he told me I had been the one screaming. That I had hit the ground. And I couldn't see the light anymore. Actually, I couldn't see anything. A sharp pang cracked through my spine, but then there was nothing. No pain. No anything."

I stopped, waiting for Kiran's interjection. It didn't come. Instead, he set those ember eyes, flickering furiously, upon mine. I swallowed.

"When I woke, my father and Az and his family were all there standing over me. I started panicking and asking for Dinah, but then I heard her voice telling me she was there. That she had been there the entire time. That's when I realized I wasn't going to see out of this eye again. I had to turn my head to see her, even though it hurt awfully. I hadn't even realized how close she was."

"I'm so sorry," Kiran said as I paused. "I can't imagine losing something so precious as an eye."

I fought back the urge to click my tongue at that statement. He had lost a wife, had he not? A wife whom he, at some point, had loved dearly. My father would have given both his eyes if it had meant we wouldn't have lost my mother. Maybe that's why I said, "It's alright. We had already lost my mother. Other than Dinah and my father, that was the worst possible thing to lose. An eye didn't seem like much in comparison." I shrugged. "Especially when the other one still works just fine."

"Still," Kiran said, shifting uncomfortably on top of the mattress, shaking my legs as his weight adjusted the sheets. "What of your back? You said you broke it on the way down."

"Oh, yeah," I said, having forgotten that part. "My father and Az's mother didn't believe our story at first. Az had been screaming that I had fallen and my back was broken, but Az's mother felt around on my spine and couldn't feel anything wrong with me. Other than my face, of course. They thought we had been playing with flint, that I had gotten burned by accident. When I woke up, I thought for sure I wouldn't be able to walk. The sound of my back cracking was still making my ears ring. But it didn't even hurt. They sat me up on the side of the bed and Az and I just looked at each other, too scared to mention it again. It's a strange thing, being horrified because you've been healed. But later Az told me that the blue fire he had seen strike my face had followed me down the fabric of my dress when I fell. That my back had broken, but that the flames had run across my robes and into my chest, without catching my clothes on fire or even leaving a stench.

"He hadn't told my father or his mother of it. Apparently, he was too terrified whatever had possessed me would be angry if he told an adult. But he told me all the same. We both figured the blue fire must have been a genie trapped in an elemental form, and that it healed me when I fell. It wasn't until that evening that I realized it had never left. That it had made its home with me," I said.

"When you told Dinah a story?"

"She wouldn't leave my side after the accident. They ended up wrapping half my face in gauze and salve to help heal the burns, and it was all so uncomfortable, I couldn't sleep. That night, Dinah curled up with me on that tiny cot. I felt so guilty she wasn't getting any sleep, either. I decided I'd entertain us both with a story. That was the first time my magic caught my voice. I might have screamed in fright had I been able to, with it controlling me like that. But Dinah didn't as much as flinch. She was calm, even as a child. She just brushed her hand against my arm and asked me to continue. And so I did. So we did. And my magic and I have been sharing this body ever since." I regretted those last words as soon as they came out of my mouth. They sounded uncomfortable.

Like I was possessed.

Which, I supposed, I was.

But I didn't care to think of it that way. And, for some reason, I didn't care for Kiran to think of it that way either.

"Hm," was all he said at first, as he brought the tip of his pointer finger to his bottom lip and scratched his chin with his thumb.

"Not as interesting as our regular story, I know," I said.

"Ours?" he asked, his ember eyes twinkling as he raised one solid brow.

I tried not to clear my throat. "Mine and my magic's." Though I wasn't entirely convinced of the truthfulness of this statement—if that was really what I had meant.

"Mmhmm," he said, pushing himself off the edge of the bed and stretching his long arms toward the ceiling. Wow. Every time he moved, every time I saw him under a different backdrop, it reminded me of how massive he was. Of how abnormally tall the ceiling of our bedroom had to be for his calloused fingertips not to scrape the top.

Our.

There was that word again. In my thoughts. On my tongue.

I considered erasing it from my vocabulary.

He shot me one last lazy smile before he sank below my line of vision onto the cot below.

I didn't sleep at all that night.

CHAPTER 46

ASHA

"Well, that was creepy," Lydia said, crossing her arms as she gazed into the shadowy hole behind the library fireplace.

I shrugged.

My sister-in-law had returned that morning, weeks before she was expected from her trip searching for answers about who had hired the lychaen. If she had learned anything, she wasn't exactly spilling the information to me.

She also wasn't spilling on how she'd traveled to Avelea and back so quickly, when I'd overheard her tell Kiran that just the journey to Avelea took over a mooncycle.

When I'd asked, all she'd said was that her contact had ended up being in town, anyway, which I would have thought was way too much of a coincidence to be true, if she actually had the ability to lie.

When I had pushed her for a more satisfying explanation, she'd insisted I train with her.

Train.

With her.

I might have laughed in her face, had I been more confident we had reached that level in our friendship. As much as I believed Lydia cared for me, I wasn't sure where her boundaries were, and I didn't care to get my face melted off.

Well, I didn't care to get the *other* half of my face melted off.

When she'd asked me if I had any skills that might be readily honed into self-defense, I'd had an idea. We'd tromped down to the library at once, and my magic had so graciously opened the wall behind the fireplace for us.

"You mean to tell me *that* is the voice that's been enchanting my brother all these evenings?" she asked.

"It sounds better in our language, trust me."

"How is that going by the way?"

A crackling noise, like the last futile breaths of a burning twig, escaped my throat. "How's what going?"

"Your story with Kiran. Have you run out of ideas yet?"

Funny that she should mention that, because I had been wondering the same thing. Well, not the part about my magic running out of ideas. I was fairly sure the Fates weren't kind enough to allow that to happen.

Watch it.

The part that confused me, was that ever since the *incident*, as I liked to call it in my head, much to my magic's annoyance, Kiran hadn't invited me back to his chambers. The first night Dinah had been well enough to stay with me again, we had waited up for hours to be summoned, but Tavi never showed.

Not that I was complaining.

Lydia just grunted, apparently impatient with my delayed response, then stooped into the hole without bothering to wait for me. I followed her, realizing the last time I'd ventured into this place, I'd thrown the lamp to the side. Now it was lying somewhere in the darkness, instead of within the ray of light cast into the room from the library.

"There was a lamp here," I said.

"Was?" Lydia demanded.

"Don't worry. I don't mean someone's taken it. I just…forgot to put it back in its place. It's somewhere in the shadows."

"No matter," Lydia said, flicking her wrist until a gentle orange flame glowed in her palm.

"I always forget you can do that," I said.

"Yeah, well, I forget you can read dead languages," Lydia said.

I gazed around the room, checking, despite myself, for any signs that someone else had visited here since the first time I'd discovered it. But everything seemed to be in its place, and the lamp was still sideways on the floor in the corner where I'd dropped it.

"And when exactly did you say you discovered this place?" Lydia asked, narrowing those perfectly arched brows in my direction.

"Not too long ago," I said, swallowing hard.

"How nonspecific."

"Well."

"And does anyone else know about it?"

I pretended not to hear her and put as much distance between us as possible. Then I made as much noise as I could as I rifled through the scrolls, hoping that if I pretended to be looking for a specific one, it would intrigue Lydia enough for her to drop the subject.

"You told that sister of yours, didn't you?" Lydia asked.

"Hmm?" I asked, turning to face her with the most innocent look I could muster.

"Human hearing isn't that bad," Lydia said.

"I don't know. Maybe my ear was damaged during the accident."

"It wasn't."

"Yeah, you're right," I said, giving up.

"Well, I figure your sister is trustworthy. She seems like the type to take a secret to the grave if she felt like it meant anything to you," Lydia said.

I chuckled. "Yeah, she's like that."

Never mind the fact I hadn't told Dinah. Tavi knew, but I didn't want to cause her trouble. Not when Lydia could be terrifying when she wanted to be. Not when Tavi was so jittery to begin with.

"So, I'm guessing opening secret doors with your voice isn't the only thing you can do?" Lydia asked.

The question had me whirling toward the far end of the room, and I realized what had felt strange when we'd first walked in.

The sword. It was gone.

My stomach sank.

"I—" I didn't know how to proceed, how to tell Lydia that I could materialize objects with my voice, without telling her I'd materialized a bloodied sword. A sword which was now missing.

Had Tavi snuck back in here and retrieved it? No, that didn't make any sense. Not only did it seem completely out of character, but there was no way Tavi would have been able to open the secret door. Not unless she was secretly hosting Old Magic in her soul.

She's not. I would have sensed it.

I wasn't sure whether that made me feel better or worse.

"Here. I'll show you," I said, pulling a scroll from the shelves. I placed it on the podium on the far side of the room.

Lydia approached me from behind and looked over my shoulder. I tried my best not to flinch. Sure, I was fairly certain Lydia and I were friends and that she had no intentions of hurting me. But she was a trained assassin, after all. An assassin who killed people who did bad things, and her demeanor left me under the impression she didn't consult a jury before deciding who was bad and who wasn't. If she misinterpreted my magic as me being a witch…and if she didn't like that…

Again, I tried not to flinch.

If it makes you feel better, she's already heard me open the wall behind the fireplace. If she's going to kill you, she's already decided to do so. No use fretting over your every move at this point.

Great, thanks.

"How old are these?" Lydia asked as I rolled out the parchment.

"I'm not sure. The parchment is crinkled. It feels fragile, but the words look like they could have been written yesterday. Here, you want to feel?" I asked, offering the scroll to her.

You left out the part about how the ink is written in Omigron blood, my magic said.

That was intentional, trust me.

"No thank you," Lydia said, curling her nose in disgust at the parchment. "I'd rather not chance destroying an artifact this old."

I wasn't sure what that meant about me.

It means you're careless.

Oh, you're one to talk, I thought.

"That's fine," I said, trying to lay the scroll back on the podium as quickly as possible, and tearing the edge of it in the process. I winced and felt Lydia's very aura tighten behind me, but I thought it best not to acknowledge my error.

If you could take over my voice and read right about now, that'd be help-ful, I thought toward my magic.

In an instant, my voice was no longer my own, and, as I read, while the words made no sense to me, smoke emerged from the scrolls. It wound around itself in a thin, curved line that swayed to the rhythm of my voice. Then, something hissed, and I realized it wasn't a sound in the ancient language, but that it was coming from the smoke itself. The dark smoke emulsified and turned a shining silver. A fork tongue licked out from the shadows.

And then it struck.

I tried to scream, but my magic had my voice locked up some-where inside me. My limbs worked, though, and I lurched backward, but not quickly enough. Not before the dark eyes of the cobra met mine. Not before its fangs flashed before my face.

But then its head dropped into my lap, its face petrified in that open stance. I screamed this time and jumped from the ground until the cobra's head rolled off my body and onto the floor beside its severed, slumped body, its fangs still glinting in Lydia's firelight.

The tip of its body, the part that had once supported its head, now hissed with smoke as fire cauterized its flesh. As if someone had taken a blade of flames to it.

My jaw swung open. Lydia's face was set, stern, and fear riled in my bones.

"Lydia, Lydia, I didn't mean to—I didn't know…"

What have you done, what have you done, what have you done? I hissed at my magic. *She's going to think we were trying to kill her! You know she's an assassin, right?* "Lydia, I never would have... I didn't know it was a snake..." My body trembled as those fangs flashed before my memory once more.

"Relax, Asha," Lydia said, offering a heavily jeweled hand to me. I took it, still shaking, and she lifted me to my feet with the effort it would have taken to lift a cooperative two-year-old. "I know you weren't trying to hurt me."

"You do?" I asked, heaving as I tried to catch my breath. My throat was scratchy from all the ancient sounds my mouth wasn't used to pronouncing.

"Of course I do. You summoned a cobra right in front of your face. So either you had no intentions of hurting me, or you're much too unskilled to pull it off. Either way, I can't say I'm trembling for my life."

I laughed, though it sounded more like an uncomfortable wince, mostly because it was.

"That's an interesting skill you've got there," Lydia said as she approached the dead cobra before us. She picked up its head from the back and turned it over in her palm. "This could be useful, you know. I'm sure the healer would love me forever if I brought her a few of these fangs to make remedies. Though I might just keep them for myself."

"I thought the fae were immune to snake venom," I said.

"True. But this is no ordinary snake. You see these markings between its eyes?" Lydia offered the cobra head to me, and I grimaced and waved my hand in deference.

"I can see them." And indeed I could. Now that I was looking, I couldn't believe I'd missed them. The markings were unlike any I'd seen on a snake, pictured or otherwise. The pattern between its eyes looked like three triangles, laid side by side. That wasn't the strange part. Above the triangles was the shape of an...

"Is that an hourglass?" I asked, and I might have reached my finger out to trace the strange symbol, if fear of the creature hadn't paralyzed my arm.

Lydia nodded. "There are tales of these creatures, legends, passed down from our ancestors. They lived in the Other, and their bite certainly could kill a grown fae."

"That's comforting," I said, remembering the mere from my magic's story, the story it hadn't told since the Lychaen attack, not since Dinah had fallen ill. The Others had been silver, like this snake.

I turned inward, toward my magic, and thought to ask it whether its story had been more realistic than I'd once thought, but Lydia interrupted my thoughts.

"Yes, you would have been dead the instant the fangs breached your skin." Sometimes Lydia spoke as if such things were dinner talk.

"If this snake is from the Nether, why would the healer need an antidote for its venom?" I asked. "It's not as if anyone's really at risk of being bitten by one."

"Well, the history is a little muggy, but the fae got here somehow, didn't we? Who's to say someone else couldn't get through?"

I groaned, but then the cobra's head shook, and I jumped backward. Except the cobra head wasn't shaking at all. It was—collapsing within Lydia's hand. Its scales turned black, and it withered, turning into ash and slipping between her fingertips.

"Why'd you do that?" I asked.

Lydia stared at the cobra's long, twisting body. All that remained was a ribbon of ash. "I didn't," she said.

Well, at least we know no one snuck in here and took the sword.

"Well, that's disappointing," Lydia said.

I, for one, could not disagree more. In fact, I felt as if my soul had returned to my body now that the horrifying snake was gone. And now that I knew Tavi hadn't somehow broken back in here. The sword must have disintegrated, just like the cobra had.

"So, are you planning on hauling around a load of scrolls on your back in case a lychaen sneaks through your window and tries to kidnap you again?" Lydia asked.

"Ummm..."

She had a point.

"Great. Well, can you do it without a scroll?" she asked.

"I can make the hearer feel like they're in the my stories." Something deep inside my body poked me in the ribcage, "—uh, my magic's stories. But they don't usually come to life and have real fangs and dissolve on the floor."

Lydia paced around the room, touching her hand to her chin and examining the scrolls on the bookshelves.

"These are ancient," she said. "I wonder..." She turned back toward me and looked me up and down in an appraising way that gave me the urge to stand up straighter.

"Try telling a story that's not in one of these scrolls," Lydia said.

"It doesn't create anything when I do that," I said.

"Yes, but what if it's not the ancient language that gives you the power to bring your stories to life? What if your magic is drawing its power from the scrolls themselves? They certainly have an otherworldly quality, don't they? Perhaps the scrolls are from the Other, and therein lies your newfound power."

That sounded good enough to me, though I doubted it would work.

I opened my mouth, but nothing came out.

Lydia stared at me expectantly.

What are you doing, I asked my magic.

It didn't answer.

Oh, come on. Just try it. We can finish the story about the boy, I coaxed.

Nothing.

"Well?" Lydia asked, her face the antithesis of patience.

"A moment." I grinned, though internally I was scowling at the wretched creature inside me.

What are you waiting for?

Nothing.

You're scared, aren't you? You don't know whether it'll work, and you're worried that, if we try, we'll fail, and then you'll be nothing without those horrible symbols, I hissed.

Still, nothing.

Please, just try. Don't you want me to be able to defend myself if another kidnapper comes along?

Finally, my magic graced me with a response. *Wouldn't you still end up having to carry a scroll around on your back so I could draw power from it? Or do you intend to live out the rest of your days in this hovel?*

I bit back my snarky retort and went with something more practical. *Well, at least I wouldn't have to carry all of them around. And I wouldn't have to pull it out and read it. And we could decide what we summoned, and—*

You mean, I could decide, it said.

Yes, fine.

"Are you okay?" Lydia asked, her face wide with concern.

"I'm fine. My magic just doesn't seem to be working right now. Maybe I used it all up reading from that scroll. I probably just need time to recharge," I said.

"Hm," Lydia said, though she appeared incredibly suspicious. "Well then, sounds like we'll have to train my way."

I couldn't say I liked the sound of that.

* * *

As much as I hadn't liked the sound of Lydia's training, I hated the feel of it even more. Specifically, the aching in my shoulder, the aching in my head, the aching in my thighs, the aching in my calves, and the aching in my soul by the time we finished. She had made me train with one of her daggers against her. Just her. No weapons. No magic.

Needless to say, she'd kicked my butt.

I hadn't as much as grazed her perfect skin with the dagger.

Not that I'd been trying all that hard.

Well.

Not that I'd been trying all that hard, at first.

I may or may not have gotten a tad vengeful after the twelfth time she knocked me to the ground, but it hadn't mattered anyway.

By the end of our session, we'd all but confirmed I'd only gotten lucky with the lychaen, and that my chances of escaping twice would be slim.

CHAPTER 47

ASHA

*A*utumn was upon us in full force, apparently. One could tell because of the parade that was scheduled for a crispy, sultry morning a few days after the *incident*, as I now referred to it—the conversation with Kiran. The one in his bed that was not supposed to happen. The acquaintanceship teetering dangerously close to friendship that had transpired between us the night Dinah had fallen ill.

We'd actually talked since then. Over bread and tea at breakfast. On my usual lone walks through the garden, when the king just happened to be strolling at the same time, despite the fact I had changed the hour I walked twice just to avoid the chance encounters. Kiran had even found a set of books in the library he needed to catch up on as it would "aid him in foreign affairs."

Dinah had recovered fully from her illness, but that hadn't stopped Kiran from asking about her, if she was well, if she had been able to resume her nightly activities of feeding the poor, if she needed assistance in that matter or in running my family's stall.

The only thing Kiran never asked was whether I needed anything. Perhaps because he knew my answer already, though even I didn't know whether I would ever be brave enough to voice it, even if he did ask.

"Don't you look brilliant?" Kiran asked, his eyes hovering over my silken dress as a servant helped me into the carriage.

"This?" I asked, glancing at the glimmering apricot dress Tavi had brought me this morning. It was simple in its shape, but not in a way that appeared anything less than ridiculously expensive, not in a way that would fool me into sipping my morning tea freely. The way the soft material flowed from my dark, exposed shoulders gave the appearance of shimmering, liquid fire. Tavi had told me I looked like a sunset when I put it on. "I'm told this is an autumn color, though I'm not certain it suits me."

"Oh, I wouldn't say that. I quite like it," Kiran said, his molten eyes flickering a shade darker to match my attire, causing warmth to crawl the length of my bare neck.

Kiran offered his hand as I stumbled over the flowing fabric, but I pretended not to notice and steadied myself on the velvet seat instead.

He cleared his throat then withdrew his hand to his side. I couldn't have him doing that, offering his hand for a multitude of tasks I was perfectly capable of doing myself. It reminded me of how everyone had acted that first year after my accident.

"I've never seen autumn," I said, doing my best to clear the silence as the camels in front of us jolted and the carriage took off over the bumpy streets.

"You speak as though it's a person or a place," Kiran said.

"I guess you could say it's a place in time, but only in certain places," I said.

Kiran turned to me and smiled. "I suppose so."

"Have you ever seen autumn?"

"A few times, mostly during foreign relations trips to Avelea...with my father," he added, and I thought I heard his voice cake and crack like mud in the desert at that last word.

"Oh. So I guess you didn't have the chance to enjoy it, did you?"

Kiran choked. "You're incredibly frank, you know that, right?"

"A byproduct of having half your face scorched off as a child," I said.

"Did your magic burn your filter, too?"

I shrugged. "No, society did that. You see, society only cares about a woman's filter if that woman is eligible to marry."

"Well, you certainly showed them, didn't you?" Kiran nudged my arm with his elbow, and my stomach tightened.

A grin tugged at the edge of my lips, and I didn't work all that hard to fight it. "Oh, I dunno. There'll be gossip that I bewitched my poor husband into agreeing to our union."

His molten eyes washed over me as a smirk emerged on his face, softening the harsh edges of his jaw, his brow line. "He's not complaining."

Heat, heat that had nothing to do with the fact that my husband wielded the power of fire within his bones, rushed over me, settling in the pit of my belly.

I shrugged and forced my focus toward the streets, where people lined up, children on their fathers' and mothers' shoulders. Purples and blues, but mostly browns adorned their shoulders and heads, protecting them from the heat.

I searched the crowd and pretended with myself that I didn't know whom for.

That was the trouble with searching for someone in a crowd. Everyone seemed to take his height, his lanky stature, his dark hair, his confident swagger, as if the entirety of Meranthi were wearing Az disguises today.

Perhaps that was why it was so shocking that my eyes found him.

Az. The real Az.

Az with a fae.

Az with a female.

* * *

MY BREAKFAST TURNED over in my stomach. I searched for an escape route, for any means to get away before Az saw me, but the crowd of faeries and humans pressed against the carriage. Not that it mattered much anyway. My limbs had hardened into wax.

Then Az turned, caught in the act of laughter at something the pretty fae in blue had said. His mouth hung ajar as he caught my eye. His wide smile morphed into a gape. He blinked, as if that might clear his eyes, fill him with relief as he realized he had been mistaken—he had only thought he had seen me. Just as I had mistaken every man with a build remotely similar to his for the best friend of my childhood, the man I loved.

His mouth clamped, and he grimaced. Lines creased his forehead between his eyebrows. He didn't have to bother mouthing it. I hadn't lost the ability to read his face in these few months.

I hadn't been gone that long.

I'm sorry, his eyes cried to me.

My eyes broke his gaze and shot down, tracing his sleeve. A dark tattoo curled across the back of his left hand.

It might have matched mine.

The female, his wife, I now realized, turned to trace his gaze. So curious about whatever her new husband had found an interest in.

I supposed that was how it felt to be in love with your husband. For anything he found remotely interesting to become worth noting, worth exploring. Worthy of utmost attention.

As she followed Az's eyes, naturally, she caught mine. I braced myself for her gaze to sour to venom—the signet of enmity between the man I loved and his fae wife.

The look she gave me was much, much worse.

The corners of those sparkling eyes turned downward, her full, unblemished lips puckering.

Pity.

Pity for the human girl shackled to the cruel king.

My throat closed up, as if the air itself were assaulting me, as if it would be safer just to suffocate.

A booming voice broke that moment, frozen in time. "Clear the crowd. Get us out of here."

* * *

317

"Asha, please wait," Kiran said, trailing behind me as if his predatory nature would not have allowed him to catch up with me within two seconds.

I pretended he couldn't and raced as fast as I could manage without tripping over this ridiculous dress that I'd be ripping off as soon as I made it to my room. The massive palace doors opened before me as wide-eyed guards questioned our swift return with uneasy grimaces. My shoes, heeled and overly bejeweled, clacked against the marble floor, each step punctuating the image of Az's tattoo. I yanked the heels off my sore feet and slung them across the foyer before proceeding barefoot, the clatter of displaced jewels ringing in my ears.

The worst part was, I couldn't even bring myself to cry. The pain, the jealousy, the heartbreak—they dripped and oozed, swirling and amalgamating in my chest until they solidified into rage, an alloy no words of appeasement could hope to shatter. A rage that would simmer and poach as long as I was in Kiran's presence. All I wanted to do was weep, to wash away with salt and tears the pain that clung like tar to the spaces between my fragile ribs, to cleanse myself of that unfading pattern that had tattooed itself to my swirling vision.

"Asha."

Kiran had stopped. The last echo of his footsteps reached my ears before vanishing into the mob of swarming thoughts in my head.

How long had it been since Az had declared his love for me? A mooncycle, if that. Was that how long it took my friend, my best friend since we were toddlers, to move on? And with a woman I didn't recognize. Someone he couldn't have known for longer than I'd been corralled inside this prison of a palace, this cage of white-washed marble.

And such a pretty cage it was.

"Asha."

I whirled on him. "I don't want to talk to you."

Kiran stood there, his usually tensed arms limp at his side, his broad shoulders sloping at the same angle at his lips.

The poor male looks miserable.

Good.

"If you don't want to talk to me, that's fine. Just please. Please listen. Just for a moment."

The image of that female's smitten flush berated my consciousness, pummeling my stupid dreams and threatening to collapse my lungs. Numbness washed over me, draining the fury from my limbs. So I stayed. Not for Kiran, but because I could no longer summon the will to move.

"I am so sorry I caused this." Kiran clenched his hands together, as if any sudden movement might send me fleeing. As if I had any reason to resist the concrete hardening my feet, my legs, my soul. "I am so sorry you're hurting. I can't—"

I didn't respond. Couldn't find the care to.

"Asha, I won't pretend it's not on my shoulders, what's happened to you, but I want you to know that you deserve so, so much better than that man."

My breath caught, and I couldn't seem to make it bend to my will, to force it into a mold of scathing words.

"I know I have no right, but do you know how angry it makes me? That he had years. *Years* with you. That, all that time, he had your precious heart secured. And he did nothing about it. He kept you waiting all that time—"

"Please, Kiran. Please just—"

"He kept you waiting, and if the fool had asked for your hand when he should have, you never would have been eligible to offer yourself—"

"You don't get to talk about him."

"Asha," he said, stepping forward and closing the space between us, so close I couldn't tell if it was my pounding heart I was hearing or his. He swept his finger over my cheek, catching a tear I hadn't even realized I'd loosed on his calloused knuckle. The sensation sent a wave of fire sweeping across my skin, tracing his whisper of a touch. When he spoke, his voice rumbled, low and deep, penetrating my bones. "He should have chosen you years ago."

His words pierced deeper than his voice, inflicting pain so intense, it was almost cathartic. A truth so raw it ripped my skin even as it cleansed me of my filth. With more gentleness than I could have ever imagined possible, he cupped my face into his massive hands and rested his chin on my forehead, pressing his lips into the crown of my braid, sending a shiver of heat down my spine, a flood of desire tinged with pain, regret. A sensation I ought not to feel for this monster of a male, this being who held my life in his hands, who could consume me in an instant if he willed it so.

So why did being consumed suddenly not feel like such an awful thing?

Fear coursed through me, and I pulled back, putting enough distance between us to free myself from the magnetic pull of his aura.

He hesitated, but the way I fled his touch must have fueled something within him, for when he spoke, his voice was steady. Sure. Indignant.

"I'm not saying it's not completely my fault," he said, advancing on me until my back hit the cool marble wall. He rested his palms against the stone on either side of my head, practically pinning me in place, so close, yet so deliberate not to touch me again.

A challenge.

A message.

One that stated oh so clearly, *I won't touch you again until you ask me to.*

An assumption that day would come.

His breathing went ragged, his voice hoarse, his warm breath tickling my cheek.

"I'm not washing myself of my horrid mistakes," he said. "But, Asha, you deserve to be cherished. And not just because someone doesn't realize the good they have until it's gone. Not because there's suddenly a fading echo where there used to be your laugh. Not because there's a void where there used to be your wit, your undying loyalty. Not because some vain *boy* finally realized having you as a companion, as a *partner*, is worth infinitely more than a thousand and one pretty faces." His fists balled against the wall, cracking the marble as waves of heat surged and swelled in the wake of his aura. And then his lips were close, that same warmth seeping into the space between us, threatening to entangle me and thaw my frozen heart. "No Asha, Queen of Naenden, weaver of tales and protector of the helpless, a girl —no, a woman—like you deserves to be cherished. Right here. Right now. To eternity and every fleeting moment in between."

My breath caught as the words cracked through the mortar between my ribs, threatening to snake and spread and rip until the heat rolling off this beast of a man devoured me whole. Until I believed every word.

But that was the thing about Kiran's words.

He was fae, so they might have been true.

But that didn't mean it was his mouth I'd wanted to form them.

And just like that, just like the mirror ceremony during our wedding, he'd stolen another moment from me, plucked it right out of my imagination and tainted it with his voice, with his image, forever.

"Please," I whispered. "Please just leave me alone."

Kiran's eyes aged to coal. His knuckles bulged white on his clasped hands, shaking against the cracked marble, sending a rumble through the wall on which my skull rested.

Fear coursed through me. Was this it? His breaking point? The part where he pinned my throat to the wall and consumed me in his rage?

"As you wish," he said, his voice crackling and dry as it scraped the bubbling air. He pushed himself from the wall, his towering form casting a shadow over me even as he stepped backward into the middle of the hall.

It was almost as if, when he stepped away from me, he took my breath with him.

When he spoke, his words hung in the sweltering air between us. "When are you going to forgive me, love?"

Love. That word hooked on the loose shreds of my heart and tugged.

"You know the worst part?" I asked, and Kiran tensed. "That you can apologize all you want. I might even...there might even be a part of me that wishes that I could forgive you. That I could forget. But I'm always going to know. I am *always* going to remember that there is a part of you that's glad Az married that girl. A part of you that felt some relief when you saw that tattoo on his hand. Because you knew it was over then. That I'd eventually have to move on—"

"Asha, please," Kiran said, closing his eyes now, as if that could somehow hide the shadows in his irises that betrayed the dark creature within, as if it could shield him from what I was about to say next.

"I might move on one day. You're probably right about that. But I will never—*never*—forget that you found comfort as my dreams were ripped from me. I simply don't know how."

I turned and walked away.

His voice, small, barely a whisper, followed me down the corridor.

"You may never forget. But I hope that one day you'll forgive."

I stopped, though I didn't turn around. And then I whispered my answer, because I knew he could hear me anyway with those fae senses he'd probably thought were an advantage before now.

"I think sometimes you forget I'm human. We don't have centuries to forgive."

For some reason, those words shattered my heart too.

* * *

I PRACTICALLY SHREDDED the parade dress off of me once I arrived in my room. Tavi knocked once, at which point I'd tried to swallow the rage in my voice and politely asked her to leave me alone. It came out sounding bitter and agitated, but I'd find her and apologize later. Right now, I couldn't, I couldn't...

I shouldn't think of Az. It only ached, burned.

But I had to.

Because if I didn't think of Az, then I'd think of *him*.

And I couldn't do that to myself.

At first, I shoved my left hand under the scalding water in the bathroom's marble basin, scrubbing at my tattoo with an exfoliating soap that smelled like wealth and excess, until my raw skin bled. Then

I launched myself onto my bed and buried my face in the lushest pillow I could find. And then I tried to cry, tried to flush all those dreadful feelings until I could create a puddle large enough to drown in. But the tears were stubborn and refused to come.

So I forced myself to sob into the sheets, my eye dry, as if that would somehow have the same cleansing effect. Eventually I punched my pillow, but my fist felt so weak against the plush material, I had to punch it again and again and again just to feel like I'd made an impact. Just to feel like I'd hurt something the way Az had hurt me.

In the end, it didn't work, and I hurled the pillow across the room at my mirror.

It didn't even crack, like I'd hoped.

But that was the thing about throwing pillows. It was a coward's choice, the weapon of a tantruming weakling too afraid to actually leave a mark on this world.

So I slept, another coward's choice. But at least it freed me from the captivity of my mind for a few fitful hours.

When I awoke, the skin on the back of my left hand had healed, leaving my tattoo looking as vibrant as the day the king had marked me as his own.

* * *

KIRAN DIDN'T SUMMON me that evening. That was just as well. I didn't have the will, the energy. Someone must have sent for Dinah—Tavi probably—because she appeared in my quarters with a hot plate of potatoes and, when I refused them, curled up next to me in the bed.

"How long?" I asked her in the middle of the night that seemed it would never end.

Her voice went small. "They eloped last week, but they didn't tell anyone. I only knew because Az came running over. He told me what had happened at the parade. That I should go to you and tell you he was sorry. That…"

She stopped.

I twisted to face her. Her eyes glowed in the moonlight coming in from the window, tears lining her lids.

Dinah shook her head, and when she spoke, I sensed bitterness in her tone. "It's not worth repeating."

"Just tell me."

"That you'd understand one day."

My heart hollowed out, and I listened as Dinah's breaths shallowed, as she succumbed to the sleep that I feared, lest my dreams trick me into thinking Az was mine.

In the morning, Tavi entered my quarters without a dress draped over her arms.

So that was it. I would die for my outburst. So be it.

"Lady Queen," she curtsied, her pale eyes bright for once. "You won't be attending the ceremony today. There will be no more ceremonies. The king has deemed you worthy."

I slumped back onto my pillow and slept the day away.

* * *

It wasn't difficult to throw myself into training after that. In fact, I searched out Lydia most days, my mind swimming for a distraction as grief gnawed a hole in my chest from the inside out.

She fell for it the first few times, probably thinking it was for the best, that it would distract me from the pain.

But Lydia was too clever to be fooled for long. After a few sessions of me welcoming her beatings, of only pretending to defend myself, of bruises that never got the chance to yellow, Lydia informed me we wouldn't be training again until I'd found the will to fight back.

As far as my brother-in-law was concerned, Fin ventured as far as to seek me out in Nagivv's sanctuary one afternoon, though he approached with hesitant feet and maintained a steady distance between us.

Nagivv snarled at him, even as I stroked the bridge of her snout. "She doesn't like you, you know."

My voice was one long line of words. I couldn't bring myself to muster the effort to speckle my voice with texture, to hammer the ups and downs into my pitch.

"I know," he said, sitting down cross-legged a stone's throw away from us. It looked ridiculous, a male as lanky as he was sitting like that. But he had that boyish aura about him, which actually fit, considering how young he was. Strange, to think he'd already been married and widowed. That he'd look like that for the next few centuries.

When it was clear I had nothing to say, no energy to scrape words from the clogged crevices of my mind, he spoke again, "Kiran's scheduled a ball."

"He doesn't seem like the type."

"He's not. It was Lydia's idea, actually."

"She seems like even less the type."

Fin smirked, though sadly. "You're not wrong about that. But they're not interested in the fun of it. They've invited kings and queens from all over Alondria."

"Is that a good idea, with someone rich enough to hire a lychaen out there trying to kidnap me?"

Fin shrugged and picked blades of grass from Nagivv's sanctuary floor, rubbing them together between his fingers. "They think it might draw the kidnapper out."

"So I'm to be bait. Excellent."

"I don't know why you're complaining. All the plan requires of you is to exist. Which seems like all you've been intent on doing these days."

I jerked my neck and glared at him, but all that did was cause me to really look at him for the first time in a while. He hadn't cut his hair since I'd met him, and it was starting to obscure his pointed ears. Tangled and messy, he might have looked more of a wreck than I did, if I didn't have the head start of only having half a face.

"You're one to talk. Don't you have a province you're supposed to be running?"

He didn't even bristle. Didn't have the energy to, apparently. But his usually soft face went cold, hard. "I'm sure it's less than pleasant to have the object of your affection go off and marry someone else, but my wife died, you know."

His words stung, the first sensation I'd felt, truly felt, in days. Shame washed over me, flooding my bones, its massive weight craning my neck until I couldn't bear to look at him. "You're right. I'm sorry, I shouldn't have—"

"It's fine," he said, even though it wasn't. "If it soothes your clearly genuine concern about the province of Talens, I've never once had the say in what happens there. Kiran appointed a council who makes all the decisions for him. For me."

That was strange. Fin's wife Ophelia had tried to seduce Kiran by saying he could control Naenden and Talens. But if he'd already had all the control...

It didn't matter how desperately I wanted to ask. There was no sense in bringing up Fin's dead wife, or especially how she'd tried to seduce his brother.

He must have seen the flicker of curiosity in my eye, because he continued. "It's not exactly public knowledge."

Did the public include Ophelia?

But that was not a question I had the right to ask. "Did you come here to cheer me up?" I asked instead.

"Nope," he said, splaying on his back in the grass. "I just didn't feel like being depressed alone. Thought you might feel the same way."

I wasn't sure that I did, but I didn't exactly ask him to leave, either.

CHAPTER 48

ASHA

The autumn ballroom had been decorated as such. The entire spectrum of reds, oranges, yellows, and greens flickered in the shape of ever-burning leaves on the domed ceiling above us, through some sort of magic only Naenden royalty could have been skilled and powerful enough to muster, and as Lydia didn't seem the decorating type, and Fin had no royal magic to speak of, I assumed we had Kiran to thank for the decor. Dancing flames floated above our heads, burning with no fuel except the air around them and the will of their master.

Autumn did not exist in Naenden, and as I had never crossed its borders, I had never witnessed such a scene. I had hoped, when I first arrived here and realized I might live into another season, that the trees in the garden outside would change colors just like they did in that book Father always read. But Lydia had informed me that the trees were evergreen, not because of their species but because of the magic that allowed them to grow in the middle of a desert city.

My neck would probably be sore tomorrow from how long I had gazed at the flickering leaves. But I would gladly suffer the consequences if it meant avoiding the stares of the king's guests. For, while

I busied myself marveling at the beauty of the scene above, and, to be honest, the talent of its artist, the rest of the room stared at me.

Gaped, more like it.

Staring would have been too polite of a word. More akin to how Kiran examined my face as if to memorize its every scar. To the king's guests, I might as well have been the night's entertainment.

A single burning leaf fell from the canopy above, swinging as it fell, as if in a soft autumn breeze rather than the harsh winds the commoners of Naenden were accustomed to. As it traced a zig-zag in the air, it flew closer to me. So close, in fact, that I cupped my hands to catch it. It fluttered for a bit, right above my palm, the scarlet and green vibrant against the backdrop of my olive skin.

At least half of the ballroom gasped as it grazed my palms. I ignored them, the little fiery leaf simply warming my cold skin. A gentle warmth. Not one anyone from Meranthi had experienced.

"Do you have a habit of playing with fire?" a low rumble of a voice next to me asked.

The leaf in my hand crumbled, its remains dissipating into cold char that crept between my fingertips and stained the marble floor. I turned to my left, but I already knew who stood there.

Kiran smiled softly down at me. An apologetic smile. A *we-haven't-spoken-since-you-told-me-you'd-never-forgive-me* smile. Subtle, but not subtle enough for our guests not to notice if they were paying attention.

Which they all were.

He wasn't wearing his traditional robes tonight. Instead, he donned a white military jacket, buttoned on either side of the midline. His dark beard had been trimmed close to the sharp edges of his face.

My husband was startlingly attractive, and I hated him for it.

Well, kind of.

"I thought playing with fire was only concerning if the habit manifested itself in childhood," I said. Kiran smirked, apparently pleased that I'd gone back to my backhanded insults rather than the silence I'd offered over the past few days.

I wasn't done hurting. And I wasn't done blaming Kiran for it. But

I was going to have to live with Kiran for the rest of my life—a blip of his, sure—but I figured I might as well get used to his presence. And sooner rather than later.

"No, I think you're getting that confused with something else. You see, it's not playing with fire that worries us in children. It's playing with the Old Magic."

At that, my jaw actually dropped. I wanted to be offended, truly, except that I couldn't bring myself to be. No one except for Bezzie, not even my father or Dinah or Az had ever made light of my injury. They had loved me in spite of it. But never had anyone joked about it. Except for maybe me.

That jagged piece of flint in my heart that had hardened against him softened, and the thaw remained much longer than I was comfortable with.

Kiran just chuckled. "What do you think?" he asked, spreading his arms out to the ballroom.

"Did you decorate all this yourself?" The ceiling had to be his work. Since Kiran's father had driven off most of the royal relatives long ago, no one else currently living in the palace controlled fire with the specificity needed to craft such a masterpiece. Except for maybe Lydia, but judging by her disdain for all things sentimental, my bet was still on Kiran. Someone had even decorated the tables with bronze leaves and ornate silver lamps, whose flames flickered blue.

And the tapestries had been changed out as well. All in the supposed colors of autumn, but each bearing each kingdom's crest, though one had to look carefully to notice them interwoven into the extravagant stitching.

He chuckled. "Well, not all of it. But I helped. Tavi's to blame. She did a lot of the delegating."

I searched the crowd for the servant girl, trying to avoid making eye contact with any of the fae guests who were still glancing at me more often than necessary, even if most of them had returned to their conversation.

"Where is she, anyway?" I asked.

"She didn't come."

"You mean she wasn't invited," I snapped. Of course, Kiran had made Tavi put in all the work of this ball before choosing not to invite her. Because who would invite a half-breed servant?

Kiran peered down at me for a moment, and I made an effort to meet his gaze. "She isn't here because I offered her paid leave to visit her brother as a reward for all her hard work."

"Oh." Heat rose to my cheeks, and I averted my eyes to my slippers. They peeked out underneath my ivory dress as if they were embarrassed by me too. I couldn't bring myself to apologize, though.

"It's nothing," Kiran said. I dared to glance at him once more, to judge the sincerity of his forgiveness. His face shone with nothing more than pleasant friendliness, for which I was relieved. "You are stunning, by the way," he said.

This comment didn't make me blush as it had during the parade. In fact, it infuriated me that Kiran believed he had the right to speak to me with such familiarity, after I'd made it clear how I felt about him.

"I don't require that sort of compliment," I said. "I much prefer candor over flattery."

Kiran cocked his head at me, tracing every curve of my face as he had made his habit. "Am I not allowed to find ferocity stunning? Or would you have me fawn over these fae females who would gladly seduce me for my money?"

I cleared my throat. This time, I did blush.

That must have pleased him, because he placed his thumb on my shoulder and stroked it lightly, his caress warm and soothing, not at all like the first few times we'd touched. More like that night in the infirmary, when he'd leaned in and whispered...

The jolt in my stomach this caused was not welcome, but apparently I didn't have a choice in the matter.

Just then, I heard a lovely, familiar voice cascade through the hall. I found Dinah, adorned in a golden dress that glittered and fell in open sleeves off of her shoulders. She spoke to Lydia and Fin, but she must have felt my desperate gaze, for she turned and waved at me with a warm grin.

"You invited Dinah?" I asked, my neck still hot from Kiran's compliment, from his gentle touch that, for the life of me, I couldn't bring myself to shrug away from.

"Just because I have to make company with these vipers doesn't mean I think you should have to," he said, his smile soft, yet strained.

You should have accepted his compliment. Look, now his feelings are hurt. Tsk. Tsk.

I don't know if that's possible; I volleyed back.

Mmm.

"I thought the point of all this was to draw out the person who's trying to kidnap me," I hissed under my breath. "Why would you risk Dinah's safety by inviting her?"

A stray leaf landed gently on my shoulder, dissolving into harmless embers on my bare skin. Before I could swat it away, Kiran brushed the ash with his thumb, grazing the notch of my collarbone as he did. "Asha, love," he said, his gaze lingering on where his fingers circled over my skin, "I would never let any harm come to someone you hold dear."

I cleared my throat. "Would you excuse me? So I can speak with her?" Before Kiran could respond, I scurried away, weaving through the crowd to get to her. As soon as I did, the fog in my head cleared, but the blaze of his touch remained. His voice rumbled behind me as he engaged in a jovial, if not forced, conversation with some high fae lord, most likely.

I had to get away from him.

I made it halfway across the ballroom when a firm hand gripped my shoulder. Thick fingertips dug into the crevice beneath the bone. I halted and turned, though the hand remained, squeezing too tightly to be friendly, though I imagined no one around could tell it was inflicting pain.

"I've been looking forward to meeting your acquaintance, Your Majesty," the high fae male before me said. His words slithered as they escaped his full lips. Vibrant red hair fell across his face and practically blended into the ceiling above, seeing as he stood two heads taller than me.

His fingers dug sharply into my shoulder, but I gritted my teeth in defiance. I would not let this fae bully see me as weak. But his fingernails seemed to grow under my collarbone, and I winced, no longer able to hold in the pain without a reaction.

As soon as I did, he released his hand and returned it to his other, interlocking them in front of his chest.

"Calias, King of Charshon. And you are?" he asked with a feral smirk.

"The queen of Naenden, as you've already said."

Don't be smart with this one.

I gulped at my magic's warning.

Calias's dark pupils overtook his sky blue irises for a moment, but he blinked, and they returned to normal.

So Calias had an icy rage. The hairs rose on the back of my neck, and he grinned, as if he could sense my body's flight response. Like an animal. Like a predator.

The music changed, the strings humming and forming into a waltz. "May I have this dance, Lady Queen?" He extended a hand, a dark ruby ring upon his thick forefinger.

That wasn't a question.

My mouth went dry, but I heeded my magic's advice for once and took his hand. His skin was clammy, cold. He pulled me in, too close for my comfort.

I had a feeling that was on purpose.

When he placed his other hand on my waist, I bit back a shudder. He smirked. "Your hand goes atop my shoulder, Lady Queen."

Right. I did as I was told, and when the beat of the music bellowed in full force, he dragged me into the waltz, sweeping us in circles that made me dizzy and had my feet aching for solid ground. Nausea crept up my esophagus as his fingers caressed my waist.

"What do you want?" My voice trembled, and I hated myself for it. For being afraid. For showing him my terror. I wanted so badly to break his hungry stare, to search for Kiran and Lydia among the crowd. To call out to them with just a fearful glance. But I wouldn't look away first. Not for all the pride I had left.

"Just to meet you, is all," he said, his blue eyes flickering. "What is your name, young human?"

I clenched my teeth and swallowed.

Before I could remind this fae that he should know my name, given I was an Alondrian queen, my magic said, *Tell him your name. This is not a fae you want to anger.*

"Asha," I said.

"*Asha*. Hmm. A bit boring when it rolls off the tongue, isn't it? Yet, you. You are not a bore at all, are you, young human?"

I didn't answer.

He flung his arm up and spun me around, guiding me with my hand as he might a horse with a bit. It didn't exactly soothe my aching stomach. When he caught me in his arms, amusement swarmed his face.

"When I heard the King of Naenden had slaughtered his young human bride and her lover, I can't say I was shocked. I was there the day he picked her as his bride. The day he plucked her out of the safety of her home just to spite his father. It was only time before the poor girl's affections wandered. Imagine how homesick a human girl might be, to be shipped from prosperous Avelea to this wasteland against her will. No wonder she resented him."

"They were in love at some point," I said, though I had no idea why I was defending Kiran of all people.

This fae likes to play games, Asha. Don't allow him in your head. Though I would advise the same regarding Kiran...

"Is that what he told you?" Calias flashed his teeth at me in a grin. Was it my mind deceiving me, or were all but his front teeth pointed at the tips? "I suppose he would perceive it that way. When it comes to the object of one's obsession, one's mind is often all too eager to paint its own narrative."

"I thought you said he married her to spite his father," I said through gritted teeth.

"Oh yes. That might have been how it started out. But the rumors... Well, there was talk among the kingdoms that the king of

Naenden had formed an—shall I say—*unhealthy* interest in his human bride."

"Is that so?" I asked. "From what I've gathered about most fae rulers, their definition of obsession would be simply having frequent conversations with their queens."

My magic groaned within me. *I have joined myself to a fool.*

Well, it's not like you were invited, so serves you right, I spat back.

But if my comment sparked anger in Calias, there was no hint of it on his face. Instead, he chuckled—a slippery sound that made my stomach uneasy.

"I can see why he hasn't killed you yet. You must provide more entertainment than he's had in a while. But tell me, young queen, how did you convince him to spare you that first evening? We both know you didn't seduce him." He nodded to the left side of my face with the upward tilt of his eyebrows. "So how did you pull one over on the King of Naenden?"

I don't like what he's doing. He suspects there is something different about you. Don't let him onto it.

Believe it or not, I am capable of coming to these conclusions myself, I retorted.

"We've already discussed this. I talked with my husband. This might be a foreign concept to you, but even fae kings need company."

"Mm," Calias said, pursing his plump lips. "I would not offend your company by lying to you, Your Majesty. I don't believe you've been honest in your retelling. Rumors making their way through the kingdoms tell a different story. That you have entranced young Kiran every evening with a tale. A tale with no end. Tell me, Lady Queen, where did you get the idea for such a preposterous thing?"

"I've always told stories. It's what you do when you're too poor to have adventures of your own," I said.

Nice.

I don't need your commentary right now, I thought.

"Still, it's difficult to imagine a story so compelling that your husband was willing to shame himself, to go back on his public decree, just for it to continue."

"You must not be well read, then, if you don't have the imagination for it," I said.

A black pit crawled from Calias's pupils, staining the blue of his eyes, but just for a moment, before he regained his composure.

"Oh, I have the imagination for it. I even have the imagination to dream that there is something missing to this story. That there is something, shall we say, lurking under the surface. And, Asha, I am just as committed as your husband to discovering the truth of the matter."

He spun me again with such force, such precision, I might as well have been a puppet flung along on a string. When I rounded to face him again, his voice went quiet, so I could barely hear it under the sound of the minstrels' tune. "Tell me, child, do you fear your husband?"

CHAPTER 49

ASHA

*A*nd there it was. The reason Calias was here.

The trouble was, I didn't know how to answer him.

His eyes widened in surprise. "You don't know whether to fear him, do you? Perhaps you're more akin to his late bride than I'd assumed."

I clenched my teeth.

"Tell me, child. How does he do it? We both know it's not his charm."

"The king has spared my life." Again, why I was defending Kiran, I did not know.

"Hm," Calias said. "How disappointing. I might have thought I could convince you to be my friend."

His hand tightened on my waist, and I had to choke back a scream as his fingernails bit through the fabric of my gown and scraped my skin. I tensed, readying to break myself from his grip, but there was no need, for a larger, darker hand intercepted it.

Kiran's.

"Surely you thought better than to lay a hand on my wife," he growled, the undercurrent of his voice crackling as the temperature in the ballroom swelled.

"Oh, come now, Kiran. We all know *you're* not laying a hand on her. Even you have standar—" But Calias did not finish his sentence, for he was forced to save his breath for a stifled scream. The grinding of bone grated against my ear, and when Kiran released Calias's hand, it looked as though an elephant had stepped on it.

As Calias drew his hand back to his chest, onyx met cinders as he and Kiran met each other's glares. For a moment, I thought they might lunge toward one another, or that Calias would erupt into flames. Kiran certainly looked ready to wield that sort of fate, his fists gleaming red, his military coat white hot.

"Careful there, young king," Calias hissed. "I might be quick to heal, but breaking bones is even better than a formal signature when it comes to declaring war."

My hands trembled at the threat. Charshon was known for its military prowess, and if Calias was right, Kiran's assault wouldn't be taken lightly by the Council, either.

Could Naenden survive if the Council ruled against us?

If Kiran's thoughts had taken a similar path, he didn't show it. Instead, his lips curved into a menacing smile, the kind of expression I imagined Nagivv must make before slaughtering her dinner. "Oh, I doubt that very much," he said. "I imagine that nephew of yours—he is your heir, isn't he? I imagine he and I could come to a peaceful agreement with little trouble."

Calias gritted his teeth in response to the threat that couldn't have been veiled if Kiran had sent the entire ballroom up in smoke. But then Kiran flicked his wrist, and Calias's eyes widened as dark plumes fled from the Charshonian king's nostrils. Panic flooded his ice blue eyes, and he grasped for his throat, gurgling and...

Oh.

Kiran was suffocating him without as much as laying a finger on him.

"Now," Kiran said, the low rumble of his voice barely audible over the minstrels' strumming of the lyre, "speaking of acts of war, should it ever cross my ears that you have as much as made my wife squeamish in your presence, I will personally crown your nephew at his coronation ceremony."

The smoke dissipated, and Calias gasped for the fresh ballroom air, his pale eyes bloodshot.

Lydia and Fin appeared at my side, and I hoped Dinah hadn't been foolish enough to follow them. But then Calias gained his composure and straightened his dress robes, his eyes cooling into that haunting blue.

"I was only asking your Queen to bless my ears with that story she's been weaving for you. From what I hear, she's quite talented," Calias said.

"Leave," Kiran said, the single word shaking in rage.

"Very well, then. I wish you two a long and fruitful marriage," he smirked before sauntering away.

"I hate him more than I hate you, Kiran," Lydia said, her violet eyes trailing Calias to make sure he actually left.

"On this, we agree," Kiran said, his growl rumbling before he stalked off.

* * *

AFTER WE RETRIEVED Dinah from the hallway outside the ballroom, where Fin had convinced her to stay after noticing Calias dancing with me, Fin escorted both of us to the gardens, just in case Calias was stupid enough to stick around and Kiran riled enough to lose his temper.

In the evening chill, Dinah clung to my arm, and I tried to numb the parts of me that Calias had touched, the bits of skin that reeled and squirmed and made me want to vomit.

There'd be a bruise on my waist later, that much I was sure of.

I couldn't allow Kiran to know that. He might have been convinced that he could slaughter the king of Charshon without invoking war with the rest of the kingdoms, but I wasn't so sure.

Fin was talking, chattering nervously with Dinah, but I wasn't listening, as much as I might have wanted a distraction from that slick, terrible voice of Calias's.

The lychaen hadn't worked, so he'd switched tactics.

He'd wanted me to go away with him. That was what he had meant, when he'd said he hoped we could be friends. No doubt he wished to drag me back to Charshon, probably to experiment on me. To find out how a human had harnessed magic, to unearth some way to use that information as a weapon.

A weapon against Kiran.

Against my husband.

That was what terrified me, what struck me to my core.

Calias was clever enough not to ask that treasonous question without confirming that I hated my husband enough to run away.

Something which, apparently, I hadn't convinced him of at all.

That fact alone was enough to fuel my nightmares for a week.

Because, in that instant, I'd defended Kiran. Calias could have freed me, could have snuck me out of Naenden. He was a monarch, meaning he had the resources to keep Dinah and my father safe, too, if I had only asked.

And when I decided I wasn't interested, it hadn't been out of fear of what Calias might do to me.

I wouldn't think about the reason, not if I had to bury it under a thousand layers of loathing. Not if I had to scrawl a list in those juvenile letters of mine and rehearse it every day—a list of all the horrible things the King of Naenden had ever done.

A ledger detailing every reason Kiran was not fit to be loved.

Someone cleared their throat behind us. I whipped around to find Kiran, still dressed from head to toe in his spotless military uniform, watching me, barely noticing Dinah and Fin.

Fin rubbed the back of his neck before offering his arm to Dinah. "Might I escort you inside?"

She locked eyes with me, a silent question brimming beneath her thick eyelashes: was I okay to be left alone with Kiran?

I nodded, without pondering too deeply why.

Fin smiled and whispered something to Dinah as he lead her away.

"He's gone," Kiran said once the others were out of earshot.

"Good." I crossed my arms, shivering in the gentle garden breeze that suddenly seemed so brash against my exposed shoulders. "It seems yours and Lydia's plan for the ball was a success."

He rubbed his temples and gritted his teeth. "Yes, unfortunately, we have no proof of such. Nothing to bring forth to the Council. Not unless he confessed to sending the lychaen after you."

I shook my head. The council. We'd learned about the Council during the short years I'd attended school. It was a union between all the kingdoms of Alondria, made of up of the kings who ruled. The purpose of the Council was to maintain harmony between the kingdoms, and if one entity threatened the peace, such as attempting to steal another kingdom's queen, the Council had the authority to take action.

"What did he say to you?" he asked.

"He knows about my stories, and he suspects there's magic behind them. He's curious how a human could end up with such magic. I think he came here to convince me to run off with him."

Kiran raised a thick eyebrow. "And you didn't take him up on it?"

I hugged my torso even tighter. "I don't exactly envision a better life as his slave than as yours."

Kiran bristled, his molten eyes flashing like lightning. But he gained his composure quick enough. "If he asked you to leave me, that might be enough to convince the Council to take action."

"He didn't though. He only implied it by asking me whether I was afraid of you."

The words slipped out, and it was only when Kiran went stiff that I realized I'd said too much.

"What did you say?"

The heat on my cheeks flirted with the cool brush of the evening breeze, and my throat caught. "Nothing, really. But that was enough for him to decide I couldn't be trusted to walk away on my own, I suppose."

Kiran stepped forward.

I didn't retreat.

"He seems to think you have some sort of spell over women or something." I wasn't sure why I said it. Why I said anything around Kiran, why my thoughts always spilled out before him like water from a cracked clay pot.

When Kiran spoke again, his voice was low, soft, as if not to drown out the echo of music carried from the music hall into the garden by the draft. "Do you trust me to give you a proper dance?"

I bristled and didn't answer. Not with my words, at least. Maybe because I knew if I let my mouth open, I'd say something nasty, push him away.

For the life of me, I couldn't figure out why that was the last thing I wanted.

"May I?" he asked.

My neck craned on its own, nodding without any authority from me. He took my hand, then grazed my waist with the other. I winced, and he frowned, deepening the furrow on his brow. "What's wrong?"

"It's nothing."

"Asha."

"Really, it's nothing."

"Asha."

I swallowed, knowing good and well I was going to regret what I was about to say next. "Calias wasn't happy about me refusing him," I explained.

Fire flashed in his eyes, and his throat bobbed. "He'll die for that," he said. "He doesn't get to survive hurting you."

"What if I asked you not to hurt him?" I said. He frowned, and I tensed. "I just don't want you in trouble with the Council. A few bruises...they're not worth losing..." My mouth went dry, and I continued, "It's not worth losing the stability of the kingdom."

He cocked his head, but his expression softened, and he grazed his hand up my dress toward my ribcage.

Then, we danced.

Slow and rhythmic and unrehearsed, not at all like my dance with Calias. Kiran pulled me close, and we swayed, the music so muffled through the walls, all I could hear was the downbeat.

Which was getting all but masked out by his quickening pulse as I leaned my cheek into his chest.

Warmth flooded me with each thrum of his heart, which knocked against my ear harder and faster with each step, as if it were trying to get my attention, desperate to rouse me from a waking dream.

"Asha?" Kiran said, and this time my name on his lips sent a shudder down my spine.

I swallowed and, despite myself, found my fingers caressing the back of his coat, stretched thin across his muscular back. "Yes?"

"I need you to know something."

"Mhm?" My throat went dry.

"Would you please look at me?"

My breath caught, and I hesitated. There was something about swaying in his arms, the left side of my face tucked into his chest, that felt so ordinary, but in a good way. If anyone were watching us from the shadows, all they would see would be a devastatingly attractive fae king dancing with a pretty girl in a pretty gown.

Most nights I didn't care much about being the pretty girl in the pretty gown.

For some reason, tonight was not a typical night.

"Please," he whispered. "I'd like to see your face."

Such a simple statement, so ordinary sounding, except that it dug its way under my ribs and jabbed me in the heart.

So I let him see me, trying with all my might to control my trembling, loathing every bit of advantage that he had over me. When I craned my neck, there was nothing between us but his warm breath caressing my cheek. That he could sense my breath quickening, that he could feel my fingers tremble against his firm back, that he could sense my skin prickle—and not from the crisp air. That he could hear my heart thudding, that undercurrent of longing—it terrified me.

That to me, now that I could no longer hear the beating of his heart, he was still just a statue, as difficult to read as script written in another language by a child new to writing.

Except for his eyes. Now that I looked at him, the tense bulge in his jaw, the narrowing of his thick brows.

I could still see his eyes.

And I knew for a fact they gave away more than mine did.

They'd gone molten again, but this time, instead of a fierce, boiling lava, instead of the berating sun in the middle of the Sahli, they'd gone light, almost as white as his military jacket, except with a hint of that golden aura that seemed to radiate through the surrounding air.

"I am so sorry for what I did to you... I...my soul is restless around you, Asha. I can't..." He lowered his face, so that his forehead pressed into my hair. "I can't even apologize, not really. Because it wouldn't be genuine. I wouldn't mean it."

My heavy, waterlogged heart plummeted, and somehow, he must have felt that too, because he said, "No, that's not what I meant. I am deeply sorry for every bit of hurt I've brought your way. For forcing you to make decision after decision that must have ripped your heart to shreds. For putting you in a position where...where you had to be so immensely brave. My tutor used to tell me that true bravery rips the soul wide open. That there's nothing that hurts more than being truly courageous. And that, if one lives through their bravery, they're rewarded with a heart immune to being ripped open by anyone else. And you've been so brave, Asha," he said, tracing his hand up my back and caressing the hair at the nape of my neck.

His fingers twisted, tangling themselves in my hair. "But I can't truly be sorry. Not really. Because I know, deep down, that if I hadn't been so entrenched in my pain and self-pity, if I hadn't allowed my heart to turn to stone, then I'd have never set out to take revenge on all those innocent—" Kiran stopped there for a moment, choking on his words. He clenched his jaw and squinted his eyes shut, as if he were having to fight to push the next words out. "All those innocent girls. And if I hadn't done that, then I would have never..." His chest heaved as he lifted those white-hot eyes to mine.

The hand still clutching mine caressed my palm, thumbing circles into my skin as if to set the cadence of his words, leaving behind tiny rings of fire I secretly hoped would never go out. "I would have never met you, Asha. And that's the worst part. Now, more than ever in my life, I know I am selfish. Because if I was given the choice to go back and do it over again, I know I'd make the same decision. Because to choose differently would be to choose to have never met you."

His face was so close to mine now, so close I felt that, if I breathed, there would be no air between us to inhale, only smoke and steam and his crackling firewood scent that threatened to suffocate me, if I would only let it.

"Kiran, I—" I swallowed and took a step back, willing myself not to trip over the tulips behind me. With space between us, I could breathe again, though barely. The distance cooled enough of the dense heat to allow room for the truth of his words to slither through me. To sink in. My next words came out only through sheer force of will, though the fog in my head wanted nothing more than to melt into him. "I can't give my heart so someone who's only changed to be with me. I'm not strong enough."

Kiran's voice quaked. "But Asha, you're the strongest person I know."

I sucked in enough of the chilled air to sting at my nostrils, to clear my head as the breeze sent needles jutting through my forehead. "No one is strong enough to carry the weight of someone else's soul."

Kiran took a step back, sealing the uncrossable gap between us, the chasm that had always existed, threatening to swallow both of us whole if we chose to ignore it.

But we couldn't ignore it, not any longer.

Kiran straightened. The stiffness returned to his shoulders, his spine, though his eyes didn't darken. "You're right. As usual," he said, and the corners of his mouth tilted into the most unconvincing smile I'd ever seen, a lifeless crescent swamped by an empty, starless sky.

"Kiran, I'm so—"

"No, you don't apologize to me. Please," he said, and then he turned away.

I watched him as he strode out of the garden. When he reached the palace doors, he paused, then tipped his chin toward the ground. "Asha?"

"Yes?"

"I'll never let any harm come to you."

I nodded and tried to blink away the tears, as if I could reabsorb them, shove them back through the ducts from which they'd escaped and pretend they never existed.

Perhaps I could do the same with the invisible current that pulled me toward the male who would only end up sweeping me under.

All the same, I managed half a whisper. "I know."

CHAPTER 50

ASHA

Kiran didn't call on us for the story that evening. Again.

"Where do you think he is?" Dinah asked, concern weighing down her delicate brow.

I bit my lip. The most comfortable answer would be to claim that Kiran was looking into my attempted kidnapping, that he was looking into Calias, but that would only worry Dinah.

But, then again, Dinah wasn't stupid. She had witnessed enough in the ballroom to know that Calias was bad news. In fact, she had been the first to spot the creep swinging me like a rag doll across the marble floor and had alerted Fin, who had alerted Kiran.

Or I could spill my guts about my sneaking suspicion for why Kiran hadn't called on me this evening. What had happened in the garden only an hour ago, emotions I'd yet to work out myself, much less untangled the words necessary to express them to someone else.

That wasn't my favorite of the two options.

"He and Fin are probably trying to work out which charges to bring against Calias when they go before the Council," I said, which I figured had a high probability of being true.

Dinah scrunched her face and sat up straight on her pillow. "I don't think so. I saw Fin heading in the directions of his rooms when I came in."

"How do you know where his room is?" I asked.

Dinah blushed. "Because I run into him in the hallway sometimes when I come to see you, and he told me one time that he was taking dinner in his room that evening, and he told me that was where he was going, so when he walked in that direction tonight, I assumed…"

Laughter erupted from me, which was unfortunate since it sent a surge of pain through my waist where Calias had gripped me with those abhorrently long fingernails of his. "I wasn't accusing you of anything, Dinah. I just didn't know where his room was, and I couldn't think of how you could."

"Oh, right," she said, grinning sheepishly. But then her expression shuttered and went right back to business. So much for distracting her. My sister could be as relentless as a woodpecker when she fixated on something. "So if he's not with Fin trying to figure out evidence against Calias, where do you think he is?"

I shrugged, flopping on my back and burying myself into the comfy sheets. "I don't really keep up with him."

Dinah's expression narrowed into a glower. At least, the closest thing to a glower Dinah could manage on that delicate face of hers. "You know I can tell when you're hiding something from me, right?"

I wasn't sure that was true, since Dinah hadn't the slightest idea when I had offered myself as the sacrificial bride for the king, but I didn't want to hurt her by saying so.

Her mind seemed to dart to the same place, because she sighed. "Just because I don't always say anything doesn't mean I don't notice. I just don't enjoy pushing anything out of you."

"So, why are you pushing now?" I grinned, poking her in the side.

"Because, until now, your story has been keeping you alive. I want to know why it's stopped," she said.

"I don't think my story has been what's been keeping me alive for a while now, Dinah," I said. "I think…I think Kiran's changed his mind."

"You call him Kiran now?" she asked. I expected a raised eyebrow like Lydia might use, but all I found were wide eyes, absorbed in my life, my happiness. You'd have thought I'd have gotten used to that by now, Dinah's ability to empathize. It was just so contrary to my nature, I had a hard time remembering she always came from a place of genuine concern. Not that I didn't consider myself a genuine person, it was just that my candid nature came with sharp edges. Hers didn't.

"We're on friendly terms, I guess." As I said it, I realized it was true. Though I knew I could never love Kiran, not in the way I'd loved— still loved—Az, I found my heart had thawed toward him. Into something I figured could resemble friendship one day, if nothing more than that.

I wondered if I should tell him such. I hadn't made that clear in the garden, that though I could never bear the burden of his soul by loving him, that I figured I could at least lend a friendly hand.

"Did something change between you?" Dinah asked.

I shot up and threw a pillow at her, to which she collapsed on the bed squealing. "Why are you so obnoxiously perceptive? Aren't the sweet ones supposed to be oblivious?"

She giggled, tapping the pillow on my forehead in return. "Supposed to be. But only because we've spent so much time pretending so we can spare everyone else's feelings."

"You deceptive little twerp!"

"Now you're just stalling."

I groaned and flopped backward onto the bed. "Kiran might have implied that he had feelings for me."

"What? What do you mean he *implied* it? And what did you say?"

"I just mean he didn't come right out and say it. He just, well, he got very close to my face and basically told me I was the bravest person he's ever met."

Clearly I hadn't sufficiently glossed over the part where Kiran got close to my face, because Dinah's eyes bulged, and she asked, "Did he kiss you?"

Heat crawled the length of my neck at the memory of his forehead pressed against mine, his breath hot on my cheek. "Of course not. I stepped away."

Dinah frowned, the crease between her eyebrows hollowing out.

"Don't worry, Dinah. I really do believe him. I don't think he's going to off me just because I spurned his advances," I said.

Dinah waved a dismissive hand in my direction, a motion I had never seen her use, not even when she'd been frustrated with the fae vendors refusing to contribute their surplus to her food bank. "I'm not worried about that. Of course, he's not going to hurt you. If he was, it would have been the dozen of other times you've offended him."

My jaw plummeted.

"Why did you pull away?" she asked, but then her dark eyes narrowed in disapproval. "You're still in love with Az, aren't you?"

"Dinah," I huffed.

Dinah bit her lip and opened her mouth, as if to push the subject, but she clamped it shut once more.

"This has nothing to do with Az," I said. *Yes, but that doesn't mean you're not still grasping at those pitiful feelings for him, does it?* "It's about Kiran. Dinah, he was fully prepared to wipe out the human population one by one. He would have killed a girl, just like yourself, every month, if I hadn't stepped in. Why would I want to kiss someone with that kind of capacity for such evil?"

"Everyone is capable of evil," Dinah said, as if the counterargument to that statement wasn't sitting in the flesh before me.

"You're not," I said.

Dinah tucked her knees into her chest. "Just because everything turns all rosy before it comes out of my mouth doesn't mean I'm not constantly filtering out the other thoughts."

I sighed. "Well, Kiran didn't filter his evil out, did he?"

"You don't know that he would have killed the girls," Dinah said.

"Yes. I do. The only reason he didn't was because he hates cliffhangers and wanted to know how a measly human got her hands on magic."

"That's not true, and you know it," Dinah said.

"Then why do you think he kept me alive those first few weeks?"

"Because he saw you were a real person, not some conniving creature he'd made up in his mind. He felt guilty about it. I know he did," she said.

My back stiffened against the cedar headboard. "Even if that's true, he only felt guilty because he didn't expect any of the women to sacrifice themselves. If it hadn't been for me, he'd have killed the first girl who was chosen. And the next. And the next."

Dinah straightened, her tiny chin held high. "You talk as if you were handpicked by the Fates themselves."

"What do you mean by that?" I asked, my voice shooting higher, growing more domineering than I'd ever used with Dinah.

"You really think that, out of all the young women in Meranthi, you were the only one willing to sacrifice yourself for the others?"

Her words struck the unguarded fragment of flesh in my heart that I left exposed for her and her alone. I balked. "I'm not saying that I'm some moral goddess. I just mean, there aren't that many women in Meranthi in my situation. Ones who didn't have a future, who could have offered themselves—"

"If you're talking about your scars, those were never going to take your future away from you. Asha, you are the bravest person I know. I'm not saying you're not. But if it hadn't been you, it would have been someone else. Someone would have sacrificed themselves."

Broken fragments of glass tinted with my sister's voice stabbed at my heart, and the worst part was, I couldn't quite pinpoint why. I couldn't distinguish between the hurt of knowing my sister's idealistic worldview detracted from my sacrifice, and the shame that I'd gotten it into my head that my sacrifice somehow made me different. Made me better than all the others, the beautiful young women I'd always known would grow up and marry and have the life I'd never quite been able to give up dreaming of.

"He told me that if he had the option to go back and do it over, he wouldn't have done anything differently. That no matter how evil that decree was, he wouldn't be able to change it, not if it meant that he'd have never met me. Dinah, I can't love someone who would choose to do harm to others, just so he could have me."

Dinah placed her tiny, fragile hands on my cheeks and stroked my scars, almost absentmindedly. Like she used to do when she was falling asleep, when we'd shared a cot back at home. "Do you think there's much use?"

"To what?"

"To asking someone to go back in time and change their decisions? I don't think even the Old Magic could do that."

"That's not the point. It's not about whether it's possible. It's about the fact that, even if it were possible, he wouldn't do it anyway."

Dinah's eyes drooped, then went sharp, focused and present. "But, Asha. If you ask Kiran to remain in the past, how will you ever change his course in the future?"

"Love doesn't change people. Not really," I said.

"If not love, then what?"

The question hung between us. Any answer I might have given fled from my mind as soon as it reached my lips.

Dinah stood from the bed and slid her feet into her slippers. "Thank you for what you did for me, Asha. I love you," she said, placing a kiss on my forehead before turning to the door.

And then she was gone.

And for the first time in my life, I realized I had fought with my sister.

CHAPTER 51

ASHA

*D*espite the fact that Calias, King of Charshon had most likely sent a lychaen to kidnap me not too long ago, despite the fact I'd fought with my sister for the first time in, well, *ever*, and the man I'd loved my entire life had eloped with a fae female who was practically a stranger—how he'd even managed to rope a fae into marriage, I'd yet to figure out—I found myself in fairly decent spirits.

And that would not do.

Because I should not, for any reason, have been in decent spirits.

Abysmal spirits, sure.

But Kiran had reached for my hand under the table at breakfast that morning.

And because I refused to accept the elation that had surged through every nerve in my poor, unsettled stomach, I'd dismissed myself from the table, telling myself it was just gas.

And then I drowned myself in the library.

Well, I didn't drown myself, not in actual water. The activist in me would have found that shameful in the middle of a desert town full of parched, poor humans.

Instead, I drowned myself in books, and that seemed to be enough to divert my attention elsewhere. Which was exactly what I needed. A diversion. A distraction. A diversion. An interference. All of the above.

All of that to say that, despite my better judgment and moral code when it came to privacy, I couldn't help but revel in the thrill of the chase when I found the next note scribbled in the corner of a fae romance I was reading.

Finally, a real distraction, I thought, instantly feeling guilty, of course, as it was at the cost of Tavi's privacy.

Well, until I actually read what it said.

It's done. Our ally is in.

I scanned over the message three times, trying to decipher whether I'd misread any or all of the letters, but after the third pass, I decided I had been correct.

What an odd love letter to write in the margins of a book. The pages thudded as I slammed it shut and went in search of another to read. It wasn't right, invading Tavi's personal love letters. How had I felt when Kiran had dared to comment on mine and Az's relationship? And Az wasn't even dead. Az hadn't even courted me.

That deep, aching drumbeat started up in my heart again, and I rushed back to the book, if only for something to steer that unending sadness away.

It didn't sound right: *It's done.* What was done? And why would two lovebirds be discussing an *ally?* Not a friend, not a companion. An ally.

Then I remembered that whoever Tavi had loved had promised to keep her name a secret. Perhaps her boyfriend had been fully fae. I kept forgetting that Tavi was only half-fae. Now that I thought about it, I realized I didn't even know if marriage between a half-fae and a fae was legal. Perhaps they'd been looking for an ally who would advocate for their marriage union.

But, then again, humans could legally marry fae. Obviously. And I had never heard of any marriage laws that discriminated against the half-fae.

353

The thought of Tavi being unable to marry the one that she loved sent my mind zooming back to Az again. To his warm hand on mine. To those biting words in the garden.

And something new, too. Guilt twisted my stomach for even thinking of him. For remembering so fondly the warmth of his hand on mine. And then I was thinking of Kiran. Of *his* hand grazing mine, *his* heart thudding against my ear as we danced, of how, the night Dinah had fallen ill, he'd propped himself next to me in bed, his fingers hovering suspiciously close to where I'd tucked my thighs under the blankets as he attended to my story. The story Az had never allowed me to talk about, because he'd claimed it brought up too many negative emotions. And how Kiran had gazed at me with those molten eyes, the ones that had set a fire in my chest—

I cleared my throat and went to work searching through the books.

* * *

THREE LABORIOUS HOURS LATER, I found it. Well, one of the *its*. It was tucked into the last page of a very dull-looking book on the accounting practices of mid-century Avelea. But there it was, all the same.

Gardens tomorrow. Sunset. Say hello to Tionis.

As I didn't have anything better to do, I figured I might as well make a visit to the blood-bather himself.

* * *

WHEN I OPENED the white double doors to the garden, the cool, steady breeze caressed my face, invigorating me. Not that I needed much of anything else to get my feet skipping and my heart pounding and my limbs hurrying.

Running from my heartbreak over Az and my unspeakable feelings regarding a certain fae king, straight into what was turning out to be a mystery, was plenty enough for that.

"Tionis, Tionis, Tionis," I whispered to myself. Lydia had mentioned her father purchasing a statue of him the day we'd gone for a walk in the garden, the day she had blown the breakfast room to smithereens. She had promised to hang Kiran's body from the statue's fingertips should he ever lay a finger on me.

Unfortunately, Kiran laying his fingers on me was the absolute last thing I wanted to think about at the moment.

Are you sure about that? Because, unless I'm mistaken, it seems Kiran laying his fingers on you is exactly what you want to think about.

I don't remember consulting your opinion, I seethed.

No, but you would do well to inquire more often.

I ignored the snickering in the corners of my mind. I was one step closer to solving a mystery, and I wasn't going to let my magic ruin it for me. Propelled by my rekindled enthusiasm, I practically skipped through the pebbled path until I caught a few of the palace guards staring at me.

"Hello!" I said in a voice that sounded much too much like Dinah's to have come from my throat. It didn't exactly help to alleviate their suspicious looks. One of the guards propped up against the stone wall that surrounded the garden, leaned in and whispered something to his companion.

"Excuse me," I said, figuring I might as well recruit their help. At least then it would look like I was not trying to hide anything. One of them raised his eyebrow at me, but I continued anyway. "I'm looking for a statue, or maybe a memorial, I'm not quite sure. But it's of Tionis."

The guards exchanged confused looks, but then one of them shrugged and stepped away from the wall. "Of course, Lady Queen. It's this way."

"Thank you," I said. I practically had to jog to keep up with the tall fae's pace. Apparently, Tionis was at the opposite end of the garden. By the time we reached the statue, pride was the only thing keeping me upright, rather than heaving for breath with my hands on my knees.

"Here he is," the guard said, motioning to the massive monument to Tionis, who was a handsome male, as all the fae were, I supposed, except that he had the look of a pampered prude smeared across his nose and upper lip.

That, and he had an extra toe. Not that I could say much about having an odd amount of body parts that were supposed to come packaged in even numbers.

Still, something about the image of him soaking his extra-toed foot in the blood of his victims churned my stomach a little extra.

"Thank you very much," I said, nodding toward the guard.

"Do you need anything else, Lady Queen?" the guard asked.

"Oh, no thank you. I was just curious about this statue, is all. I read about it in the library and wanted to come see it for myself."

Apparently, my tendency to hole myself up in the library and not come out had made its way around the palace, for a look of understanding replaced the confusion on the guard's face, and he actually smiled. "Very well. Good day, Lady Queen. Let me know if you need my assistance."

"Yes, thank you…" I paused, realizing I didn't know his name.

"Rayes," he said, and he blushed a bit. I wondered if Lydia went about asking the guards their names. My guess was probably not.

"Thank you, Rayes," I said, and he walked away.

Once I could no longer hear his footsteps, I counted to thirty, figuring he could still hear mine. Though I wasn't sure why, as the instructions in the book had simply said to say hello to Tionis, not scale the statue or blow it up or anything.

"Hello," I said, just in case it was as simple as that.

I stared at it for a bit, but after a few minutes, my neck cramped, and my pride as well. I felt a bit like an idiot just watching the statue as if I expected it to talk back to me.

So I figured it was better to explore it instead. I approached the statue and placed my hand upon the stone, deceptively chilled in the pleasant garden, but I found nothing unusual.

What were you anticipating? Another secret door?

Don't mock me, I thought, *We already found one in the library. Why would it be so strange to find another?*

But my cheeks went hot nonetheless. I circled around to the back of the statue, wondering whether there was a secret entrance on the other side, but the back seemed just as solid as the front. I even knocked on it a few times, but it didn't sound hollow.

Something rustled in the leaves behind me, and I jumped, causing that uncomfortable vibration within my bones that gave me the unpleasant sensation that my magic was laughing at me.

I chose to ignore it. Especially once I realized the cause of my distress had been a bird, which was hopping from one leaf to the next. I smiled at it. It reminded me of home, the little scavenger. I had always thought their dark feathers, red eyes, and long beaks were quite unattractive, but for the first time, I didn't loathe the nasty creature. There wasn't much of home in this place, except for Dinah and occasionally Father. What a happy surprise that someone had bothered to put a crow in the garden.

And how strange.

I cocked my head and peered around. Exotic parrots and colorful song birds flitted by, rustling the bushes. There was even a peacock that was known to strut around like it owned the palace. Why would anyone have brought a common crow into this sanctuary? At first, I supposed it must have flown over the wall, but then I remembered that the garden was surrounded my a magical membrane, one that trapped the cool air within. One that wouldn't allow a bird to fly through. I'd seen them before, pecking against the air as if it were solid.

I scanned the area, but none of the guards had meandered to check on me, so it seemed. So I tucked my head and pushed myself through the bushes. Unfortunately, these bushes were the type that came to a point at the tip of the leaves, and they scratched at my cheeks as I waded through them.

Eventually my face slammed against the stone wall.

Can we be done, now?

I rolled my one eye before wrestling myself out of the bushes. I stood before Tionis with my hands resting on my hips. Az had told me that during his travels to Avelea during his merchant's apprenticeship, he'd met someone who'd told him of a secret passageway into the palace. If only I had been a little less distracted by his proposal and had pushed him to tell me exactly how he got in that night. It couldn't be a coincidence that Az had gotten into the palace grounds through a secret passageway in the gardens and that the lovebirds writing in the library notes had planned their secret meeting in the gardens as well.

There is another statue of Tionis in the palace, you know.

I crinkled my brows. When the realization hit me, I almost smacked myself in the face.

Of course there was another Tionis.

Fin had pointed it out to me in the servants' wing the day I'd first met Nagivv.

I practically raced across the palace, sure that, if I searched the statue carefully, I would find some lever that opened up a passageway, some note carved into the statue's exterior, some ancient script that served as a key, much like the writing over the fireplace in the library.

When I finally arrived in the servant's wing, the only thing I found was Nagivv, licking her paws at the eleven-toed feet of the statue.

CHAPTER 52

ASHA

"You're distracted," Lydia said as she swung a wooden pole at my head. I ducked, but as I looked up, I noticed the pole hovering just above my forehead. "You're too slow. That would have smashed your skull if I hadn't lifted it at the last second."

"I'm aware of that," I grumbled, standing back up and placing my sparring stick in a defense position, which I considered a fluid term, since there was no way this piece of wood was going to do me any good if Lydia suddenly decided she wanted me dead. "Why are we even doing this? I'm never going to be fast enough or strong enough to defend myself from a faerie if one ever attacks me. You can teach me as many strategic moves as you want, but the most I'm going to accomplish is amusing my attacker."

"Exactly," Lydia said, stalking me. I groaned and shuffled my feet to face her. As confident as I was that Lydia was skilled enough in fighting that she knew exactly how hard she could land a blow without causing me any permanent injury, the welts on my back still hurt like crap, and my bruises from our last training session had only just turned yellow.

"What do you mean, *exactly?*"

"I mean, that you're prepared at all will catch them off guard. Even if it only gives you a few seconds, seconds can make the difference between life and death."

"Haven't we established Calias doesn't want to kill me?"

"Do you trust him to pick kidnappers that won't give in to the allure of snacking on your flesh?"

I grimaced.

Lydia rolled her eyes, stalking a circle around me like the predator she was. Man, would I hate to be someone she actually wanted dead. "Would you rather work on your magic then?" she asked. "If you're so confident your human nature is too much of a disadvantage to make fighting worth it, perhaps we should take another stab at your strengths."

"Yes, I'll just paralyze them with my fast-paced narrative and buy myself enough time for you or Kiran or Fin to come rescue me," I said, but then I lurched, crying out as pain rippled through my belly. "Ow!" I yelled, grasping at the place where Lydia's stick had just collided with my stomach.

"What?" Lydia said, shrugging. "You said it yourself. You'd rather keep fighting."

"That's not what I said at all," I grumbled under my breath, but Lydia's attack seemed to have the desired affect anyway, because I dropped my stick and walked over to one of the dark, dusty bookcases and plucked a scroll from the wall.

"Un-uh," Lydia said.

I shoved the scroll back into its place on the shelf. "I couldn't conjure up a butterfly without them," I said, turning to face her again.

She placed her hands on her hips and flashed a grin that could have flayed the hide off a boar. "Then we start with a caterpillar."

* * *

NEEDLESS TO SAY, no caterpillars were conjured during our four-hour training session. Not even a caterpillar egg, for which I was immensely thankful, as I thought I might vomit if any of those materialized. Especially if they looked anything like spider eggs.

Blech. I retched twice during training just thinking about it.

Even Lydia, the Princess of Collected, allowed her frustration to show when, on the four hundred and thirty-fifth attempt, not even a stray tail of smoke furled from my voice, which happened to sound just like my own, as my magic refused to participate.

Just like I had told Lydia it would.

"Alright, that's it. We're done for the day," she said, gesturing at some invisible conjuring that should have been there, according to her, yet wasn't, according to me. "Meet back here tomorrow at nine."

At least she's not making us get up so early.

I was pretty sure I would have rather gotten it over with.

* * *

Why are we down here? If I recall correctly, we aren't supposed to be meeting Princess Lydia again until morning, my magic complained.

Maybe you were asleep, I thought.

You need more practice in veiling your fishing remarks. If you want to know something about the nature of my existence, you could just ask me.

I huffed, *Fine, do you sleep ever, or do you just eavesdrop on every one of my experiences?*

Are you referring to the romantic evening with the king you've been hoping for ever since the night of the ball?

I hissed, which echoed off the stone walls of the secret library, where I had decided to sneak into after dinner, hoping that, if I could convince my magic to at least try to conjure something, then maybe I could persuade Lydia to go easy on me tomorrow too.

We just talked and danced that night, I thought.

Mhm.

I thought if I wanted to know something, all I had to do was ask, I pushed.

I said that was the best way to get information out of me. Not that I was obligated to answer.

Well, then maybe stop bothering to ask me what I'm up to, I thought.

Why do I have the feeling you're going to tell me anyway?

I groaned. My magic wasn't wrong about that. As I scanned the room, the countless scrolls, my heart skipped. All that power my magic could conjure from the words scrawled into the pages before me—the power to materialize, the power to *make*... But could it do more than it was letting on?

Listen, I said, though that immediately felt silly, as I was pretty sure my magic was always listening.

It's a plague, really. Perhaps I should have chosen a host whose mind wasn't whirring with twelve thousand unrelated anxieties every waking moment.

I groaned, *They're all related, okay? Trust me. Besides, I'll gladly deposit you with the swine if you'd like. Maybe that would solve my problem of whoever is coming after me.*

Perhaps another time.

After lighting the discarded lamp, I read the inscription on the other side of the fireplace behind us, and the wall reappeared, sealing us inside for the moment.

"I know you are capable of more than you'd like Princess Lydia to know about," I said, continuing my admonition once I was confident no one could overhear us from the library.

And how do you reason that?

"Because you don't even bother to try when she's around."

Has it ever occurred to you I don't enjoy making a fool of myself? That I don't take pleasure in others witnessing the limits of my power.

"I know that's not the reason, so help me."

Help you do what?

"Help me conjure something. Something that could protect me. Something that could protect us if Calias sends someone to take us again."

I'll aid you by infusing your words with the power that dwells in this room. But I'm too tired to come up with a tale at the moment. You'll have to do that yourself. Besides, are you planning on carrying the entire library on your back at all times?

I ignored that comment, mostly because I hadn't figured out the answer myself. Yet.

Comforting.

"Shut up," I said. Then I shimmied my shoulders, shaking out the nerves, or attempting to, at least. I wasn't looking forward to my magic witnessing my limited skill in oration.

"As the Queen of Naenden gazed at the... As Asha looked at the scrolls surrounding her, she felt the power of their Otherness tingling at her fingertips—"

This is compelling prose, really. Stop talking about yourself and just speak of what you wish to conjure.

"The hidden room in the library was no longer a room at all, but a forest." I paused, but nothing happened. The room was definitely still just a room.

What kind of forest?

"A rainforest?" Still nothing.

You aren't even convincing yourself. How do you expect to convince this realm?

"Okay, fine," I said, taking a breath, closing my eye, and channeling the voice I'd so often resented for overtaking my throat, "*Hidden deep within the broad leaves of the tallest tree in the rainforest, a parrot peered down upon the Queen of Naenden. As he cocked his head to the right, the vibrant red feathers around his neck bunched, and his indigo and yellow tail feathers—I don't know—rustled or something. What a strange voice this woman had, he thought. One he'd very much like to imitate, as he'd become bored with imitating the travelers who frequented this forest. He'd memorized all of their voices and could impersonate each of them well, as long as the person he was trying to prank believed they were hearing their friend from a distance. But even the pranks had gotten old, and this woman's voice...well, it was deep and resounding, and hardly sounded like a woman at all. In fact, he thought the voice might be especially good for pranking, as it had almost frightened him off of his perching branch when he had first heard it.*

"*'Is anyone here?' the woman called.*"

"Is anyone here?"

I jumped, that sentence echoing more loudly than it should have off the stone walls. As if... I opened my eye, and before me sat a parrot, perched upon the podium.

"Is anyone here?" he asked again, his head jerking from side to side, the magnificent colors of his feathers brightening the drab room.

My heart leaped. "We did it," I whispered.

"We did it," the parrot echoed.

Ah, yes. We summoned a parrot. Should anyone attack us, I'm sure we could sick the bird upon the trained attacker until it plucked said kidnapper's eyes out.

I shrugged, my elation too high at the sight of the majestic bird, who looked real enough to touch, that even my magic's snarky pessimism couldn't bring me down.

"Now to try something else," I beamed.

"Now to try something else," said the parrot.

At least someone agreed with me.

CHAPTER 53

ASHA

Sore and defeated from a morning wasted training with Lydia, I didn't have the energy to leave the library once my sister-in-law decided I was a lost cause.

I had to admit, continuous failure had left me in a foul mood.

It didn't matter that, after conjuring the parrot, my magic and I had managed to materialize a monkey as well. That didn't mean my magic would perform for Lydia.

And so my fresh, purpled bruises bandaged my yellowing ones, though I did manage to block at least three of Lydia's blows.

I was pretty sure it was only because she felt sorry for me, though. She had asked me to breakfast afterward. Needless to say, I hadn't been in the mood.

By the time the vizier walked in, there were over a dozen piles of books, not so neatly stacked, sprawled across the floor as if in a desperate attempt to take cover as I wrenched them off the shelves and ripped through the pages.

"Looking for something?" he asked, a wiry brow lifting.

"Yes," I said, the behemoth of a book in my hands almost too heavy for my wary fingers to hold onto. "Has anyone ever bothered to organize these shelves? You'd think in the palace library there'd be a pattern, an organization system or something. They're not arranged in any sort of order," I huffed, hoping that I could at least force all my aggravation into the lack of structure in this library, rather than send it hurtling toward the vizier.

"Actually, it is organized," the vizier said, then, sweeping his eyes over the wreckage of books in the floor, he added, "Or, at least, it was."

"What do you mean?" I asked, sure that it wasn't possible that both Dinah and I could be so uneducated as to overlook a sensical organization system.

"It's organized by author name and the first character of the book title. Just not in our language. The library system was set up over five hundred years ago, back when our ancestors spoke an ancient tongue."

"How is that helpful? Does anyone know that language anymore?" I asked, dully.

"Only scholars. Thankfully, a few of them keep the library directory updated. I'm sure they'll be thrilled to come back in and, erm, update their catalog after they hear what you've done with the place."

"I'm sorry. I'll clean it up," I said, slumping and a tad embarrassed. Had I really been irritated with Lydia this morning, or was I simply ignoring the scattered mess of feelings that had pooled in my chest since the parade? Since the ball.

Since yesterday morning at breakfast, when Kiran's hand had brushed mine under the table.

There was a reason I would be eating in my quarters today.

"With the careful organization system you've used to make sure everything goes back where it belongs?" the vizier asked, his eyes practically chuckling for him, though not a hint of amusement escaped his mouth.

"Is there any way I could get my hands on this directory?" I asked, sheepishly.

"Actually, it's made public," the vizier said.

I snorted. "Public? Why? The public isn't allowed in the library."

"As I've told you many times, my dear queen, I do not make the rules."

I actually smiled at that. "Right. Would you mind bringing me a copy? So I can clean up my mess?"

"I'd be delighted, actually," the vizier said. "The scholars who organize this place are so snooty and up in their own educations, they're a pain to deal with."

He strode from the room and came back a few minutes later with a huge scroll. "There you are. Organized by author name in the order of the ancient runes, but translated into our language," he said.

"Thanks," I smiled. "Really. And thanks for not getting on to me about the mess."

The vizier turned around, his blue eyes glittering. "I've been informed my favorite queen has had a difficult few weeks. I'll resign my post before making such a time worse."

My eyes burned, although I had no desire to cry in front of the vizier. "But you won't resign before you make me clean up my own messes? Even on a difficult week?"

The corners of the vizier's lips tugged upwards. "I find organizing therapeutic." Then he strode away, and I found myself alone once again.

It took me a good five minutes to find a section of floor clean enough and large enough for me to roll the scroll out. Eventually, I found a spot in the northwest corner of the room, and after heaving a few stacks of books out of the way, I smoothed out the crisp parchment on the floor.

It read:

Directory of Books and Scrolls
Naenden Palace
In order by author name
Translated into the Common Tongue by Rathe and Nosti

Veringtan the Fifth
To Rule the Unruly (608 p.r.)
Of Bowels and Exploits (790 p.r.)
The Weary Minstrel (690 p.r.)

Lost in the Sahli (740 p.r)
Rules and Wagers (1023 p.r.)
A Game of Will (803 p.r.)

I allowed my eyes to slip down the page, the boredom of having recognized none of these names or book titles opening the dam where thoughts of Az and his new bride were threatening to drip through and unleash a flood. Eventually, in the third column, I found a book I'd actually read.

Even better, I found a book the secret admirers had read too.

Horatiaunus the Ancient
Charshon Tax Law (1805 p.r.)
Avelean Tax Law (1803 p.r.)
Naenden Tax Law (1804 p.r.)
Laeien Tax Law (1803 p.r.)
Mystral Tax Law (1805 p.r.)

Charshon Tax Law. It was the book with the note that read, "Gardens tomorrow. Sunset. Say hello to Tionis." Fairly sure this was an official document, not just a copy, I refrained from grabbing a quill from the library desk and circling the name of the book. Instead, I kept a finger on it and scrolled down the rest of the columns with my right hand.

Selvius the Lovesick
To Love a Human (2026 p.r.)
To Seal a Bargain with a Kiss (2028 p.r.)
The Forbidden Merchant (2030 p.r.)
Love and Fae (2029 p.r.)
Death and Betrayal (2031 p.r.)
Love doth not Wait (2025 p.r.)

There. *The Forbidden Merchant.*
The romance book that had been inscribed with, "I'd wait a

millennium if I thought I'd have the slightest chance of seeing your face again."

It didn't take me long to find the next. A Naenden law book, the one containing the first note I'd found, the day Kiran had accused me of manipulating him.

My nostrils should have flared at the memory, but I found myself grinning at his rashness. That was bad news, so I shook Kiran from my head and replaced him with the note. *"I can't stop thinking about you."*

Probably the kind of note Az's new bride might have written to him.

The thought sent a wave of hurt through my bones, and I kept looking until I found the last book on my internal list, *1001 Ways to Serve Sythgreens.*

Three more days.

I really wished I could scribble all over this with a pen, because the more I looked at them, the fewer connections I could find between the books. Some were history, some romance, one was even a simple cookbook. The authors had names that didn't sound similar at all, and they were all written in different years.

Sighing, I lifted myself off the floor and strolled over to the desk, where I found some loose parchment in the drawer. I grabbed the quill and settled back in my spot next to the directory.

What was I missing?

Then I felt stupid for grabbing the pen and paper, because I wasn't sure what to write, where to begin. Figuring I had to start somewhere, and the words would just come to me eventually, I wrote all the book titles that contained notes in a column. Then I stared at that column for quite a long time before I pushed the parchment away and strode to the first bookshelf on the library to the left of the cedar doors.

There his name was, Veringtan the Fifth. It took me two trips, as Veringtan wrote epics, but I transferred our entire collection of his work to my brainstorming space. Then, I turned pages. And pages and pages. Finally, on the sixth and last book, *A Game of Will*, I found a note.

Been a while. You look better than I remembered.

My heart did somersaults. Maybe it was an author's sixth work on the list? Or perhaps the last volume listed? But when I checked my theory with the other books on my list, it didn't pan out. One book was the first listed under its author's name. Another was the third.

I groaned.

How long would it take me to go through every book on this list?

* * *

THAT NIGHT, I waited in my chambers for Dinah to come, but when the knock sounded on my door, and I invited her in, it wasn't Dinah who entered, but Kiran.

My face went as hot as the sweltering aura that seemed to emanate from my husband, and I jolted from where I'd been lounging in bed. "Oh. I—I thought you were Dinah."

In fact, I'd been avoiding Kiran since yesterday at breakfast when his hand had grazed mine, sending my mind catapulting to all sorts of unsavory places. I'd even gone as far as taking all my meals in my chambers.

Kiran smiled, a half grin that almost appeared shy, hiding beneath his beard that just so happened to be trimmed perfectly to frame his insanely angular jawline. "She sent word that she got caught late at the stall. Tavi came by my quarters to inform me, so I could determine what to do for the evening. And, well, I thought I'd ask you to tell me a story."

"I'd hate for Dinah to miss any of it."

"Then perhaps you could tell me a different tale? One you grew up telling, that way Dinah doesn't have to miss out?"

"I don't always get to choose which story my magic will tell."

"I don't want to hear your magic's story. I want to hear one of yours."

A smile tugged at my lips, despite myself. "I'd like that."

"Good. Me too." He closed the door behind him, and my throat constricted. Then he strode across the room and plopped on the floor, still too polite to dare sit on my bed. I followed suit and sat next to him, leaning against the bed frame.

"Well," I said, raising my palms to the ceiling, "What sort of story are you in the mood for?"

To my surprise, the color in his face deepened, and I replayed my words in my head to figure out what I could have said that was so embarrassing. But then he shook his head and said, "Your favorite."

"Oh, well, in that case, I'll tell you a story I told Dinah every night for years when we were growing up."

"How fitting."

"Long ago, because as you know, all stories must take place in the distant past lest we be forced to think too much about their modern applications..."

He chuckled at that, but I sent him a faux glare, and he pursed his lips.

"Long ago, there was a princess. Because who would want to hear a story about a pauper? Unless they were extraordinarily beautiful, but that's beside the point, I guess. Well, this princess found herself being courted by an equally attractive prince—they have to both be attractive, because that way you know they're the two people who are supposed to fall in love."

"Naturally," Kiran said, nodding his head.

"The prince was more exciting than any of the other princes she'd been forced into courting. In fact, he was so interesting, it was hard to believe he was a prince at all, as princes' jobs are fairly stuffy and not nearly as interesting as they'd like others to believe. Well, one night she followed him as he left the palace, and when she did, she found he lived, not in his own palace, but in a shabby tent on the edge of town. And this shabby tent was full of all sorts of things, things he'd clearly stolen. His mother was there, ill and bedridden. As the princess watched, he presented his mother with the food he'd snuck from his very date with the princess that evening."

"I can see how that would be a problem."

"Well, not at all. Because they're both the most attractive people in the story, you see. And while most women would have had nothing to do with a man who lied about his identity, witnessing the thief care for his ailing mother only made the princess love him more. Because that's how love works."

Kiran grinned, his perfect teeth gleaming, wrinkles forming around his molten eyes. "Is it now?"

I shrugged, glad for an excuse to hide with my bunched limbs the heat blotching my neck. "So they say. Anyway. Then she married him and made him a prince, and they lived out all their days under the sun and probably died within hours of each other, they were so in love."

Kiran tried, unsuccessfully, to stifle a laugh, and my lips broke into a grin. "You should have asked for my magic's storytelling. It's much better at it than I am."

I'd say.

Kiran examined the callouses on his thumbs, then lifted his eyes to meet mine. "I don't know. I believe I prefer yours all the same."

Warmth spread deep in my belly, flushing my legs and waist. "It's my insightful social commentary, isn't it?"

He shook his head, his eyes gleaming. "It's your brutal honesty. It's so genuine. So pure. I envy it, in a way."

The snort that escaped my nostrils was about the most unattractive sound I had ever mustered. Of course, I'd wait for this moment, alone in my room with the King of Naenden, to reach my peak awkwardness.

And why should that matter to you?

I pushed my magic, far, far back into the recesses of my mind, as far as the dark corners where I'd once stuffed away the memory of obtaining my magic.

If I wasn't mistaken, I thought I heard a muffled grumble.

"What?" Kiran asked.

"You're *fae*. Why should honesty impress you? You are literally incapable of lying."

The corners of Kiran's smile flinched, and the wrinkles around his eyes sagged, but the grin remained all the same. "Being unable to lie and telling the whole truth—those are two different things entirely. We fae like to wallow in the muddy line between the two."

Something uncomfortable clenched in my chest at the idea of Kiran and Lydia and Fin all being expert deceivers. But was Kiran even talking about himself, or was he referencing his horrible father? As far as I knew, Kiran didn't know what their father had done to Lydia, how he had abused her. Did he sense his father had been deceptive by omission? By hiding the assassin he'd formed within his daughter's heart from his son, the heir to the throne?

As I had only a handful of coping mechanisms for such discomfort, I reached for the nearest in my mind and plucked out one of my personal favorites—self-deprecation as a means of deflection. "Like when merchants who wanted to make a deal with my father would compliment me by saying I was a vision to behold?"

Kiran tried not to, but my comment had the desired effect on him. He coughed and put his fist to his mouth in an attempt to disguise his laughter, but he wasn't fooling anyone. There was no one in the world around whom people put their foots in their mouths more than me. So I continued. "Never mind that they neglected to specify what kind of vision I was. Nightmares are visions too, you know."

My comment stifled the sound of Kiran's laughter, and his dark ember eyes seemed to melt in a white fiery glow. His jaw went slack and his cheeks softened. "I think you're stunning." His gaze lingered around my mouth, sending through me a simultaneous flood of desire and the suffocating urge to cover my face and all its blemishes under the nearest pillow.

"Yes, I stun people into losing their speech when they see me," I said, trying and failing to dilute the blatant self-deprecation with a chuckle.

"No." He frowned, taking my hands in his. Heat, and something else I didn't recognize, prickled up my arms from the places his callused fingers touched my skin. "I think you're beautiful."

Pain swelled into a lump in my throat. "And what kind of work-around is that? It's not polite to tease me about my lack of education, you know, if there's another definition of beautiful that I don't know about."

There was no smile on his face now. No hint of teasing. No jokes. No games.

Only intense, unadulterated desire.

Crap.

My heart accelerated.

"Only the truth," he said, his white-hot eyes boring a hole through the very intentional walls I had erected around my heart.

But I could work around that. "Oh, I see," I said, though my throat was closing up now, and I was becoming ever more aware of how he stroked my hands in his strong but gentle grasp, tracing the lifeline of my palms with his thumbs. "You said '*you're* beautiful,' not that I *look* beautiful. Because beauty can be an inner attr—"

I stopped talking.

But only because his lips were on mine.

He'd cleared the space between us faster than lightning could strike, faster than the jolt of shock and euphoria could travel from my lips, crashing down the rest of me in a rushing wave. His kiss was firm but gentle, hesitant and intentional, urgent and patient and unyield-ing, all at the same time.

I melted into it, into him.

When he pulled away, something deep within me ached.

I sat there, mouth ajar, the remnant of his kiss still smoldering, lingering on my lips.

Kiran's eyes widened and flickered, a wildfire behind those irises of his. When he spoke, his voice was rushed, gravelly. "I apologize. I shouldn't have—" He cleared his throat and stood, turning toward the door.

It had almost closed behind him when I found the breath for words. "You could stay a little longer. If you wanted."

Maybe it was the way he was back in my quarters within a second, maybe it was the intensity burning in his eyes, or maybe it was the way he'd scaled the room in the blink of an eye, his mouth on mine before I had time to process what was happening, but it seemed he wanted to after all.

CHAPTER 54

*A*s much as the Old Magic enjoyed tormenting Asha about sharing her consciousness, he was not one to disrespect the privacy of a loved one. So at the first hint that the King of Naenden wanted more than just a story, at the first sign that Asha returned his desires, the Old Magic had made haste to distract himself.

It had hardly taken any time at all to transport his thoughts back to the story of Mother and Farin. In fact, any time he allowed his mind to drift in that direction, he would find himself completely absorbed in its tale. Even though it appeared evident by this point that Kiran's intentions toward Asha had altered and that her life no longer hung in the balance of this never-ending story, the Old Magic had grown fond of its characters, the manner in which they acted independently of his will.

As if they had minds of their own.

As if they were the ones telling the story.

He found himself worrying on their behalf.

That was silly, he reminded himself, considering they weren't real, and he could give them a happy ending if he wanted to.

Of course they couldn't have been real. It wasn't as if he had that sort of power, to know things he shouldn't have otherwise known.

Besides, the characters, the places, the voices—they were the abstract sort, the kind of faces whose details he'd found himself having to fill in for his hearers' benefit, the features he'd been forced to guess at to create a full picture.

So they couldn't have been real. He was the one who'd made them up, filled in the empty spaces, padded the areas of their character that would have made them seem one-dimensional.

Yes, that was all it was—a story that had gotten away from him.

He was more than sure of it.

TEARS FLOODED Mother's face as she watched her kinsmen shove her friends to their knees.

Friends.

That's what her magic had given her, really. Its power flowed through her veins, a power she should have anticipated when the magic informed her that magical abilities varied based on the body in which it inhabited.

The magic.

Her magic.

That's what she'd come to call it, come to realize. She'd thought it was a creature at first, a creature with the power to grant her access to magic.

But the voice inside her didn't harness magic at all.

It *was* magic. Its very essence, wrought from the fabric that bound the worlds, separated them into hundreds, thousands, millions of realms.

It was a thread loosed from the invisible blanket that inhibited the realms from bleeding into one another.

And it was hers.

And it had given her friends.

Because her magic was not one, but many.

The others—its siblings, as it called them—had found their own homes, forged their own bonds, all with humans, just as her magic had done countless times before it had found a vessel to outlive the rest.

But now they were caught.

Soon her friends would be dead.

She had only just made them.

At least the others were out running errands. Perhaps they'd be delayed in returning. Perhaps they'd stay safe.

A fae guard dressed in an armor of forged metal—a specialty of Alondria—grabbed Anika by the hair at the base of her neck and twisted, shoving her to the floor of the dingy cottage Mother had come to consider home. Anika cried out in pain, and Mother lunged for her, but the sharp backhand of a nearby soldier cracked against her cheekbone. Spots the color of blood spattered across Mother's vision, almost disguising the face that had struck her.

Almost.

Except Mother would have recognized a patient of hers anywhere.

There was something about clinging to the hand of a dying male, anchoring him to this side of the sun, pulling him back from the brink of death, that branded his face in one's memory. He had been a member of her tribe, back before Father had crossed through the Rip and brought them over to safety, back before he'd become their savior and turned the prey into predators. She'd healed him after a mere attack. Father had wanted to put him out of his misery, but she'd laid across him, stood between her husband and the helpless male, begging for more time.

He spat in her face.

Anika whimpered, chattering under her breath what must have sounded like nonsense to the guards as they dragged Malik from the room next door. Blood stained his dark forehead, pouring from a gash the size of mother's forefinger. She crawled toward him, her bare knees scraping the wooden floor. If she could just touch him before…

Something lurched through the door. A fiery orange mass blurred across Mother's vision as a fox lunged itself at the fae twisting Anika's neck. It plunged its teeth into his hand, defending its friend, her nonsensical muttering having summoned him. The fae male yelped and snapped his arm, sending the fox flying across the room. Its body smacked into the wall, sliding and landing limp on the floor.

The sight reminded Mother of Teeth, the playful Other that had become Farin's pet. The dog—as she now knew to call it—who occasionally accompanied her son when he made his public appearances.

The fae male on behalf of whose life she had once pleaded yanked her by her ankles until splinters from the floor lodged themselves into her forearms. She rolled over and kicked, but he was stronger, and he only twisted harder on her leg.

Her knee snapped.

Her magic healed it before her mind could even register the pain.

The fae male's eyes widened as her twisted leg righted itself under his grip.

She took the opportunity to spin, throwing her weight to the side and knocking the male off-balance. He stumbled, loosening his grip on her foot lest she pull him to the ground with her. She slid from his grasp and hopped to her feet, slipping his knife from his side as he fell.

The knife's serrated edges, meant for ripping through human flesh despite the fact it was unnecessary, despite the fact that fae could snuff the life out of a human in an instant, painlessly, without much effort, glittered in the candlelight, begging to be used upon the man who hadn't remembered.

The male who'd begged for his life, and when she'd granted it, had spat in her face.

His eyes widened. Unnecessarily, though he didn't know that.

She wouldn't kill him.

Not because she was a healer, not because she'd fought off Death since she was old enough to beat roots into dust with her homemade mortar and pestle. Not because her magic had amplified those gifts, allowing her to heal others with the slightest brush of a hand, teaching her to mix the herbs of this new world into salves and potions and antidotes that could erradicate plagues, not because killing was contrary to her very existence. Not because she'd never taken a life before.

She hadn't.

But only because she was saving it, that first kill. Saving it for *him*.

That male witnessed what you did, her magic warned, as it always did, so afraid of who might come for it if the secret of what she could do reached the wrong, pointed ears.

I meant for him to, Mother thought back.

She uncurled her slender fingers and allowed the knife to clank to the floor a hairsbreadth away from his reach.

Then she turned on the others, their faces gaunt with fear.

They were stronger, faster.

But what could they do against a fae whose body healed itself before the damage was inflicted?

If they were wise, they'd listen.

"Release my friends," Mother said, trying her best to slow her racing heart as it fretted over what could go wrong if the fae twisted too hard against their fragile human necks.

"That's not our orders," the one to blame for Malik's blood said.

"Whose orders, Aechen?" Mother asked.

The fae male trembled, betraying the truth, telling Mother all she needed to know. That he remembered.

"Surely not the orders of the male who commanded your father and mother slain?"

Aechen's lip trembled, but Mother sensed him tighten his grip around Malik's neck. Malik shot her a questioning look, as he often did, and she returned it with the slightest tilt of her head. A request to trust her. "My father and mother were a threat to the tribe, a threat to themselves," he said, his voice lacking the coldness Father would have preferred in a soldier.

"Is that what he told you to comfort you?" Mother asked.

Aechen swallowed.

"Yes, I believe it was. And did he tell you of the root I'd mixed for them, one that would soothe their groanings, render them peaceful until they met their natural end with open arms, holding the hand of the son they adored?"

Aechen's hand trembled around Malik's neck. The other two fae didn't move.

She knew why.

It had been foolish of Father, haughty, to send these three.

But that must have been the problem with being utterly cruel. If a kind person committed a cruelty, they'd remember it forever. If a cruel person committed a cruelty, well, it must have been like trying to recall what one ate for breakfast on a particular day a decade ago.

He simply hadn't remembered.

But Mother had.

These fae had.

"I begged him to let me help them," she said, measuring her words. "Reminded him what they'd done for our tribe when we were only children. Begged him to allow me to do this one thing for our elders, the male and female who'd kept our tribe safe when we were but help-less babes. He stole the root mixture from me. Hid it. Told me I could have it back when there was a younger fae who needed it, someone who stood a chance of bringing food into the tribe, rather than wasting it."

Aechan's hands twitched.

So did the fae next to him, as well as his brow. She could read the question on his face—this fae whose wife Father had ordered murdered because she had disobeyed the laws and become pregnant.

Because her pregnancy would have put them all at risk. The female hadn't even screamed during her execution, lest she attract the Others and put her husband in harm's way.

Mother had borne Farin a month after the female's death.

Aechen released Malik, who heaved a sigh of relief, stood, then patted the fae male upon the back as if he were a friend.

Perhaps now, he was.

Anika seized the opportunity to rush over to the fox, to scoop it up in her arms and cradle it, whispering words no fae or human could understand. Her tears stained the fox's pelt, as she put her hand on its chest and felt the shallow ebb and flow of its ribs.

She brought it to Mother.

Who healed it with a touch.

Because that's what Mother did. She healed. She restored. Not just her own flesh, but that which belonged to others. Mother could mend frayed garments with a brush of her hand, render a rotted grape as ripe as the day it was plucked from the vine, all with the gentlest touch.

You shouldn't show them your gift.

They're friends, Mother explained.

Her magic rustled uncomfortably inside her.

It was the perfect moment to ask her question. The question whose answer she already knew before it formed on the fae's lips.

Except she was interrupted by another sound, another voice, another question.

"Mother?"

FARIN HAD GROWN. Mother had known that, of course, she'd seen him in the ridiculous parades his Father had forced him to join.

But up close, his hand resting upon the doorway to hold up his sturdy frame, he looked like a man.

He was a man, she realized, pain seizing her gut.

She'd missed it. She'd missed it to the point that she hadn't recognized his voice. Only the word. The word she'd dreamt of hearing every night for the past eight years.

Mother?

He barely had the chance to stumble toward her before she'd wrapped him in her arms, her tears soaking his too-broad shoulders, shoulders that hung on a wide frame, one that should have still been tiny, fragile.

"I've found a way for us, my son," she whispered as her tears soaked his sandy hair. "I've found a way."

CHAPTER 55

ASHA

The next morning at breakfast, I didn't flinch away when Kiran's hand brushed over mine under the table. Didn't wish away the soothing heat that washed over me at his gentle touch.

I did, however, take one too many furtive glances across the table at Lydia and Fin to be sure they hadn't noticed a change in the air.

"If I have my breakfast on my face, you can tell me, Asha. We're friends after all," Lydia said.

I blushed, but Fin answered before I could. "She's not staring at you, Lydia. She's staring at me."

"And why would she do that?" Lydia asked.

"Because I'm so handsome. Obviously."

Kiran stifled a laugh, but not well enough. Lydia and Fin snapped their gaze at their eldest brother, then slowly traced the path between his face and mine. Back and forth, back and forth.

They looked like they'd been hypnotized.

Well, except no one could mistake Lydia for being under anyone else's influence. Ever.

She opened her mouth then, mercifully, shut it before placing her napkin over her porridge and standing from the table. She cleared her throat, but when she spoke, her voice was calm as the face of a cat before it pounced. "Kiran, may I speak with you in private?"

He shot an apologetic look in my direction, then slipped his hand from mine before standing and following Lydia out of the breakfast room. I returned to my porridge, noticing for the first time how fascinating it was to count all the little black specks in the grain.

When I chanced a glance at Fin, he was still staring at me, his eyes wide with horror.

"We didn't—"

Fin's neck turned the color of fresh beets, and he shook his head like a dog trying to shake water out of its ears, even as he raised his palms in front of him. "I didn't ask."

For some reason, my fumbling lips couldn't seem to catch onto the escape rope Fin was tossing me. "But I just wanted you to know that nothing... Well, not exactly nothing... But nothing like you're thinking—"

"It's fine, Asha. You have nothing to be embarrassed about. You and Kiran are male and wife, unconventionally so, perhaps, but these things happen."

The muscles in my windpipe clamped down, causing my attempted throat clearing to come out sounding more like a squeal. Nothing had happened, nothing more than kissing. And then we had talked, Kiran and I, until we'd both fallen asleep against the baseboard of the bed, my head on Kiran's shoulder, his forehead resting in my hair.

Fin must have recognized my distress, because he took in a deep breath. When he spoke, his voice was low. "If you're not okay, if he's pressuring you to do anything you don't want to do..."

If my face had flushed before, now it was as red as a river reflecting the sunset. "No! Is that really what you think of him?"

The grimace on Fin's face was answer enough. My heart sank. Right. Kiran had killed Fin's wife. They weren't exactly on the best of terms. Fin tolerated Kiran, but mostly to numb himself to his brother's existence, not because there was any love between the two of them. But Fin and I, well, we'd become friends, had been so before Kiran and I had become…whatever it was that we'd become.

You mean married.

Now was not the time.

"I…" What was there to say? Fin looked up at me expectantly, but what was I supposed to tell him? That I was sorry that Kiran had killed the love of his life, but that he really was a good person when you took the time to get to know him?

For some reason, that didn't seem like it would land the way I wanted it to.

Fin smiled grimly. "I just want to make sure you're happy. Are you happy, Asha?"

Well, no. Not anymore, I wasn't.

"If he hurts you. At all. Ever. I want you to tell me," Fin said.

My breakfast threatened to make a second appearance. "He's not going to."

"For his sake, I hope not."

I didn't have to ask what Fin meant by that. The onyx that had consumed his fiery eyes told me enough.

* * *

KIRAN AND LYDIA were gone by the time I left the breakfast room.

She'd probably dragged him halfway across the palace so she could lecture him in peace.

Nerves shifted in my stomach, as if my mind couldn't decide whether I was floating from my evening with Kiran, or sinking from the fact that the weight of my feelings for Kiran had landed on Fin.

But of course they had hurt Fin. We were friends. Friends who had bonded over the pain Kiran had caused us both.

And Kiran and I were too many conflicting things to count.

Opposites, in temperament, in experiences.

Enemies, because wasn't that what fae and humans were? Well, I definitely didn't feel that way about Fin and Lydia, so it wasn't fair to feel that way about Kiran.

Did Fin and Lydia ever threaten to kill you? Ever force you to perform rituals where they decided whether you were worthy to live through the day?

Well, no.

But, that was just it. As much as Kiran had threatened, he'd never actually laid a hand on me. Never actually hurt me. Any time he'd had a chance, he'd relented.

And that somehow excuses his behavior?

I snapped, *If this was how you felt about him, why didn't you speak up last night?*

I make myself scarce during such situations.

At least I could find comfort in that.

It was almost as if the Kiran I knew, and the king who'd ordered innocent girls to be slaughtered every mooncycle, were two different people. Two distinct entities who shared a name but nothing more.

There was no other way to think about it. Because the King of Naenden was unlovable.

But Kiran.

Well, Kiran, I'd grown to...something. I'd grown to something Kiran. I couldn't think of a certain forbidden word, not with Fin's disappointed face looming in my mind.

But something.

I could think something.

Because surely Kiran was worthy of at least that much.

For the first time, it occurred to me that he hadn't had what I'd had, a realization so strange it didn't seem possible. Because how could that be said of a king? But it was true. I'd had parents who loved me, who cared that I grow up to be a decent human being.

But Kiran.

That phrase is starting to grate on my nerves.

His father had forged the evil in Kiran's heart. The paranoia, the anger, the need to project strength and brutality. It hadn't been there to begin with, not within the child who'd loved literature more than combat. And sure, Lydia and Fin had the same father, at least in name, but not at all in person. Lydia's father had tried to break her, not forge her, and Fin's father had ignored him.

But Kiran reneged on his decree. He had been willing to show weakness to his kingdom, to the entirety of Alondria, because he didn't want to hurt me.

Let's not forget how he strangled then unleashed his Flame upon your friend's wife.

The pit in my stomach twisted. That wasn't exactly to his credit, but when he had explained it to me, I'd understood. And Ophelia had been plotting to kill Fin...

The battle between the long list of sins Kiran had racked up and the softness I nurtured toward him in my heart became too much to bear, too tangled to sort out. Fondness for Kiran—it was like being cut, but after the scab had crumbled, and only soft, pink, untouched skin was there to take its place.

How many times can a cut heal before it leaves a scar?

Somehow, my feet found their way to the library all on their own.

If I couldn't sort out how I should feel about Kiran, I'd at least solve the puzzle of the notes in the margins of the library books.

I pulled out the directory and took another look, just to be sure I hadn't circled the wrong books or anything.

I hadn't.

In an hour, I made no progress, despite my using the directory as scratch paper—for which I would surely pay with a stern look from the vizier. My mind had almost given in to thinking about Kiran again.

But then I noticed that whoever had ordered the books in the directory hadn't done it by the date of the books' publication date. They must have organized them alphabetically in that ancient language. I grabbed the quill and scribbled down the works of *Veringtan the Fifth*, but this time I ordered them by date. *A Game of Will* turned out to be his fifth work, chronologically speaking.

My motivation renewed, I tried the same technique with *Charshon Tax Law*. Sure enough, it was the author's fifth work.

Not bothering with the quill and parchment this time, I ran my fingers over the next author's list until I found the fifth in order by date. When I reached the shelf, I found a small teal book wrapped in a patterned paper covering.

The note was on the second to last page.

Of course I do. I've been upgraded.

I jerked my head back, confused by the meaning of this particular message. Regardless, there was no use trying to figure it out. Not until I had all the notes lined up in order, at least.

* * *

BY THE TIME I finished the list of notes, my stomach was growling, throwing fairly intense threats my way. On my loose piece of parchment, I had rearranged what I figured was the entire conversation in order, noting the two distinct handwritings.

Been a while. You look better than I remembered.
Of course I do. I've been upgraded.
Pleased with the change?
Bored.
What if I could change that?
I'd think you a fool with aspirations that outspend your station.
Perhaps my true station outranks my supposed.
Am I supposed to believe you on faith, or that handsome face?
Gardens tomorrow. Sunset. Stand and watch Tionis.
Too dangerous.
I waited all night.
All night?
I'd wait a millennium if I thought I'd have the slightest chance of seeing your face again.
Tomorrow? Same place?

At this point, I noticed the one with the boxy handwriting had written two notes in a row.

I can't stop thinking about you.
Then we're of one mind. Did you give thought to my words?
Yes. I'm agreed. Expect next note two weeks following Starfall.

It happened again, the same handwriting twice.

It's done. Our ally is in.
Meet me. Tomorrow.
Three more days.
Two more days.
Tomorrow.

Then, in the same handwriting again. That last note.

Your name will die with me. Know that I loved you to the end.

MY MIND RACED. Clearly, there were conversations I was missing. The couple had talked when they met at the statue of Tionis. But about what? Whatever it was, it seemed the one with the boxy handwriting had needed to take time to consider it. Perhaps it was a marriage proposal?

That's not seriously what you think was going on, do you?

I gulped. Tavi seemed so sweet, so gentle. And she'd been my first ally here, other than the vizier.

You're just using that word in your head to make it sound like it's a word someone would normally use for a friend.

My magic was right. The term *ally* gave me pause. It was the one word in the string of notes that made my stomach turn lopsided, that indicated these were more than simply love notes.

Have you forgotten about that part about being upgraded? Who talks about themselves like that?

It was true, it certainly wasn't the most endearing thing to write, but for all I knew, it was meant in jest, and the humor simply didn't come through in the writing. And why did one of the lovebirds seem to think it was too dangerous to meet the other in the garden? Why did they have to hide their relationship in the first place?

And what changed on Starfall?

And why did one of them know they were about to die?

Maybe this isn't Tavi, I thought to my magic, and a stark nausea lingered in my throat. Something wasn't right about these notes, and it made me even more uncomfortable that I couldn't quite put my finger on it.

"Lady Queen?" a small voice asked.

The voice ripped me out of my thoughts, and I spun around. Tavi stood before me, looking down at me with a pleasant smile.

Those pale eyes darted back and forth between me and the pile of books. Between me and the list I'd made on my parchment.

"Yes, Tavi?" I asked, trying to position myself between her and the parchment without being so obvious about moving it behind me.

"Lady Lydia sent me. She wants to know if you'll be joining her at dinner."

"Oh. Um. Not tonight, Tavi. But thank you for checking on me."

Tavi cleared her throat and shuffled her toes. "Lady Lydia said that, if you declined dinner, I was to tell you she said it was not a request."

"Is she the queen now?" I asked, slightly agitated at my friend.

"She thought you might say that. And she said to tell you that queens don't…"

"Don't what?"

Tavi looked as though she might rather swallow her tongue than tell me.

"Tavi, you can tell me. I know you're just the messenger," I said.

Unless these notes suggest otherwise.

Shut up.

Tavi nodded. "She said to tell you that queens don't sulk."

My jaw tightened, but I scraped out a kind tone. "Very well, Tavi. Tell Lady Lydia I'll only be a few more moments. That I have a mess to clean up."

Tavi's eyes flickered back behind me to the parchment I was trying so desperately to hide. "It's quite the mess, Lady Queen. Are you sure you wouldn't rather me clean it up?"

"I wouldn't want you to miss dinner over my mess," I said.

"I've already eaten, Lady Queen."

"Really, it's fine, Tavi."

Tavi looked as if she might protest, but then she clamped her mouth shut and turned to the door. I almost thought I'd have a chance to breathe when she turned back around. "I'd really rather not upset Lady Lydia," she said, timidly.

"Right," I said, pushing myself to my feet. "I'm serious, though. Leave this for me to clean after dinner. That's an order. You deserve a break."

I couldn't decide who was trembling more when we left the room, me or Tavi.

* * *

I SCARFED down my meal with Lydia in less time than it took her to eat a single carrot. She eyed me with distaste when I left the table, but apparently that I had finished eating placated her enough, because she said nothing as I left.

When I arrived at the library moments later, the books remained.

Except my parchment and the last book, the one with the note *Your name will die with me*, were gone.

CHAPTER 56

ASHA

J asked the first servant I could find to point me toward
Tavi's room. The plump forest faerie did, and after a few
moments of swirling hallways and finding myself lost not once, but
twice, in the South Wing, I found a door with her inscription.

Tavi
Queen's lady's maid.

When I knocked on the cedar door, no one answered.
"Tavi?" I called, with as much composure as I could muster.
Again, no answer.
I turned the knob, and the door cracked open. Regardless of the
fact that, being queen, technically, made it absolutely ridiculous of me
to do so, I searched the hallway in both directions to make sure no
one saw me as I entered the room.
The small room was a mess. Books, papers, boxes, candy wrappers.
If it could be considered a belonging, it was cluttering the floor, the
bed, the dresser. It amazed me that someone who cleaned for a living
could be such a sloppy individual.
Technically, it's not her job to clean, remember? She takes that upon

herself when she cleans the library. Her actual duties are to the queen, said the know-it-all parasite sharing my mind.

Right.

Are you conceding that I can be helpful?

Only on occasion.

I closed the door behind me and went immediately to the bed, but then doubled back and turned the lock to the door. Just in case. As far as I could tell after a few minutes of searching, if Tavi had brought my notes to her room, she hadn't left them out in the open. When I plundered through the drawers to her dresser, all I found were servants' clothes, so wadded, I wondered how Tavi got them looking presentable, short of placing her clothes on the roof and allowing the sun to burn the wrinkles away before she got dressed in the morning.

Unwilling to give up yet, I pushed at the heavy cedar dresser until its legs groaned against the wood floors. Something thumped on the ground when I did.

When I reached behind the dresser and through a considerable volume of sticky cobwebs, my fingers wrapped around the edge of an object that felt like a book.

I pulled it out, only to find that, instead of a book, I'd found a pack of letters. I opened the first and grinned.

That looks like familiar handwriting.

Indeed, it matched one of the handwritings written in the library books, the script of the person who had mentioned Tionis as a meeting place.

I stuffed the letter into the envelope and pushed the dresser back into place.

We're leaving? You haven't even found what you were looking for.

Tavi could be back any minute now, I argued.

And you're afraid of a servant girl. Why, exactly, Lady Queen?

I'm not sure yet. That's what worries me the most, I thought.

When I opened the door, Tavi stood in front of me.

* * *

"Lady Queen," she said, though the usual jitter in her voice had gone stiff. She slid her eyes down to my hands, where I grasped her letters.

"Tavi," I said, because what else was there to say when she'd caught me breaking into her things?

"Are you in need of my personal letters?" she asked, her voice sickingly polite, even as her pitch rose with every word.

I clenched the letters in my balled fist. "Who else wrote the notes in the library books?"

"I'm not sure what you mean."

"What were you and your boyfriend planning before he died?" I asked.

Rage flashed in those usually pale eyes of hers, and, to her credit, her voice remained calm when she spoke through gritted teeth. "We were planning to marry."

Doubt reared in my stomach, horror striking me regarding the pain I would cause her if I was wrong. But I wasn't wrong.

Something was going on here, and Tavi knew more than she was letting on.

Tavi was only half-fae, and just because I didn't have proof that half-fae could lie, didn't mean I lacked an educated guess.

"May I have my letters back, please?" she asked.

I looked back and forth between her and the letters clutched to my chest.

"They're family letters. I don't see much of them, living in the palace, and all. Most of them are from my mother."

When I didn't budge, her voice strained. "Please. She died two years ago in the plague."

And that was all it took to ruin my resolve. The grief of a dead mother.

You're going to regret that, my magic chastised as I handed them over. Tavi ripped them from my hands a bit too quickly, then stepped out of the doorway, politely dismissing me, her Queen.

But she knew better than to let that title invoke fear. We all knew better.

So when she slammed her door behind me, I knew I had lost, that those letters would burn before I laid my eye on them again.

* * *

I PACED outside Tavi's room, ready to rip my hair out of its braid. While I had a few options, none of them sounded especially advantageous. I could tell Kiran, of course, but...

But what would you tell him?

Stop finishing my sentences, I snapped.

My magic shrugged, unsettling my mind with the way it shuffled inside my consciousness.

It was right. What would I tell Kiran? That I'd found love letters written in his library books that told of a plot to...

To nothing. They never actually said what the plot was, did they?

I didn't bother to chastise my magic for interrupting me this time.

Good, glad you've come to your senses about that.

My skin crawled in irritation.

The other option was to burst back into Tavi's room and demand the letters. Technically, I was the queen.

But I had already lost that battle the moment I let my embarrassment get the best of me. Even if I forced Tavi to hand over the letters, by now she had probably chewed up and swallowed any of them that might have contained important information.

Then there's the possibility you were wrong and invaded her private letters from her dead mother for no reason at all.

Then there was that.

I wasn't making any progress toward a plan when a low, rumbling whine ripped me from my thoughts. I turned to find an sleek black tail flitting on the ground around the nearest corner.

That was right; Tavi's rooms were in the South Wing, where Nagivv liked to roam when she got out of her sanctuary. I took a deep breath before stepping around the corner and hoped my not-so-little friend hadn't swallowed one of the kinder guards.

She sprawled on the cold floor, scraping her massive snout against the feet of one of the marble statues that lined the hall. Her whines pierced my heart, and when I kneeled to pet her, her whines grew louder, until she was meowing at me, scraping her claws gently across my robes.

If I hadn't known better, I would have thought she was trying to tell me something.

When did knowing better ever do you any good?

I frowned and tickled the fleshy folds behind her ears in an attempt to soothe her, but she shook her colossal head and forced my hand away, clawing instead at the feet of the statue.

The eleven-toed feet of the statue.

Tionis. Yet another piece of the puzzle that didn't seem to fit any of the others. His face peered down at the saber like an annoyed pet-owner might a cat scratching their feet.

Maybe Fin had been right that day when he had joked that Nagivv liked this particular statue. I'd found her down here again, that day I had attempted to find a secret passageway in his twin statue that resided in the gardens.

But that was just it. I hadn't found anything.

Coincidences. Az finding a secret passageway into the gardens. Tionis's statue in the gardens. The conspirators planning to meet by the statue. Nagivv clawing through guards, swallowing them whole, just so she could paw at the feet of this horrific historical figure, the ancient fae who had passed his time washing his feet in the blood of his captives...

Wait.

I bit my lip in an attempt to yank myself back into reality and far, far away from the idea that had just occurred to me.

Surely you're not thinking of doing what I think you're thinking of doing.

I didn't grace my magic with a response. I only caressed the fur between Nagivv's brows before tracing my finger down the bridge of her snout, until my fingertips hovered before her mouth. She licked them, as if expecting some sort of treat, her leathery tongue prickling my skin.

Before she closed her mouth, I pushed the padded part of my palm against her canines.

She recoiled in surprise as she tasted the blood on her tongue.

Are you trying to get eaten?

"You're not going to eat me. Are you, Nagivv?" I asked, but I yanked my hand away from her maw all the same. Blood pooled in my hand, glistening in the torchlight as pain throbbed through my wound.

I hope you get an infection from that.

Before my magic could scold me any further, I fisted my hand and extended my arm. When I tilted my fist, hot blood rolled off my palm, dripping onto Tionis's feet.

The stone drank my blood until there was no sign of the spill at all. Not even a stain.

Tionis shuddered, then lifted, before swinging open so hard, it would have knocked me over if it weren't for Nagivv, who pushed me out of its way with her tail.

Behind where the statue had been was a hole in the wall, and within the hole, darkness.

Nagivv sniffed the musty air of the tunnel, whimpering even louder. Then her eyes sparkled, her hind legs kicked, and she was gone, disappeared into the darkness.

I'd barely taken a step, barely wrapped my bleeding hand in my garment, when my magic filled my head with its voice.

Asha.

Don't try to stop me.

I will not. But think carefully, child, of what you might find down there. The truths you might uncover.

I'm not afraid of the truth, I thought back, before stepping into the darkness.

I was wrong.

* * *

When I reached the end of the dark tunnel, brushing my hand against the cold, stone wall to guide me, my foot stumbled on thin air. I regained my balance, and pushed my foot further down, where it met solid ground. Same for the next foot. A staircase.

The staircase curved, round and around, until torchlight shone through a doorway at the bottom.

And at the bottom was a cell with metal bars, each the size of my forearm.

And within the cell was a woman.

A woman with pale hair and pale skin.

A woman I would have recognized anywhere.

CHAPTER 57

ASHA

*I*t couldn't be her. It couldn't.

But there was her ashen blond hair and her pale face that, speckled with dust as it may be, could have never been mistaken for belonging to a native of Naenden. Her brilliant blue eyes shone through the watery tears that glazed them.

"Who are you?" I asked, more to the Fates than to her. I begged, begged for a response, an explanation other than the one that had run away with my sanity.

The beautiful girl pushed herself onto her hands and dragged herself to the cell bars. Her pale fingers curled around them, her yellowed, pointed fingernails scraping against the metal. When she spoke, her voice was barely a croak. "I could ask you the same question."

Nagivv whimpered and scratched at the metal bars, which shrieked in a high-pitched tone that ground against my senses.

The girl's watery blue eyes swept over me, taking in my robes. Scarlet. Reserved for royalty and royalty alone.

Except that even though soot had covered her from head to toe, a few speckles of burgundy, dark as blood, punctured the thick coating around her gown.

A wry smile curled the corners of her lips. "I'd introduce myself as the Queen of Naenden, but, given the way you're dressed, it seems that is no longer the case." Her eyes swept over my robe, the scarlet that signaled my royalty status.

My heart thudded, landing lifeless and hollow on the stone floor beneath us. No, no, no. That couldn't be.

"You're dead."

The girl's laugh rattled with mucous, sending bile up my throat. "Obviously not."

I dug into the recesses of my mind to confront my magic. *You showed me her death, you showed me Kiran burning her alive...*

What? Did you think I was omniscient? All I know is what I see from your eyes...pardon me, eye. What I hear from your ears. The heralds claimed she was dead. All I did was embellish.

No. Kiran had said she was dead. And the fae couldn't lie, so either this was not Queen Gwenyth, or Kiran didn't know…

My mind raced. Who could have trapped her down here without the king's knowledge? And why?

The girl's shrill, bitter voice interrupted my thoughts. "Is that what they've been telling people? That I'm dead?"

I curled my fists, flexing and retracting my fingers, as if my body suspected the girl behind bars might attack. "I don't know who *you* are, but Queen Gwenyth is dead."

She cocked her head lazily to the side with such little effort that I wondered if she might pass out. "Now, who told you that?"

My voice trembled, and I hated myself for it. "Th-the heralds, for starters, and then Kiran."

"Oh, you and my husband are on a first name basis already? He must have had his hands all over you pretty early." Her blue eyes blazed behind that watery veil, her words commanding the blood rushing to my neck, my cheeks.

I willed my feet to turn, to flee, to leave this wretched bully of a girl, this liar, here to rot in her cell. But they didn't listen. I couldn't leave. I had to know.

Know what, exactly?

Shut up.

We're verging on dangerous territory, girl. You could leave while you have the chance.

We both knew that wasn't an option.

"Tell me, Lady Queen." Her coarse voice went silky on those words, *Lady Queen,* as she kneeled and stroked Nagivv's pelt with her cracked fingertips. "Did you notice anything odd about the king's heralds?"

"What are you talking a—" I stopped, because a memory swept over me, the voice of a faerie, a stranger in the marketplace that day. *Seems our king is lowering his late father's employment standards. Did you see that herald? Human as they come.*

How odd it was, the stranger had noted, that a palace who typically exclusively employed the fae had broken tradition and hired humans as heralds.

I was pretty sure my heart had stopped beating. I shook my head. "No. Kiran confirmed it. He said you were dead. The fae can't lie."

She blinked those icy blue eyes at me, and the urge to throttle her surged through my limbs. Liar. She was the liar. "Is that so?" she purred, her voice melding with Nagivv's content rumbling. "Tell me, did he ever say those exact words? That I, Queen Gwenyth, was dead?"

My mind rummaged through its memories, every moment that Kiran and I had discussed his late bride. I would find it, I was sure of it—the exact moment he had said the words that would condemn this girl as a phony.

That night I'd found him weeping—he must have said it then. What was it that he'd said, exactly?

Yes, I regret it.

Because I miss her.

I hate her for what she did, yes.

No, surely I was missing something. Some specific phrase that couldn't be worked around, something he'd said that would have been a lie, if this girl was telling the truth, which would confirm she was lying.

But that doesn't stop me from wishing she was here. Isn't that what Kiran had said when I'd asked him why he was upset? But how specific did the word *here* have to be for that sentence to have been untrue?

Not specific enough to keep my guts from hardening into pebbles.

Because he hadn't said she was dead. In fact, I'd noted it, thought it was his way of coping—refusing to say the word aloud, lest saying it aloud would make it true.

It was as though the girl's words had hung my mind by an invisible noose, that my image of Kiran was kicking its legs as fast as it could, as if trying to run but gaining no traction. Nowhere to kick off, nowhere to launch, nowhere to land.

"Mm. That's what I thought."

My legs were shaking now, because this couldn't be happening. The late queen; she couldn't be alive, rotting down here, the prisoner of my husband, the male I had...

My fingernails dug into my collar of their own volition, tugging at my clothing as it suffocated me, fighting for more room to breathe. "No."

He had said she was dead.

No.

He had allowed me to believe she was dead.

The realization crashed down upon me like a landslide, trapped me between itself and the life I had made for myself, the frame of the male I had trusted, the male I'd kissed, defended.

"You might want to sit," Gwenyth said, shrugging as she picked the filth from her overgrown nails. "It's kind of a long story."

* * *

I SAT, trying my utmost not to cradle my knees to my chest, to expose the truth, that my world was caving in on itself stone by stone with each word that escaped Gwenyth's cracked lips.

"I don't know what all he's told you about me. Obviously, nothing blatantly false, but you'll learn this about the fae—they can weave the most cutthroat lie out of broken strands of the truth."

I didn't have the energy to respond, the energy to do anything but hang on to every sound, waiting for the one that would send the rest of the barricade I'd created around myself, my new life, crashing down upon me, suffocating me.

"We met at a ball. His father, the late king—curse his rotting soul—had decided it was time for his beloved heir to marry. Sure, he wanted a proper bride for Kiran to solidify his bloodline, but more than that, he wanted to shame the other kingdoms. We were all so afraid of him, even in Avelea. So when he sent a request to my father, a wealthy merchant, to host a ball, my father didn't question it. I know it's hard to believe, but the late king was even more paranoid than Kiran. He abhorred the idea of inviting other nations to his home, to his own ballroom, lest they sneak through his palace and seduce his slaves and children into offering up his secrets. Worse than that would have been to host the ball at another royal's palace. Think of all the traps they might set." She scoffed in amusement, her thin fingers twirling around the loose hairs bordering Nagivv's feline ears.

"It was up to my father, a human merchant, to provide the Prince of Naenden with a betrothal ritual fitting of a bloodthirsty king, and he succeeded. You couldn't imagine the work that went into preparing for it. Then they came, that host of preening princesses from all over, each one more slithering than the next. King Rajeen made them perform in front of Kiran." She sneered, and my stomach recoiled as I hoped she wouldn't describe what went into such performances. "They weren't even allowed to tell Kiran their names, and he was to pick, purely on beauty and performance alone. The late king didn't even allow them to speak. You see how that might have shamed the other nations a bit, put us in our place?"

I nodded, my throat stinging with bile, the contents of my stomach swirling, threatening an uprising at the base of my throat.

Gwenyth's eyes went hazy again, as if she were back in that ballroom, immersed in the scene that changed her life forever. "I was serving drinks when it happened. Strange, how that detail is still branded into my memory. Maybe because I can still feel the sting when the goblet I dropped shattered and the glass pricked my ankles."

"It was time for the great Prince of Naenden to choose his bride. Except he surprised us all. We'd all assumed he'd turned out just like his father, since the rumors whispered his father had groomed him from infancy to be a monster. But what the late king hadn't realized was that Kiran despised his father for forcing him into the sadistic ritual, for using his marriage as an excuse to squeeze his thumb down on the other kingdoms."

"When it came time to pick a bride, he called for me, the human girl pouring drinks."

The bulge in her neck bobbed, as if she were trying to swallow but couldn't due to dehydration.

"And you said yes?" I asked.

Her head snapped over to me at a rate that made me wonder how her withered skin didn't rip with the force of it. "Did you say no?"

"I—" My words had offended her. Guilt plagued my stomach, a feeling I couldn't explain. Not when it was for the very girl who had gotten me into this situation in the first place. The girl who had tried to kill my husband.

Something twisted in my stomach, wrestling with the loyalty to him that swelled within me.

So I decided to explain, because surely it couldn't hurt anything, not when Gwenyth—I supposed I believed her now, as much as I didn't want to—was locked down here in the dungeons. "After you betrayed him, Kiran was angry." Those sounded like reasoning words. Excusing words. Why was I making excuses for him? I tried to go on, to explain what exactly had happened, but I couldn't bring myself to say it aloud. Not after the shift that had happened between us since the night of the ball, not with the thought of his hand brushing mine at the breakfast table. With what had occurred last night. I couldn't reconcile any of it. "I made a deal to marry him to save my people." That was the most painless way I could come up with to say it.

She made a high-pitched, almost mocking sound that made my skin want to crawl. But when she spoke, I was drinking up her words again, as if I were a cupbearer, checking a glass for poison but gulping it down in one swallow to get the death over with, if it was.

"I wish I could say mine was as noble. Or that I had a choice. But I didn't. My father was thrilled with the price the king offered. He didn't care that I had a man back home I intended to marry. So he sent me away with Kiran.

"I was terrified of him at first. But he was gentler than I expected. He didn't force himself on me like the other fae I'd heard of. Instead, he tried to get to know me. He'd brush his hand against mine, or occasionally lean in for a kiss on the cheek. And, after a while, I felt my fear of him wane. We would talk after dinner until we were both laughing. And one night, when he followed me up to my chambers, I allowed him in." Her blue eyes sparkled, and something sharp and icy burst in my chest, prickling my nerves and fanning the urge to leave this girl to rot in her cell. I tried and failed to smother the feeling. "And after that, everything was blissful for a while." That flicker in her eyes faded, and a dullness washed over her pale, pretty face.

"But Kiran had his father's assassination to deal with. It happened on the way back from our engagement ball, but there were no leads on who had finally managed to snuff the old creep. Some of Kiran's spies thought they found a lead in Avelea, so Kiran rushed away to chase it. Not that he cared that his father was dead, but he wanted to be sure the assassin wouldn't come after him. The longer he was away, the more I felt the peace begin to fade, the fear return. And I started to remember, remember things he had done to me. Times he'd allowed his flames to whip at my wrists when I'd displeased him. Times I hadn't wanted him in my chambers, but he had forced down the doors, only to have a servant repair them the next morning.

"It was then that I realized Kiran possessed a gift, one distinct from the Flame, one he shouldn't have had. You see, the more Kiran touched me, the more he could control my feelings, soothe my fear of him."

I shook my head. "You can't possibly know that."

Her mouth spread, revealing pale, sickly teeth. "Oh, but yes I can. Because that was my magic's power, before he stole it from me."

* * *

No. That wasn't possible. That was too much of a coincidence. And Kiran, he couldn't just take—

Can you feel magic in her? I asked my magic.

No, but she's claiming she doesn't have it anymore.

But you would have felt that power in Kiran, if it were true.

I felt a gust of wind roll through me, as if my magic was sighing. *Not necessarily. The fae suppress magic, absorb it into themselves. If Kiran had taken Gwenyth's magic, then I would be no more able to sense my kin than I would my lost relative who first sparked Kiran's ancestor's power.*

I opened my mouth to retort, to speak until some word fell from my lips that could explain why it couldn't have been true. But Gwenyth cut me off.

"Once I realized what he had done, I grieved, of course. But I couldn't let him know I knew. He was under the impression that I had never realized my powers were anything more sinister than simply excelling at being manipulative, so he never suspected that I'd figure out what he had stolen from me. Still, I found ways to avoid him, his touch. Illness, that sort of thing. I was so alone then. And then Tiberius—" Her voice caught on the name, telling me all I needed to know. That must have been the name of her lover, the guard with whom she'd conspired against Kiran. "He was kind to me. Gentle. He'd sneak me to that wretched healer and make her bandage me up after Kiran had lashed out. We couldn't be seen together, of course, but we came up with a system."

"The notes in the library books," I said.

Her brow raised, something like sick delight sparking in her eyes. "Someone's been bored."

I swallowed my annoyance, forced it down my throat. "Who was your ally?"

"Tiberius found a smuggler, someone who would get us both out of Naenden, someone who said he could find us a new life."

"If that was the case, if you were planning on running away, then why try to murder the king?" I asked.

She sighed. "That's what Tiberius said, too. But I—" She shivered, and I wondered if it was from the cold, or the memories. "I couldn't imagine we'd ever be safe. I kept having these dreams, you see. That he'd catch us, right on the edge of the Sahli. I knew that if he died, his brother Fin would take the throne. I wasn't ever nearly as scared of Fin. Even if he searched for us, I knew he'd give up, eventually. Not like Kiran. Not like their father would have. Especially when it came to light what Kiran had done." She turned to me, her eyes wide and milky, her face the sickly ghost of a once beautiful girl. "I couldn't live like that. Running from him forever. The night Tiberius asked me to meet him by Tionis, he tried to convince me to run away with him. Since you found my dungeon, I'm sure you're aware the statues of Tionis mark secret passageways. Kiran's father bullied the King of Charshon out of the one that now resides in the gardens. Of course, he never knew what it did, that the statues create magical passage-ways that don't require digging. The only reason I knew was that one of the Charshonian advisors got drunk at Kiran's betrothal ball and blabbed about it to a table full of merchants whose drinks I was pouring."

The pieces started to click together in my mind. Az must have been one of the merchants sitting at that table. He had overheard the secret to getting onto the palace grounds the same way Gwenyth had. There must have been an entrance somewhere in the city that covered a tunnel leading to the one in the palace gardens.

No wonder the lychaen had been able to slip into the palace grounds unnoticed. Calias was the King of Charshon, meaning if his advisor knew, he also knew how to breach the palace's security. Calias must have told the lychaen about the passageways.

"I wanted to run away with him that night. I wanted to so badly," Gwenyth said. "But I knew as long as Kiran lived, our happiness could only be temporary. I thought if we could poison him—" She blinked hard, swallowing. "But we were caught in the end."

"How did they catch you?" As much as I didn't like this woman, I couldn't help but be curious.

She groaned. "My lady's maid, of all people. I kept the vial of poison between the cut out pages of one of my tattered books. Apparently, she got it into her head that she would surprise me for my birthday by getting it rebound. When she found the poison, she went straight for the Captain of the Guard, who immediately had me arrested. They knew I must have been in contact with a smuggler to get my hands on a poison lethal enough to kill a fae. It wasn't long after that they tracked down the smuggler, and he gave them Tiberius's description."

"Where do they keep him? Tiberius?" I asked.

Her eyes bore into me, and when she answered, her words with tipped with venom. "They strangled him right where you're sitting. They made me watch."

"Who? Kiran?"

She scoffed, flitting her hand so hard it startled Nagivv out of her content slumber. "Kiran gave the orders for them to keep me down here. He never came to see me after he learned what I'd done. I guess, even with all the trickery he used, he still had the audacity to feel betrayed. Like he'd let himself believe I actually loved him."

"If that's the case, why not kill you?" I asked.

"Because he's obsessed with me. I hurt him, so he can't bring himself to visit me. But he can't quite let me go, either." She slumped against the metal bars, her cheeks pressing between the openings.

My heart sank like ash at the bottom of a river.

When she turned to me, her voice was barely a whisper. "Yours is the first face I've seen since Tiberius's. Since they killed him."

"That was months ago. If that were true, you'd have starved by now," I said.

"That's the thing about fae magic. What they're capable of isn't natural. He had one of his servants enchant my body to keep me alive without food or water."

The muscles in my throat tensed as the stench of rotting flesh in the streets of Meranthi soured in my memory. If that was true, if the fae had the power to keep humans alive without sustenance, then why did so many of Kiran's subjects starve? Surely, he didn't know. Surely.

Gwenyth sprawled on her back, the absence of her touch causing

Nagivv to stretch her claws in agitation. "Oh, don't worry. It's not a curse I would place on my worst enemy. I might be alive, but the hunger, the thirst—they make me wish I wasn't."

"What did you mean earlier, 'when it came to light what Kiran had done?'" I asked.

She rolled her eyes. "That my charming husband had forced himself onto Ophelia."

My ribs shook at the accusation, but something wasn't right. If my timeline was correct, Gwenyth had been caught with the poison before the news ever made it to Meranthi of the almost-affair with Ophelia, Fin's wife. She would have been locked away already, and I doubted anyone would have slipped her the news. Besides, Kiran hadn't forced himself on Ophelia. It had been the other way around. "How did you know about Kiran and Ophelia?" I almost snapped, thankful for a reason to doubt the truth of Gwenyth's words.

Her eyes widened for a bit, then narrowed. "How did I know? The real question is, how was I the only one to know? The way she shrunk in his presence. The fear in her eyes. The shame when she looked at me. I befriended her when I realized what was happening. That it was happening to both of us. That's how we bonded."

That made little sense—not when compared with the story I'd heard. Gwenyth hadn't been there the night Ophelia tried to seduce Kiran, the night he'd killed her.

"Wait, are you saying this happened more than once?"

She laughed. "So he finally got caught, did he? Made it public?"

Rage boiled within me. "How can you be so calloused? When you claim to have been her friend?"

She snapped at me. "Because, *Lady Queen*. At least, if it's come out in the open, it won't happen to her again. She's safe now, can't you see?"

A shudder swept its way down my spine. "You don't know."

"Know what?"

CHAPTER 58

ASHA

*W*hen Kiran arrived in his chambers that night, I had to clench my fists to ground myself, to force the trembling out of my body. I'd chosen the evening robe especially for this—a soft, lavender gown with sleeves made for long fae arms. Tavi hadn't gotten around to hemming it yet, so the sleeves hung well past the length of my fingers, hiding the one mechanism I had left to control.

The smile that broke across his face when his molten eyes fell on mine might have broken me, had Gwenyth's words—the fact Gwenyth possessed the breath to even speak such words—not already shattered me.

Liar. Just because my fae husband had no such ability didn't make him any less of one. He'd just found ways around his supposed limitations. In fact, he'd used the fact he couldn't lie against me, to convince me to trust him while he worked on me from below the surface. A touch here, a caress there, a human speaking the lie he'd commanded them to tell.

Still, the joy on his face when he beheld me, the spark in his eyes, might have melted me. And I couldn't look away, not without raising suspicion.

So when he wrapped his arms around me, warmth radiating

through me at the gentleness of his touch, I allowed his power to course through my bones, to soothe my trembling. If he was going to manipulate my feelings, I'd use it against him. I'd use it to hide my fear.

Because he could take my feelings, twist them into whatever he wanted, but he could not take my memories.

Not with me here to remind you constantly.

I didn't have the energy to force away my magic's voice. Not today.

"I've missed you," Kiran said as he pulled me close and pressed his hot lips against the bridge of my hairline, a wave of unnatural contentment rippling through me.

I could forget if I wanted to. I could melt into these arms forever, choose to cling to this peace that radiated wherever he touched.

Not if you don't want him stealing me.

Did I really care, though? My magic had cut me, burned me, bruised me. Kiran hadn't. There were no scars on my body, no burn marks on my face to testify against my husband.

Not yet.

Even if he did, he could make it not hurt, dissolve the pain, make me not care.

That thought was enough to snap me out of it, to buoy my logic to the surface, to snatch my determination from drowning in the sea of warmth that was all Kiran, and none of me.

I drew away from his embrace, and the tiniest trickle of dread broke through the wall of golden warmth as it leaked into my belly. It was enough to steady me, though Kiran's influence kept me from trembling, from completely giving myself away. He frowned. "Is everything alright?"

Given my newly revealed knowledge that my husband was keeping his ex-wife alive in the dungeons downstairs? "Of course. I'd just like to hear about your day. That's all."

As if to prove the truth in my words, I hopped onto the bed and propped myself against the backboard, patting on the sheets to invite him to sit next to me. He grinned, a sight that sent a flood of heat

411

through my chest, and complied, settling in next to me and wrapping his powerful arm around my shoulders.

A wave of surrender crashed over me, but this time, I'd prepared myself for it.

My thoughts and my feelings were separate entities, easily clouded by one another, sure, but I could suspend my thoughts, allow them to float. I could examine my feelings from a straying cloud's vantage-point to see if they were true.

"Well, it wasn't all that interesting. Mostly meetings. You know how the vizier is, going on and on about the budget and our foreign relations with Mystral. Luckily, I had other thoughts to distract me." He turned his face into mine, his hot breath caressing my cheek, threatening to soothe the dread right out of me, to remind me that, if my husband had locked away his wife in the dungeons, there had to be a reasonable explanation.

I shuddered and pulled away, the teasing come-and-get-me grin on my face way too easy to be fake. "As honored as I might be, should a king really be daydreaming about women during meetings?"

"Not women. You." His lips grazed mine, and for a moment, I found myself lost in the pleasure of it all.

Asha. You are aware that I am a witness to everything.

That was enough to jerk me backward.

Kiran frowned again, a look that his magic tried to convince me was one of genuine concern. "Are you sure you're alright?"

I coughed, as if that somehow could expel the influence he had over me. Somehow, it gave me an edge. "I just don't want to be a distraction. Your rule is important. So many lives depend on your decisions. I don't want to be selfish with you. Even your mind." Even as the lies escaped my lips, it shocked me to find that I was brushing his forearm with my thumb. That hadn't been part of my manipulation technique.

Stop touching him. You're only doing yourself in.

Right. It took considerable effort to draw my hand back to my side, but I managed it all the same.

The tension between his brows relaxed. Good, I'd been convincing. He smiled, his eyes burning into that deep ember. He brushed a loose strand of hair from my face, leaving behind a ribbon of warmth where his fingertips had grazed. "I was only trying to be charming. Apparently, I'm not very good at it. The truth is, I had to force you out of my head all day to focus on my work. But don't worry, Asha. I haven't forgotten our kingdom. Our people."

It occurred to me what nuance existed within a fae's inability to lie. So much so that Kiran could claim having to push me from his mind all day without that statement being considered an outright lie by the ancient magic that restricted him. Probably because such a statement only implied adoration, when he very well could have been distracted with plots to steal my magic.

Fortunately, the ancient rules would only bend so far.

"Do you have any other abilities? Other than the ability to control fire?" I blurted out the words before the tender flame welling within me could soothe away my resolve.

Kiran jerked his head, taken aback. He blinked quickly, then sat up straight and rigid.

Thinking.

"What do you mean?"

He's avoiding answering the question.

As if I didn't already know that.

One can never tell when you're under a spell.

It took physical restraint not to roll my eyes. Kiran had backed away from me, lifting the fog just enough so I could trace out the path, though he held on to my hands.

I laughed, trying to play my facial expression off as innocent. That had always been a difficult one for me, what with the intimidating scar slit across half my face.

"It's just that I know so little about the fae, other than what gets spread around the humans in Meranthi, or what you or Lydia or Fin have told me. You've sparked my curiosity, I guess. I'd like to know more about my husband."

A blue flame flickered in his eyes, though with what emotion, rage or desire, I couldn't tell. But his face softened. Or, at least, that's how I perceived it. One couldn't really tell these days. Then he raised his eyebrows, as if trying to figure out where to start.

Or trying to figure out how to deceive you without lying.

Or that.

When it seemed he'd come up with a suitable answer, he let out a smooth, controlled breath. "Sorry for being so defensive. It's just that you're not the first person to ask me that. I...um..."

His eyes flitted across the room, as if he were thinking of someone else.

Perhaps his wife he keeps locked away in the cellars? Mm?

Then he withdrew his arms from me, fully this time, and rested his hands in his lap. He turned to face me, shifting the bed as he sat cross-legged in front of me, reminding me of that first night we had talked. Really talked.

His warmth oozed from me, leaving behind a void glacial dread.

"It's not common among fae to possess multiple gifts, certainly not within my family line."

I scanned his words, searching for one that would confirm he hadn't stolen it from Gwenyth.

I couldn't find one.

"How did you end up with it, then?" I dared to ask.

His eyes went dark, suspicious. "What do you mean?"

I'd pushed too far. He couldn't know I knew about Gwenyth. I forced that abashed grin onto my face, the one that made me seem embarrassed about my lack of education. "I don't understand how the line of magic works. How it gets passed down from parents to their children."

The tension in his broad shoulders released. "There are plenty of scholars who would love to understand it fully."

A non-answer.

"How does it work—your magic?"

His eyes went cold. Empty. Drooped. "If you're asking about it, I think you already know."

A shiver ran up my spine, enough for at least ten that must have built up under the surface while he had his hands on me.

I searched my mind for a reason to have figured it out without Gwenyth's help. "The way I feel when you touch me. It just seems," I tried my best to soften my words with a shy smile, "a little too intense to be real."

He grimaced, and I realized too late that my words had wounded him.

I wouldn't go about stinging a lion if I were you. That never ends up well for the bee.

"That's not what I meant. I..." But without his hands on me, his influence had faded, and my limbs trembled. The words shuddered as they left my mouth, revealing my fear, my terror, stronger now than ever after being repressed, overpowered. As if Kiran's calm had simply been the lid on a pot of boiling water, keeping the trouble contained, but bubbling all the same.

"Asha." He reached out to touch me, but I flinched, drawing my arm to my chest.

Our eyes met, and a dark shadow of understanding passed his.

"You don't have to be afraid of me," he said, trying again to brush my arm with his fingers, but I lurched, hobbling from the bed. I toppled over onto my back, scraping away from him on my hands and knees, much like I had attempted with the lychaen, fear consuming me.

Animals. That's what fae thought of us. Animals consumed by our primal urges.

And here I was on all fours proving them right.

He stood, towering over me, his eyes wrought with sorrow.

Was he going to regret killing me for discovering his secret? Or would he lock me away next to Gwenyth?

"Just say you've never used it on me," I whispered. Begged. "Just say you've never forced me to feel something that wasn't real."

His response was quick. "Asha, I promise I haven—" But his throat caught on the words, and his lips writhed under his beard.

He couldn't say it, because it wasn't true.

I'd caught him in a lie.

He closed his eyes, took a breath, and started again. "I promise I haven't—"

"I don't want to hear it," I hissed. A snake, that's what I was. A cornered snake, hissing and coiling, and preparing to strike.

Except I didn't have any fangs.

"Whatever you're about to say, it's not the truth. It's just some non-lie you've come up with. Some way you've found to skirt around the truth." As the words poured out, so did the fear, and in its wake, all it left behind was resentment, anguish. Because Kiran had made me believe I'd fallen for him. That there was a man out there who could love me, despite everything Meranthi had ever taught me. Years. Years I'd spent training my heart never to expect the impossible, to be okay with the fact that my appearance made me unlovable. That it was simply against a male's nature to develop a romantic attachment to a woman whom they could not possibly find physically attractive. The only male I'd allowed to slip past the wall I'd constructed around my heart had been Az, and only because he'd been my friend for so long, I knew he alone could see past the surface.

Yet even Az had said it. There were things he had to work through. Things, meaning the blotches across my cheek where my skin was irreparably damaged, the cavern where my left eye once was. Even with all our history, it had taken him years and the threat of losing me to get him past the repulsion of my appearance. Years.

And I had been stupid enough to believe that, for the immortal fae king whose previous wife's face and body could have been personally crafted by the Fates themselves, it had only taken a few months.

My mind raced through our every encounter, second-guessing every blink, every attempt he might have made not to look at me. When we kissed, had he hesitated? I couldn't seem to remember. Or perhaps he had simply thrust his lips onto mine, hoping to get it over with, like one might do with an unpleasant meal, shoveling it down before the taste could settle in.

Stupid. To believe I could soften the heart of a cruel fae king. That I could trust him.

I'd fallen in love with a male who kept his wife locked away beneath our home.

I might have vomited had I eaten anything in the hours since discovering Gwenyth was alive.

He took a step forward, and I recoiled into the corner. "Don't touch me."

It wasn't any use. He would do to me what he wanted.

I just wouldn't let him convince himself any longer that what he had done was excusable.

The flames in his eyes went out. He backed away and straightened his robes.

He said nothing as he strode from my room and slammed the door behind him.

CHAPTER 59

ASHA

I half expected Gwenyth to be dead by the time I found her.

An ancient scroll rolled around in the pack I'd found in my closet and strapped against my back before sneaking down to the library and plucking the scroll from the hidden shelves.

Then I'd found myself barefoot on the cold, stone staircase. Just in case my slippers caused the whisper of noise that made the difference between my life or my death.

Either I was way louder than I had thought, or Gwenyth had known I was coming, because when I rounded the curve of the staircase, her glittering blue eyes reflected the flame from the lamp I'd lit once the secret door had closed behind me. Nagivv was asleep on the stone floor, her snores rhythmic. Had I not been sure my life was about to be cut short, I might have found the steady beat soothing.

"You came back."

Gwenyth didn't sound surprised. A sly smile crossed her cracked lips. "I thought I might have made a friend."

Not by her charm alone, she didn't.

I don't have time for your commentary right now, I snapped back.

Will you have time when we're rotting away in this dungeon in this unsavory girl's place?

I ignored my magic, which turned out to be easy to do in Gwenyth's presence, since I would have rathered ignore her. "What exactly is your plan?" she asked, eyeing me with uncertainty as I slung the pack from my back and onto the floor.

"Remember how I told you I have the Old Magic?"

"Until our dear husband steals it from you, you mean?"

I tried not to let the pit that the word *our* had dug in my stomach cave in any farther. "Right. Well, it can draw extra power from these ancient scrolls. Something about them originating from the Nether. I'll let it harness my voice to morph the bars of your cell until there's an opening wide enough for you to fit through."

"And have you done this before? Morph something that already exists?" she asked, her eyes glittering with the apparent high of insult.

"Do you want me to break you out or not?" I asked, not wishing to delve into the fact that, so far, all I'd managed to do was create a false replicas of an ancient sword and conjure a few temporary imitations of rainforest animals. How was I supposed to know whether I could bend metal?

As I untied the clasp on my satchel, the ancient scroll rolled out, and I scrambled to my hands and knees to fetch it before it rolled away. I dropped it at least twice, my jittering fingers betraying me.

"Careful, or your nerves will land you in here with me. As much as I'd enjoy some company, I don't figure you're in need of a roommate," she said.

My magic stirred. *You're an idiot if you think that was anything other than a jab regarding your relationship with the king.*

Oh, as if you haven't done the exact same thing?

You're right, it said, *but the difference is, I care about your wellbeing.*

Only because my wellbeing is your wellbeing.

That might be the case, but can you say the same for this girl?

Again, I ignored it. I couldn't let her rot down here. If it was my fate to be a prisoner here in the palace, so be it. But there was no reason for her to continue to suffer. Not when I understood what it was like to be ripped from one's family.

Is that really why you're doing this? Because this girl has been so kind to you? Or are you doing it out of the goodnesses of your altruistic heart?

Why else? I almost hissed aloud.

Oh, I don't know. Perhaps to lash out against Kiran. He used his magic to make you believe you loved him. To make you believe he loved you back. How better to punish him, but by releasing the girl he can't seem to let go of? How better to avenge yourself?

I didn't give myself time to consider that possibility. Instead, I clutched the scroll in my hands and spoke.

The story was a simple one. Short and sweet. One of a girl trapped in a dungeon by an evil king who'd stolen her from her family. Except, the Fates seemed to pity her, even for her crimes. Because one night, the bars to her cell bent and curved, creating a space just large enough for her to slip through.

There wasn't enough time between the part of the story where the bars resumed their previous form and the part where I regained my true voice for me to open my eye. Not before Gwenyth was already wrenching me to my feet.

"Where to next?" she whispered, a fire sparking in those bright blue eyes of hers.

* * *

WE HAD to go by feeling alone, grazing the palace walls with our fingertips rather than risk allowing our lamp to burn, lest we spark a guard's attention. While I had expected to lead the way, once I'd told Gwenyth of our escape route, she had taken my hand and led me through the corridors herself.

She took a different route than I might have, curving along the corridors in a roundabout way that left me disoriented, unable to place our position in the palace.

I'd forgotten. She had lived here longer than I had.

She had snuck out this way before.

It served to our advantage. We didn't meet a single guard along the way, though we'd had a plan for that too. If we were caught roaming, Gwenyth was to pull her hood over her head. I would claim my sister Dinah was very ill, and I was taking her to the infirmary, that the wind had snuck through an open window and snuffed out our lamp, and that we'd had to feel our way about the palace until we became quite lost.

If the guard happened to check under Gwenyth's hood, the plan was simple.

Run.

Thankfully, it hadn't come to that, and we reached the garden doors with little issue. Moonlight shone through the glass, lighting a spot on the marble floors.

We stood on the brink of the shadows.

Only one guard paced outside the door. Good. This should be simple enough. Gwenyth squeezed my hand, and I steadied myself, waltzing up to the door.

I knocked softly, and the guard lurched. But when he turned and found nothing but the weak human queen, his gaze softened, and he opened the door.

"Yes, my Lady?"

It wasn't Roe. So that, at least, was a good sign.

Consider this a plan endorsed by the Fates, do you?

I cleared my throat. "I can't sleep. I'd like to take a stroll in the garden."

He frowned. "It's dark out here. I'd hate for you to take a fall." From the look on his face, he meant it. Discomfort twisted in my belly. But, then again, the guard shouldn't have been so trusting.

"Maybe you could accompany me, then?"

He shuffled a bit on his toes. "I'm not supposed to leave my station, Lady Queen."

"Right. Silly me. Of course not," I pretended to laugh, though it took everything in me not to scream in panic. This wasn't going to work. They'd catch us and send Gwenyth back to the dungeons. And what would they do to Dinah? What would they do to Father for my part in the attempted escape? "I understand. But please, it would mean ever so much to me if you'd allow me to take a quick stroll. I won't be long. I believe it would help me sleep."

The guard's resolve wilted, and he opened the door to let me through.

I'd have to act soon. He'd surely lock it before Gwenyth had the chance to slip through if I didn't do something. Fast.

So I tripped and, despite every survival instinct my human body had come equipped with, forced my arms not to catch me. The results were a pounding headache, a mouthful of dirt, and a gasp from the guard. He rushed to my side, wrapping his arms around me. "Lady Queen, are you alright?"

He tried to lift me, but my knees stumbled. As strong as the fae were, apparently that didn't protect them from cumbersome, flailing objects. At least, not when they were trying to be gentle.

Out of the corner of my eye, I glimpsed the slightest distortion in the shadows. Gwenyth had gotten through.

I clambered to my feet. Falling really had hurt, and I pretended to laugh. "I'm fine. I'm used to tripping over things," I said, pointing to my missing eye as evidence, and as the guard didn't seem to know whether he was allowed to laugh, he shifted uncomfortably before releasing me.

"Glad you're alright, Lady Queen."

"Thank you." I smiled, relief flooding me. Gwenyth had gotten through.

I made to go back inside, but the guard stopped me. "Aren't you going to take a stroll, Your Majesty?"

Right. I swallowed. "I suppose the fall startled me. Perhaps I should go back inside."

He frowned, a look of genuine concern washing over his face that made my heart clench with guilt. "Forgive me saying so, Lady Queen, but wasn't the whole point of a stroll to calm you?"

"Of course, I suppose you're right." I faked a smile and strode past him. "I won't be long."

When I reached the curve of the bushes, I hurried my pace. A few minutes later, I found myself facing Tionis, wondering how far

Gwenyth had made it by now. What would she do with her life as a fugitive? Sure, she had made plans to go on the run before all this, but that had been when Tiberius, the guard who had shown her kindness, the male she loved, still breathed. What would her life look like without him along for the adventure?

A hand gripped me, and I almost screamed, except that another hand clamped over my mouth. "Sh. Don't get us caught now."

The hands released their grip and spun me to face Gwenyth, a few strands of her pale hair poking out from her hood and glowing in the moonlight. "You ready?"

Confused, I shook my head.

"Aren't you coming?" she asked, cocking her head.

I frowned. I wanted to. Really, I did. More than anything, I longed to escape from this marble prison where even my feelings weren't my own. I'd considered leaving with her, had even dressed in traveling robes, but...but if I fled, Dinah and Father would suffer my punishment. I couldn't do that to them.

"My father and sister need me here," I said.

I expected her to disappear into the bushes. In fact, it surprised me she had stuck around to wait for me at all, but instead of leaving, she frowned. "We could take them with us. I'm sure my smuggler wouldn't complain about a few extra passengers, for the right price."

She eyed the coin purse that hung from my belt. I unwound the string that attached it to me and pressed it into her palms, shaking my head. "My father's health wouldn't allow it. And Dinah would never leave him."

"Very well, then. Good luck to you, Asha. Make him pay one of these days, won't you?"

I bit my lip and nodded, though I was fairly certain my Fates would work out the opposite way, and that I would be the one to pay with my life, no doubt.

She scraped her palm against the thorns of a nearby rosebush and sprinkled her freshly drawn blood on the feet of the statue. It shuddered, then shifted, revealing a hole in the ground. She spared one last look at me, then turned to go, but a voice interrupted us from the shadows.

"Lady Queen?"

On instinct, we both turned.

The guard from the garden door stood there, his eyes fleeting back and forth between the two of us, lingering on Gwenyth as if she were a ghost.

Because that's what she should have been.

She was gone before the cry escaped the guard's lips.

My legs wouldn't let me run.

My love for my sister wouldn't let me run.

CHAPTER 60

ASHA

When Kiran swept into the garden, his red cape billowing in the restless breeze, no one seemed to know what to say. Even the guard who'd caught me, who'd called for one of his men to follow Gwenyth, the other to wake Kiran, was at a loss for words.

"Your Majesty. I summoned you at once. This seemed a matter in need of your guidance." The guard clutched the hair on the nape of my neck, forcing me to look Kiran in the face.

Kiran's eyes swept the guard's arm, honing in on the fist that squeezed so hard it made me want to gag, and snarled. "Get your hands off her."

Right. Because using his hands against me was his right, and his alone. Still, the guard loosened his grip on me, and the pain ebbed.

Kiran advanced toward me, but I backed away, pressing myself into the guard's steel armor. Kiran froze in place, frustration bubbling underneath his stark features, then addressed the guard once more. "I expect a reasonable explanation for why you called me outside in the middle of the night."

"Of course, Your Majesty." The guard fumbled for words, probably because he, of all people, was well aware of his employer's murderous tendencies. "Her Majesty, the Queen approached me at my station, requesting that I let her into the garden for an evening stroll. She said she couldn't sleep, that a stroll might soothe her—"

"And it seemed good to wake me?" Kiran said, his voice snapping like thin ice in the evening breeze. "To ask my permission? Queen Asha can do as she wishes."

Right. As long as I remained within the confines of this palace.

"No, Your Majesty. My thoughts were the same. So I allowed her into the garden, at which point she tripped. I assisted her up before she commenced her stroll. When she disappeared from my sight, I worried she might trip again in the dark, so I went after her..."

Kiran stepped forward, and I fought the urge to step back in the shadow of his massive frame. Not that there was anywhere for me to go with my back pressed against the guard's chest. "You abandoned your station?"

The guard's teeth were clattering now. Fear. I'd used this poor guard for my own purposes, and now he would suffer at Kiran's hand. I couldn't bear it any longer.

It was my turn to snap, to sign my death wish. "And it was a good thing for you he did."

Kiran's brows raised as he examined me, my robes fit for traveling, not for sleeping, and I watched as half of the truth clicked into place. Half of the truth—that was all the fae deserved, all they ever supplied. It was as if Kiran had forgotten the guard was even there, because his head jerked when the guard spoke again.

"Your Majesty, when I followed Her Majesty the Queen, I found her conversing with...with the late queen."

I flinched, preparing for the wrath of the king, but Kiran's eyes softened, confusing me. "I see her sometimes too. Especially in this place where she belonged. But the spirits do not come to visit us."

The guard shook his head, his breath quickening as he stumbled over his words. "No, Your Majesty. Not the crown mother. It was Lady Gwenyth I saw."

Kiran's jaw flinched at the name, and swifter than light, his eyes darted toward the hole in the ground, noticing for the first time how the statue of Tionis had shifted. Cold, calculated understanding dawned on his face and he glared at me before returning his attention to the guard. "You're relieved of your post for the night. You may return tomorrow. Leave us be."

The guard's hands trembled on my shoulder. "Your Majesty—"

"Now."

The guard scurried away, leaving me alone with the king.

The king with fire for eyes.

* * *

HE PACED in silence for a long while, as he contemplated what to do with me—the best manner in which to kill me, most likely. His monstrous feet thudded against the ground, shaking me to my already shaken core.

Just kill me, I wanted to force myself to say. *Just kill me and forget about Dinah and my father. Unleash your vengeance now, until there's none left over.*

But my mouth wouldn't form words, and my feet refused to shift.

When Kiran slowed to a stop, my world fell out from under me.

This was the end.

The thoughts that used to haunt me, the ones Kiran's hands had soothed, had numbed, all rushed to the surface. Die by noose. Die by fire?

No, something told me my passing would occur between the calloused tips of his warm fingers.

When he turned to face me, his eyes had gone dark as the night. When he spoke, his words were slow. Deliberate. "You deserve an explanation."

The words shocked me to my core. Since when had he treated me like I deserved anything? "And what explanation is there for locking your wife up in the dungeon and convincing your wife—forgive me—your other wife, that she's dead?"

Pain strained his brow, and the wrinkles around his eyes slumped, softening the sharp lines of his face, until he almost looked boyish.

"She's not my wife anymore. You can ask the vizier for the records if you don't believe me."

"I thought fae marriage bonds were unbreakable," I hissed. "Or did you marry her like you married me, without vowing a thing?"

He winced, which should have terrified me, which should have reminded me it was in my best interest to soothe my husband's temper, rather than unleash it. "The affair and the plot to kill me were enough to dissolve the marriage."

The affair. A cruel laugh escaped my lips. What a hypocrite I'd married. How long had he been sleeping with his brother's wife, yet he dared point a finger at Gwenyth? But I couldn't say as much, couldn't loose my tongue. I had to protect Dinah, my father. No matter how much I despised it, that meant I had to protect the king's fragile ego too.

"You lied to me."

"You know I can't do that."

I threw my hands into the air. "Is that supposed to make me trust you? When all you've done is spin the truth, manipulate my feelings to make me believe a lie? What's the difference, *Your Majesty?*"

The acid on my tongue, that title he hated so much spewing from my lips, sent his jaw rigid. "Please. Just let me explain."

"Yes, please do. Please explain why you keep your ex-wife rotting away in the dungeons. Go ahead."

Nothing. He had nothing to say to me. Not in response to that. Finally, he let out a cool, long breath, as if he were trying to temper the rage boiling within him, lest he lash out at me, as if he hadn't already crushed me, as if he wouldn't deem me unworthy in front of my people when all this was over. "Did you think better of me when you thought I'd murdered her myself?"

My throat caught. How dare he pin me into a corner like that? After all he had done to deceive me? Kiran took a step forward, and I recoiled. "Don't touch me."

His eyes flashed, but he held his hands in front of him all the same, a silent surrender I had no desire to believe anymore.

I knew better now. "You're obsessed with her. You always have been. And when she betrayed you, you couldn't let her go. So you buried her and made everyone believe she was dead. And then you took all your rage out on us. On me."

He shook his head, groaning with such depth I might have believed him, had I not maintained a safe distance from his deceptive grasp. "I would never hurt you, Asha."

My mouth dropped open in disbelief, and by the wounded look in his eyes, I took it he caught my meaning.

"You already have."

A commanding voice raged through the bushes, shortly followed by Lydia rounding the corner. Her violet nightgown flowed behind her in waves, fury blazing in her eyes. "You."

She took Kiran by the collar and wrenched him toward her. Still, he stared at me.

"Look at me, you idiot."

He surrendered, craning his neck toward her, the flicker in his eyes deadening.

"How could you? How could you *lie?*" She gritted her teeth on the word, as if it physically caused her pain.

I didn't stick around to hear his excuses. Instead, I slipped through the trees, pacing until Lydia's screams faded into the nothing that now inhabited my heart.

Maybe it was because my feet were well acquainted with reality— that I had nowhere else to go—that they led me through the halls, now buzzing with soldiers, up the staircases, and to my room, where I slumped on my bed and lay, for what I decided might be forever.

CHAPTER 61

ASHA

*O*n any other occasion, I might have been impressed that it was customary for the queens of the kingdoms to attend the annual Council meeting. Never mind, it probably had more to do with the fact that one of the kingdoms, namely, Mystral, was ruled by a queen alone. Whether my attendance was due to the outnumbered queen pushing for an increased female presence in the meeting, or the kings attempting to distract the Queen of Mystral with fellow gossipers, I tried not to ponder.

Mostly because I was in a sour enough state to believe the latter.

Besides, I was inclined to be offended on behalf of Lydia, who had not been invited to join the Council, as she was technically neither a queen, nor an heir. And no matter how much she'd tried to convince me that she would enjoy getting to stay behind and run Naenden for a change, I couldn't help but get the feeling she was just masking the hurt, like she always did.

It didn't help that the annual Council meetings rotated location based on the various kingdoms involved, and that, this year, it was to be held in Charshon.

I might have refused to go, had I still dreaded Calias. At least if Calias kidnapped me, I could be certain I would maintain my right to hate him for it without having to worry about him magically convincing me he was anything other than a monster.

Kiran had visited my quarters the night before to reassure me of the safety measures he would employ during our journey to make sure Calias couldn't lay a hand on me.

I had informed him that it wasn't Calias's hands that concerned me.

We embarked from Naenden in the latter weeks of autumn, although the Council meeting was in early winter.

Apparently, Father hadn't been exaggerating about how long it took to cross the Sahli desert. Even for the fae.

The coach assigned to me was pleasant, the temperature regulated by magic. I assumed Kiran had enchanted the carriage to deflect heat away from itself. Cool. Comfortable.

Which only accomplished the opposite.

As the gentle breeze designed to keep me cool ruffled the loose hair around my face, my bitterness produced plenty of heat to boil me from the inside out.

This was all it took. A little magic, barely enough to wear down the king, and an entire caravan of royalty, servants, advisors, and camels could cross the Sahli.

Could escape.

I glimpsed the camels from the small window in the front of my carriage. There wasn't even a servant manning them. I supposed it would have taken too much effort on the king's part to enchant an outdoor space like the one that kept the garden back home cool. But somehow, the camels didn't need a guide.

How many times had they made this journey?

Despite the many comforts Kiran had afforded me, I could have been sick.

It was all I had ever dreamed of, leaving this wretched place, this wretched city that, my whole life, had spat me out as if we hadn't gotten used to drinking warm water.

But this was not at all what I had imagined. In my dreams, it had always been me and Az, taking my father and Dinah by the hand and traveling as far as we could by night, stopping just in time to make dens in which we'd sleep during the day to escape the broiling sun. In my dreams we'd make it to the border, but just barely. Dirty and burned and sand-stained, we'd scale that last dune, and rejoice to find that the bordering city, hazy in our eyes, wasn't a mirage, but our refuge.

Instead, I could nap the entire way if I wanted.

Except they weren't beside me, Az and Dinah and my father.

Except I'd be coming back.

Despite the attempts to keep me cool, the air in my chest went hot, my ribs constricting against my lungs. The collar on my gown seemed to shrink, cutting off my air.

Trapped.

I was finally escaping Naenden, and I was less free than ever.

The door to my carriage creaked, ripping me from my panic. I flinched, readying myself for a private audience with the king, alone with him in my comfortable little prison cell, unable to escape his warm hands, his magic that could force me to revel in my mouse trap.

But the silhouette, darkened by the backdrop of the glaring sun, was too thin to be Kiran, and when the figure closed the door behind him, my eye adjusted to find Fin kneeling so his head wouldn't scrape the ceiling.

"Do me the favor of keeping me company for a while?" he asked. "I've tried to enjoy the scenery, but it's dreadful."

I nodded, trying to swallow the lingering trepidation that was too slow to leak from my face. Maybe I should have been afraid. Maybe I was a fool to trust Fin over his brother.

He took the seat next to me, his shoulder brushing mine in the cramped space. It was only in comparison that I considered Fin a slight-figured male. Just because Kiran was a beast among the fae didn't make Fin tiny.

The walls of my mobile prison closed in on me again, and it took all that was in me to slow my breathing, calm my pulse.

"By the Fates, Ash, you're shaking." Fin raised a hand to my shoulder, but I flinched, the sight of which made his eyes go wide. He slowly brought his hand to his side and scooted away from me, pressing himself to the side of the carriage so he wouldn't have to touch me.

Rather, so I wouldn't have to be touched.

I tried to avoid looking at him, but the heat of his stare bore into me until I could no longer ignore it. When I turned to face him, the disquiet on his face was palpable, and his eyes burned with concern.

"I'm your friend," was all he said.

The words shattered me, the sincerity in his voice that I wanted so badly to be genuine.

"Oh, come on now. My feelings are going to be hurt if you don't say it back." That mischievous, teasing grin overtook Fin's boyish face, but his eyes didn't take part. Was that sorrow over losing my trust, or worry that I might suspect the truth about him? That all the fae were slithering liars underneath their curse?

"Did you know?" I whispered.

"No." He didn't even have to ask about what.

We sat in silence for a moment, Fin staring across me and out my window to the exact patch of desert he'd just now complained of being bored with. When he finally spoke, his voice was bleak. Empty. "Funny how he didn't mind executing Ophelia for her treachery. But when it came to Gwenyth..." He shrugged his shoulders and craned his head back against the window.

"Are you going to kill him for it one day?" It was only a whisper, a half-formed thought that rattled me more than it seemed to unsettle Fin.

"Oh, no. It's illegal. Really illegal."

I choked on something that mimicked a laugh. "Yes, I suppose decent society tends to frown upon murder. But, then again, you'd be king, so I don't think you'd have to worry about suffering the consequences."

He laughed, but as he did, tears bridged his eyes. "Are you making the same offer to me as Ophelia did to Kiran?"

"Sorry, but I'm already queen, so," I shrugged, and wry laughter glittered in Fin's eyes.

He let out an exaggerated sigh. "It's well enough. Probably for the best anyway. When I said it was illegal, I wasn't kidding. The Council has rules against such things. Even royalty can't get away with it."

I raised my brow.

"The Council isn't fond of turnover. They believe the more frequent the change in power, the more cracks threaten to sever the alliance. I suppose they figure the largest threat to royalty is their family."

"That's depressing."

"Well," Fin said, "depressing as it might be, the Council is usually right. The punishment for royalty murdering their own blood is execution by the Council."

"Welp. So much for that plan."

"I suppose we could plot and scheme and make it look like someone else did it."

It was my turn to lean back against my window. "Too much work." I flitted my hand, dismissing his idea.

I closed my eye, and silence followed. The carriage bumped gently across the sand, and had almost lulled me to sleep when Fin spoke again. "Will you hate him forever?"

"Will you?"

"I have longer than you to forgive."

My eye shot open, shocked that he might actually side with Kiran on this subject. "What is that supposed to mean?"

He frowned, the creases in his forehead reminding me of wrinkled silk against his youthful features. "It means, if I spend the next century hating him, I'll have ten times that to get over it. To have a relationship with my brother. If you spend the next few decades hating him—"

"Then I'll die a bitter old lady."

"Well, I wasn't going to say it that way."

"I don't think I'm too upset by that possibility. I'm already withered away on one side, anyway."

My joke didn't land, as evidenced by Fin's lack of laughter. "He didn't have the lives we did, Ash."

"Last I checked, our childhoods weren't exactly similar."

"No, but neither of us were groomed to be bloodthirsty, to treat others like they're as disposable as sand. Neither of us ever learned that the only way anyone could love us was through keeping a tight grip on our power."

"Kiran's childhood doesn't excuse him for what he is."

Fin leaned forward earnestly, his molten eyes flickering, reminding me of Kiran, the last person I wanted to see in Fin's gentle face. "But think of how he turned out compared to what he could have been." I grunted, but Fin continued. "Believe me, I want to hate him as much as you do. But think what it meant to Kiran, to the boy inside him, who our father taught to believe weakness would make him worthless. Think of what it did to his reputation when he decided not to kill you that morning. When he went back on his decree."

I rolled my eye, an action I tried not to do often, as it had a tendency to unsettle others. Then again, some statements demanded an eye roll. "A decree that was wicked and prejudiced in the first place."

"What about Gwenyth? He could have slaughtered her for what she did. That's what my father would have—" Fin's breath caught, and his face twisted. Confusion warped his brow, as if he were accessing a memory for the first time in years—one he'd forgotten he had. Then he shook his head and continued. "That's what my father would have done. Would have had him do. But he didn't."

"He didn't seem to have a problem slaughtering your wife."

Fin flinched, and guilt washed over me. "I'm sorry. I shouldn't have—"

He shook his head, straightening against the carriage door. I might have found the look comical, such an oversized male stuffed into such a tiny cabin, if shame hadn't consumed my conscience. "It's fine. You're right. But don't you see? He could have plotted with her, could have devised a way to get rid of me, to secure the entirety of his power in Naenden. But he didn't. He protected me. In his own sick, twisted way."

"Well, I'm not fond of sick and twisted. Besides, didn't you say Kiran pretty much rules Talens anyway?"

"You have a point, I admit. But what about you?"

"What about me?"

"Kiran was distraught when the lychaen attacked you. He barreled through the palace trying to get to you, knocked over half a dozen busts of our ancestors on the way to the infirmary. And I've seen how he looks at you. I haven't seen him look at anyone like that since—"

"Since Gwenyth? You mean, the wife he kept locked up in the dungeons? How comforting."

Fin reached out to me, placing his hand on the back of mine. I resisted the urge to recoil. It burned with leftover heat from having just been outside in the blazing sun, but…

But nothing more. The grip around my chest didn't loosen. No abnormally calming sensation flooded my body.

If Fin had the same gift as Kiran, if he'd hidden the power away and only pretended to be magicless, he wasn't using it on me.

"My brother is still somewhere in there. Somewhere in that shell my father crafted around his soul. You know that better than anyone, I'd think."

"It's not my responsibility to dig him out."

Fin shook his head, a deep melancholy overcoming his features that should have been foreign to a face as young as his. "No. But you're the only one with the opportunity."

My heart turned to stone in my chest. No. No. I'd already done enough. I wasn't going to let anyone put this weight on my shoulders. But even as I pushed the implications away, Fin's words had the desired effect. The little wide-eyed girl from the parade flashed before my eyes. The girl who looked up to me. Who expected a better life because of me.

But then I felt Fin's hand on mine again. Normal. And I remembered he didn't know. He didn't know what his brother was truly capable of. What he could do to our minds.

Had Kiran done this? Asked Fin to come talk to me, to win me over? Embraced his brother and made him to believe he felt good about convincing me to forgive the devious king?

Sadness washed over me, but gratefulness all the same. Because despite everything, I believed Fin when he claimed to be my friend.

"So," I said, unwilling to broach this conversation any further, "about Dinah."

Hot blood coursed up Fin's neck. He opened his mouth, his white teeth barely touching in a startled grin. Then he coughed into his fist, grinned, and dismissed himself from the carriage.

CHAPTER 62

The Old Magic didn't like where the story was going, but he couldn't find a way to stop it. He was used to steering his tales, to deciding the fates of his characters.

Well, these characters had chomped down upon the bit and spat it out before crushing it under their hooves.

He didn't want to hear the end of this story anymore. Didn't want to test the pit that was developing in the stomach he shared with Asha.

But the Sahli desert stretched long and far, and there was nothing to distract him.

Nothing to keep him from sinking.

MOTHER'S MAGIC wasn't speaking to her.

It wasn't that she didn't care. She did. But the hole in her heart where her son belonged was full, and there was no room left for missing her magic's voice.

Besides, it would speak to her again. Once it realized what she'd done. That she'd freed its sibling's host from slavery to the fae.

That she'd freed them all.

Father hadn't aged a day since stepping foot into Alondria. Mother hated him for it, for eluding the aging process while their child had grown up before him, without his Mother to witness it.

It seemed that was how things worked in this world, at least for the Fae. They developed through childhood normally, then settled into adulthood, unfazed by time, unaffected by the way it would have weathered their skin back home.

"Hello, my dear," Father said to her, his voice as silky as the day he'd asked for her hand in marriage so many years ago.

For some reason, it didn't land quite the same way now.

He met her on the base of the hill, her peering down on him from its crest, the same hill she'd sprinted down eight years ago in a footrace to their son.

She'd failed him that day.

She wouldn't fail him again.

Farin stared meekly at her from beside Father. He'd outgrown his sire, Mother now realized, and shame washed across his face as she examined him.

He played his part well.

"Did you really think my son would choose you? That he'd forget all I did for him? That I made him a prince? A god?"

Mother couldn't help the shiver that ran down her spine, the quick prayer to the Fates that they would not hold Father's blasphemy against her son.

"Did you believe he'd run away with you? That he'd want to go back to that place, to filth and squalor and being hunted? To being silenced?" Father taunted.

"You were the one who silenced him," Mother said, holding her chin high.

Farin's cheeks flushed, and Mother's heart ached. He'd spent too long with his Father if deceit came so easily to him that he could manipulate his blood, feign a flush to sell a lie.

She hated Father for that. For the way the ruining of her innocent son played to her advantage.

That she'd had to recruit him to her treacherous plan in order to execute it. In order to free him.

In order to free them all and make up for the evil she'd introduced into this innocent, helpless world.

You assume I'll assist you after you betrayed my trust. After you told your son of my existence. Of my siblings.

Shame pinpricked Mother's heart, but she doused it in the love she had for her son.

When he reigns in the place of his father, she promised, *you and your siblings will be safe at last.*

Her magic didn't answer. It didn't have to. She knew it knew she was correct. That it would forgive her in time.

When all was made right.

She'd made it wrong. And she would make it right.

"How long, Farin, do you think it will take the Others to hunt down your mother?" Father drawled. "How long do you think she'll survive when they scent her blood?"

Farin's voice was cold, calculated. Just as Mother had needed it to be. "This world has softened her, made her forget. She won't last the hour."

Father chuckled, a hateful noise Mother was thankful she hadn't had to hear all those years he'd forced the quiet upon them. "I have a gift for you, son. You may perform the honors."

Farin swallowed, then nodded. His boots dug at the soft earth as he climbed the hill.

Just as he had all those years ago, as she'd followed him, watched him from afar as he, not her, not his father, had led their people to their salvation.

He had been their salvation.

Father had ruined that.

But they could fix all that. Together.

When her son reached her, when he drew his serrated blade and held it to the inside of her arm, she met his steely gaze with a grim determination of her own.

Farin's arm trembled, the jagged edge of his knife scraping against her skin, letting her know it was there without drawing a drop of blood.

That was critical.

"Son," Father called from below, his voice littered with impatience. Disappointment.

Farin pushed farther with the blade, bending Mother's skin with such delicate precision, Mother knew the slightest breath, the slightest unsteadiness would push too far, reveal their cards too early.

"Son."

"Father," Farin said, his voice trembling, pleading. "There are other punishments. She is weak, outcast. Is that not enough for us?"

Father's footsteps had barely reached the wind by the time he reached them, before his hand swept across Farin's ribcage, knocking him to the side, with a gust of strength that Mother felt, that bruised her in the place it bruised her son.

She'd kill him.

She'd been saving up the courage for it, and now she was over-flowing.

"You," Father said, wrapping his broad, gnarled fingers around her throat and squeezing until her vision was littered with speckles of void. "You ruined him. You took my heir and babied him until he was weak. You did it to punish me, didn't you?" he said, grinding his fingernails into her throat. Pain spiked and ebbed as her body healed itself of the injury, the injury her husband couldn't see under the cover of his calloused fingertips. He leaned close, pushed his plump lips against her ear, as he'd done so many nights, so long ago, whispering excuses, excuses, excuses, making her believe her wounds were inflicted by herself. "As they flay your flesh, know that I am flaying his. That I'll sire a dozen heirs to take his place. And when he meets you in the shadows, out of reach from the sun, you can tell him who it was who really did this to him."

He sliced his blade across her throat with the precision of a preda-tor, a predator who preferred his prey to die slowly, in whirlwind of pain and sharp clarity.

Mother smiled.

Father's eyes dipped to her neck, where blood should have flowed, serving as a beacon for the Others he intended to throw her to for breakfast.

He released his grip, as if to check that he hadn't accidentally obscured the gash with his hand.

It was a stupid thought.

But then again, he was a stupid male.

His eyes widened, providing just enough time for Farin to slice his Father's neck and shove him through the Rip.

MOTHER HEALED.

It was what she did. What she had always done.

And what was the Rip, but a wound in the Fabric binding the realms?

So when she touched it—that beautiful ray of light that had tantalized her son so long ago—the light hummed with warmth, as if her touch soothed its pain.

When she withdrew her hand, the wound was gone, and so was the sliver of light.

She might have regretted not being able to watch as the Others tore Father's flesh to shreds, had her son—her son she so longed to take far away from this place, her son she couldn't wait to feed, her son she'd find a female for—not, after signing his father's death sentence, let out a laugh that chilled her weary bones.

"Well, that was almost too easy," he said, his voice cold and hard and not at all what she'd remembered it to be.

She turned toward her son, toward his face, the one she'd known, deep down in her soul, had changed. The change she'd attributed to age, the change her magic had warned her about when she'd confessed her secret, when she'd told him she could close the Rip, that she could free him forever.

"Well?" he asked, cocking his head to the side in a gesture so unfamiliar, she found herself searching his face for some sign this creature wasn't Farin at all, that she'd been duped by a prince lookalike with a grudge against the fae king. "Aren't you going to bow to your king?"

Mother's knees crumbled from underneath her, but not out of reverence.

She simply could not hold herself up anymore. Her limbs shook, and her son's fingers brushed her chin, forcing her to crane her head to look at him, to acknowledge what she'd done.

"You've been granted this chance, this responsibility, son. You could use your power to heal," she said, searching for the glimmer of kindness that was absent from his cold stare.

His lips tilted, revealing a feral grin, one that warped his face, angled his bones in directions she didn't recognize. "Healing is your power, mother. Not mine."

A wail ripped over the trees, a song of sorrow and pain carried on the wind from the nearby village, the village where Mother's friends lived...

She shook her head, confused. "Something is attacking them. We have to go to them," she said, panic flowing through her as she tried to decipher whose screams berated her ears. Malik's? Anika's? The others?

"I was disappointed at first, I'll admit," Farin said, pacing across the crest of the hill now. "I don't know. Perhaps I thought my gift would be like yours, some concentrated version of who I am at my deepest core. That is how it's supposed to work, isn't it? I mean, I assume your friend Anika was always an animal lover, wan't she? Even before the magic found her?"

Mother shuddered, something about Anika's name on her son's lips churning the bile in her stomach.

"I apologize about her, by the way. But then again, how was I supposed to know that when magic binds itself to a host, it attaches itself to their soul. That when that magic abandons its host for a more worthy, more durable body, the old body has no way of surviving the tear? I do wonder if the same applies to us fae. I imagine not, though I intend to find out."

Mother's chest caved in on itself. "No," was all she could manage.

"Now, Malik," Farin said. "Malik I do have to take responsibility for, I'm afraid. But, if I'm to be king, I need commanders whose power is rivaled by none other."

Mother shuddered, her heart spiderwebbing into a million tiny cracks. "You killed them."

Farin lowered his brow, gesturing toward his chest. "Me? No. Really, I blame it on their magic, finicky as they were. Hardly any of them hesitated when we offered them immortal bodies, equipped with strength and speed and youth. One would think that at least one out of six of them would have resisted, at least taken time to consider..."

Mother sucked in a breath. Six. All of them. Her son had murdered all of them. All of her friends. Every last one.

She listened for the wail inside her head, for her magic to abuse her, to scream, to remind her its warning, to weep for its siblings. She banged against the edges of her mind, but she could not reach it, could not make it answer her, tell her what to do.

"Tell me, Mother? Have you forced your magic into submission yet? What am I saying? I'm sure you tolerate its voice prattling on in your mind."

"Farin..." she begged, clutching her stomach as it ached. As it hurt from a wound even her magic couldn't heal.

He kneeled over, placing his hands on his knees so he could meet her at eye level. "The magic that coursed through your friends, they were so eager to get a taste of our power, they never stopped to consider that they might no longer be the ones in control. That their fae hosts might not be their hosts at all, but their masters." His eyes glinted. "We swallowed them whole, Mother. Absorbed them. You could do it, too, you know. Wouldn't you like to have that mind of yours back? Without a grating voice infiltrating every thought?"

Please, Mother begged her magic. *Please tell me what to do.*

It did not answer.

I'm sorry, I'm so sorry, she thought.

It didn't seem to matter. Why would it?

Perhaps she'd already done it, absorbed the magic into herself

444

when she'd forced it to close the Rip. Perhaps it was gone forever, its consciousness ripped away, just like its siblings'.

"Why?" Mother asked, barely able to keep control of her stomach as she let the one word slip out.

The wails coming from the village swelled, threatening to burst Mother's ears, drive her to insanity.

"I didn't understand at first," Farin laughed. "I suppose it was the child in me, but I wondered if my gift would allow me to create something from nothing, to taste flavors not known to fae-kind, to see colors one couldn't imagine if they tried. So, why pain? I've never enjoyed inflicting it, you know, even if it was necessary to gain our rightful place in this new world."

The cries broke her, splitting Mother's head, causing her to see white.

"But then I realized, Mother. The power to inflict pain wasn't the point, was it? It wasn't about the pain at all. It was about the screams."

The blood seemed to drain from Mother's limbs as understanding dawned on her.

"Can't you hear it, Mother?" he asked. "Can't you *taste* it? The catharsis of that beautiful sound. It's relieving to them, you know. Or perhaps you don't. I certainly never did. It most likely shouldn't, but you know what?" he asked, his face tilting. "It does make me feel better. Because when they scream, my pain melts away."

Mother's heart broke. Shattered.

A look that she might have once mistaken as sorrow crossed her son's face. "Not the gift I would have chosen for myself. But perhaps the Fates had my best interest at heart."

"Farin, my boy, this isn't you," Mother cried.

He shook his head. "No, Mother. It's not." He let out a heavy sigh. "Your boy was weak. I like this *me* better."

Her son extended a hand, offering to help her stand. Mother tried to swallow, but there was no moisture in her mouth to assist her.

"I have hopes for this magic, Mother. Hopes that, as it's bonded to me fully, submitted to my control, that it will pass down through my line. I plan to sire an heir when I return to my palace."

Mother stared at the outstretched hand, unable to look any longer into the face she no longer recognized. The one Father had ruined.

The one she had ruined that day, when she'd led Father straight to him.

"You won't take my hand?" he asked. "I have no intentions of hurting you."

His fingers twitched.

His breath caught.

The screams stopped.

Silence filled the air as Farin fell to the ground, dead.

CHAPTER 63

ASHA

The king and I were to share a tent.

As was customary.

My empty stomach gnawed on itself as a servant led me to the extravagant habitation that could have been an apartment complex in my neighborhood.

Tents of all the Alondrian courts' colors speckled the meadow, servants weaving in and out as they set up for the day.

Rivre, though technically part of Charshon, was near to the Adreean Coast, quietly tucked away from civilization, the perfect meeting place for a bunch of paranoid fae leaders who refused to set foot in one another's homes.

The section reserved for Naenden might as well have been an artist's rendition of a flame. In fact, the more I examined it—the way the tents, some of them orange, some scarlet, some yellow, tipped into curves at the top, flowed into the adjacent tent as if they'd been engineered to curve into the shape of the next—the more I convinced myself it was all on purpose. That our entire section was designed to remind the others of the power that blazed from our house.

From their house, I reminded myself.

Kiran's tent was the largest and most menacing of them all, most of its fabric a deep, bloodred crimson, with sections of burnt orange woven in to match the pattern of the rest of the tents. The sheer size of it would have been menacing, even without the implication of who it belonged to.

My husband. The murderer. The flame.

The flame that could make you enjoy burning, if he wanted you to.

A shiver of dread ran up my spine as the servant led me to the bedchambers.

It was massive on the inside, twice the size of Father's and Dinah's hovel. Cedar wardrobes and trunks lined the dark red fabric of our temporary room. Graciously, there were no mirrors to be found.

Maybe Kiran had remembered I hated them.

I shoved the thought down, the implication that he might think of me, ever.

Because then there was the bed, reminding me of a menacing lion slumbering in the middle of the room. Scarlet curtains draped around its four cedar posts, each one sharpened into a stake at the tip.

My throat closed up at the look of it.

I couldn't sleep here. Not with him. Not when I wasn't strong enough to fight off his magic, his influence.

A few of the servants followed us, each rolling a rack of garments packed with all of my most elegant dresses.

This was to be an occasion, after all.

When Kiran strode in, they all scattered, leaving me alone with him, the male who could force me to love him, to forget every act of violence he'd ever committed, simply by tucking my hair behind my ear.

Except for the brief conversation we'd had when Kiran informed me of our upcoming journey, I hadn't seen him since that night, since I'd screamed at him in the garden after the guard had caught me freeing Gwenyth. How long ago had that been? Weeks. I'd locked myself in my room ever since then, until Tavi arrived, painfully less talkative than normal, to prepare me for our journey.

The worst part of the past few weeks was that he hadn't forced himself in. Hadn't acted how I'd expected. Hadn't fulfilled the nightmares. Not until now, at least.

"Your Majesty." My voice came out hollow as a wooden flute.

The only thing that changed in his hard, angular face was the slightest droop in the skin where his jaws met his cheeks.

He lingered at the entrance of the tent as the last of the servants rushed away, as my gaze lost them in the crowd swarming in the pathway cut by the royal tents.

It was only then that he advanced.

My feet begged to run, to retreat, but I didn't let them, wouldn't give him the satisfaction.

I braced myself for the part where he stripped me of my dignity. The part where he made me feel things I didn't want to feel. Things no sane human would feel toward a murderer.

But he stopped, farther than an arm's length away, and stared.

He broke the silence first. "I'm glad you came."

I didn't actually have a choice in the matter, but okay.

"The Council meeting is tomorrow evening, as I'm sure the servants have already informed you. I should warn you, Calias will be there—"

"I'm not afraid of Calias."

Kiran bristled, the implication of my words clear as the water reserved for Naenden royalty.

"Well, you should be."

I couldn't help but bite back. "Why? What's he going to do? Cage me up in his castle and try to figure out a way to steal my magic from me? At least I'm pretty sure he'd allow me to hate him for it."

Kiran closed his eyes, squeezing the bridge of his nose between his fingertips. "I haven't touched you in weeks."

"And is that supposed to make up for the times you did?" Kiran's molten eyes flashed a warning, but the words were coming out now, the ones that had built up in my weeks of solitude. "Is that supposed to make it okay, the things you made me feel for you? The feelings you convinced me were my own?" Saying the words out loud made me sick. Made me feel dirty, used, barely allowed a proper washing before being plunged in the grime once again.

Kiran sighed. "I apologize for not being honest about my abilities earlier. Though I'm sure you can now infer why I don't reveal them to many. It has a tendency to break trust."

I scoffed, not missing his condescension. "If trust was what you were worried about, you never would have used them on me in the first place."

"Asha, I—"

"Just tell me outright. You're fae. You can't lie. So just tell me you never used them on me."

Kiran burst, a wall of flames licking the air around my flustered cheeks, close enough to warm, to warn, but not to burn. And then, as quickly as they emerged, the flames died, quenched by their source. Kiran trembled, though whether it was from surprise at his outburst, or rage, I couldn't tell.

All I knew was that it had me trembling, too.

When he spoke, his voice was too cold for someone who could wield fire at will. "Do you think it's always so easy to control?"

I didn't know what to say, so I took a step back.

He advanced, even his massive shadow overtaking me. "Do you know how many hours my father spent teaching me to control my flame? And yet, it still takes hold of me on occasion. In times of distress."

He closed the space between us, his hotter than natural breath stinging my cheeks now. "There was no one to tell. No one I could trust wouldn't use my abilities for their own gain. If my father used my fire, imagine what he would have done with...with this." He stared at his hands, palms up, as if they were a curse. "I tried to teach myself, but there was so little opportunity. So I tried to suppress it."

"Until?"

The flames in his eyes flashed. "Until you were in pain."

The lychaen venom—the pain that had dissipated faster than the healer had ever witnessed.

Only after Kiran had arrived.

The dreams had stopped after he'd touched me, after Lydia had let him anywhere near me.

It didn't matter, though. "And what? You think because you used it to numb my pain that gave you the right to mess with my head? To make me believe I felt something for you?"

His eyes melted again, as if that golden hue might stream like tears at any moment, staining his razor sharp cheekbones with sunlit paint and scorching his skin. "As far as I'm aware, I never used my abilities to alter the way you felt about me."

I took a step back, away from his heat, the heat that was smothering my thoughts, scrambling them. It was a lie. It had to be a lie.

But he couldn't lie.

"That's not true. You made me feel calm around you. You might not have made me love you, but you took away the fear. The fear that would have kept it from happening."

But Kiran shook his head. "Again. I never used my power to alter the way you felt about me. Gwenyth had been lesson enough. I hadn't realized what I'd been doing to her until it was too late. Until she figured it out and despised me for it. Like I said, it isn't always within my control, but I was careful with you."

No. I took another step back, and the curve of my spine hit the bedpost. He stepped forward, pinning me between the post and his heaving chest, though we still did not touch, though only a sliver of a hair separated us.

What he was saying couldn't have been true. Because he had stolen the power from Gwenyth rather than being born with it. Because that was the only thing that made sense, the only explanation for why he had allowed me to live once he realized I possessed the Old Magic too.

"You're lying. I don't know how. I don't know which part of your story is a half-truth, how you get away with it," I hissed.

"I'm not lying. I can't lie."

"I don't believe you."

A painful twitch of a smile broke the hard line of his lips. "And why is the truth so hard to believe?"

451

The words cut. Because until now, I hadn't known the answer. Not really.

"Because if it's true, then I fell in love with a monster all on my own. Without anyone's help."

His lips were near to mine now, but he was careful not to close the gap, only to let his breath linger. "My love, would that be so awful?"

I gritted my teeth and nodded, afraid that if I allowed the breath to escape that was necessary to form an answer, I'd lose all control and fall right into him.

"And if I weren't a monster?"

That did it, gave me the footing I needed to catch my breath, the strength to resist. To spit his words right back at him.

"Then we'd never have met, would we?"

He pulled back, my arrowheads for words having their intended effect. The air surrounding us cooled as his eyes chilled into that dark, familiar void.

Then he cleared his throat and turned, leaving the same emptiness in his place.

* * *

Roe, the Scriel who'd begrudgingly allowed me into the vizier's office the day I'd offered myself as a sacrificial bride, had volunteered to be my guard, the one in charge of making sure no ill befell me at the hand of Calias.

That was convenient for me, as Roe and I both had about equal concern for my longevity at the moment. In fact, I figured he'd offered himself for the job, hoping to turn his attention away from whomever Calias sent to kidnap me this time.

I wouldn't seek death. The guilt of what it would do to my father and Dinah was enough to dissuade me from that. But if I was to suffer as a caged animal for the rest of my life, and this was my only chance to see the world outside of Naenden, I wasn't going to spend it locked up in a tent.

If Calias captured me, so be it. I'd already doomed myself to be a prisoner either way. Maybe at least I'd get to see snow.

The price of a handful of gold, which I didn't bother to count, was enough to buy me a few hours of a blind eye from Roe. When I slipped a hood over my head, obscured by the evening shadows, I might have been just another servant in the bustling crowd.

If the tents had seemed extravagant in daylight, they were majestic in the lantern light. Some of them swayed in the gentle breeze, the firelight bouncing off their gilded fibers, giving the impression that we were standing in a crowd of oversized candles, flickering playfully about. Chatter buzzed around me, the excitement of servants who had the night off after their hard day's work of setting up the tents.

I wove through the crowds, and the strangest feeling settled in my stomach. That I'd been here before, somewhere, sometime. But I supposed last time I'd woven through a crowd this packed had been the day of the decree. The day that had changed my life forever.

It wasn't hard to allow the crowd to sweep me away this time, to push and poke until I could only see the tip of Kiran's tent, and only if I looked back, which I sought not to do.

Music swelled in the distance. There must have been a traveling band playing somewhere ahead. That would have made sense with the rest of the festivities. Perhaps I'd go for a stroll and listen. After all, I could count on my left hand the times I'd heard professional musicians play.

They tended to avoid deserts.

Apparently, they weren't fond of getting sand in their instruments.

It didn't take long to follow the beautiful tune, especially since my nose would have taken me to them anyway, as they were stationed near an Avelean food stand that smelled of rosemary and something else I couldn't place, but certainly would have liked to.

The melody carried me away with it, somewhere far from here. Somewhere with a trickling river, and peach trees, and wild dogs, and...

I gulped, realizing I'd been thinking of my magic's story. The one we'd yet to finish.

I could tell it to you, if you'd like.

I shook my head. I didn't want to know. It hadn't seemed to be leading anywhere happy. Besides, it was Kiran's story now. He'd done that, taken everything I enjoyed and tainted it with his smell, his heat.

No, thank you.

"Cheerful for such a serious occasion, don't you think?"

The voice coming from my left side made me jolt. I turned my whole body to face its owner. Standing much too close was a human girl so beautiful, her features were almost unreal. Her eyes were teardrops the color of grass after a morning shower, her hair a river of vibrant red curls that poured out, unable to be contained by her dark green hood.

A human servant, maybe? But that didn't seem quite right. In fact, I thought I saw two points bulging from either side of her hood. And then it hit me. The girl was half-fae, like Tavi.

"I didn't mean to startle you," the girl said, with an apology injected with just the right amount of sincerity, without sounding like she pitied me for the reason I'd been so easy to sneak up on.

"It's fine. It's a natural byproduct of my circumstance," I joked.

Fates direct the girl, she didn't shuffle or seem unsettled by my self-deprecation.

Oddly enough, she looked suspicious. "You'd think a queen would have someone keeping an eye on her blind side."

I tensed and shifted my weight to my toes, preparing to launch through the crowd to flee. It had been stupid to leave the tent, where Calias must have had eyes everywhere. "A lychaen didn't work, so he sent you instead?" I asked.

The girl frowned, confusion washing over pixie features. She placed a gentle hand on my arm, a gesture that had the heels of my feet finding the ground again. Then she leaned in close and whispered in my ear. "Are you in trouble?"

I recoiled, the question shaking me to my bone. Was I in trouble? The answer should have been simple. I'd married a king who, at one time, had decided to self-soothe by marrying then murdering a human girl every month of the year until he got over his ex—his ex he pretended to have slaughtered with his own hand, but had kept locked away in the dungeon instead. I'd bonded myself to a male who could warp my feelings into anything that suited his interest.

A king who'd had the power, yet had refrained from using it on me. A king who, as much as he was capable of cruelty, was capable of repentance. Capable of remorse.

It was only when I shook my head that the weight of it all crashed down upon me. The realization of how deeply my trouble had burrowed itself into me.

The girl didn't look convinced, but she straightened all the same. "Probably for the best. You're not really my ideal cargo anyway."

I frowned at the acid in her voice. Was it directed at someone else, or at herself?

Something bulging from her satchel caught my attention. A flute. "Will you play with them?" I asked.

She laughed and waved her fingers in the band's direction, as if to lump them all together in a group. A group very distinct from herself. "This is all a little too public for my tastes."

An artist that didn't care for fame. Interesting. "So, you hate money, then?"

Her head jerked, but a smirk spread on her face all the same. "I don't work for money."

"You're a servant?"

Her face contorted, if only for a moment. Only long enough for me to catch the pang of resentment in the flicker of the lantern light. But she had the wall back up within an instant. The trained composure was impressive. Who was this girl?

She turned to leave, but it was my turn to place a hand on her shoulder. "Who are you?"

"I shouldn't have come here," was her only answer as she gently shrugged my hand away.

"Then why did you?"

She smiled, a sad little thing, paired with sorrow and another emotion I couldn't place. But then there was something else too.

Hope.

"I had to see the face of change."

When she slipped into the crowd, it occurred to me I'd only seen the girl because she'd wanted me to.

And that I'd never see her again.

I didn't know why that made me feel so sad.

"You're making all sorts of new friends, aren't you?" The sly voice ripped me from my thoughts as another girl stepped in front of me. A girl with hair like moonlight and a feral grin to match the shadows.

Gwenyth.

Her gaze searched through the crowd for the red-headed girl who had just disappeared. "I've been watching that one for the past few days. She's like us, you know. I can feel it, her magic. Can you?"

I swallowed, unsure what to make of Gwenyth being here at all, much less the mystery girl who apparently had her own magic. Magic that Gwenyth could sense, but I couldn't.

I certainly felt nothing.

"You shouldn't be here," I whispered, scanning the crowd for Kiran, Fin, a servant, anyone who might recognize my predecessor, the human queen who was supposed to be dead. The girl who was supposed to be far, far away from Kiran.

"You're right about that." She nodded her head to the trees that lined the meadow. "Well, are you coming?"

CHAPTER 64

ASHA

I don't like the feel of this place. There's something about it... My magic trailed off, seemingly at a loss for words, which was especially unnerving.

I just need to know what she wants, I insisted.

Gwenyth strode through the meadow, moonlight streaking her silver dress and her ash-blond hair, causing both to glow. Now that she had cleaned herself up, I could see even more why there had always been talk of her immense beauty. Her features might have been fae-like, with her wide eyes and sharp cheekbones. I imagined, growing up with the rich humans who coveted the attributes of the fae, she had probably received that as a compliment throughout her upbringing. Food of actual substance had filled her sallow cheeks in the weeks since I'd set her free.

"You're looking thin," she commented, her blazing blue eyes sweeping over my gauntly form that barely filled out my gown. Tavi had needed to take it in three times over the past few weeks. "What, did he lock you in the dungeon too, then let you out just to make an appearance?"

I shook my head. "No. I've barely left my room."

"Hm." That tiny, high-pitched noise made me want to squirm. I couldn't explain the feelings I had toward this girl. On one hand, I still wished to throttle her, to erase her from my memory, the girl whose existence had ruined, first, my life, and second, the life I thought I had rebuilt.

But then again? How could I hate her for telling me the truth? How could I hate a woman who had been given less of a choice than I had in marrying our manipulative husband? Gwenyth had watched them slaughter Tiberius, the guard to whom she'd given her heart. They killed him right in front of her. How could I truly hate her?

My limbs trembled in the moonlight. "What do you want?"

She furrowed her already perfectly arched brows, as if I was capable of offending her. "To help you, Asha, like you helped me."

I replayed the words, scanning for guile, for mockery, but found none.

A weak smile broke my grimace. "You shouldn't be here. You should be on the other end of Alondria by now."

"And leave you to suffer? I think not," she scoffed, waving her pale hand at the moon to dismiss such a silly notion.

I halted as we crossed the meadow. "Is that what this is about? You trying to rescue me? Because I can't run. Not like you. He'll kill Dinah and my father if I do."

Are you so sure about that?

My stomach clenched, my intestines swimming with unease, with confusion. I wasn't so sure about anything anymore.

Gwenyth stopped and turned toward me, frowning, the intensity of the expression only accentuating her perfect features. "I know."

I nodded. "Good."

"That's why we have to make sure he can't follow you."

My numb heart faltered. "And how are we supposed to do that?"

"We're going to kill him, Asha."

* * *

I BLINKED what must have been forty times before I responded. "The last time you tried to kill Kiran, it didn't work out so well for you." *Or the people you loved*, I kept to myself.

"That may be true. But that was before I had you as a friend."

I could have laughed at that, could have said that I didn't have any friends. But I didn't have that kind of energy. Not when whatever Gwenyth had planned was likely to get not only me, but also Dinah and my father, killed.

"And what can I do?"

"Well, for starters, you can bend metal with your words."

I groaned. "That's not really—"

"Asha," she snapped, her blue eyes greedy with what I now recognized, not as undiluted concern for a friend, but a hunger for revenge. "You can bend metal with your words. Think of what else you could bend. What else you could crush. What you could stop."

Her words hit me then, the full weight of them.

What I could stop.

Nothing short of a fae heart.

Was that even possible?

The question, directed at my magic, received no answer. Which was answer enough.

A shudder that had nothing to do with the breeze coursed the length of my spine, freezing the marrow in my bones.

I shook my head frantically. "I can't do that."

"Why not?"

"Because my family—"

"Are already in a safe place," Gwenyth smiled, placing a hand on my shoulder. "Some friends of mine got them out of Meranthi a few days ago. They're safe. And anxious to see you."

Tears stung at my eye as I searched Gwenyth's face for any sign of deceit. Again, I found none. Her face was softer than it had been in that cell, and so was her voice.

"Why are you doing this?" I asked.

That sinister nature reappeared, flickering over her soft, girlish face. "Because I want him dead. Where he can't hurt or steal from anyone ever again."

My head swam with the gravity of what she was asking me to do. I'd resolved myself to break her out of her cell, planned to shut myself up in my room for eternity, as long as I could shut him out of my heart, avoid his touch. I'd resigned myself to be his eternal prisoner.

But to cut off his life, to kill? That hadn't even crossed my mind.

Then there was the problem of Gwenyth's story about Kiran stealing her magic not matching up with Kiran's, and as much as I was inclined to believe her over him, that didn't change the fact he was incapable of lying.

"You told me Kiran stole your magic, but Kiran said he's had the ability to warp other people's feelings since childhood," I said.

She stopped and swept her gaze over me, assessing me.

"He can't lie," I added.

"Did he specifically say, 'I've had the magical ability to change other people's emotions at my will since childhood?' Because if he used generic words like 'I've had *it*,' then there's no way you can know what he was referencing."

I groaned. My conversation with Kiran had been so heated, I hadn't exactly been keeping an internal record of his word choice.

"That's what I thought," she said. She kept walking, and as we approached wherever she was taking me, something sweet and earthy and tangy wafted in the evening wind. I struggled to keep up, my slippers useless in the dewy grass. "The Council meets tomorrow night. We'll do it then, together. I've already talked with a few of the guards. They were close to Tiberius, and they hate Kiran for what happened to him. They've agreed that, during all the commotion, they'll sneak you out. All you have to do is make their hearts stop."

"Their?" I shuddered.

"Kiran's and Fin's."

I shook my head, swallowing, as if that would somehow fix the pressure in my ears that had obviously caused me to mishear what Gwenyth had just said. "Why does Fin have to die?"

Gwenyth placed her hands on my shoulders again, squeezing them gently. "Isn't it strange to you that, after Kiran slept with and eventually murdered his wife, that Fin's been fine with it all?"

"I—"

"No, think about it, Asha. In the past two years, between the two of them, they've married three human girls. Two of us had magic, which isn't exactly common. That's too much of a coincidence, don't you think? I keep thinking, what if Ophelia had magic too? And once one of them, Fin or Kiran, figured out how to steal it from her, they killed her together. There weren't any other witnesses, were there?"

"Not that I know of, but don't you think that's a stretch? What if Fin doesn't have any idea what Kiran has been up to? What if he believes Ophelia's death happened just the way everyone else believes it did? Then we would be killing an innocent male. That's even if I had the power to kill a fae at all, which I don't. Not without a source from the Nether."

Her lips curved into a mirror image of the crescent moon lurking in the foggy sky above us. "What if I told you we have a source from the Nether?"

I frowned, which only seemed to fuel her.

"What if I told you we could access the Nether itself?" She twirled, her silvery robe fluttering in the moonlight in the middle of the meadow. In the distance, a stream hobbled over pebbles, rushing and playing and pivoting. There was an orchard to our right, where peach trees grew. That must have been the smell I'd caught—ripe, crushed peaches painting the ground where their flesh had spilled.

Sweet and tangy.

My heart jolted. "Where are we?"

A smile slipped over her pale face, just as I noticed the ominous hill coming into view in the distance. "Asha, dear. We're where it all began."

* * *

I SHOOK MY HEAD, fear coursing through me, swarming my mind and scrambling to make sense of her words. If it was true, if Gwenyth had brought me to the location of the Rip.

No. No.

I'd seen what dwelled just on the other side of the curtain. The silver beasts that raged, moonlit blood dripping from their fangs, the monsters that wiped out the fae, that sent them fleeing to our world for refuge.

"We can't be here." I stepped backward, tripping over my robe. My hands dug into the soft earth, dirt cramming itself under my fingernails, as if to seek shelter.

That's when I felt it.

The pulsing—even, and a thousand times stronger than the energy that coursed through the ancient scrolls. It sang on the edges of the gentle breeze, thrummed through the dewy grass.

No. No.

I launched myself to my feet, scrambling to regain my balance as my head spun. "This isn't safe. We need to get out of here."

Gwenyth approached me, taking my hand in between hers. "It's okay, Asha. You don't have to open it. You just have to draw power from it."

I don't like this, my magic protested.

"You don't understand. There is power that lurks—" My throat caught on the words as fear filled my chest. It had been true. The story had been true. The little boy, Farin, and the beasts with the dripping fangs.

Because as much as I wanted to will it away, to blame the story on my magic for having visited this meadow and coming up with the story itself, I couldn't ignore the energy.

I could not ignore the power.

This is my fault, my magic rumbled, *I should have seen it, should have felt it...*

Why didn't you tell me your story about Farin was real?

My memory is a slippery thing, elusive in nature.

Gwenyth's whisper ripped my attention away from my magic. "But

I do understand. You feel it, don't you? It's calling to you. You don't have to be afraid of it. It knows you, and it wants to help. Can't you hear it calling to you just like it called to you that day from the lamp?"

I dropped her hand.

"How do you know about that?"

Her brows faltered over her pale, sparkling eyes. "You told me. The day you set me free, you told me that you got your magic from an accident. That you touched a lamp—"

"I never said anything about the lamp," I said, my heartbeat frozen in my chest.

She let out an exasperated laugh. "Well, I'm sure you did. How else would I have known?"

I took a step back.

Because, other than Kiran, only one other person in the world knew about that lamp.

Gwenyth turned toward a tree to our left, her eyes pleading to the shadows.

Or rather, the person who stepped out from the shadows.

"Hi, Asha."

I knew his face before the moonlight highlighted his handsome features, the boyish eyes and windswept hair I could have sketched from memory, if only I'd had the talent.

Az.

CHAPTER 65

ASHA

Seeing him there, in the wrong place, in the wrong time, with the wrong amount of stubble, was as if, all this time, my mind had only been pretending to blend my thoughts together, only putting up a farce, an illusion that I could access any memory of mine at any time I wanted. In that moment, I realized my mind had simply set up a system of organization in which every bit of information I'd ever held onto was stacked next to the other bits that my mind considered relevant. So that when I saw him, my childhood friend, standing here, responding to Gwenyth's call, there was a delay—the time it took for my mind to scramble around to find the document that matched his face with his name. He might have been a stranger to me in that lapse of a moment.

In fact, perhaps he was a stranger, after all.

"Az?" I gasped. "What are you doing here?" I started toward him, preparing to wrap my arms around him, but something stopped me, warned my heel to dig into the mud.

What was he doing here?

"Asha." Az smiled as he breathed my name, but there was something in his voice that was strained. How many times in my life had he said my name? Thousands? Yet, it had never quite sounded like that.

High pitched. Forced.

Fake.

As he stepped out of the shadows, Gwenyth met him, her fingers finding the spaces between his as she peered up at him with her doe eyes.

He didn't look at her—only at me as I traced the path between them with my eye, as my gaze bounced between their faces, followed the curves of their necks down their shoulders to their interlocked hands and back up again to be sure this wasn't some wild illusion.

What I wanted to say next was that I didn't understand.

Except that, for the first time, I thought maybe I did.

Az pursed his lips together into that forced, bashful smile. Even in the moonlight, his cheeks blushed, a pink that might have occurred at the hand of our overbearing Naenden sun, had we been in Naenden, and had Az's skin not darkened to adjust to its battering rays long ago.

My heart went cold and motionless, as if it might miss the explanation if it beat too loud. As if it needed to hear it to decide whether to continue beating.

"When?" That was the best I could do with the little breath I had in me, the only word I could pluck from the swarm of questions buzzing around in my head, making my ears ring and sweat bead on my clammy forehead.

Az's shoulders hunched in that all-too-familiar tell, the one I could have recognized in a market crowd, the posture he assumed when he should have been ashamed of something and wasn't. When he hoped those who loved him would find his shortcomings endearing. "Since my trip to Avelea last year."

My internal calendar flapped in the breeze as I scrambled to find it —the exact date the boy I'd loved my entire life had fallen for a married woman. For Gwenyth.

What was it that he had said when he'd returned, when he'd told me of the human queen? *I was there when he chose her.*

"The ball. The one where Kiran chose the queen, chose you," I said, looking at Gwenyth, before addressing my best friend once more. "You came back beaming. You came back *beaming.*" The last sentence, I almost whispered to myself. "You said you were high off travel. That you were going to take me with you someday."

Az blushed again, and he and Gwenyth exchanged a look of pity that made me want to shove my head into the dregs of a deep well and breathe in slowly.

Gwenyth nodded, and Az slipped his hand from hers before taking a step toward me.

I stumbled backward, my slippers treacherous in the damp grass. "But you're married. I saw you in the crowd the day of the parade." My gaze slipped to his left hand in search for that swirling tattoo, and there it was, fresh and bright as mine in the moonlight.

He sighed. "There's so much I should have told you, Asha."

I shook my head, if only to disorient my thoughts, to keep them from going down the inevitable path of reason, from taking one step in front of the other until they arrived at the destination I could already smell from a distance.

Swift as a hawk, he reached me and took my hands in his. They were warm, soft, just as they'd always been, even in his fingertips that hard labor had once left calloused. "Please sit down with me. I'll explain everything," he whispered.

He kneeled to the ground, and I followed, my knees promising to give out soon, anyway.

We sat like that for a long while, his wide brown eyes pleading with me before he even opened his mouth.

To please, please listen.

I nodded.

"When my mother was on her deathbed, she sent my siblings out of the room. She told me..." He swallowed and winced. "She told me I had another sister, one I'd never met, who lived in the palace. That I should find her. That twins deserved to know each other. She said there had always been something missing in me, in my soul, and she blamed herself for separating us when we were children. At the time of our birth, she'd thought it was for the best, because my sister didn't grow up like we did. My sister never lacked for food or water. My mother had tried to convince the same family to take me, but they needed children who could work at the palace, and I didn't have my sister's traits…"

"Your sister's traits." The words brushed my lips in a whisper, echoing his own as I traced that familiar face, the face so handsome I'd always teased that he belonged with the fae, not with us. The wide, crescent eyes, the strong jawline, the flawless skin that would have been enough evidence to convict him in the courts, the silent testimony I'd somehow overlooked. The features that had the fae females in the marketplace swooning over him. "Your father was fae."

He swallowed and nodded, but I frowned as my mind attempted to force some of the oblong pieces together. "But your ears are rounded."

He choked a bit, then shrugged, as if this knowledge didn't completely shatter his identity. "Apparently, it's not a trait that's always passed down. Something about how the fae magic mixes with certain types of human blood or something." He ran his fingers through his dark, wild hair, a motion that might have caused my stomach to swallow my heart whole a few short months ago, before the rock in my gut weighed me down, prevented me from launching into his arms and embracing him.

"You said your sister works at the palace. Is her name Tavi?" I asked, though I thought I already knew the answer.

He nodded, and a whir of memories came back to me. How her expressions had reminded me of him, but I'd simply brushed them off as symptoms of being heartbroken. How she'd mentioned a brother, one for whom…

For whom she found the books.

"You're the one who wrote the messages in the books. Not the solider Tiberius." I looked back and forth between Az and Gwenyth, and their silent expression confirmed as much. When I spoke, I directed my words at Az. "You asked Tavi to check out books from the library for you. She thought you were just a quick reader, but you were using them to communicate with Gwenyth."

Az swallowed before answering, "Yes, Gwenyth and I worked out that particular method the night Kiran chose her as his bride."

"And Tavi did what you asked, never suspecting what you were up to, didn't she? She must have put it together when she found me in the library with the stack of books and a list of your notes in order. That's why she took them. Because she was trying to protect you, her brother."

"Stupid girl," Gwenyth said. "Wish she would have put in the same amount of effort to protect me. Instead, when I found that someone had taken the vial of poison from my hiding place, I knew I had little time to get one last note to Az." Her gaze lingered on him, the hunger she harbored for my friend evident in the way she curled her full lips. It was revolting. "I'd barely gotten the book back onto the shelves before the Captain of the Guard came to arrest me."

I shook my head, trying to ignore Gwenyth lest I throttle her. "I still can't believe you and Tavi are twins."

Az let out a long exhale, and his breath fogged in the cold. "That wasn't all my mother confessed, Asha."

CHAPTER 66

ASHA

*M*y heart sank. What else could there be?

"The late King, King Rajeen, often had women scouted out for him from the city when he grew bored with his queen. My mother was one of those women. When she discovered she was pregnant, she feared for her life. For our lives. You see, the king forced the women to take a special brew afterward. He didn't want any unwanted offspring getting the idea they deserved an inheritance. But the brew he forced on my mother failed, and my mother was so poor, even poorer than when she was married to my stepfather. She knew she would have to scrape by on alms to provide for one child, so when my sister and I were born and shocked her with the burden of twins, she knew she couldn't keep both of us. My sister looked fae, with her pointed ears, so my mother convinced the kitchen servant at the palace to adopt her; they were only employing fae in the days of Rajeen. Mother kept me, but her heart ached for Tavi for the rest of her life. I think that's why she told me in the end who I really was."

It felt as if time had stood still. Az? My Az, was the son of King Rajeen?

Wait.

That meant Az was Kiran's brother.

I thought I might fall ill.

Before I could grapple with that unpleasant truth, Az spoke, interrupting my thoughts, "When I found out, well, I couldn't process it. So I set off on that merchant trip. That's when I met Gwenyth. We had planned to elope when Prince Kiran picked her, of all people, to be his bride. Through Tavi, we were able to exchange messages and even meet from time to time.

"We thought we could carry on like that and be happy. But then, Gwenyth kept having moments she couldn't remember with Kiran. As if he was suppressing her memories or something. And she would have these bruises that she couldn't explain. So we came up with a plan. A plan that wouldn't just free Gwenyth, but that would free everyone. All the humans of Naenden."

I nodded. Because I understood now, and the sting of that insight threatened to cauterize my stomach. "A plan that would make you king."

He whistled, as if the thought knocked the wind out of him. As if he hadn't considered it millions of times in the past year. All without ever mentioning it to me.

"When we met by the statue of Tionis—"

"Tionis," I said, barely whispering the wretched name, the name that condemned me to my own stupidity. Because that was the name —Tionis, Tionis, Tionis—that had linked Az and Gwenyth together all along. Hadn't Gwenyth placed them within feet of each other when she'd admitted that she'd heard a diplomat blabbing about the statue that housed magical passageways, as she had poured drinks at Kiran's ball? I'd even assumed Az had been sitting at that very table, that he'd heard of Tionis from the same source, and used that information to sneak into the garden. The note from the book in the library had given instructions to meet there. The note written from Az to Gwenyth.

The limited contents of my almost-empty stomach threatened to swirl into my throat.

"Asha?" Az asked, concern brewing on his familiar brow.

"Go on," I said, my dry voice cracking.

"When Gwenyth and I met by Tionis, I proposed a plan. There's a decree amongst the kingdoms that it's illegal for royalty to murder their own siblings."

I nodded, remembering how Fin had explained this to me in the caravan while we journeyed across the Sahli. "Yeah, it has something to do with keeping order and the Council not having to deal with overthrown governments all the time."

"Exactly. So—"

I didn't need him to finish explaining. Because, suddenly, the part of the story that made no sense... It had struck me as strange that Ophelia would use control over the province of Talens as a motivator for Kiran to conspire against Fin, since Kiran's board of advisors already ran Talens anyway.

But Ophelia hadn't known that.

Gwenyth hadn't known that.

Az hadn't known that.

There was a reason it made no sense, and that reason was standing in front of me in the skin of my best friend. My stomach hollowed out.

In the dungeon, Gwenyth had mentioned the ordeal between Kiran and Ophelia. Except, Gwenyth was supposed to be in solitary confinement when the news of Ophelia's death returned. But when I had asked her how she knew about it, she claimed Kiran had been forcing himself on Ophelia for a long time. And then she had acted like she hadn't known Ophelia was dead.

Which, I suppose she hadn't.

Our ally is in, that was what the note had said, the one that came after the note mentioning Starfall.

Kiran and Gwenyth had visited Fin and Ophelia during Starfall.

She hadn't known about the affair from Ophelia.

She had known about the affair, because she had been the one to plan it...

Ophelia was the ally.

"So you somehow convinced Ophelia to persuade Kiran to murder Fin. To convince him they could make it look like an accident, but then she would have the evidence you needed against Kiran to bring in front of the Council."

They both nodded, turning my heart to stone. Without the smallest bit of inflection, I asked, "And how did you manage that?"

Gwenyth interjected this time. "We didn't exactly have to beg her. As much as Fin carries himself like a gentleman, he's no better than his brother. He kept her prisoner. She was glad to be rid of him."

I rifled through my memories again, to the conversations I'd had with Fin about his late bride. He'd seemed so heartbroken that she was gone. So gentle. Could he really have been such a monster that his wife had conspired to have him murdered without a second thought?

"And then," I bit my lip, "with Kiran and Fin out of the way, you'd be the next in line for the throne."

Az breathed out again, and the tendrils of smoke that escaped his mouth curled between us before dissipating.

"And you think the fae would accept that?" I asked.

Gwenyth laughed, answering for my friend. "They'd have to. I did quite a bit of research on it when I was queen. Az is the next in line for the throne after Fin, considering it would never go to Princess Lydia—not in Naenden, at least. The law doesn't specify whether the heir must be legitimate. Or that they have to be pure-blooded fae. Besides, even if the Council has any objections, we already have the support of a few of the noble families on our side."

My eye flickered to Az's hand again, to the swirling tattoo, to the memory of the fae woman in the marketplace, the one who had shattered me with her look of pity. "Your wife is the daughter of a noble family?" This had to be a joke, a nonsensical nightmare. "And how exactly did you manage to get their blessing?"

Az bit his lip, but Gwenyth giggled. "Oh, Az can be quite seductive when he wants to be, especially to those with weak minds."

My stomach twisted in revulsion, and Az at least had enough decency to stare at the grass. "Alright, so you seduced the girl. I fail to see how you convinced her parents to let you marry her."

Az cleared his throat, as if to signal Gwenyth to give him time to explain himself, but she rattled on, the truth bursting forth like the juicy piece of gossip that I supposed it was. "As it turns out, fae nobility are prudes, and while their sons are off doing whatever and whomever they wish, they tend to have a tighter rein on their daughters."

"Exactly," I said. "And I imagine most of them aren't keen on marrying their daughters off to humans. Poor ones at that."

"True," Gwenyth said. "But the only thing worse than having your daughter marry a human, is having your daughter sleep with a human, and the news slithering its way into the ears of your fellow nobles."

My jaw went slack as I turned on Az. "You seduced a girl so you could blackmail her parents into letting her marry you?"

He buried his hands into his face, allowing his fingers to skim through his hair. "She'll have a good life as queen. Better than she had in her abusive mother's house. Believe me, her parents won't be so upset either, once they realize they've inadvertently secured a marriage for their daughter with the heir to the throne. They'll support my ascension fully, and my heir is less likely to be challenged with a fae mother of noble birth."

My mind had gone numb by this point. "And you're alright with this?" I asked Gwenyth. "Allowing this girl to take your place as queen? It doesn't bother you that Az slept with her? That he'll sire heirs with her?"

Gwenyth shuffled but gained her haughty composure quickly enough. "It's never been about being queen, little girl. If it were, I'd have suffered through that bore of a husband that we share." I had to hold myself from biting the bait, from reminding her that we didn't share anything, that Kiran divorced her and left her to rot. But I held my tongue, if only because sick curiosity had me wondering how in Alondria a woman could bear it for the man she loved to sleep with another.

She cast a hungry look in his direction, and her blue eyes lit up in the moonlight. "It's only ever been about being with Az. Whatever that takes, I'm willing to offer," she said, though her voice caught on the words, breaking, bending to his will.

He offered his hand to her in return, and I stared at my feet to avoid puking lest I catch the same longing in his eyes.

Instead, I let my mind wander to that nightmare of a night, the one where Az had come for me, the one where I'd rejected him. I turned to those cool green eyes, the eyes that should have seemed familiar, that I hoped would bring me comfort. And maybe they would, depending on how he answered my next question. "That night in the garden, when you claimed you'd always been in love with me and wanted to run away with me. Where exactly did that fit in?"

Az shifted uncomfortably in his seat, but the fact that Gwenyth didn't as much as look fazed told me all I needed to know. "I thought Gwenyth was dead. I was mourning. My head wasn't in the right place. And I love you, Asha. I always have. I needed you in that moment, as confusing as it was."

"And you're sure it had nothing to do with the fact that I was suddenly in a position of close proximity to the king." It wasn't a question. I didn't need an answer.

"Asha," Az took my hand in his once more, brushing his thumb over my palm, a gesture that would have once sent a surge of warmth coursing through my blood. Now, it heated my blood alright, right to a simmer that threatened to boil over the edges of my sanity. "Please. You're the only one who can help us. Not just me and Gwenyth. This is bigger than the two of us. Bigger than the three of us. How many nights did we sit up on that rooftop dreaming of a world where humans ruled? *Fair* humans. And now, we have that chance. The Fates have gifted us—no, entrusted to us—the opportunity to make a world that's a haven for the humans, the ability to have a voice on the Council."

His dark eyes twinkled in the moonlight, and the evening wind chilled my skin, just as it always had. The part of me that ached for the time when it had been me and Az against the world jolted to life.

But I had to kill it.

Because now there was something in his eyes I didn't recognize.

Something that had been there the entire time.

Something I'd chosen to overlook.

"And what about Tiberius?" I asked.

Az blinked. "What about him?"

I searched myself before I asked the question. For any plausible answer that would win me over to Az's side. I found one and only one. But first I addressed Gwenyth. "You claimed you loved Tiberius, but he was executed because his name was on the list with yours for who was supposed to be smuggled out of Naenden. He was your safety net, wasn't he? Someone to blame if you were caught and people started questioning how you had communicated with the smuggler? That way, even if you were found out, Az would stay safe. You put his name in the note to the smuggler, and then had him deliver his death sentence himself. Did he even know what was in it?"

Gwenyth only sneered. "Of course, he didn't. He knew better than to open a correspondence sent by his queen."

Hatred washed over me, directed toward this shell of a woman, but I turned my attention to Az instead, pleading, "What evil did he do to deserve to die?"

There it was. A line for my best friend, one I'd practically shoved into his palms. I would have accepted the right answer in a thousand different currencies. A tear welling up in his eye. Burying his face into his hands. An even-keeled statement of remorse, regret. That they hadn't ever intended for anyone innocent to come to harm.

Instead, Az's face hardened, and that something I'd chosen to over-look stared me right in the face, refusing to be ignored any longer. "They're fae, Asha. They're the enemy. They've always been. And don't look at me that way, like I should feel something for them because I have fae heritage tainting my blood. What have they ever done for me. For us?"

My ballooning heart didn't shatter, because that would imply that it left behind pieces, pieces I might could pick up, even if it cut my fingers to do so.

My heart burst, spilling its contents on the dewy ground, which was all too eager to soak them up. "No. Not all of them. Not Fin. I won't hurt Fin."

Az and Gwenyth exchanged a nod, a signal indicating they'd

prepared a plan, in the case I answered this way. Gwenyth strode over to us and kneeled next to me. "He asked you nicely," she hissed through her teeth. "What he was too kind to mention is that the little safe house we set up for your sister only remains such on the condition you do as we say."

Fear sliced through my ribs, making it hard to breathe. I turned to Az to examine that face I knew so well, to see if it was true. The only hint I found was the crease of disappointment marking his forehead. "I don't want it to come to that, Asha. You know I don't."

"Oh, don't worry," Gwenyth laughed. "I might have stretched the truth earlier. We only have your sister. We thought it best to leave your father behind. That way, if you allow your sister to die, you can relive the experience by explaining to him what happened. I've heard he's not in good health. Hopefully her death won't come as too much of a shock."

This wasn't happening. This was some horrible nightmare. Lychaen venom still coursed through my veins, and this had all been some dreadful dream. Falling for Kiran. Finding out his wife rotted in the jail cells. Az's lies. It wasn't real. It couldn't be. None of it made any sense.

"No. No, it won't. It's Dinah, Az. She's your family." I choked on the words as I squeezed his hands, pleading.

Gwenyth rolled her eyes, a look that awoke some violent beast in me, a longing that someone would rip those arrogant, rolling eyes out of her head. Her, she had done this. She had seduced my friend with her promises of power, of purpose, and she'd morphed him into someone I didn't recognize. "Technically, *Lady Queen*, Kiran and Fin are closer relation, and he doesn't have a problem killing them off, does he?"

I turned my attention to Az, to the bond between us, the one that had endured so much more than he and Gwenyth had.

"Az." He stared at his toes, refusing to look at me, so I tipped his chin, forcing him to hold my gaze. "I know you're good at heart. This isn't you," I whispered. It was all coming together now, the source of all this wickedness. Gwenyth had poisoned his mind, just as she'd poisoned mine against Kiran, against Fin. It all made sense. He must have confided in her his heritage when they met. But when the opportunity presented itself, she married Kiran instead, because why marry a king's illegitimate son when you could marry a prince? But her marriage to Kiran hadn't been enough for her. She'd needed more. Power, danger. So she'd manipulated poor Az. And then she'd manipulated me. Me, Kiran, Az—we'd all been chips in the palm of this girl's hand.

"This isn't you. You wouldn't hurt them. I know it."

Az shifted, the muscle at his jaw jerking. Gwenyth laughed, an insult at the tip of her tongue.

Except she never got the chance to speak it.

Because Az jolted up. His blade sliced her throat, trapping the words so they'd never reach the raw wind's air.

Her limp body crumpled to the ground, a mass of silvery thread in the moonlight. I choked on a gasp as my hand reflexively went to my mouth.

Mingled fear and relief flooded me. Fear at what my best friend was capable of. Relief that he had used his newfound capability to protect me.

To protect my sister.

Az wiped his blade on his pants, staining them with Gwenyth's blood. Then he kneeled, his face a hair from mine, and whispered, "Consider that the least of what I would do."

CHAPTER 67

ASHA

I couldn't tear my eyes away as Az lifted Gwenyth's limp body by her armpits and dragged her into the trees. Blood smeared the grass in little streaks, tugging at a memory of the time Az and I found a bunch of poisoned berries that we'd quickly crushed and used to finger-paint the clay walls of our neighboring apartment building.

The neighbors had found it later in the day, and by the streaks of dark red splattered across the wall, had assumed a brutal murderer had left the marks of their sin as a calling card.

We'd been in so much trouble.

Az disappeared into the shadows of the woods, and my feet tugged at me to run. But there was no use in that. I'd always explained away the fact Az could so easily outrun me, reasoned it was due to the difference in our sexes, even when we were too young for it to have mattered. But Az had fae blood running through his veins.

If I ran, it would only inconvenience him.

And that wasn't a side of his I wanted to be on, alone, in the dark, with acres of trees that would be more than willing to hide a body for a friend.

When Az returned, I searched his face for the boy I knew. And somehow, I found him. Not where I expected, though. Where I expected to find shivering limbs and cheeks drained of color and eyes full of the daunting realization that he'd just separated a human soul from its body, I instead found cool determination. A quality I recognized from the countless times a snake had ended up in our hovel, and Az had been the one to come to our rescue. He'd been our knight, our fearless protector who could behead a viper without shrieking. Then he'd go off to bury it, and he'd returning looking... Well, looking like this.

"You didn't have to do that," I said, forcing my voice to stay even, collected, though I wanted nothing more than to wail.

"She made it necessary. Gwenyth was a foolish girl. In the end, her conniving nature couldn't make up for the fact she didn't know how to keep her mouth shut."

I swallowed. His meaning was clear enough. In Gwenyth's quest to win me over to their side, she'd been too eager. Back in the dungeon, she'd slipped information about Ophelia that she shouldn't have known. Of course, she'd recovered easily enough by claiming the affair had been going on for a while. But the part about her knowing that my magic came from a lamp. There had been no explaining that away.

A question tapped against my mind like a loose shutter in a sand storm. "Was this your plan all along?"

Az didn't answer. He didn't have to.

"Gwenyth said she was caught because Tavi planned on rebinding one of her old books for her birthday," I said.

"Is that a question?"

"Did you tip Tavi off about the poison Gwenyth had in her possession?"

Az sighed before looking up at me. "Tavi admitted to me one night that she was terrified about Gwenyth's birthday coming up. She was afraid if she presented Gwenyth with the wrong gift, Gwenyth would find a creative way to punish her. I gave her the idea to rebind the book. Tavi's such a timid creature. I thought for sure she would put the vial back where she found it and not tell a soul. At least, not until the king was poisoned. But once the king was dead, I knew she'd have a guilty conscience and give up what she knew. I never expected her to be brave enough to go to the Captain of the Guard immediately."

"So you meant for Gwenyth to get caught in the end?"

No answer.

"Right. Is that what you were doing in the garden that night? Did you figure out that she was alive? Were you coming to finish her off so she wouldn't rat you out eventually?"

Again, nothing.

I sighed. "Was anything Gwenyth said true? About Kiran and Fin, I mean?"

He turned his dark eyes on me and ran his fingers through his hair, a habit that had stopped my heart so many times before.

Still did.

But for another reason entirely.

Gwenyth's blood dripped from his fingers and stained his hair.

He must have noted that the familiar movement didn't have its desired effect, because he dropped his hand and shrugged. "How am I supposed to know? Whatever Gwenyth told you in that dungeon, she was going off on her own. I didn't even know she was alive until a few weeks ago, when she came sauntering up to my door. Does it matter? They're fae, Asha. Human life holds no value to them."

That was a *no*, then.

Lies. Gwenyth had fed me lies about Kiran just to turn me against him. Just to plant doubt in my soul. But, then again, she'd been right about Kiran's secret ability, his power to alter others' feelings with a simple touch. He'd admitted as much.

She conveniently failed to mention that she had been plotting to kill him from the beginning.

My heart sunk. I'd felt pity for Gwenyth. I still did, in some twisted way. She might have been a master manipulator, but she was the one who'd been duped in the end.

We both had.

I wondered how many questions I'd be allotted before Az's

patience ran out, before I ended up slumping next to Gwenyth, both of us in the same boat, simply for trusting the wrong male.

How ironic that my human friend had become more of my enemy than the fae king who might have slaughtered a thousand human women had I not stepped in and changed his mind?

Changed his heart.

If not love, then what? That was what Dinah had said to me that night.

Dinah.

Did she even know to be afraid yet? She trusted Az as much as I did. So probably not. Fear dug its filthy nails into my heart, planting an infection from which I might never heal.

"How did you know about the Rip? Gwenyth wouldn't have known about it. Neither would Tavi." Because the location of the Rip had come to me with the Old Magic, tucked within the tale of Farin and Mother.

"I asked Dinah to tell me the stories," he said. "I missed you, and it helped me feel connected to you. But it wasn't long before I realized the gravity of what your magic knew. The location of the Rip has long been lost to history, but a connection of mine knew of a place where a hill jutted from a peach orchard—one next to a river. It was a long shot, but here we are."

And are we supposed to believe he never intended to gain anything from it? Ha!

Something wasn't adding up.

So the Council just happened to choose the location of the Rip as a meeting place?

My thoughts exactly, I said.

But what had Fin said? That it was Calias's turn to host the meeting site? And if it was Calias's turn, that meant Calias had chosen Rivre above all the other possible cities, which meant...

"You're working with Calias, aren't you? He's your connection."

He glanced at me, wariness lining the corners of his eyes. "It's not safe for you to know that."

Because clearly your safety is all this pure soul has in mind.

481

"Since when?" My mind whirred, and I found the answer before he opened his mouth, right in the mouth of Calias himself, when he'd forced me to dance with him all those weeks ago. "Since the ball where Kiran met Gwenyth. You and Calias both attended."

He clenched his jaw. "Calias can never find out that you know."

But I wasn't finished. "Was it your idea, or his to send the lychaen after me?" I ripped my sleeve up my arm, exposing the long, jagged scar where the lychaen had marked me forever.

He winced, the shame in his face so convincing it almost tugged at my heart. "When you refused to come with me that night in the garden, we had to find another way…"

Az, the boy who'd held me all those nights ago when I'd wept over my scars and how they'd never leave me, never let me forget.

My pulse stalled. "You've wanted to use me as a weapon since the beginning."

Az shook his head. "No. No. Please. When you offered yourself as a sacrifice to the king, I grieved you. I grieved you, Asha. You know why? Because I was going to lose my best friend, and it was going to be my fault, my failure that caused it. I was in a low place. I couldn't even…" A guttural noise rattled in his throat. "I couldn't even bring myself to come to the wedding, to be there for you in your last moments. So when I heard the king had spared your life, I knew the Fates had given me a second chance. And yes, I contacted Calias and told him about your magic. Neither of us had any idea what you could do at that point, of course. But Calias has been researching a way to weaponize the Other and the Old Magic for a long while now. We thought if I could get you away from the palace, even for a moment, his mages could teach you how to wield it. That we could hide you until the Council meeting, until you had grown into your powers. But then you refused to come. Not long after, Tavi told me she had seen you wield a sword out of thin air in the hidden room behind the library fireplace. That's when Calias and I knew we had to get you out of there before Kiran figured out what you could do."

My mouth went dry, my jaw numb in the cold winter air. "For my own safety, I'm sure. That's why you sent a flesh-eating monster to escort me from the palace."

Az sighed and ran his hands through his wind-tossed hair. "I argued to send someone less…feral. Clearly, I lost that argument."

"And what does Calias have to benefit from this arrangement?"

"We have an agreement. He thinks I'll be more easily swayed by his arguments than Kiran is. Rather than negating his vote on the Council, I'll double it." He scanned my face, noting the disgust in my snarl. "I know it seems like trading one evil for another, but we can't change the entire world at once. We'll start with Naenden first."

Speaking of trading one evil for another.

"And Ophelia? Was she really as willing as Gwenyth made her out to be?"

Az reached out, making out as if he would stroke my cheek, but he hesitated a hair's breath away from my skin.

Blood still coated his fingers. To touch me would be to mark me, and that would be inconvenient to his plan.

"What? Are you worried that if I have blood on my face, it might make it difficult for me to get away with murder?"

He spoke, his fingers still hovering there next to my cheek. "Your heart has always been so pure, Asha. I know this is difficult for you. But remember the life we've always dreamed of?" *I'm assuming he means what* he's *always dreamed of.* "We always thought those were just silly wishes to carry us through the days when our stomachs were empty or our bodies had wilted in the sun. But this is *real*, Asha. This is our chance. You and me. We're going to change the world."

I smiled weakly, wryly, and swallowed. When I spoke, my voice was dry. Empty. "Is that what you told Gwenyth?"

Rather than go cold and steely, the corners of his eyes sunk. Hurt punctured his face, and his hand dropped to the side.

By Alondria, he actually meant it.

"Gwenyth cared for no one but herself. Do you really think so little of me you believe I'd manipulate a decent person? It's always been you and me, Asha. Always. Anything else was just a bump in the road on the way to this. Can't you see? This is what the Fates want. Why else would everything have come together so perfectly? What are the chances that you found your magic—magic that could kill a fae king—and that you ended up his wife? And that I would be the heir once he's dead?"

"You mean once he and Fin are dead?"

Az exhaled, exasperated. "You know I'm right."

I shook my head. "But it wasn't chance at all. You were the one who sensed the magic that day in the alley; you were the one who wanted to chase it. Not me. It must have been your fae nature calling to you. So this," I said, pointing to my missing eye, "this was, in a way, caused by decisions you made because you're half-fae, because you're the next heir. And then *you* plotted against Kiran, which was the whole reason he made the decree to begin with. And it was because of my magic, my scars, that I was unmarried and able to give myself up as a sacrifice. I chose to do that, Az. *Our* choices led us here. To look back and say the Fates caused all this to come into place is one thing, but to presume the Fates intend for us to commit murder? That's putting your voice in their mouths."

To my surprise, a smile overtook his face. "Okay, then? So let's make our own Fate." He took my hands in his, this time so overcome with the elation that sparked in his eyes that it no longer mattered to him he was smearing my hands with blood.

In fact, that was exactly what he intended to do.

I went rigid at the touch. "How did you convince Ophelia?"

His brows slumped, and he placed his bloodied hand on his forehead as he shook his head. "You have to understand. We didn't mean for her to die. We never intended for any humans to die."

Except for Gwenyth, he must mean.

"Ophelia had a brother who was a part of the royal guard. I met a friend of his who had joined in Tijan's merchant caravan. We stayed connected when we returned to Meranthi. After Prince Fin's wedding, there was such a buzz about it in Naenden, the guy was so proud to tell me he knew a family secret of the royals. That Ophelia's brother had killed a fae male who had harassed Ophelia when she was young. The whole family worked together to cover up the murder.

But the laws in Naenden are plain. It's an offense punishable by death for a human to kill a fae."

"But her brother did it to protect her." My voice was only a whisper now.

"Don't you see now why something has to be done? We can't sit by and allow them to oppress our brethren. Not when we have the power and opportunity to save them." His voice was shaking now, though not with fear. With conviction.

I frowned, wanting more than anything to be convinced of anything other than the truth—that my best friend was sick, ill with a thirst for power.

But there was no lying to myself, no being deceived, not anymore. "You blackmailed her. She loved Fin, and you made her choose between her husband and her family." I backed away, my slippers squeaking on the wet ground, reminding me there would be no use in running.

He shook his head and advanced, nostrils flaring, emitting that horrid fog that now reminded me of a dragon preparing to spit fire. "We didn't mean for her to die."

"But you meant to kill the male she loved."

"You don't understand."

"No. I think I do."

He halted, stunned by my words. "You could be queen, Ash. I want to make you queen. Imagine what you could do."

"And what about your wife? Are you going to murder her too? Or will you wait until after she's borne you a son or two?"

Az sighed, his green eyes pleading. "I know it's not ideal. This has all turned out so differently than I wanted. She might be my wife, but there's nothing in the law that forbids multiple marriages. My bond with her means nothing to me, Asha. Do you hear me? Nothing. There's nothing stopping us from taking the life we've always wanted for ourselves, from me making you my queen."

"The thing is, Az, that title's already mine."

His brows narrowed into an expression I'd only ever seen him use against the fae males in the market who'd baited me. "You'd choose him over me?"

So here we were again, having the same conversation I'd played over so many times in the garden, imagining how my life might have been different had I taken his hand and run off with him, forgetting the little girl in the crowd whose future held promise because of my pain.

Had I made a different choice.

Strangely enough, it was Kiran's voice that rang in my head. *He should have chosen you years ago.*

Wasn't that the truth.

When I answered, the resolve in my voice shocked me. "I will always choose those who choose me."

It was enough to solidify the ice in his dark eyes. "Well then. If that's the case, I'm afraid you're going to have to make a choice between your fae lover and your sister."

I tried not to let the tears fall, not to give him the satisfaction. "I know."

CHAPTER 68

ASHA

*K*iran had already returned to the tent by the time I made it back that night. He sat atop the bed, his large hands clenching into the scarlet sheets.

Calm. I had to remain calm.

His head had whipped in my direction as soon as I lifted the heavy leather flaps that served as our door. "Where have you been?" There was no anger in his question, no judgment. Just anxious nerves. It was strange that I could recognize that now. A few hours ago, I would have interpreted it as my obsessive captor's lust for control.

Kiran had his faults. Ones I couldn't ignore, but he had never possessed me. Never manipulated me.

Kiran might have had the power to force feelings upon me, but it was Gwenyth who had convinced me to let her do as she wanted with them.

"I needed to get out for a bit. Take a walk. I was getting restless cooped up in here," I said. A morsel of truth to cover up the rest. How fae of me.

Kiran's eyes drooped on the sides in what I assumed must have been exasperation. Tired. He was tired. That wall of fire, that blast of anger he'd used on me earlier—it had all but withered. He wouldn't fight me anymore, wouldn't try to win me over. "I assumed you'd been taken when I arrived and you weren't here, until the guard told me otherwise."

I wondered how few minutes had passed between Roe returning from his revelries and when Kiran arrived at the tent.

"I just needed to stretch my legs. To think, that's all." I shuffled uncomfortably. It was true, I had wanted space to think, had hoped that moving outside the confines of this tent would have sent the answers flowing through my blood and to my brain.

I just hadn't imagined it would happen at knife point.

At the hand of my best friend.

In the forest where the Rip lay hidden, undisturbed, though not for much longer.

"It would have been so easy for them to take you," Kiran said, placing his elbows on his knees and rubbing his temples with his palms.

You have no idea, I thought.

"I know. I'll be more careful in the future." Not that the Fates would bless me with one of those.

But that didn't matter. Not when Dinah had a chance, not when she was...

No, I couldn't think about what Dinah would suffer if I failed. Not when I was trapped in the same tent with a being who could detect quickened heartbeats, who could smell the sweat forming on my brow. Come to think of it, it was amazing he didn't smell Az on me.

But then again, this was only the same reaction I'd had around Kiran for weeks now, ever since discovering that Gwenyth was alive. Since discovering what he could do.

And there Gwenyth was, too. Planting the seed of fear so long ago that Kiran wouldn't notice the difference when my dread fixated on the life of my sister.

Too bad she'd been so preoccupied with staying ahead of me, she hadn't noticed Az sneaking up behind her with a dagger in hand.

Az had always been the one in the lead, so much so, I hadn't even seen him from a distance. Not even when he'd left a clearly marked trail behind. One I should have followed. One I did follow, but just not quickly enough.

You need to breathe.

Right. Breathe.

Kiran locked eyes with me then, and I crumbled on the inside. Those molten eyes, so full of life, so earnest.

I had refused to see it before, to acknowledge that willingness to be molded in his demeanor, that longing for someone to take him by the hand and lead him into the person he might have been, had his father not had other ideas. It had been easier that way because it had made my decisions for me. No need to consider whether to take a chance on a male who might or might not be capable of being saved, not when I had condemned him as evil to his core.

Would those eyes still burn with that yearning for a different life, once I displaced him from under the sun?

Or would they turn to ash?

I figured I knew the answer.

When he spoke, the tenderness of it shattered me. "Please. Hate me, if you will. But, Asha, I beg you. Please don't be afraid of me."

My heart pounded, which he could surely hear. Sweat beaded on my forehead, which he could surely smell if not taste. There was no hiding that I was upset, wildly so. Panicked for Dinah, aching, guilty for him. For Kiran, for the male I...for the male I desperately did not want to kill.

And he thought I feared him.

He should have been more concerned with fearing me.

My awareness flickered to the sides of the tent, as if I would catch a shadow looming just behind Kiran, placed for only me to see. A threat.

Before I'd left the meadow, Az had informed me that Calias had ears in our tent. That they would know if I tried to warn my husband.

Of course, whoever Az had sent to eavesdrop on us would be nearby, but not close enough to be seen. Only close enough to hear.

So I told him the truth. The only part of the truth I could free from the suffocating serpent coiled tight around my airway, the only truth that wouldn't give the command for my sister's execution.

"I'm so sorry, Kiran. For all I said. None of it was…" I gulped, stopping myself, and hating myself for it. Even knowing that, tommorrow evening, I would attempt to assassinate him, I still couldn't bring myself to recant my words, to claim that what I said hadn't been based in truth.

What a hypocrite I was, unable to absolve Kiran of his intention to murder when, come tomorrow evening, he wouldn't be the only one with blood on his hands.

His blood.

My eye stung at the thought, but I blinked the sensation away.

"True?" Kiran asked, his molten eyes glittering. "Now, don't feel pressured to lie just because you're the only one in the room who can." A warm smile spread across his face, hesitant, but genuine, shocking me. But why should I let him surprise me with his warmth, when it radiated from his very core, his very being?

I straightened, though I studied his feet rather than his face. "I'm sorry I didn't give you a chance to explain yourself before I went off and did something rash."

Rash. What a pitiful word to describe what I'd done in freeing Gwenyth. In providing Az with yet another tool in his arsenal, a tool he'd been all too willing to dispose of. Whose hands were wet with Gwenyth's blood? Her own for conspiring against Kiran? Mine for setting her free? Az's for slicing the blade across her bared neck?

Or did it sprinkle all of us, staining our flesh with guilt and marring our souls?

"I'm sorry I wasn't honest with you from the beginning," he said. "That there had to be a beginning at all. I forced you into giving your life away to protect Dinah from me."

Irony of ironies. And now I would sacrifice him for the same purpose.

I might have choked on my next words, had the thought of saving Dinah not kept me steady. "Bitterness is a nasty thing."

"Bitterness doesn't excuse what I did," he said.

I lifted my face to meet his gaze. "What you almost did," I corrected. "You didn't actually kill any of the innocent girls you threatened to."

Except for Ophelia.

Yeah, and I wasn't about to mention that fact. Not when it would have overwhelmed Kiran with guilt. Perhaps if I succeeded in killing him, I could at least allow him the dignity of fading from under the sun in peace.

As it turned out, I didn't have to bring her up. "I might not have lied to you directly, but what I did to you in hiding the fact that Gwenyth was still alive was hardly honest. Nothing I'm about to say makes that any better, and I know it won't mend your broken trust, nor should it, but I hope it will... I don't know what I hope it will do, but I have to explain myself, if you're willing to listen."

I nodded, swallowing, almost wincing, as the saliva fought to glide over the welt threatening to burst my throat from the inside out.

"Thank you. Asha, I'll never forgive myself for what I did to Ophelia. What I did to Fin when I killed her. I've never..." He placed his hands on his knees and inhaled. "I've never felt my Flame slip from my control like it did in that moment. It's not as though I'd never killed before her. My father forced me to slaughter many of his enemies with my bare hands as a child. But I'd never killed in anger, I'd never slaughtered in a rage. But that didn't mean the rage wasn't there, that it wasn't constantly lurking beneath the surface, waiting for me to stumble, to crack the window for it to escape.

"So when Ophelia betrayed Fin, when she ruined my chances of having any positive relationship with my brother, I...I lost it, Asha. And once I'd lost it, once I got a taste of her fighting for breath, it was like my magic took over, like it'd been waiting my whole life to play this game. Fire may feed on wood, but it lives by the air it steals when we aren't looking. And it wanted more than anything to feed on hers. And I let it."

My stomach churned, and I thought I might be sick as the scent of Ophelia's charred flesh stained my imagination, as the molten eyes of my king blazed while he wrenched the air from her chest and used it to feed the Flame that consumed her body.

As I remembered she was innocent, and that Kiran still didn't know.

"To be completely honest, by the time it was over, I was shocked that my Flame hadn't consumed me with it, it was so out of my control. I've told you before that the fae's relationship with magic is different than humans. Your magic possesses you, but we fae, at an early age, must learn to conquer it. In the moment of Ophelia's betrayal, my Flame no longer wished to submit to my will.

"That thought, along with the knowledge I'd crushed my brother's heart, followed me the entire journey home. I could feel my Flame scratching at my skin, burning it from the inside out." He shuddered, brushing his dark arms with his hands as if to scratch an unrelenting itch. "The only thought that got me through was that, if I could just make it home to Gwenyth, she would fix it. She would figure out a way to make it better, to tell me everything was going to be fine, to help me get my Flame back under control. Because I could feel it slipping—"

"Your hold over your magic?" I asked.

He frowned, his brow furrowing. "My hold over my mind."

I exhaled, fogging up the chilled air of our tent.

"When I arrived in Meranthi and the vizier informed me that Gwenyth had taken a lover, and that they had plotted together to murder me... Asha, it was like my mind cracked, like there'd been hairline fractures on its edges, and they just...they just burst. It was everything I could do not to take the vizier and the palace and all of Meranthi down with me, all I could do not to unleash that agony on the world in a blaze of fire, one that would rip through the Sahli and the kingdoms until there was nothing left."

Fear, horrible, gut-wrenching fear rippled through me at the gravity of his words, at the seriousness in his eyes that told me he wasn't exaggerating.

"How did you stop it?" I asked.

He swallowed hard. "I let it take me instead."

My heart faltered. "What does that even mean?"

"Magic is a strange thing. It somehow resides both in the world we can see and the world we cannot. It straddles the material and the immaterial. Why would it have taken the material world when it could have my immortal heart, my mind, my soul, my being?"

A single tear salted my cheek. "You let it feed on you?"

He nodded, pressing his eyelids shut.

I shifted uncomfortably, and my magic answered my unasked question. *I am not aware of the exact state of my kin, but I do not believe they possess the same sentience that I do, nor can they partake in conversation with their hosts like the ones we enjoy. It does not surprise me that they would feed on the souls of their captors if given the chance.*

I offered a mental nod to my magic, an expression of gratitude for sharing such sensitive information.

"What was that like?" I asked Kiran.

"Um." His heavy breaths filled the air between us with smoke. "It was like being lost, except in your own head. Without any of the usual markers you'd normally use to get around, to know left from right, right from wrong. It was like wandering in the dark, except the stars had gone out, and the sun never rose to let you know that time had passed."

"And now? Are you still lost?"

A smile cracked at the edges of his lips, and his molten eyes welled, fire mingled with water. "Yes. But I can tell I'm getting closer."

I suppressed the sob threatening to burst forth at any moment and forced a comforting smile. "You seem pretty close to finding yourself."

"Not a step closer."

"I thought you said—"

"I haven't found anything. On the contrary, I've been found."

I couldn't tell if it was the heat rippling off my husband, or the surge of his emotions as his fingers grazed mine, or just my natural reaction to such an admission, but warmth flooded me, brushing my cheeks and swelling in my stomach.

No, no. I couldn't do this. I couldn't feel this. Not when I'd already decided who I would save.

"So why not execute Gwenyth?" I asked, clearing my throat and returning my hand to my lap, a perfectly safe distance from my king's reach.

My king, hm?

Kiran frowned, then slid his hand across the sheets, folding it under his thigh. Something about the small movement sent a dagger through my stomach. "Even in that dark place, I knew better than to put myself in a situation where I might let my magic get the best of me again. I figured if I saw Gwenyth again, that I'd break, and my Flame would take everything."

"Then why not have others execute her for you?"

"Even in that dark place, I feared that, if she died, that agony would be worse than the first. That I'd already given too much of myself, that my magic would have nothing else to take but the material world." A shiver fled down my spine, even in spite of Kiran's radiating heat, but he continued, "So I forced the vizier to hide her away, somewhere I would never find her, in case I got it into my head that I was strong enough to see her without consuming her. Without losing everything. Since fae marriages contain clauses in the case of infidelity, I had the vizier dissolve our marriage, then sign a fae contract, a binding agreement never to tell me where she was."

My heart skipped. "You had no idea she was in the palace."

He shook his head. "No idea."

That shouldn't have made me feel better, but it did.

But there was one last question. One last answer that, similar to the line I'd tossed Az, would cement Kiran's character in place in my mind. Az had failed that test.

What kind of world did we live in where the king who had once intended to murder a woman every mooncycle might exceed my best friend in character?

"I need you to answer my next question as directly as possible," I said.

"I promise to do so."

"No getting around the question, no talking in circles."

"Asha, please. Whatever you want to know, I'm more than happy to

494

supply. If it were up to me, you'd know all of me. Every inch. Every shadow."

Heat washed over me, and I tried my best not to let my mind explore the full meaning of *all of me*.

The question, the one that would clear my husband of his guilt and condemn me as a murderer in one go. "Do you have the power to steal the magic of others?"

"No. I don't."

Something like relief tainted with bile filled my stomach. "Did you take Gwenyth's magic, either through your power or someone, something else's?"

"I didn't take magic from Gwenyth. I wasn't aware that she possessed the Old Magic."

"Right, well I'm beginning to think she didn't. Unless you count being extremely manipulative," I said, my voice tinged with bitterness. Now that Gwenyth was dead, it seemed the net she'd strung around my mind had loosened, allowing me a chance to break free. My father had warned me of con artists from a young age, people who would take minute observations about me and use them to craft a story, to use the information I'd given them to weave something believable. She'd garnered the hints—my scars that must have reminded her of the girl back home Az had told her about, the girl inhabited by the Old Magic, my robes that must have told her I'd taken her place as queen—and she'd used those details to figure me out, to provoke me to jealousy. She'd assumed that deep down I'd believe I couldn't be loved, and she'd used that against me, to convince me that Kiran only could have wanted me for my power.

"Is that how she convinced you to break her out of her cell?" Kiran asked, frowning, wrenching me from my too-late realization.

"Well, yes. And no. I think…I think I was hurt. She told me you kept her in the dungeon because you were obsessed with her."

"And you believed her?"

I shrugged, the slight movement putting pressure on my throat, and I had to keep a soft sob from squeezing its way out. "It didn't seem like too much of a stretch—that the only reason someone like you would want someone like me would be because you wanted to take my magic for yourself."

Kiran pursed his lips, his face made of stone. When he spoke, he almost had to force the words out between his gritted teeth. "What do you mean by *someone like me?*"

My shoulders went limp, my hands flopping into my lap. My throat went dry. "I don't know how you even stand to look at me."

His throat tightened, and he extended his hand, his fingers hovering just over my scars, so that only the heat from his fingertips brushed my cheek, not the skin itself. He traced them with his invisible touch, the touch I so wished to lean into, to feel against my skin as I'd felt that night in the infirmary when he'd swept my hair from my forehead. But even that longing made me sick. Because how could I deserve to feel him, how could I deserve to touch him when...

"If you're talking about these," he whispered, "all they do is remind me how lucky I am to have ever met you. All they do is remind me that I could have lost you before I ever had the chance to find you. Your body, Asha, as much as I would like to..." His gaze lingered on my lips, his voice catching. "Your body is the vessel that tethers your soul to this side of the sun. It's what keeps you here with me. That, and that alone, is what I love it for."

I couldn't breathe, not with him so close, not with what I wanted in this moment. What I didn't deserve to want, considering what I would do to him tomorrow. My body might have tethered me to this side of the sun, but it also harnessed the power to sever his soul from his.

I couldn't do this. I couldn't give in. Couldn't do that to him. "She told me you had forced yourself on Ophelia—"

And just like that, the tension between us snapped in two. The particles of air between Kiran's body and mine popped, like wood crackling under the consumption of a flame. My husband's eyes darkened to soot, so that I could not distinguish between the color of his eye and his pupil. His hands shook as he fisted them. "She what?"

"I know, I know—"

"No." Kiran clenched his teeth. "Asha, listen to me. Never in my life have I forced myself on a woman. I would never. I *will* never. If I have ever done so, or if I ever do, may the Fates rot my body alive at the hand of my fae's curse."

I wasn't sure if I was imagining it, but I thought I felt the air shift, as if something had clicked into place. A fae vow. Kiran had made a fae vow, the terms of which, should he break, his flesh would rot where he stood. The gravity of it shook me. "I know that now..." Oh, how I knew. Oh, how it wouldn't matter in the end. I swallowed, forcing myself to look my husband in the eye, as much as it pained me to do so. He needed to know I believed him. "I know, Kiran."

The air cooled, and his face softened as I touched his cheek with my palm. As soon as I did, a wave of deep, intense longing passed from his body to mine. It crashed against my senses, a torrent of desire breaking against an insurmountable cliffside. My breath hitched, and I recoiled my hand, tucking it into the safety of the folds of my skirt.

My cheeks heated, and the way the muscles in his neck strained told me that he'd seen, that he knew exactly what I'd felt roll off of him.

His labored breaths roared in my ears, but when he spoke, his voice was soft. "I'm sorry, Asha. It just slips out of me sometimes. Like I said before, I've had this curse since childhood, but I spent years hiding it rather than learning to control it. You shouldn't have to deal with that."

That. Was that the word for the aching he felt for me? For me, the woman with half a face—revolting by most people's standards, unattractive to the rest? Because as much as that surge of attraction I'd felt through his touch betrayed his physical desire for me, it hadn't been lust that I'd felt.

"When I met you, I thought I'd never be capable of love again. The thing is, I was wrong, just not in the way you'd think. The truth was, it wasn't that I'd never love again. It was that I had never actually loved. Not really. No one had ever showed me how. And then you burst into my life, offered yourself to save your sister. That shook me to my core, love. Because I knew I'd never do that for anyone else. And I knew there was no one in the world who would do that for me. That's why I was so hard on you those first few weeks. I couldn't bring myself to believe it—that there wasn't some scheme I'd uncover that would explain it all. But once I realized what was inside you—pure, unadulterated love—I wanted that inside me too."

My breathe caught, and I shook my head. "Kiran..."

"I love you, Asha."

My heart must have stopped then and there. Agony bit through my soul, leaving nothing but tattered shreds behind, the truth naked and cold in the damp pit of my empty chest.

Because I loved him too.

I just loved Dinah more.

"Kiran..." I pulled away from him, forging a chasm between us, one I knew we wouldn't cross again.

The hurt on his face crushed me, but taking my cue, he pulled away as well, clearing his throat and averting his gaze. "Right. I shouldn't have... I had no right to put all that on you. You didn't ask for any of this." He stared at the swirling tattoo on his left hand as he fisted and extended his fingers. "I've decided that, when we return to Naenden, I'm freeing you of your bond."

My heart faltered. What did he mean? That he'd divorce me? Fae marriages were even more serious than human unions. That fae could not lie meant that breaking a vow... In Gwenyth's case, the infidelity clause had allowed divorce, but with me... That was impossible, that would... "You can't. That would kill you." I didn't even have to notice the uncomfortable rumbling of the magic within my soul for the irony of that statement to sink my heart.

Kiran's mouth lifted in the saddest smile I'd ever witnessed. "I know. Don't worry, I'll remain somewhat of a coward. The fae tend to be wary of our wedding vows. I don't know if you noticed or not—I'm sure our wedding day was quite traumatic for you—but I said very few words."

I nodded, remembering how disgusted I'd been.

"You can go where you wish, Asha. I'll support you fully. If you want to return to your father's home, you are free to do so. If you want to take him and your sister," I fought back the urge to flinch at the mention of my family, "and relocate them to a cottage in Avelea, I will provide the means for you to do so. I will even see to it you remain guarded, though from a distance that would ensure you'd never notice the intrusion. Yours is a soul I never could have imprisoned, even if I wanted to, but that doesn't give me a right to keep you for myself."

Tears flooded my cheek, and the lump in my throat burned and swelled with such vigor, I thought I might stop breathing.

Kiran turned to me and, seeing the tears washing my face, smiled weakly. "That's all I want. To see you happy."

"Thank you." Those were the only words I could manage without spilling the truth, without sending Dinah's execution order ringing through the air.

"Any time," he chuckled nervously; then, as if realizing where he was, he sprung from the bed. "I should leave this for you."

I shook my head in protest, unable to form words now that the weeping had begun. Now that my sobs welled in my throat and the tears flowed freely. Tears that Kiran would mistake for relief, for joy.

Tears he wouldn't understand until his heart was on its last beat.

"I want you to have it," he said. He crossed the room and returned with a quilt that he rolled out onto the floor before settling onto his makeshift pallet.

When it seemed he wouldn't budge from the floor, I resigned myself to the plush, inviting bed I didn't deserve. The very mattress felt like it would rise to my nose and mouth and suffocate me during the night.

I didn't shun the thought as I rocked through the endless evening, my silent tears soaking my pillow until a single ray of light from the tent flap signaled I must rise and face my Fates.

CHAPTER 69

*A*sha hadn't slept that night, and it hurt the Old Magic. It hurt him to feel her affliction, not simply because the sharing of her body meant that he felt her torment as keenly as he might his own, but because he would have suffered on her behalf anyway. He would have hurt, simply because she hurt.

Still, he couldn't stop the story. He wished he could, wished he could shut it down, refuse to witness its ending.

It would only result in more pain, of that much, he was sure.

He simply couldn't tear his mind away.

MOTHER CLUTCHED her son's chest, grasping for where his heart lay hidden underneath bones and tissue and sinew. Then she relaxed her hands, allowing the power to seep out of her, just as she had done to heal the Rip.

Nothing happened.

Mother tried again, but she couldn't seem to remember how she'd done it before. It had never taken much effort, much thinking, ever since her magic had inhabited her. She'd only wanted someone to be healed, and at her touch, it was done.

So why did her hands lay flat, flaccid against her son's chest?

No, no, no.

A pallor washed over her child's face, a sickly white she'd become all too familiar with back in the Nether, where the roots could only do so much.

But she wasn't in the Nether. She was in Alondria. Alondria where the air itself healed the fae. Alondria where magic...

"Please," she choked. "Please help him."

Silence.

Mother coughed, tears burning at the edge of her swollen lids. "Please."

No one answered.

Mother gasped, the brevity of Farin's life lingering at her fingertips. She fisted her hands and shoved them into his heart.

Something cracked, though she couldn't tell whether it was her child's ribs or her soul. She shoved and shoved and shoved, for if she couldn't heal her son's heart with magic, she'd do it the typical way, without cheating.

Surely the Fates would reward her for not cheating.

Mother pushed and pushed and pushed, but the cracking—that, she could hardly bear. She longed for her ears to go numb, to spare her from the awful, clattering noise that somehow echoed over the wide expanse of the field in which her son lay...

Lay...

She couldn't process the end of that thought. She wouldn't.

Nausea washed over her in a wave so torrential, she thought it might drown her. She had barely crawled out of range of her son's still warm body before she stained the hillside with vomit.

Even as she trembled, some innate need for cleanliness had her wiping her mouth—the sour of her bile still lingering—on the hem of her robe.

Something about digging her fingers into the earth to brace herself gave her an idea. Her magic might not be speaking to her, sure, but she still remembered all it had taught her. The abilities granted to her by her magic hadn't been limited to healing at her touch. She'd also been gifted with a plethora of knowledge regarding how to mix the materials of this world in an infinite combination of salves and potions.

If her boy was sick, she would simply heal him the old fashioned way.

Her mind swarmed with possibilities, with the ingredients she could salvage from their immediate vicinity. But it would do her no good to gather various components without knowing the end goal. First she must diagnose the problem.

But when she returned to her boy, she saw it.

The way his face had gone stiller than sleep. Too pale for blood to be coursing through his veins.

She cradled her child's head in her lap and screamed.

HOURS LATER, her voice's ability to wail dwindled, her cries into a series of labored rasps.

Mother didn't understand how this had happened. She stroked her child's hair, noting how peaceful he looked, how much he resembled the boy he once was, the child who had led her to what should have been their salvation.

Until she'd traded the wellbeing of an entire realm for the life of her son.

She'd thought the Fates were punishing her, when Father had sent her away, forced her to wander through this new world without the company of her son.

Now she realized that had only been the beginning of what the Fates had in mind for her.

Her boy, her sweet, kind, imaginative boy. She traced his closed eyelids with her fingers, her tears splotching his brow as she wept.

She had done this to him. She had been a coward, and when it had come down to the choice, she'd traded his soul for his life.

And now he was left without either.

I doubt either of us will ever forget this day.

Mother stiffened, the voice of her magic reminding her of that night in the forest, the night they'd met, before its voice had joined her own in her mind, back to a time when it seemed to carry itself on the breeze. Even the same, faint blue light blurred the edges of her vision.

"You could have helped him," Mother said, gagging as her dry tongue scraped the roof of her mouth. "You could have helped him, but instead you left him to die."

I did not leave your son to die.

"Liar," Mother hissed, rage boiling inside her chest now, anguish for her lost son. Her only son. Her only child.

Interesting that you would call me the liar, when you are the one who broke our bargain. The one who told your crafty son, not only of my existence, but my siblings'. Your son struck a deal with my foolish siblings, and they jumped upon it—the chance to dwell within an immortal body. Your son and his wicked friends tricked them, overpowered them. Extinguished them. Even now that your son is dead, I cannot feel my siblings—cannot sense them or hear them. I am afraid they are just as gone as your son is.

"Is that why you're here? Is that why you came back?" Mother hissed. "To gloat over my pain?"

I see you've guessed the truth, that when you used my power to heal the Rip, I channeled the surge in energy to sever my ties with you, to free myself from your body. It seems your fae nature allowed you to survive the separation.

That was well enough, Mother thought. She never wanted to hear her magic's voice again. Not after it refused to help her son, refused to save him.

Why would I attempt to save the life of a being I killed?

The whisper hung suspended in the breezeless air, her magic's words repeating themselves in Mother's mind, whirling around in her brain, scrambled until she could hardly make sense of them.

She didn't understand.

You see, when I channeled the power of the Rip to free myself from your body, that wasn't all I did. The agony you feel for your son—I feel it too. Felt it deeply, even before I learned of what your son had done to my siblings. I didn't know yet that they had been absorbed into the fae, no longer their own entities, never to speak to me again. But I could sense their absence like a blind spot in the eye of a human. Just out of reach, hardly noticeable until one knows to look for it. And who else to blame, but you? You, for telling our secret, the one I'd entrusted you with, thinking you were good.

A dry, mirthless laugh curled on the edges of Mother's voice. For all the pain she'd endured at the hands of Father, now for this creature to claim...

You are good until it comes to your child. And then, you are selfish. So can you really call yourself good at all? Listen, my dear. What do you hear?

Nothing. Mother heard nothing.

Exactly. While your son lived, there was only pain and torment for the humans he and his father had subjected. You mourn his loss, and this is fair. But to claim your son should have been allowed to live, even if it meant the continued suffering of countless others...that is not goodness, my dear.

Mother spat at the wind, hoping her magic would find itself at the receiving end. "You know nothing of what his father was like, what he did to Farin. The abuse my son endured. You know nothing, what I could have done for him once his wretched father was out of the way. I would have taught him better. I would have shown him how to heal, rather than destroy. And you *took* him from me."

The magic went silent for a moment. By the time it spoke again, the evasive blue light intensified, pulsing just out of Mother's direct sight. *Do you know how I killed him?*

Mother didn't want to know. She didn't. But, for some reason, she couldn't bring herself to say so.

You lied to me. Your son lied to my siblings. He deceived you about his reasons for helping you rid yourself of his father. So many lies, my dear. Lies that bred destruction. You fae, you encroached upon this helpless world, its people who had no way of defending themselves from you. The fae—stronger, faster, with lives that do not fade with the passing of time—it was unfair. You must understand that. You upset the balance of nature.

"I thought you operated outside of nature," Mother said.

I do. Which is why, when you healed the Rip between realms, I was able to harness the power and alter it into a curse.

Mother's heart might have snagged on those words, had she cared about anything at all other than the way her son's body was limp in her arms, never to move again.

Your son died because he lied to you.

The point of Mother's ears curved toward the voice. "What did you say?"

That was the curse, the one I placed upon you and your son and all the fae, and every descendent who comes after you. At least, until the effects of the curse wear off, becoming less potent until there's no curse left at all. For now, though, any fae who lies will die. Immediately.

Mother's mind split, racing in opposite directions, one fumbling for her son's last words, that last lie that ended his life, the other funneled toward her magic, concentrating her hatred all in one place.

"How dare you?" she whispered.

"How *dare* you?" she screamed.

How dare I? Do you even remember your son's last words? If you'd only remember, you might not be so harsh with me.

Thoughts swirled through Mother's mind, but she fumbled every time she thought she had caught hold of those words. Every time she thought she might have grasped them, they slipped through the cracks in her skull, the cracks Father had made with his fists...

She couldn't remember, couldn't recall her only son's last words.

I am leaving this place. I intend to slumber, perhaps for eternity, as it is evident I am incapable of doing any good for this world, for its people.

Mother wasn't listening. She didn't care if her magic faded from existence just like its sibling. All she desired was to remember the last words of her child.

And then, as clearly as if her magic itself had deposited the words into her mind, she heard them.

She heard them in her child's voice.

She thought she heard her heart shatter too.

For the words that had slain her son, the lie that had stolen his breath, were the worst of all.

"I have no intentions of hurting you."

CHAPTER 70

ASHA

*T*he plot was simple enough, at least in theory.

In execution, not so much.

At a time of his choosing during dinner, Calias would call on me to grace his guests with a tale. After all, what kind of host would he be if he deprived his guests of a few words from the infamous queen who had saved her own life night after night with her delightful stories?

And then I would murder my husband and my friend.

Az had made it clear enough that he and Calias didn't care which method I chose, as long as it displayed my power and killed Kiran and Fin only. One wrong move against him or Calias, or the other guests, and there was a messenger in the tent at the ready to send word to my sister's safe house demanding she be executed. Brutally.

Try to kill everyone, including the messenger, and the males guarding Dinah knew that, if they received no word by midnight, they were to slaughter my sister anyway.

I wouldn't find her on my own.

Az had made sure of it.

* * *

THE TENT where the dinner and treaty negotiations were to be hosted was up and adorned by sundown, when the invitation indicated the dinner was supposed to begin.

I had chanced glances at it all day, as servants dressed in all the colors of the various courts had driven long wooden poles into the ground, as they'd climbed ladders to lay white linen and string ever-burning candles, supplied by Naenden, of course. All the while I'd tried to keep my secret, Az's secret, from spewing out of my weak stomach. Servants had offered me refreshments all day—cheeses cured for years in Avelean creameries, olives plucked from the vine-yards of Charshon, breads freshly baked in stoves carried all the way from Dwellen.

I had turned them away, my empty stomach flaring in protest as soon as the savory scents reached my nostrils. I wondered if I would vomit after the deed was done. If that would displease Calias enough for him to command Az to send the messenger to kill Dinah.

I couldn't stop thinking about her, though I tried during weak moments throughout the day. I tried to push the sounds of her screams from my ears, the images of torture I was sure she would endure if I failed.

And I would fail, one way or another.

The images would push too far, become too graphic, and I would erect a mental wall to keep them out. But then I would remember that Dinah might already be suffering, and the least I could do was suffer with her, keep her from having to go through it alone. So then I'd allow the graphic images to swarm into my mind again, stinging at every turn, every bloodstain, every crackling of bone.

Kiran had tried to check in on me that morning, but I had avoided him all day. There was no use in risking Az's spies growing suspicious. One wrong move, and they could interpret something we said to one another as conspiring together, an attempt to save Dinah. They would assume I had tipped him off.

That, or Kiran would push me to talk about what was wrong, and they would think he had grown suspicious.

I'd wandered the hills of Rivre all day, unable to decide whether I wished the hours to accelerate, to be over with already, or to languish. To bless me with as much time as possible before I did what I had to do.

Before I failed.

Before I failed, and Dinah was dead.

I figured that much was inevitable.

It didn't matter how much power leaked from the Rip. It didn't matter if it was equivalent to ten thousand scrolls. What I knew I had to do; it was too much. I had hardly been able to create a parrot from my own words, from my own story, before it had fluttered away into ash.

I couldn't do this. It wouldn't work.

We have a plan. It will work.

Oh, shut up, I seethed. *You don't care whether Dinah dies or Kiran dies or Fin dies or the whole lot of them. You'd just rather me not die. I'm sure it would be extremely inconvenient for you, wouldn't it?*

It will work, it replied with causal certainty I couldn't bring myself to trust.

What are you going to do when they finally get around to killing me? Because that's what they are going to do.

My magic didn't answer.

That unpleasant realization had settled in during my long, sleepless night. I wasn't just a weapon for Az to wield. I was a scapegoat.

He would try to save me when they crowned him king. I was sure of that. But if Az had proved anything to me last night it was that, if he couldn't save me, and my death cemented his place on the throne, it would have been worth it.

But, as much as I had willed the day to slow down, to keep my sister alive a little while longer, I could tell the sun was already setting behind the hills.

It's time.

And it was.

When I reached my tent, I shooed away the servant who had arrived to dress me. If I was about to have all control swept away from me, I'd adorn myself.

* * *

"YOU LOOK ILL," Kiran said, peering down at me with those molten eyes.

"Exactly what a woman wants to hear after she's put so much effort into her appearance." I gestured toward my evening gown, a silky, beautiful thing that shimmered silver or gold depending on its light source.

"That's not what I meant. You're stunning." Kiran's eyes swept over my gown once before landing on my face. I swallowed the dread crawling up my throat, but it wouldn't budge as he examined me with those intense eyes. Fire burned behind those irises, a gentle flame I had never seen him use on anyone else.

I wondered what color they would turn when he died.

Cold, black, empty eyes stared up at me. I shook them away. Promised myself that I wouldn't look at them when the time came.

He took my arm, and I clung to his powerful bicep with all my might, hoping that if I dug my fingernails tight enough into his evening coat, that I'd somehow suppress my shaking limbs.

"You're trembling," he said, sliding his hand down my arm and wrapping his fingers around mine. A shot of pain went through me at the kind gesture, one that he interpreted as a wince. Kiran dropped my hand, and it hung limp by my side. "I'm sorry, I..."

I interrupted him by grasping his arm again. "It's fine." I tried to smile. It must have looked like a pretty weak attempt, because he frowned.

"I know this meeting makes you nervous. It does me too. Especially with Calias here. But you'll be by my side all night. You have nothing to fear." He looked at my hand as if he might reach for it and squeeze, but I cleared my throat.

"I'm afraid I don't deserve your concern. Not after the terrible things I said to you." I stared at my slippers, unable to meet those eyes once again. Somehow, I knew something earnest would stare back at me. And earnest wasn't something I could handle at the moment.

"None of them were unfair or untrue," he said, his voice soft. Meek. Forgiving.

I couldn't do this, I couldn't do this.

But you have to, said a voice, but this time, not my magic's. Mine, but dark. Empty.

"That doesn't mean I'm any less sorry I said them," I said.

Kiran cocked his head, and, without smiling, softened his eyes. As if he could feel the bridge rebuilding itself between us.

As if that bridge wasn't made of ice and my voice wasn't the sharpened edge of a pick.

I decided then and there not to look at him for the rest of the evening.

We entered the tent behind the Mystrian envoy, the Queen of Mystral donning a dress that looked to be made of snowflakes, with a high neck that swooped against her shoulder blades, then cascaded down to the floor like a torrential avalanche.

Rumor had it that she had murdered her king. Not that anyone could prove it, otherwise they would have frozen her head on a stick and lodged it somewhere in the middle of the tundra. In her presence, I could see why no one had dared to question her. With her long, slender neck held high and her eyes sharp as shattered glass, I wondered if anyone had even bothered to bring forward allegations. She still wore that awful necklace adorning her collarbone, with its matching bracelets. The whisperers said she kept the rest of the wine that had killed her husband within the crystals of her jewelry. The blood-red jewels provided the only contrast to her stark white outfit. As I watched her offer her hand for Calias to kiss as we entered, a shard of bloodred ice dangled from her wrist.

Perhaps I could at least allow the Queen of Mystral some relief. Surely no one would talk about the queen who had slipped poison into her husband's wine once I stopped the hearts of the King of Naenden and his brother.

Fin. My stomach fell out from under me when he joined himself to my right side, whisking his arm into mine at the last minute to help escort me in. He grinned at me, a smile that utilized every wrinkle and divot on his face, which only made me wonder if I would lose the contents of my stomach as soon as the servants set the food before us.

"Just in time," I said at the same time that Kiran said, "You're late."

Fin just shrugged and, when we reached the tent opening and Calias offered his hand out for mine, a hungry smirk smeared across his face, Fin simply offered him his own bejeweled hand.

The disgust on Calias's snarling lips only appeared for a fleeting moment before he regained his composure. Still, he looked upon Fin's outstretched hand with a curled nose. "Not the hand I had been hoping for, I'm afraid."

We passed into the tent, and Kiran turned to whisper to Fin over the top of my head. "I'd be inclined to say you shouldn't have done that, poked the beast like that, but—"

"But there'll be a blizzard in the Sahli before he lays a hand on Asha?" Fin responded, with a fierceness to him that had me questioning how he kept that propensity for rage hidden underneath his carefree demeanor.

"Exactly," Kiran said, something about which made my eye sting.

They were protecting me, Kiran and Fin. Because they considered me—I wasn't sure quite what, but something resembling family or friend.

In fact, somehow, after all their father had done, after all Kiran and Az and Gwenyth and Ophelia had done to soil their relationship… somehow they'd bonded over protecting me.

And I was going to kill them.

I couldn't even bring myself to hope it didn't work. Not when I knew what Calias's soldiers would do to Dinah. I wished I could somehow apologize to them. Tell them I was sorry, see the hurt in their eyes, and hear them tell me they understood. That they would do the same for one another.

I wondered if that was the case now, or if some wounds never healed, even between brothers.

The tent was unlike any I'd ever seen. Far from the shanty tents in the marketplace of Meranthi, this tent stretched long enough to accommodate a table double the size of the one in the dining hall in the palace. And the lights, there must have been thousands of lights flickering above us. Someone had even enchanted a fog above the candles to give off the impression that we were standing under the stars.

Why we weren't, on such a clear night, I had no idea.

The dining table was made of a dark, chestnut wood and lined with a velvet indigo runner with golden stitching. Someone had carved names into the face of the table, as if the Council had commissioned it for simply this purpose, and no one had any intention of using it again.

Why use it again if two of the names would be irrelevant?

I ignored my magic. The whole day, I'd vacillated on whether I wanted it to be my friend, my comforter, or whether having someone witness what I was about to do was too much.

At the moment, I'd settled on too much.

My heart lurched as Az, dressed in servant's coats, silver with green thread, caught my eye and smirked at me from across the room. He stood with the other servants on the edge of the tent wall, each of them with a plate in hand, ready to be set before us.

Az, my friend. That smirk, so familiar, it was etched into my very soul.

The man who would make me his queen, if this all turned out perfectly according to plan. The boy who'd drive the dagger through my heart, if that was what the mood of his audience deemed necessary.

An usher hurried us to our seats, which, to my dismay, were positioned so that our backs would be toward Az, though we would remain within earshot.

Someone had carved my name between Kiran's and the Queen of Mystral's. For a moment, I thought it must be some gross oversight on Az's part. Surely he would not want his assassin sitting next to Queen Abra, the one being that intimidated the rest of the kings so much that no one had dared to question her when she'd probably poisoned her own husband.

"After you," Kiran said, gesturing for me to sit first, at his right hand. I did, and he followed, Fin sitting at his other side. As I looked around the table, I noticed that the other groups were arranged similarly, with the king seated in the middle, the queen on his right, and any heirs to his left.

Queen Abra sat alone.

Well, alone, next to me.

As I sat, a presence appeared just a hair from my back and set the table in front of me. Again, I had to fight back the shiver.

"Your Majesty," Az whispered before returning to his place.

No one touched their plates until Calias returned from the entrance. He sat at the head of the table, next to Fin, interestingly enough, and I remembered from my brief schooling that this meant that Calias had placed the kingdom of Naenden in the seats with the lowest preference.

I wasn't sure what infuriated me more, that he had openly shamed Fin, or that he had been so confident that I wouldn't tip Fin off that he had sat himself next to the person he was plotting to assassinate.

"Friends," Calias said, gesturing toward the array seated at the table. "I am so grateful you've all responded to my call. I hope that, as we commune together over this grand meal, which my servants have been eagerly preparing, that we will put aside our differences and learn the pleasantries of one another's companies, and that this will provide an opportune foundation for a negotiation of peace."

Yes, and I'm sure he'll have even more to say about the importance of peace once he's pretended to apprehend you.

That was it. The rest of Az and Calias's plan that Az had conveniently forgotten to mention. Because there had to have been a reason we were doing this publicly.

So that when Az took the throne, there would be no one to question who had murdered his two older brothers.

Framed. That's what was happening to me. I might have been powerless enough to go through with it, but at least I wasn't stupid enough not to see it coming.

"Now please, enjoy your meal," Calias said. Most of the table did, and I picked at my food with a fork, hoping no one would notice that I wasn't eating.

"You also prefer not to eat without a beverage?" a cool voice beside me asked.

I almost jumped and was even more surprised when I found that the Queen of Mystral was addressing me. I stumbled for words for a moment as she stared me down with this wide, piercing blue eyes of hers.

The drinks. She's talking about how they haven't given you anything to drink.

"Oh," I said, glancing down at the table and realizing neither I, nor anyone else, had goblets next to our plates. "No, I find the food sticks in my throat," I said, feeling that was an idiotic thing to say, but figuring stupidity was the least thing I had to worry about under the circumstances.

"Calias claims it's a Charshonian custom. Yet I've been to Charshon, and not once have I met one of his people who doesn't lap up the first drop of liquid they can afford to get their hands on," the queen said, not bothering to hide the look of disdain on her face as she scowled in Calias's direction. "I've decided he made up the practice just because he enjoys making his guests feel uncomfortable."

I couldn't say I disagreed with the theory, though I wasn't sure why she was sharing such thoughts with me. "Do we not get to drink then?"

"It's served between the first and second course," Abra said. "The least he could do is give us empty goblets, so I could fill them."

"Dinner would probably be over before they melted," I said. Abra cocked her head at me with such ferocity, I stumbled over my words to add, "At least, I would hope it would be over."

Abra's pale lips parted into a grin, and she laughed. "You've made quite the wave in the history of Alondria," she said.

If only you knew...

"So have you," I said, really not wishing to get into questions about my magic, my story, or, most especially, my family.

My heart sank again at the reminder of them.

"Only rumors." Her lips parted again. It unsettled me, the way she could smile with such ferocity; she had a similar effect as a female wearing a scarlet lipstick, though she boasted not a hint of paint on her pale face.

She lifted a forkful of potatoes to her mouth, and my eyes couldn't help but linger on the scarlet jewels dangling from her bracelets.

"Is there enough poison in them to kill?" I asked, trying to keep my voice lower than the chatter about the tent.

Abra turned a wide, curious eye at me as she ate from her fork. Then she delicately placed it next to her plate, shifting her gaze away from me. Without looking in my direction, she whispered, "High-fae? No. Only enough to cause a minor illness."

"Isn't a minor illness a big deal to the fae?"

She snorted. "To some it is."

My mind buzzed. Perhaps if the poison could make a fae ill, it could incapacitate a half-fae for a time. "Would they melt if you took them off?"

"Theoretically, yes. But they're much more valuable dangling from my wrists, keeping everyone from opening their mouths around me—well, everyone but you, apparently—than they would be causing a minor bellyache. I can't say there's anyone I dislike that little that I dislike enough for the consequences to be worth it."

I nodded and stared at my plate, bringing a pile of creamed rice to my mouth just to have something to do, something to distract me from Abra's piercing stare and allow my mind room to think. If I could only get the poison to Az and Calias somehow. Sure, I couldn't take down Calias with it. But even if I could impair him for a while...

"You and I are not all that different, you know," Abra said, regaining me attention, and I noticed that something had thawed that hard expression on her brow. That her eyes no longer appeared cold enough to burn to the touch.

"You have no idea." And then I realized exactly why Az had seated me next to Abra. Because if anyone was going to stand aside while I murdered my husband, it would be her.

The sound of metal clanking against metal drew my attention, and

I watched as Calias rose from his seat and tapped his fork against a silver goblet. Immediately, Az was at my side, leaning over my shoulder to take my plate. He brushed his shoulder against mine. A threat. One that Abra couldn't hear. The plate in front of me disappeared with him.

"Attention, all," Calias boomed. "It is time for the second course, and, as is tradition, the goblets will pass from my left-hand side around the table, a sign of my goodwill to you, that I will be the last to receive my drink from the servants."

I might have rolled my eyes had the stakes been any less paralyzing. Az appeared next to Calias's side with a cart full of silver goblets. Calias passed his own to his left side, then took another from Az. Before long, the goblets had reached the opposite end of the table and were being passed back around toward us.

"Are you one for taking risks?" Abra asked me.

"It depends on who I'm doing it for," I said.

"What about yourself?" Abra reached to her right and took a silver goblet from the heir of Dwellen before pausing, then passing it to me. I gave it to Kiran and then reached for the next goblet, repeating the motion.

It was only after my own goblet lay before me and the table went still that I realized something was different about Abra.

Her jewels were gone.

* * *

I HAD to swallow hard to keep from gaping. Abra must have caught the shock in my face, because she simply smirked, clearly pleased with herself. As if she'd checked off her good deed for the day. I turned toward Kiran and Fin, but they had both already downed their glasses.

What were you going to do? Warn them not to drink poison when you're supposed to be murdering them?

Stomach aches. Minor illnesses. That's all that poison would do to them.

Wouldn't all this be easier if it actually killed them and you could blame it on the Queen of Mystral?

Tears burned at my eye, and I had to blink them away, to wash my magic's words from within me. Anything that made what I had to do sound so flippant. So easy. As if my soul would not expire with the brothers. As if it wouldn't die with Dinah if I failed.

"Now, Kiran," Calias said. "I think I can speak for everyone here when I say we've all been curious about your bride here, how she went from being a criminal to, well, here with us now." Calias waved his hand toward me and an uncomfortable chuckle echoed across the guests. "Won't you do us the delight of allowing her to share a tale with us? We're all dying for her to captivate us as much as you—"

Kiran might have lunged at him, had Fin not just projectile vomited all over Calias's plate.

Calias jumped backward, and Kiran launched himself for his brother, placing his hand on his shoulders and pushing him toward the exit.

"Come with us, Asha," he said, turning toward me, but then his face paled, the contents of Abra's jewelry setting in, and he pushed Fin faster in an attempt to make it outside.

I stood to join them, unable to think with the fear swirling in my head, but Az's arm stopped me in my place. He glanced behind me, surely at Abra, who I imagined was watching us closely.

"Allow me to assist you, my lady," Az said, his voice unnervingly friendly and charming. Familiar, except for the title that had replaced my name. The way he could warp back into that someone I knew. Someone I'd thought I knew... It made my skin crawl. "I wouldn't want a lady to witness such a vile thing."

He pulled me to the side by my arm so that everything looked in order.

Even though his nails were carving into my flesh.

Once we were safe from Abra's earshot, at least over the chatter of the crowd, he whispered, "What have you done? One word to the right guard, and she's dead. And if you plan on thwarting that message, Dinah dies anyway."

"I didn't do anything," I hissed through my teeth. "I would never do anything that put my sister in harm's way."

Az recoiled a bit. I wondered for the first time what had become of Tavi. Fear shivered through me, but I didn't have time to dwell on it now. I glanced over at Calias, who was assuaging the crowd with a joke and a handsome grin on his face. He must have felt me watching him, for he turned his head to face me and flashed me a warning smile. Then he took one look at Az and tilted his chin down ever so slightly.

"Looks like you already have," Az said with a tsk. He opened his mouth again, and the meaning of Calias's nod hit me.

They were going to kill Dinah.

They thought I'd foiled their plan to kill Kiran and Fin. Panic welled inside me.

"Wait," I whispered. "Please."

"I can't disobey direct orders," Az said. As if he cared. As if he regretted any of this.

"Just wait. Trust me," I said. Then I ripped my arm from his grasp and waltzed to the head of the table, to Calias's right-hand side, my chin held high.

What do you think you're doing?

For a moment, I didn't know. But then something, the loose threads of an idea, fluttered before my mind.

I grasped onto them and spoke. "Ladies and lords, I apologize if my husband's and his brother's ill stomachs have ruined your meal. Please, allow me to make it up to you, and to His Majesty, the King of Charshon, with the tale for which you've been holding in your chatter all this time."

Calias seized up next to me, and for a split second, I thought he'd cover my mouth, stop me.

I spoke before he had the chance.

CHAPTER 71

ASHA

*B*y the time my voice, my magic's voice filled the chamber of the tent, everyone else had gone silent. As if my magic had taken hold of their voices too.

"It was a cool evening in Rivre when the king and his brother fell ill. Little did either of them know that the illness was planned, the doing of the human bride they had been so careless to bring into their midst. The girl they had been so foolish to assume would be docile, all because they had watched her offer her own life in exchange for her sister's, and misinterpreted her loyalty as weakness."

Calias tensed beside me, but otherwise he didn't move. No one did. I scanned the crowd, making sure to force eye contact with each of them as the story flowed through me. A few of them glanced down at their plates when I caught their eyes, wide with wonder. Some curiosity. Others fear. Some hunger for violence, drama.

Even Queen Abra sat subdued with curiosity.

"But, in all the months the woman had been weaving her story, she'd also been weaving a plan—revenge for the life the king had stolen out from under her, the decision she had made only because his vengeance had backed her into a corner. How many times had the woman had the opportunity? How

many times had the king been so near, her voice could have closed his throat before he had the chance to reach for her?

"But a quick death wouldn't be enough for the king who had taken her youth, her family, her dignity. The being who had assumed her wicked without knowing her, then decided her meek once he'd subdued her, once he'd seeded the wickedness inside of her.

"No, the queen decided a spectacle was in order.

"Oh, how it thrilled her to discover the Council had invited her to attend with her cruel husband. Because where better to humiliate the one who'd put her to shame than in front of his peers, those he so desperately wished to impress?

"The queen poisoned the drinks of her husband and his fool of a brother. Not that she needed to weaken them in order to destroy them. No, her power was far more vast than they'd imagined."

Abra's eyes flickered in the shadows. The candles overhead had gone dim at the sound of my voice.

I reached out to the Rip, to the energy that rippled out from it, pulsing beneath my feet in the soft soil.

My hands shook by my side, and for a moment, I thought I had lost the audience by pausing. But then the entire table leaned forward, as if they feared they might miss my next words.

"She called them into the hall with her voice alone, and they came."

The crowd gasped, and I turned my head to follow their gaze. There, in the entryway, stood Kiran and Fin, both kneeling over in pain, both clutching their stomachs.

My gaze caught Kiran's, and a wave of realization crested on his face. His molten eyes went wide with what I wished was simply fear, dread.

But the hurt in his eyes. The way he looked at me as if all I had to do was drop this charade and repent, and he would pretend as though nothing had ever happened.

As if I hadn't committed treason.

As if this couldn't be the second time this was happening to him.

The reality of those eyes, the intensity of them, shook me to my core, obliterated my ribcage and left my heart bare, naked, raw in front of him. In front of all of them.

But I had to keep going. I swallowed the lump in my throat.

"Had they not realized," I shook with the bile, the greed, the slime in my voice that reminded me of Az, of Calias. But no one was watching me anymore. All eyes had turned to the King of Naenden. To his brother. To the two fae under the control of a mortal woman.

I was going to die for this.

That was good and well.

"Had they not realized that within her lie, the Old Magic, that bane of old, who had slumbered for centuries, had awoken to her touch. The being that had taken her sacrifice and blessed her with a power beyond the mortal senses."

"Asha, please. This isn't you." Kiran lifted his chin toward me, though a fit of violent pain sent him stumbling to the ground. He steadied himself on a nearby pole with a wavering, outstretched arm.

The cold, cruel laugh that rippled from my throat unsettled me. It wasn't mine. Not that strange mingling of my voice with my magic's that I was so used to.

No, this was my magic's voice. And it was no longer content with hiding in the shadows, sheltering its power in a human girl with half a face.

My magic fed on the Rip, the energy leaking from its home.

"When she demanded they kneel, they kneeled."

Metal clanked against the hard ground as Kiran and Fin's feet collapsed out from under them. I allowed my focus to wander to Fin.

That was a mistake. He didn't address me, didn't ask why, at least not with his voice. But his eyes had gone dull, powerless, and when he looked upon me, it was as if all the sadness this young fae had ever felt had simply accumulated in this moment. As if he figured it had been leading him here the whole time, and now it was time to resign to it.

The realness of it sent a surge of fear coursing through my bones.

No, no. I couldn't do this. This would not work.

But it was too late. I'd surrendered to the power. To my magic.

"She could have told them to slit their own throats, if she desired."

Not a hushed whisper echoed through the air this time. Not a soul moved.

"Perhaps she would." And that's when I realized it was my voice again. Because it was trembling. Trembling in agony, in fear, in dread of the hatred that would shackle my mind for as many days as Calias and Az allowed me to live.

Not that the crowd would notice the difference. They would assume the hatred causing my voice to quake would be for these two.

"The king and his brother placed their fists upon their chests."

Their arms moved as if led by invisible strings at the hands of a cruel puppeteer. My hands. My voice.

Kiran's whisper, kind and forgiving, broken and confused, was what shattered me in the end.

"Asha, my love. Why?"

But I didn't have time to shatter, didn't have time to collect the scattered fragments of my heart, to slice my fingers on the jagged edges of my splintered soul.

And so, I spoke.

"In front of those the two had so desperately tried to impress, the King of Naenden and the Prince of Talens ripped out their own hearts."

CHAPTER 72

ASHA

I closed my eye, but there was no stopping the sound that rippled through the air, the echo of ripping flesh, the vibration of ribs cracking under the weight of the powerful hands that smashed through them.

A dense thud, then another, followed by the slump of two heavy bodies.

Don't look, my magic whispered.

I didn't want to, but my eye seemed to open of its own accord.

"No!" Someone shouted, and then I was falling toward the ground, and dirt had filled my mouth, and Calias—of course the voice was Calias's—was on top of me. Something ripped behind me, and just as quickly, a wad of cloth was being shoved into my mouth.

But none of that stopped what I had seen.

Neither Kiran nor Fin had closed their eyes in death.

The flames, the flickers had gone out, and there was nothing but white in their eyes.

"Treason!" Calias called out.

Chairs scraped against the dirt as the weight of what had just happened sank in. As kings and queens and heirs came closer to get a good look at the woman who had slaughtered two high fae royalty by their own hands.

"Dinah," I tried to whisper through the cloth, but the word came out garbled, unintelligible. Calias must have understood my meaning anyway, because he called for a servant to come help, and Az's musty scent was in my nostrils, fueling my urge to puke.

"You didn't tell me she could control living beings, that she could control fae," Calias hissed so quietly, even I, from a foot away, could barely hear.

"I didn't know, Your Highness." Though there was nothing in Az's tone that suggested that he regretted his underestimation of me.

"Send word to the guard keeping her sister," Calias said, and I let out such a long, weeping sigh I thought I might choke on the air trapped inside my mouth by the wad of cloth.

"Very well, sir."

"Send word that the sister is to die."

I strangled on my gag, sent an arm swinging in Calias's direction, but he was on top of me in a moment, pinning and twisting my arm to my back.

For a breath of a moment, I managed to free my neck. To find Az's eyes. Those eyes I'd known since childhood.

I pleaded with him. In one look, I retold all our adventures, all the promises we'd made to each other.

That we'd always protect each other's families.

But the light I searched for had already been snuffed out.

"Gladly, Your Majesty." The words sank me, cast a grip around my throat stronger than anything Calias could have mustered. Az rose to his feet and sauntered to a fellow guard, one of tall stature, long legs. Probably the fastest of the messengers here. Tears streamed down my face and I gargled on the water building up in my mouth, soaking the rag.

Dinah was going to die, Dinah was going to die. My sister was going to die.

Calias ripped me to my feet, but I could barely stand. My legs, my knees, my resolve had all given out. I willed my mind to fling my feet at him, to kick, to scream, to lunge after the guards, but he only clenched the nape of my neck tighter, and a paralyzing pain shot down my spine.

"This girl, this child of woman, thought to rebel against her master this day. She believed it possible to rise against the high fae. To alter the balance. To change the order. That order being her place above us. Above us!" Calias yelled as he twisted the knot of my hair in his fist.

Someone in the crowd yelled a word at me I'd only ever heard used to describe ladies of the night. I didn't see who it was, couldn't bring myself to lift my head.

Calias solved that for me. He ripped at my hair until my neck overextended, exposing my neck, as if the crowd were a pack of wolves who could sniff my blood and were ready to pounce, to rip out my throat.

That was what Calias would do to me.

Or worse.

Whatever it was, I wished he would get on with it. Let me join Dinah in that blissful abyss.

My vision went blurry for a moment, faded, then came back into focus on Abra's face. Her lips pursed, her eyes a blue only observed on the tip of a flame.

I wondered if Abra could produce an ice so cold it burned like fire.

I wondered the point of even wondering such a thing.

For a moment, I thought she might strike, try to free me, but then her gaze flickered to something behind me.

In fact, as I scanned the room, I realized no one was looking at me anymore, despite Calias's attempts to lift my body above the table by my hair.

Calias must have noticed too, for he whipped around, yanking my neck with him, and gasped.

Kiran and Fin's bodies, both slumped onto the ground, had turned dark as onyx.

As we watched, something wry and bitter and harrowing swelled in my stomach.

I laughed.

A dry, muffled cackle that I knew I would hate myself for later, after I learned Dinah was dead.

Because Kiran's and Fin's body withered to ash and settled into the dust beneath them.

CHAPTER 73

ASHA

*C*haos dispelled in the tent. Kings and queens and their heirs gasped, volleying their heads between me, Calias, and the dust that had once been Kiran and Fin's bodies.

"Sorceress!" Calias cried out, twisting me by the neck and pointing a long, bejeweled finger at me.

It worked, Asha, you did it. My magic pushed something urgent through me, shared a sense of comfort and launched it rolling through my veins. But it was no use. Because it hadn't worked at all.

Sure, I had kept from murdering the real Fin and Kiran.

But Dinah was still going to die.

My sister. My sweet, selfless sister was still going to die.

I'd trusted the fact that fae couldn't lie outright. Except I had forgotten that Calias hadn't promised me anything at all. That he was free to change his mind on a whim, since the promise had merely come through the mouth of his messenger. Sorrow overtook me, and I wanted nothing more than for Calias to put me down, allow me to sink into myself, curl up on the dirt floor and offer myself as a fertilizer for the earth.

"I suggest you release her," a familiar voice said. It drew my attention, and my neck seemed to move without my direct permission, as if I were a mosquito and the voice was an evening flame.

Fin stood in the entryway, staring down Calias and not even bothering to glance at the pile of ashes where his conjured, dead body had just lain. Even in my distress, I admired his self-control.

Fin and Kiran. They were still alive. They could save her.

I thrashed against Calias's restraining hand, but to no use. My warning, that a messenger was on his way to order the death of my sister, garbled in my mouth behind my gag.

"I said, 'put her down.' And free the Queen of Naenden of that gag while you're at it." Fin's voice was a command. One he must have conjured up within himself just for this moment, as I was almost sure he'd never used it before.

"She's a sorceress and a trickster. Can't you see?" Calias paused dramatically, though I figured he was simply fumbling for his words but not wishing to convey such to the crowd. Apparently, he found his footing, for he started up again. "Fin? Not you too? Can't you see, brother? The woman has enchanted you with her Old Magic."

A hushed muttering broke out in the crowd at the table, but if it bothered Fin, he didn't show it.

"To what end, Your Majesty?" Fin flourished toward the ashes on the floor. "Surely if the queen had the power to convince a room full of educated fae royalty that she had murdered the King of Naenden and its prince, she could have just as easily conjured a beast to murder us before it vanished to dust. The Queen of Naenden clearly had no intention of harming my brother or myself. With that in mind, I suggest you let her go. If you don't, I can't imagine how many ordinances you would be violating, but I'd be happy to count them for you later, my duties as a prince being rather dull."

Calias's arm faltered for a moment, but he didn't release me. Tears rolled down my cheek. Every second this gag bound my voice was another second that Fin wouldn't race after Dinah to save her.

If they'd kept her close by, she might already be dead.

"I'm afraid I can't do that," Calias said. "Not when we're still unsure whether the sorceress has cast an enchantment over you that would incline you to protect her."

Fin approached, stepping directly through the ashes so that they fluttered around his feet.

Where was Kiran? Why wasn't he here? I tried to ask Fin with my pleading eye, but he didn't look at me. He didn't break his cool, fearless stare from Calias.

"From what I can gather, the only beings the lovely queen tricked were the lot of you." Fin whisked his hand around the room toward the guests. "And you." He tucked his hands into his pockets and nodded toward Calias. "How disappointed were you when you realized you had let yourself be fooled by a human woman? I'm sure you thought yourself above such things. There seems to be an idea going around that humans are less clever than the fae. Bless our lovely Queen Asha for rendering the humans a voice, and your respect, finally." Fin grinned with that casual smirk I was sure was boiling Calias's blood, that I would have found endearing, had the seconds of my sister's life not been dripping away.

"Remove her gag. Now. That's an order," Fin said, stopping in place.

"Under whose authority?" Calias sneered.

Fin reared his head back in faux surprise. "My brother's, of course. Or have you forgotten that I'm the heir to the King of Naenden? What kind of heir would I be if I allowed my brother's queen to be mistreated when she's broken no ordinance, done nothing worthy of being bound?"

"You and your brother have fallen prey to her deceit." Calias backed away as the slight Fin approached. I had no doubt that, had this conversation occurred in the dark shadows of the hills, Fin would be dead.

But we were not in the shadows. Calias had planned to kill the King of Naenden and his heir in the light of glowing lanterns.

In front of the Council.

The only force strong enough to put him down.

Fin advanced, his eyes glittering. "Why do you wish to keep her gagged, Calias? What are you afraid she might tell us?"

Where was Kiran?

Calias snorted. "What she might tell us? I'm fearful of what she might *do* to us, with that voice of hers, that filthy magic that possesses her. Her mind is not hers to rule, child. The Old Magic could strike us all. The girl must be silenced. Aren't we all in agreement?" Calias flourished toward the Council. No one dared make a move. They only stared.

Not at Calias. Not at Fin.

At me.

At the woman bound and gagged. The woman who had possessed the power and opportunity to murder them all, yet had not taken it.

"For all we know, you're simply a conjuring of the girl's voice, and the real Fin has dissolved to ashes before us," Calias said.

This must have sounded reasonable to the crowd because they all began muttering again.

"I appeared after you gagged her, remember?" Fin said.

"Yes, but aren't you supposed to be ill?"

The crowd stirred.

"Vomiting does wonders for an upset stomach." Fin grinned, though his eyes were as icy as fire could be. "What do you think, friends? Do you believe the Queen of Naenden has committed any crime?"

"She poisoned you and your brother," Calias hissed through his teeth.

I strained my eyes to catch a side-long glance of Abra, who sat sipping on her chalice. She hadn't even flinched when Calias slung his accusation at me, the accusation that should have been directed at her.

Perhaps her motives in poisoning Kiran and Fin hadn't been on my behalf at all. Or maybe she had been looking out for me, but refused to risk her throne by being less than covert.

"And as the victim of her crime, I feel I should have the most say about whether she's punished for it," Fin continued.

Victim. That was what Dinah would be. I screamed through my gag, croaking like a strangled chicken.

"I'm only going to ask you once more. Let her go," Fin said.

"If I'm not mistaken, are you not the brother born without a gift from the magic?" Calias said, his voice sickeningly sweet. He dropped me to the ground, though he kept his firm grip on my neck. My tears formed puddles in the mud beneath us. This was all taking too long. Even if Fin and Abra could wrestle the gag from me, we would be too late.

Dinah was dead.

I was sure of it.

Fin's banqueting robe made a muffled thud as it hit the ground. He rolled up the sleeves of his tunic, revealing the lean muscle of his forearms.

No.

I shook my head, my protests silenced by my gag.

Dinah was dead.

Fin was going to be dead.

And where was Kiran?

Where was my husband?

Calias tsked. "You foolish boy. Do you think you'll land a fist on me before I swallow you whole?"

Fin shimmied his shoulders, reading his fighting stance. "What are you going to do? Kill an heir of Alondria in front of the Council? Pretty sure that's a no-no. But that would be convenient for you, wouldn't it? If you killed me here and now? Wasn't that the end goal of this evening anyway? Excuse me—half of the end goal."

Calias shuffled behind me, but subtly enough I doubted anyone noticed. "My dearest brethren," he said, gesturing to the Council as Abra bristled. "Do you not agree that our poor Phinehas is clearly enchanted under this temptress's spell? That the most obvious course of action is to execute the witch in the hopes that the enchantment over the prince might be severed? All in favor?"

At first, no one moved. No one uttered a word.

Someone cleared their throat, and Abra rose from her seat at the table. "Aye."

My heart seized in my chest as the other rulers followed suit, each rising, each echoing her approval. Abra must have seen the pleading in my eyes, either that, or sensed the fear that sent my pulse skyward, because she offered me an almost apologetic nod.

No, Dinah.

Killing me, that was fine, but not before I got the message to Fin to save Dinah.

"I would have thought the vote to execute a fellow ruler's queen would have had to be unanimous," Fin said, taking a step forward. "Killing my brother's king will be nothing less than an act of war."

When Calias spoke, the faux concern that oozed from his voice crept down my spine. "You say that now, but once the enchantment is br—"

Fin launched himself at Calias, scaling across the expanse between them in a single leap. Calias lurched backward, but Fin was faster, and a horrid crackling noise echoed through the tent as Fin's fist collided with Calias's cheekbone. Calias staggered, releasing his grip on me, and I crawled out from between the two fae, fumbling with the knot that secured my gag. My fingers shook, and I could barely get a hold on the tightly wound fabric. Just when I managed to get my fingernails between the folds, pain slapped my entire body, sending me flying, spinning, whirling, until I landed on my back, next to...

Next to Fin.

We lay there side by side in the mud, our bodies imprinting the soaking ground as the wave that had just floored us crashed against the ground, retreating into the earth as water dispelled across the tent.

Water.

The gift of the Charshonian ruling line was water.

Panic swelled in my chest as I tried to swallow the mouthful of water collecting in my mouth, but the gag was shoved too far down my throat. Liquid stung at my nostrils as I breathed, unable to expel any of the water I had inhaled when Calias's wave had knocked me backward.

And Fin.

He craned his neck to get a good look at me, his magicless, caramel eyes streaked with sorrow. He smirked when he caught me looking at him, a sad little attempt at comforting me, but I appreciated it nonetheless. "I thought you might want some company. That way you don't have to die alone."

I choked on a half-laugh, half-primal-wail, Fin's dismal humor never failing to shock me, not even at the end. Love swelled in my heart for my friend, but so did anger, burning equally as hot, a vengeful fire racing in my veins that wanted to burn everything in sight at the thought of Fin dying.

But that was the unfortunate thing about fire.

Neither of us had it.

And, even if we did, water trumped fire.

Calias advanced, a blue orb swirling in each of his outstretched palms. "It pains me to do this," he said, the sheer pleasure swelling behind his ocean eyes so obvious it made me wonder just how stupid the rest of the Council was if they thought he hadn't been hoping for this outcome, "but I think it's clear to everyone here that the witch's influence is too strong to be severed by her death alone."

Something clammy grabbed hold of my hand, and as I craned my neck, Fin's fingers intertwined with mine. Salty tears stung at my eyes, or perhaps Calias had simply been cruel enough to sick saltwater upon us.

Calias wrenched his left hand, and water spewed forth like a raging waterfall, shooting straight for Fin's mouth, curling in tendrils up his nose. His back arched as the water flowed through him, drowning him. His fingers clawed for mine, struggling to grip onto me, but they slipped, and I watched in horror as Fin's body seized, his eyes rolling into the back of his head as he convulsed.

No. No, no, no.

I grasped for his hand, but I missed, for as soon as I moved, Calias flicked his other wrist.

Pain.

Pure, unadulterated agony exploded through me, painting the

inside of my skull with the guts of my brain, scorching the space behind my eye with the sting of bursting stars. Water rushed into my mouth, soaking my gag, shoving it further down my throat, until I thought I might drown on my own vomit. It forced its way into my nose, stealing the breath from me, flooding my lungs, agony popping like inflamed pustules in my chest.

Death, this is what death felt like.

Not death, strangled at Kiran's hand. Not death, stabbed in the chest, at Kiran's hand. Not burned to a crisp at Kiran's hand.

Now, those deaths that once paralyzed me with fear seemed merciful.

Could the Fates have been crueler? Had it not been enough that my death would come as the man I had loved my entire life stood idly by, prepared to sacrifice his best friend and use her lifeless body as a stepping stool on which to propel himself to the throne? Was it not enough to watch Fin die trying to save me, when I had been prepared to end his life to save my sister's less than an hour ago?

My sister.

Was she not enough?

Perhaps I would see her again, when we both faded from under the sun. Perhaps she already waited for me, her hand outstretched, ready to take me into her arms.

But not before this grand finale the Fates had planned for me. Not before this sick bit of poetry—the part of the story where the girl raised in the desert, the girl who lived so much of her life for a palmful of water—the day that girl drowned.

Seemed fitting enough.

So I surrendered, surrendered to the roar berating my ears, succumed to the river I would have had to cross eventually anyway.

And once I surrendered, once I embraced the darkness as I swam through it, hoping to find my sister's warm touch somewhere in this void of a place, everything went quiet for once.

Perhaps death wasn't so bad after all.

Maybe Fin would be here too.

Maybe he would get to introduce me to Ophelia.

I thought I might like that.

But Kiran.

His name deflated that thin layer of peace I had deceived myself into thinking went on forever.

What would Kiran think, when he found my body, Fin's body, swollen and bloated with that cruel, deathbringer of an element masquerading as a giver of life?

The thought made me sad. And I didn't want to be sad. Not here. No, sad was for under the sun, not above it or within it or...

Or without it.

It was so dark.

Panic rapped on the glass of my pleasant illusion, fracturing its surface, spiderwebbing out, cracking, cracking, cracking.

"Asha?"

Those sounds, I'd heard those sounds before. What was an asha? I should have known, but the meaning of the word escaped me.

"Asha!"

CHAPTER 74

KIRAN

I watch as Dinah flings herself at her sister, pounding the heels of her palms into Asha's chest. I watch as that tiny human girl cracks ribs, the sound of which grate against my ears, taunting me, reminding me that I am too late.

Too late.

Too late.

Half an hour ago, I made a choice. A choice to go after Dinah. A choice for Fin, my magicless brother, to stay with my wife, to protect her, if not by his power, then by his words. I commanded him to stall the Council until I could return with Dinah, her life spared and her kidnapping sufficient evidence to take Calias down, to save Asha from their legal hand.

Half an hour ago, Calias's guard fled the tent, just as Fin and I finished puking out our guts. Half an hour ago, I'd almost strangled him, thinking Calias had been the one to poison us, hoping for evidence to support my suspicions. Half an hour ago, he'd told me through guttural breaths that Calias was holding a human girl captive. That he'd been sent with her death sentence. That if he didn't make it to his destination, that within the quarter hour, she'd be dead anyway.

I'm the faster of the two of us, so I'd made the decision.

I would go. Fin would stay.

The worst part of it is, it doesn't matter that I went after her. It doesn't matter that I abandoned my wife in the hopes of returning her sister to her alive.

Because by the time I got to Dinah, she'd already been saved. By the time I got to Dinah, the stench of fae blood soaked the evening breeze, riding the wind and signaling a warning. A calling card.

By the time I got to Dinah, the Umbra had beaten me there.

When I burst into the cave tucked deep within the cascading hills of Rivre, a bloodied array of bodies separated from their heads had lead me to Dinah, her almond eyes set with determination, even as she stood, fists trembling, before the Nightslayer.

For a moment, I'd been convinced he would end me, that being who was said to be cloaked in darkness itself. The creature who had spilled a sacrificial amount of blood without sullying his dark robes.

Why the Avenger of the Innocent chose to spare the male who had vowed to slaughter a human woman every mooncycle, I would never know.

All I know is that I chose wrong.

Because Dinah was alive without my help.

I sent my brother to his death sentence, and by doing so, I might as well have killed my wife.

Anguish ripples through me, splays my ribs, guts that pulsing thing within me that apparently is still made of flesh after all.

They lay beside one another, the olive of their skin paled underneath their swollen cheeks.

"Asha!" Dinah screams, panting as her delicate torso hinges, as her fists plunge into my wife's sternum.

Her rounded human ears can't hear it.

But I can.

The squishing of liquid with every beat of her tiny hand, with every unnatural pulse of Asha's chest.

And Fin.

But I can't think of Fin. Can't think of my brother splayed across the ground, can't think of the laugh that would never escape from lips so bloated, can't think of Lydia.

Lydia.

She'll die when news reaches her.

And then she'll kill me too.

Perhaps that will be a mercy.

Perhaps she'll do it out of love, as a demonstration of her affection.

But no, Lydia won't kill me. How silly of me to forget. She won't get the chance.

Because the Council will kill me; they'll have me executed publicly.

For killing Calias, of course.

Because that's what I've done.

They always say that water trumps fire. That, in a fight between the two ancestral magics, the life-giving force is the more destructive of the two.

They are wrong.

But that's because they don't account for pain, for anguish so consuming, it devours everything in its wake.

It would be kind of the Council to kill me, to release me from the image that imprinted itself to my mind only moments ago. Asha and Fin, my wife and my brother, their bodies flailing lifelessly in the mud as water shoved its way down their throats, into their noses, as it puffed their skin and possessed them.

And of Calias, that wretched sense of self-satisfaction smeared across his putrid face, the gluttonous high of victory as he killed my brother. My kind, lighthearted brother.

As he killed my wife.

My friend.

In that moment, I'd erupted.

The water defiling my loved ones' corpses had evaporated, cooked until it was little more than scalding steam floating, pushing against the fabric of the tent until the ropes holding it to the stakes had frayed and popped, sending our covering soaring, lost to the night sky.

I hadn't minded. In fact, I had wanted the sky to watch, to sit idly by as I'd *consumed* him.

In the end, it had been too quick, the flash of horror in his eyes as I turned him to ash, as I returned him to the dust from whence he came. I should have drawn it out, made him suffer longer.

But he had touched her. Bruised her. Tortured her.

Murdered her.

And I had wanted him dead.

And now he was.

"Asha! Asha, please wake up. Please." Dinah's cries break through the fog suffocating my mind, the one protecting it from reality. "Kiran, please. Please help her."

I jolt to my senses, noting the way an aura of dread emanates from the Council members. Pure, raw cold radiates from the nearest end of the table, where Queen Abra stands rigid, unreadable. The House of Dwellen is here, the mud beneath their feet sprouting vines, their thorns reared back like wolves awaiting the pounce. I can only thank the Fates that the King of Avelea declined his invitation to the Council meeting, claiming illness, lest I face the ferocity of his magic.

They will slaughter us.

If it was just me, I might even welcome death.

I could go to Asha, to Fin, to my mother.

But who would look after Dinah? Who would make sure she came to no harm? How could I face my wife in the shadow where the sun does not reach if I give myself up without protecting her?

But my Flame is almost gone, depleted after my outburst against Calias. I can't protect the girl.

I might laugh, if the situation weren't so dire. All my life, I've been raised, no, molded, to slam my iron fist into the spines of the innocent, the helpless. And now, now that I'm finally ready to wrench myself from my father's will—his will that he so easily convinced me was my purpose—now that I'm finally ready to avenge the innocent, to protect the weak, I lack the power to do so.

Perhaps my father was right after all.

Without power, we are nothing.

Except my father hadn't known Asha. Somehow, in the centuries he sold searching for power, he had missed her. He'd missed the person whose words yielded such might, she had shattered this heart of mine. The one my father had worked so hard to fortify, to forge.

If she were here, if that vile excuse of a fae hadn't bound her lips, crushed her mightiest weapon, she would have saved us all.

I don't possess that kind of power.

But I know who does.

I clear my soot-filled throat, the words scraping the dry air. "You may finish me if you so desire, but first, you would do well to hear what this young woman has to say." In a moment, I'm at Dinah's side, melding with the rhythm of her frantic hands, taking her place at Asha's chest. My heart breaks with my wife's ribs as I throw my weight into my palms, scanning her face, my brother's face.

My brother who I'm abandoning to save her.

Fates, forgive me.

To my relief, a faint pulse patters at my calloused fingers as I leave a smudge on the curve of her neck. Asha is alive, if barely. And if Asha is alive...

"You must tell them what you know."

Dinah shakes her head, her sweaty, untamed braid tossing in confusion. "No, I have to stay with Asha. I have to make her wake up." Tears carve caverns into her soot stained cheeks.

"I'll stay with her."

"I can't leave her."

"If she wakes, they will only slaughter her again."

Understanding strikes Dinah's innocent face, and she stands, hands trembling, to face the Council. When she speaks, her voice quakes, but I've long since abandoned the idea that such is a sign of weakness. "Calias of Charshon gave the orders for me to be kidnapped in a plot to force my sister to kill the King and Prince of Naenden publicly, so he could frame her for their murder and win your support by acting like he saved the day."

Now that Asha's heart is beating, I switch my attention to Fin, pounding against his chest with my palms.

"But my sister wasn't like all of you," Dinah continues, her pitch going shrill as the evening wind. "She wasn't the kind of person to stand by and watch as innocent people are slaughtered. You were going to let her kill the King and Prince of Naenden, weren't you? Because you *feared* her. And then, when you saw the evidence that she'd tricked Calias, that she had spared their lives instead of murdering them, you stood by and watched as Calias drowned her." Fin gargles, a stream of water spewing from his puffed lips. His eyes flutter open, sending a wave of relief crashing into the swell of agony in my chest. He might be magicless, but he's still fae, meaning his body can withhold Calias's drowning longer than a human…longer than Asha. I gag as I fumble for her pulse, for the smudge on her neck that marks where I last felt it. Nothing. No. No, no, no.

Fin's gaze crosses, then fixes on Asha, then rises to meet her sister, whose voice has gone quiet, barely a whisper, yet it carries through the night as if suspended by the wind itself. "Asha wasn't like all of you. When she saw that innocent people were in danger, she gave herself in their place. In *my* place. And it wasn't because she wasn't scared. It wasn't because she wasn't terrified. It was because my sister wasn't a coward. So, if by any chance the Fates look down upon her with kindness and allow her to wake up, if after all she has done, if any of you lay a finger on her—"

"Then what?" the King of Dwellen scoffs. "What is a fragile human girl going to do?"

Fin flinches, but there is no need, for Dinah crosses the muddy distance between herself and the King of Dwellen, crushing his thorny vines beneath her muddied slippers as she cups his rigid jaw within her palm. As if he were barely weaned, and not five centuries her senior. "Then I will find comfort in the fact that my sister dwells in peace beyond the sun while you live out your miserable immortal existence unable to escape the cowardice rotting your soul."

I ready myself to pounce, to scale the distance between us and throw myself between Dinah and the immortal king.

But when she turns and walks away, leaving a trail of trampled vines in her wake, and a jagged thorn shoots from the earth, aimed straight at her heart, it turns to crystal just as it grazes the spine of her coat.

541

No, it turns to ice.

"There will be none of that," Queen Abra says, looking upon the King of Dwellen with disdain as a frozen tear clings to her cheek. She flicks her wrist and the icy thorn shatters.

Dinah nods in appreciation, leaving the stunned council behind before running toward us and kneeling at Asha's side. "Help me wake her up," she says.

Pain claws at my throat. "I can't. It was too much. I can't find a pulse."

Dinah's gaze snaps at me, her caramel eyes blazing with such intensity, I could be convinced she's Flame-blessed. For a moment, I think she might lash out at me, yell at me like she did the Council, blame me for her sister's death. The thought terrifies me. But then she grabs my hand, her tiny, warm fingers interlinking with mine. When she speaks, there's nothing but certainty in her voice. "All your life, you've been made to believe that you exist to destroy. That your power exists to destroy. That changes today. Today, you're going to use it to heal."

I shake my head, the sureness in her brow only breaking my heart more. "I don't have that kind of power, Dinah."

She closes her eyes and presses both of our hands to Asha's chest. "Can you feel the water?"

I frown. "Yes, but—"

"Then make it go away. Evaporate it like you did the flood of water Calias was using to drown her."

"You don't understand. My power isn't like that, it's not that controlled. If I unleash it, I'll hurt her."

Dinah's wide eyes snap open, and where I expect scolding on the hard line of her lips, she smiles. "You won't hurt her, Kiran. I know you'd never hurt her."

Tears sting at my eyes as her words carve their way into my chest, as they burrow into my soul. I inhale, and as I let the breath out, I allow the warmth to flow through my fingertips, seep through her skin and fill her up. Steam escapes her nostrils, fleeing her open mouth in swirling tendrils.

"Good. See?" Dinah says, her lips tilting.

I want it to matter. I do. But no amount of clearing my wife's lungs will restart her still, lifeless heart.

"I know you can heal her. I know you can," Dinah whispers. "Just like you healed me that night you carried me to the infirmary because my stomach ached."

My heart sinks, plummets, slams through the muddied earth and buries itself there. Dinah believes I have the power to heal others. That night she fell ill, I only assuaged her discomfort; I didn't heal her of the illness itself.

She believes I can heal her sister.

But all I can do for Asha is comfort her in death.

"Dinah, I can't—"

"Of course, you can. You've done it to me—"

"Dinah."

She peers up at me with those wide eyes, those eyes I want nothing more than to say 'yes' to, to please, to fill with joyful tears.

"I can take the pain away, if she still feels any," I say, my voice breaking as my throat caved in.

Dinah blinks, and with the shutter of her eyelids, realization dawns in those beautiful irises. Pain. Pure, undefiled pain ripples through her face. "No."

"Dinah—"

"No, no, no, Asha." She collapses onto her sister's limp frame, flooding Asha's already soaked gown with tears. "Please, please, no, you can't take her away from me. Please don't take her away from me," she mutters, and I realize she isn't speaking to me, but to the Fates.

Fin groans and crawls to Asha's side, his fingers finding Dinah's hair, pulling it away from her face as she weeps.

I try to swallow, but the lump in my throat won't let it go down. Then I pull Asha's limp, cold hand into my lap, caressing it with my thumb, sending any pulse of comfort I can muster through to her.

But there's so little comfort within me, who knows if I'm doing her any good?

Perhaps I'm just sending her pain, agony, loss, making her feel all the anguish that one should be free of after passing from under the sun.

She is dead.

My wife, my friend, the only person in this world to ever see me for the ugliness inside and come away from it harboring anything other than disgust, is dead.

My storyteller, my laughter, my all, is dead.

I'll never hear that voice again.

Shock—blinding, excruciating shock—jolts through me, electrifying my bones and paralyzing my muscles. This is a nightmare. This is all just a nightmare, and this pain is too overwhelming to be real. It surges through me, pulsing through my hands, thrumming through the air, seizing my hands until they grip Asha's gown...

"Do you hear that?" Fin groans, his lips barely moving.

I hardly have the will left in me to summon the air necessary for speech. "Hear what?"

But he doesn't have to answer.

Because I hear it too.

Thu-thum, thu-thum, thu-thum.

Asha's heart.

Her heart is beating.

CHAPTER 75

ASHA

*D*inah caressed my face in my tent, the soft candlelight highlighting the scars and bruises on her brow, under her left eye and on her cheeks. Her touch hurt my aching, bloated skin, where Calias's wave had slammed into me, but I couldn't bring myself to tell her as much. Not when she was alive. Not when we both were. "Lie down," she said. "You've had an awful day. You need to rest."

My eye stung at that comment. Dinah had been kidnapped, trapped in a dungeon in the hills of Rivre, and, from the looks of it, abused. Yet somehow, all she could think of was taking care of me.

"I'm so sorry, Dinah. This was all my fault," I said, the words scraping the inside of my throat as my salty tears burned the scratches on my face. Apparently, drowning hadn't done much to improve the resonance of my voice.

"Don't you dare blame yourself, Asha," Dinah said, taking my chin in her hand and forcing me to look her in the eyes. "Listen to me. You saved us. All of us. Calias and Az had months to plot, to trap you in an impossible situation. You had a day, and you still outwitted them."

I buried my face into her shoulder, the words, the admission knocking against my insides. The truth that I knew would never let me be, that would never let me sleep soundly again. "Please don't act like I'm so noble. Dinah, I would have..." I stopped, unsure my guilt would allow the words to escape my mouth, unsure that my conscience would ever allow me such relief, when I by no means deserved it.

"You can tell me," Dinah whispered. "I'll love you just the same, I promise."

The words sent me gagging as I wept, and it took a few minutes for me to regain my capacity to speak. When I'd stopped sobbing, I opened my mouth multiple times, but I couldn't seem to catch the words.

"If you get the first five words out, the rest will come," Dinah said.

I nodded and exhaled. "I would have killed them," I managed to choke out, but Dinah was right, the admission seemed to have made way, shaken loose the rest of my confession. "If Abra hadn't mistaken my curiosity about her poison for me wanting to poison Kiran and Fin. If they hadn't gotten sick and left the room and given me the chance to conjure up apparitions that looked like them...I would have killed them, Dinah," I gasped, the sobbing roaring out of me now, "I couldn't bear for you to die. I was going to do it..."

Dinah said nothing for a moment. She only stroked my hair as I soiled her nightgown with my tears. When she finally spoke, her voice had that determined quality. Gentle, but sure of herself. Just harsh enough that I knew her words demanded respect. "You wouldn't have killed them, Asha."

"I know you want to believe that, but I intended to. You don't understand," I said, weeping.

"No, listen to me," Dinah said, taking my head from her shoulder and forcing me to look her in the eye. "Do you know how I know you wouldn't have killed them?"

I shook my head, feeling more and more like a child. A child with the capacity to murder.

"Because you didn't. You found another way."

I gagged. "That was only chance. Good luck. I had no control over Abra poisoning them. If she hadn't, they'd be dead right now, at my hands."

"No, they wouldn't." Dinah shook her head. "Don't you see? You would have just found another way."

"There was no other way!" Shame washed over me at my outburst as I remembered what Dinah must have endured, the horrors that would probably haunt her the rest of her life, and I crumbled.

But Dinah only smiled. "Do you think it was just some coincidence that Abra mistook your intentions? That you were seated next to her at the dinner? That Fin and Kiran were gone just long enough for you to turn the conspiracy in your favor? No, Asha, I don't believe that. I can't. You're a good person. A good person who sacrificed your life to save me on the off chance I might have been in danger. And you used your time to make sure you took care of your family. You're the kind of person who can soften a hardened heart. You're not a murderer. I know that. Kiran knows that. The Fates know that. There was always going to be a way."

The tiniest smile tugged at the edges of my lips. I wasn't sure that I was convinced, but it was nice to hear all the same.

Dinah sat up and shook her shoulders, "Besides, maybe now you'll have a little more empathy for Kiran and not judge him for what he *might have done* had he not fallen in love with you."

I jerked my neck back in shock. Then something incredible happened. My broken ribs shook, and in between sobs, agonizing laughter cut its way through the air. Then Dinah was laughing too, and we cackled until our bellies ached with joy and pain and relief.

* * *

DINAH STAYED with me that night, though I didn't sleep at all. I simply listened, listened to the way her lungs stole little huffs of air from the universe, piece by piece, as she slept. As if they thought the world wouldn't notice if they took so little at a time.

But that's what we were as humans. So little in the universe. *In the multiverse apparently*, I thought, as the anxiety of the Rip only half a mile away tugged at my belly.

Sometimes Dinah would take too long between breaths, and panic would seize me. I had to clench my fists together to keep from shaking her shoulders, forcing her awake just so she could tell me in her own words that she was alive.

Perhaps that was why I was still awake when Kiran returned from the Council meeting that had been called to discussed the happenings of the previous Council meeting.

* * *

"You're still awake," he whispered.

My limbs seized up, and fear coursed through my body. A million questions swarmed my mind. Would he be able to sense what I had almost done? What I had been willing to do? And if he couldn't feel it, would it eat away at me on the inside for the rest of my life?

"I would like to speak with you, but I understand if you wish to rest," he said.

We both knew I wasn't getting any resting done.

Clenching my fists, I rolled over in bed and slipped out. He offered his arm to me, and I hesitated, but took it, even though my hands shook in protest. Would he sense my fear of him? My fear of myself, my secret? Or would he assume the shaking was simply the aftermath of the traumatic day?

As soon as our skin collided, a blissful neutrality washed over my aching bones, melting away my pain. "Thank you," I whispered. The onsite healer had given me a potion to heal my ribs overnight. Other than my concern over Dinah, that had been another thing to blame for my lack of sleep. The discomfort of my ribs suturing themselves back together had been less than pleasant, but I was happy when she had said I should be able to walk by the time I woke up.

Never mind that I didn't exactly go to sleep, and that she probably wanted me to wait until morning to test out my stride, but the healer didn't have to know that.

We stepped out of the tent and into the cool evening. My limbs shivered, and Kiran stripped himself of his coat and placed it over my shoulders. Something about it felt warmer than it should have, and I realized he must have enchanted it. The thoughtful gesture sent of flurry of guilt rushing through me. One I was sure would burst out of me if I wasn't careful, so I stopped it with a question before it could.

"How did you know Dinah was in danger? And how did you know where to find her?" I asked.

He exhaled, the fog of his breath glowing in the starlight. "You sure you want to relive that at this exact moment?"

"I'm sure."

He nodded, then gestured at the ground, beckoning me to sit with him as he lowered himself. Once I followed, he said, "I thought that might be the case. When Fin and I fell ill, I assumed someone at the dinner had attempted to poison us. Well, I assumed it was Calias. So when his messenger came racing out of the tent, I caught him and tried to force him to admit that Calias had poisoned us. He didn't, of course, since Calias *hadn't* poisoned us. But I suppose he figured I planned on snapping him in two, because he told me he was simply a messenger, and that Calias had a human girl in his possession that he had ordered to be killed. That he was simply carrying the message. Eventually I got it out of him who the girl was, and I threatened him with his life if he didn't take me to her. Before I left, I ordered Fin to get you out of the tent safely. We had heard most of what was going on from outside the tent and guessed Calias had set you up to kill us. From the looks of it, you were trying to make it look like you had. You're a genius, you know," Kiran said, looking down on me with such warmth in his eyes, I could have thrown up.

"And Dinah? Do you know… She swore she was fine when I asked her. That nothing happened to her. I don't quite believe her," I said, unable to formulate the question we both knew I was asking.

Kiran grimaced, a sight that made my stomach coil. "Dinah's guards were dead by the time I arrived."

"What?" My jaw dropped. The words didn't quite register. "But… but how?"

"Ever heard of the Umbra?"

Heard of her? I'd been rescued by her, when that guard had attempted to assault me.

Not that Kiran knew that. Nor did he know that the Umbra was a *her*. A her who happened to be his sister.

"The Umbra?" I said, the surprise in my throat all too genuine, but for reasons other than what Kiran would assume. "How...how?" I stopped myself there before I said too much.

Kiran shrugged. "How does the Umbra know anyone is in danger?"

How indeed. I shuddered thinking of the bruises on my sister's face that might have never had the chance to heal had it not been for Lydia's intervention. Neither Dinah nor Kiran knew that it was Lydia who had come to her rescue, of course, and I wasn't keen on telling either of them my friend's secret. If they were to discover the truth, it would have to come from Lydia's lips. I'd have to find a way to thank her, but how did one really thank someone for saving their loved one's life?

But that didn't stop me from wondering how in Alondria she had known Dinah was in danger, or how she'd reached her in time when she was supposed to be in Meranthi overseeing the kingdom in Kiran's absence.

Kiran twirled his thick, calloused thumbs. "I thought he was there waiting for me. My personal angel, there to escort from my place under the sun."

My mind hitched on the *he* part of Kiran's statement, and I remembered Lydia possessed that glamoured ring that allowed her to appear as a male. My throat went dry at the self-condemnation layered under his simple statement. "Why would you think that?" I asked.

My husband clasped his hands, rubbing the heels of his massive hands together as he rocked. "Honestly, I'd been expecting him. Ever since the day I had my heralds announce that wretched decree. Thought he was late, actually. Though I can't imagine what other evil must occur in Alondria if I didn't make the top of his list. I thought he'd come that day—the day I intended to execute you."

I pursed my lips, watching my husband as the pain struck his perfect features, bending and twisting his brow like hands to a clay sculpture. "You thought? Or you hoped?"

He swallowed, clamping his eyes shut, and the sight clenched itself around my belly, wringing me dry as the Sahli.

"I didn't know how to stop it, how to put an end to what was overcoming me. How to resist the growth of what my father planted so many years ago." He opened his eyes then, turning those white-golden irises upon me. "But then came you."

Guilt in the form of a shard of glass lodged in my throat as he leaned closer, his presence warming my skin with a pleasure and excitement I didn't deserve. It should have been comforting, so why did it feel as though it would suffocate me instead?

I couldn't do this.

"Asha, is something wrong?" Kiran asked, wiping my hair from my forehead and tucking it behind my ear, leaving behind the whisper of his touch. "Other than the fact Calias kidnapped your sister and almost forced you to murder someone as kind as Fin, I mean." His teasing smile sent my stomach into cartwheels.

Was something wrong? Everything was wrong.

"Calias wasn't working alone."

"I would think not, with an army at his disposal."

"No, I mean, he was working with Az."

Kiran's thick brow raised. "Your childhood friend who attempted to steal you away from me?"

"That's the one."

A wicked grin broke across Kiran's lips, showing off his perfect teeth.

"Why does the news that my best friend tried to frame me for murder and threatened to torture my sister make you look like Winter Solstice came early?"

"Because," he said, nudging my arm with his elbow, "now when I kill him, I don't have to worry about you giving me the silent treatment for a decade."

"I thought a decade was like an hour to the fae."

"Not when my time with you is limited."

My heart lurched, catching in my throat, and I turned my face from him, burying it in my hands.

"Asha?"

Just tell him.

I can't.

My magic huffed. *Well, I'm going to get seasick if I have to live with your conscience hurling itself about as if it were a fishing boat in the middle of a hurricane.*

You know, I thought, *I had hoped the one benefit of dying would be ridding myself of you.*

The definition of dying is fairly subjective. Personally, I'm grateful to your husband for shocking your heart back into action, even if it was an accident.

"Kiran, I—" When I peeked around my fingertips, I found his molten eyes golden and glowing. As if he were basking in my presence.

"You're so clever, you know," he whispered. "You found a way to save all of us. And Asha, that show you put on. That power inside you…" He shook his head in disbelief. "You're incredible."

My nose tingled, and my eye stung. "Please don't say that."

"I think I will anyway," he grinned, but his smile faltered when he beheld what must have been the semblance of a cornered antelope on my face. "What's wrong? Calias's dead. Are you concerned about Az? Because we'll find him, Asha. And I was kidding about the murdering him part. Well, I wasn't kidding, but I could be talked out of it."

"I'm not afraid of Az," I said.

Kiran's eyes went slack, and I recognized his interpretation of what I'd said immediately.

"Not you. It's not you I'm afraid of either," I said, and his tense shoulders relaxed a little. I inhaled. "Kiran, I have something to confess. I… It was pure luck that Abra placed the poison in yours and Fin's cups."

Kiran's eyebrows lifted. "You're telling me that Queen Abra is plotting against us too?"

"Well, no. Not exactly. I asked her about her poisoned jewels, and she misinterpreted it as me wishing to poison you and Fin."

Kiran nodded and grimaced. "I could see how her history would incline her toward helping you out."

Then immediately turning on you, my magic grumbled.

"Kiran, if she hadn't made that mistake, misinterpreted my intentions, if you and Fin hadn't left the room," I sighed, blowing all the air out of my lungs, expelling the fear that was between me and the next words, "I would have killed you and Fin. To save Dinah, I would have done it."

Kiran looked away from me for a moment and exhaled heavily. He stared up at the stars for so long, I wondered if he was trying to count them to soothe his thoughts.

"I am so sorry. I know what this means, and I'm fully ready to accept the consequences—"

Kiran jerked his neck back at me. "The consequences?"

"Yes, I know I've committed treason. Or, at least, conspired to—"

"Asha, you do realize that the entire reason we know each other was because I pretty much decided to have you killed without ever having met you, right?"

"I—"

"No, please. First, tell me why you asked Abra about her jewels to begin with. Knowing you, I imagine it wasn't because you cared about the fashion tips."

I almost yelled at him, screamed at him to listen to me, not to make light of this.

Just answer his question, Asha. Do you remember?

"I had an idea. I thought that if the poison in her jewels was strong enough, I could somehow poison Calias. That maybe I could... I don't know how I was planning on saving Dinah with that idea. I'd hardly had time to come up with it before Abra put the poison in your goblet instead. I just thought that maybe there was a way to—"

"A way to save us?" Kiran asked, a glint in those warm eyes.

"It was just a thought. Hardly even a thought. A kernel of a thought," I said.

"And did you have other kernels of thoughts throughout the day?"

I slammed my fist against the ground. "You're missing the point!

Don't you get it? If one thing had been different, I would have killed you!"

Kiran smirked. "Well, then I suppose we're even."

I gaped.

"That entire speech you gave me in the palace about me being a murderous monster? Feel free to recant that now," he said, waving his hand dismissively toward me. "Go ahead. Admit that you're just as much of a monster as I am. That we both intended to kill one another, and that puts us on the same playing field."

"You..." I fumbled for the words as the rage enveloped me. I shot to my feet. "Don't you *dare*. I almost killed you, almost ripped my soul out to save my sister. You...you...ugh...you almost killed me over hurt feelings and prejudice and—" I stopped, because Kiran had stood, too, and was now leaning over me, his warm breath fogging the air, brushing against my cheek.

"Feel better about it all?" he asked, his voice low and rumbling.

I gulped. "I would have killed Fin. There's no excuse for that. Fin's never hurt anyone."

Kiran leaned in closer, and his pure massiveness, the way his body seemed to halt the crisp wind in its wake, struck me. The way he thawed my limbs, my heart without even touching me, just by being near. "We both know you wouldn't have harmed Fin. Not when it came down to it."

Hot salty tears poured down my face as his words, as the truth, settled in. As mingled fear and longing rose within my chest, fired through my blood, tingled in my cheeks, my arms, my fingertips as he drew nearer. Our noses were almost touching now.

But there was another question. One that had gnawed at me all night. "You knew I might die, that Calias might try to kill me, that Fin doesn't have magic, but you saved Dinah first anyway. Why? Wouldn't it have made more sense to send Fin after Dinah?"

My heart begged for the right answer.

"You said it yourself. Fin doesn't have any magic. We didn't know what awaited him where Dinah was being held. I'm the stronger of the two of us, but I'm also faster. I couldn't risk Dinah's life on Fin's speed."

"But you risked mine on Fin's strength. Not that I'm mad about that, of course. I would have made the same decision. What I don't understand, is why did *you*?"

"You," Kiran said, taking my cheek in his palm, setting my entire being on fire. A fire that didn't consume, only warmed. "You are the woman who sacrificed your life on the one in a thousand chance your sister might come to harm if you didn't. How…" He leaned his forehead against mine, fogging the air above my lips, stealing my breath. "How could I claim to be the male who loves you and allow your greatest fear to come true, simply to save myself pain?"

"I'm sure it would have hurt to die," I said, attempting to break the intensity of this moment with a poorly timed joke. "Actually die, I mean. Have my spirit leave my body kind of die."

"Not when you're you. I believe those who sacrifice themselves for others come to peace when they drift from under the sun. Asha," he said, taking my hands in his. The warmth of his fingertips caressed the back of my hand, my palms. My feet were floating off the ground now. "Please. Please find it in yourself—"

I slid my forehead up, tipped my chin. As if that had been the answer he'd been waiting on for weeks, that he'd been dreaming of for ages, he leaned into me. His lips met mine, warm and gentle. My face went hot, and I melted into him, allowed his fingers to trace my arm, my neck, tuck themselves behind my ears and absentmindedly caress my hair.

"Can I share something with you?" he whispered.

"Yes," I said, knowing exactly what I was agreeing to.

This time, when Kiran unleashed his power, when he loosened whatever reins he'd used to secure it within his ribs, when he finally let go…

This time, the waves didn't crash against the cliffside.

They flooded it.

Longing, urgent and intense, surged through me, bursting the dams the two of us must have spent our entire lives building. But the water was warm, heated by the glowing ember that coursed from his lips. It melted my aching bones, saturating my chest, my stomach, my limbs with molten gold. For a moment, I thought it might drown me, thought I might let it.

By the time he pulled away, I might as well have been intoxicated.

"That's it?" I asked, having to steady myself on his ridiculously solid chest to gain my balance as my legs quaked. "I mean...not that it wasn't good. That's not what I meant."

Kiran's eyes flashed with mischief, desire. "For now," he said. "I would hate to ruin my reputation as a gentleman."

A huff of baffled irritation escaped my lips. "You do know we're married," I said, sure my face was the color of a beet as desire mingled with embarrassment rushed up my arms.

Kiran laughed, a hearty chuckle that rang through the night. He took my hand and pressed his soft, warm lips against it. "That doesn't mean I won't be courting you first, love."

I let out a suppressed chuckle.

He nodded toward the tent. "Why don't you go to bed? You'll be grateful for the rest tomorrow. Don't worry, I'll stand guard out here, though I imagine Azrael is as far as the wind by now."

He led me to the entrance of the tent and watched me curl into bed next to my sister.

I think we both knew that last statement was garbage, that I definitely wouldn't be getting any sleep that night.

CHAPTER 76

ASHA

"*A*re you going to tell him?" The vizier's blue eyes were warm as I shook the scroll in my hand, jittering with the nerves, with the weight of what I'd just read.

The broken wax seal beat against the back of my hand as I shook it and paced through the vizier's office.

"We don't keep secrets from one another," I said, biting my lips, for the first time in a while wishing that were not true.

"You mean to tell me that birthday party you threw him wasn't a surprise? What will I tell all the petty gossips on my staff who almost died having to hold it in?" the vizier asked.

I turned to him and sighed, tossing the scroll on his cedar desk. He peered up at me with those wistful blue eyes, the ones that looked so innocent.

"You know I'm mad at you at the moment," I said.

"I figured that might be the case," he said.

"You knew the whole time," I said through gritted teeth, though I had to admit, my tone wasn't as harsh as I had intended it to be. I could never seem to find the anger toward the vizier I would have needed for such a thing. Not when he'd been the first to be kind toward me, toward Dinah. Not with those cruelly innocent, unaffected blue eyes twinkling up at me.

"If, by that, you mean I knew that the late king Rajeen had many affairs, at least one of which brought about unwanted offspring, then yes, I knew. I also knew that the late king would have murdered me in my bed had I not sealed the records and paid off the maid so that she would never speak a word of the twin's parentage to anyone. What I did not know, is that she would break the vow she made and tell at least one of her children. That her child would grow up to be a devious and manipulative monster with a grudge against his late father and his siblings. A child who would feel entitled to the throne and conspire against our dear king by manipulating his kindhearted sister and his childhood friend. So yes, it depends on what you're accusing me of, whether or not I accept your accusations," he said.

A groan escaped my lips, and I rubbed my aching forehead with my palm. "You know that isn't all of it. That it's not the worst of it."

The vizier frowned, guilt deepening those sea-blue eyes of his. "I know. And I truly am sorry."

"I should make you tell him," I snapped.

"Perhaps from a justice standpoint. But we both know that you've surpassed me in the ability to comfort Kiran while he aches," he said.

This caught my attention, and I searched his face. I searched for disloyalty, greed, anything that would make the vizier's concealment of this information sinister, but I found none. Just an elderly male, weary of bearing tens of lifetimes of mistakes.

"Are you going to bring charges against me?" he asked, his eyes drilling into mine. Not pleading. Just curious. Not for the first time, it struck me how old the vizier was. That even fear of death had become too wearisome, too boring to bother with.

I exhaled.

"I see."

"I haven't decided yet."

"Not that it's much consolation, but I regret not informing Kiran about Azrael and Tavi earlier."

"And the rest of it?"

The vizier furrowed his wrinkled brow, and a deep sadness washed over his iron face. Tired. The vizier was so, so tired. "I'm sure you've wondered why I age faster than the rest of them."

I shrugged. "I always assumed you were much older. That fae only seem immortal because none has lived long enough yet to die of old age."

"That may be part of it. But I am not as old as you might suspect. The healers have always believed there was something off about my magic. That I was born without that little something that keeps the rest of my brethren eternally young. They claim it's a rare disorder, almost unheard of."

I shifted on my feet. "And what do you think?"

He sighed. "I think I've spent my life keeping one too many secrets. Secrets that were not mine to keep, yet, not mine to tell."

That seemed like the understatement of the millennia, considering what I now knew. What I had uncovered in the dreadful scroll now trembling between my hands. I should burn it, never tell a soul.

"I think I'd have to agree with the healers."

"Perhaps," the vizier said, "but, Asha, my queen. Secrets have a magic of their own. A dark and terrible magic, with the power to rot a fae heart from the inside."

"Then why did you keep them?"

He shrugged. "For her. For them. Never mind, it didn't matter in the end."

I sighed. As frustrated as I was with the vizier, I couldn't help but feel indebted to him. When I'd arrived back at the palace, my first course of action had been to confront Lydia, in secret, of course, and ask how in Alondria she'd known Dinah was in danger. Apparently, when Dinah and Az both went missing, my father had hobbled all the way to the palace in a frenzy, beating on the gates and demanding an audience with Princess Lydia. The guards might have beaten him to a pulp, had the vizier not heard the commotion and stepped in.

He had taken my father straight to Lydia, but not until he'd disposed of the two guards and called for replacements. Lydia had known enough about Dinah's behavior to know she'd never run off with a married man, so she'd left Meranthi in the vizier's charge, threatened a few smugglers within an inch of their life, and garnered information on the underground caravan that had transported a young male and his *cargo* across the Sahli for a hefty sum. A trail of gold-thirsty mercenaries had led Lydia to the cave where they'd hidden Dinah, and carnage had swiftly followed.

When I'd asked her why she hadn't stayed in Rivre to help, she'd informed me that, if Kiran was ever going to learn to be the king Naenden needed, he was going to have to learn to sort out his own crap. Plus, she had to get back to Meranthi before news got out that she'd left. I hadn't pressed her after that.

I examined the vizier, the male who had rescued my father from the guards, the male responsible for sending Lydia to my sister's aid. It had me wondering if he knew Lydia's secret too, if he was a vault of knowledge that, if cracked, could send the kingdom of Naenden crumbling. He had known about the statue of Tionis in the South Wing from his time serving Kiran's grandfather, back when the cruel male tortured his enemies in those dungeons. That was how he had known to take Gwenyth there when Kiran had commanded he lock her away somewhere Kiran would never find her. When I'd asked him about it when Kiran and I returned from Rivre, he'd said he had thought the statue in the South Wing was the only one to be enchanted. Had he realized the statue of Tionis in the garden had possessed the same ability, he would have told Kiran immediately. Or so he claimed. The vizier might have kept secrets—the detrimental sort, but I couldn't will myself to despise him for it. I swallowed and nodded. "When I tell him, I'll do my best to make your case."

"Thank you, Your Majesty." The vizier stood and bowed until I waved an irritated hand in his direction.

"You know I hate when people do that," I said.

"So you've told me," he said.

I rocked back and forth, clawing my lips with my fingertips. "What am I going to tell Kiran?"

The vizier shrugged. "The truth, I suppose. What else is there?"

CHAPTER 77

KIRAN

I'm poring over the records I retrieved from the vizier, a tower of scrolls piling up on my office floor, as a knock sounds on my door.

I know it's her before the cedar door creaks open, before she strides in wearing an ivory silk gown that glides like moonlight against her olive skin, her long braid teased and unraveling like she's been messing with it. Asha does that when she's thinking—wriggles her fingers between the segments of her braid to the point other visiting diplomats must think Tavi incompetent. I'm pretty sure Asha has no clue she does this, and I haven't brought it up, because it's too stinking adorable to risk her trying to break the habit.

"Find anything?" she asks, carrying an armful of scrolls that, if I know my wife at all, will probably burst from her hands any moment now.

I'd offer to help, but it'd only get on her nerves.

On second thought...

"No, but do you need me to carry a few of those?" I ask as innocently as I can muster.

She shoots me the exact glare I was hoping for, the one that has her brow furrowing and my heart jolting. "They're just scrolls. You and Fin act like being human is a crippling disease or something." When she attempts to flit her hand in my direction, dismissing my concern, a loose scroll slips from her arms, clattering to the floor as it rolls in my direction.

I snicker, and even my stubborn bride can't hide her smirk. "Well, at least I got them up the stairs," she says, shrugging as she drops the pile of scrolls. They whirl away from her like they're afraid she might step on them if they don't.

Asha, still clinging onto the only scroll she didn't drop, lowers herself to the floor next to me and tries to plant a kiss on my cheek, but I'm too fast for her and sweep my head around, intercepting it, her lips landing on mine, considering for a moment, then apparently accepting the change of plans.

When she pulls away, I note the moment in my mind, tracing the curve of her scars, the ones I love for reminding me each and every day what a lucky male I am for not losing her before I even knew she existed. I tuck away the flush of her cheeks in my memory, saving her laugh for a lonely night centuries down the road.

My stomach threatens to plummet, but I don't let it. Not when I have her here with me. Right here. Right now.

I'd cherish her if I couldn't keep her forever.

"Kiran, I've found something," she says, her laughter fading.

My chest tightens as I search her face for answers. She's wearing the same expression she used the day she told me the truth about Ophelia, about how I'd murdered a girl whose family was being threatened by the woman I'd thought I loved. Asha had encouraged me to tell Fin, though she'd promised she'd do it if I couldn't. In the end, I'd been the one to break my brother with the truth.

Fin hasn't spoken to me since, but Asha claims he'll come around.

I wonder if it will happen within her lifespan.

I wonder if I'll deserve his forgiveness by the time it does.

We might have won against Calias the night of the Council meeting, but the wounds he and Azrael and Gwenyth inflicted are far from healed.

The wounds I inflicted are far from healed.

It had only taken us a few moments once we returned to the palace all those months ago for the gravity of Azrael's disappearance to slice through our beautiful illusion of bliss. Azrael knew about the Rip. He knew its location, that Asha had drawn immense power from it, even more so than he had foreseen.

That left us with a question dangling over our heads. A question Asha and I were gravely confident Azrael was exploring at this very moment.

If Asha could draw power from the Rip, could she open it?

And, even worse, if she could open it, could someone else? Someone else endowed with the Old Magic?

"What is it?" I ask.

She takes the scroll she was careful not to drop and starts to unfurl it in the floor, but she hesitates, her fingers stroking the thick paper. "I want you hear it from me before you see it." She takes my hands, pulling them into her lap and stroking them with fervor.

Dread cakes my bones, and it takes everything in me not to allow it to rush through my fingertips into hers, infecting her mind with the mire clogging my veins.

"It's bad, isn't it?" I ask, though I don't have to. Not with the way her skin has paled.

She nods, the simple motion puncturing the bonds I've clasped over my emotions. Her eye twitches, and I realize I must have allowed some of my fear to seep through her skin on accident. I go to pull my hands away, to relieve her of the burden that should be mine to bear, but she tightens her grip around my fingers.

I can't help but adore her for it.

"Az was telling the truth about his heritage. The records were sealed, but they exist all the same," she says.

I let out a strained laugh, surprising myself. "Is that all?" I ask, relief flooding through me. I allow a bit of it to transfer through my fingertips, as repayment for the dread Asha experienced on my behalf. "Well, we already knew that, didn't we? You're so sweet to be worried that would hurt me, but Asha, my father—he was a horrid excuse for a living, sentient being. Unfortunately, he bragged about his conquests to me my entire life. When I was seven—" I stop there, my laugh dying with the unsavory memory that springs to my mind. I stare at the partially unfurled scroll. "Though I'd rather not read it, just the same."

She squeezes my hands, pulling me back from the cliffside of unpleasant thoughts. "This scroll isn't the record of Tavi's and Az's birth."

I stare at her for a moment, confused. "Then what is it?"

"The vizier took an oath when he entered service to the castle. Part of that oath was to document every royal birth."

"And?"

She lets out an exhale, and I can see it hidden within the recesses of her frown. I can hear it as she tries to steady her voice, her attempt to keep the truth from crushing her husband, from crushing me.

She nods toward the scroll. "And this one's yours."

I swallow and say nothing.

"After Lydia was born," she continues, "after your parents had tried so long for an heir, and their long-awaited child was born female, your father didn't take to it well."

I nod. I know this part already, but Asha is well aware of that. She's telling me this to ground me, to comfort me with the known before she shatters my reality.

"He pressured your mother into trying for another child to produce an heir. Years passed, and it didn't happen. And your father's behavior toward Lydia grew more and more violent. He hated her, resented her for not being a male. For ruining his one shot at an heir."

"And then Fin and I were born."

She swallows and traces circles on the back of my hand with her thumb. "Yes. And then you were born. But only after..." Her voice catches, and her thumb rattles against my skin. "Your mother became suspicious that their infertility had more to do with your father than with her. And she was desperate to save Lydia. She thought that if she didn't produce an heir, your father's wrath would go too far, that he'd kill Lydia. So she—"

I jolt to my feet, wrenching my hands from her fumbling grip. Her fingers slip from mine just in time for the flames to lick the lifeline of my palm without harming her. The realization of how easily I could have hurt her crushes me. "I don't wish to hear any more," I say, not because I'm angry at her, not because I wish to silence my wife.

I'm just so afraid.

She nods, biting her lip. "Okay," she whispers. Something about the softness of her answer soothes me, cools the air in the room I hadn't even realized had begun to boil. I return to the ground to sit across from her, but I shake my head when she tries to stroke my knee.

I just hope she understands.

Thousands of questions swarm my mind, along with the impossible decision of which to ask first. Whether to ask at all, ever.

"Do we have a record of who he was?" I finally settle on.

She shakes her head. "No. She never gave the vizier a name."

"And why did she tell the vizier about her infidelity in the first place?" I can't help but hiss through gritted teeth.

"He said the secret was killing her. That she couldn't bear it by herself."

The snarl that escapes my lips is feral, primal. "But she didn't keep it all to herself, did she? It takes two, after all."

If the way my fists have clenched, the way my spine has arched like a beast reading to attack…if any of that terrifies her, she doesn't let it show. "I believe she disguised herself," she says. "I doubt the male ever knew who she was, who he had sired."

Her calm in the wake of my fiery storm grounds me, reminding me, despite every fiber of my being screaming otherwise, that I am safe. That she is safe. "If my fa—if the late king wasn't my father, wasn't Fin's father…" I shudder, placing my hands on my forehead. "Did my father—Rajeen, I mean—did he ever know?"

She pauses, and I can tell she's weighing her answer. "The vizier didn't think so."

I sigh in relief, but…but then my heart hardens, darkens as a sickening realization washes over me. The same realization that made my wife the bravest human to ever walk Alondria for sharing her knowledge with me.

Because if Fin and I were sired by an unknown fae...

That means Azrael is the rightful heir to the throne.

That he's always been.

CHAPTER 78

ASHA

*I*t took the better half of an hour for Kiran to calm his boiling rage into a simmer.

I couldn't understand it, not really, the emotions that must have been coursing through him.

That was the thing about Kiran. He had the power to make anyone feel whatever he wanted them to, but so little power over himself.

I hadn't been sure what to tell him when he'd asked me if King Rajeen had known about Kiran's mother's affair. The vizier hadn't thought so. But then there was that moment in the caravan, when Fin and I had been discussing why Kiran hadn't slaughtered Gwenyth for betraying him. Fin had almost said that was what his father would have done. Except he'd stopped and looked confused, as if some repressed memory had come back to haunt him, a memory he'd assumed was a bad dream.

And then there was Lydia. Her secret. Who her father had forced her to kill.

But I couldn't say such things. Not without proof.

Besides, Kiran had enough to digest today without me throwing speculations his way.

When the air cooled and a gentle breeze escaped the stuffy air through the window, I smiled.

"You're getting better at that."

He let out a weary, exasperated laugh, but returned my smile all the same.

It would hurt. For a long time, it would hurt. And it would do more than hurt. He explained that to me once he'd regained enough composure for words.

"I don't know what I'm supposed to feel, Asha. Anger at my father for pushing my mother away, for treating Lydia like..." He bit his lip. "I feel hurt that my mother kept this secret all those years. That she didn't tell me herself. Regret that I'll likely never know who my father is. And Fin... I don't know how to tell Fin, if I even should. If Az really is the rightful heir..." He huffed, pushing his fingers to his temples. "Either way, Az is out there somewhere. And is probably miles ahead of us when it comes to finding a way to open the Rip. He won't even need to discover he's the true heir to the throne if he rains down the Others upon us," Kiran sighed. "If only this information helped us track him down. But we've already questioned Tavi, and she barely talked."

"I'm almost certain Tavi didn't know what Az was up to," I said, nervous that Kiran seemed to think she was on Az's side. I'd felt guilty about bringing her up as a suspect of conspirators, when I was fairly sure she'd aided Az unwittingly. When we had arrived at the palace, she had burst from a room upstairs and flung herself into my arms, weeping about how she hadn't known, and that she'd only realized what Az was up to when she found my notes, that she'd tried to confront him, but he was gone, and that she hadn't made it back to the palace in time to stop our caravan.

At first, I had been suspicious and asked her why she hadn't sent word, but as it turned out, she had. Only, the guard who'd received her note had forgotten about it, figuring nothing a half-breed could say would be of any importance to the king and queen.

Kiran had fired that guard immediately.

I didn't wish Tavi to come to any harm just because she hadn't told us who her father was. "She probably doesn't even know, Kiran. I doubt Az told her."

"You're probably right," he sighed. "All this searching, just to find out that the answer leaves us nowhere."

"Not nowhere," I offered, rubbing his back. "At least it will put some flame under you to get the law changed, so Lydia's next in line."

Kiran laughed dryly. "Yes, and put her in danger."

"I'm fairly sure she does plenty of that on her own," I said. "So, we just have to figure out another way to track Az. What if?" I grinned, wondering why the thought hadn't come to me earlier. "If we think he'll try to open the Rip at some point—"

"I've already stationed guards around the perimeter," Kiran said.

I glared at him, and I wondered if the fact that I only had one eye made the *did I sound like I was done talking* look more intimidating than the average woman's.

Kiran cleared his throat. "Continue, please."

I grinned. "Well. If he's looking to open the Rip, he'll need someone to open it for him, won't he? And I doubt he's stupid enough to come after me again."

Kiran nodded. "So he'll be hunting for someone else."

"Exactly," I nodded.

"So we just have to find them first," Kiran said. "Great. Should be easy."

"Maybe easier than you'd think." My mind fluttered back to Rivre. To music and dancing and the girl with curly red hair and a flute in her satchel. The girl Gwenyth had found an interest in.

She'd said the girl was like us.

At the time, I'd thought Gwenyth possessed some supernatural ability to sense others who hosted the Old Magic.

I knew better now, of course.

But I also knew better than to ignore *what* information Gwenyth harbored just because she'd been lying about *how* she retrieved it.

Az's plan had rested in my willingness to channel the Rip. He'd even had a backup plan in case I refused—threatening Dinah. But Az was smart. Too smart not to have an alternative to fall back on.

When I'd confronted him about murdering Gwenyth, he'd claimed he'd done it because she couldn't keep her mouth shut.

What if he had been less concerned with her giving him away, and more worried about what she might reveal if he left her alive?

Like the fact that there was another person who possessed the Old Magic?

Perhaps he feared whoever acquired that information could get to her first.

A knock sounded on the cedar door. "Kiran, open up. I just had a talking to with our dear vizier and you'll never guess the information a headlock can get out of someone." The door knob cracked and Lydia burst through the door.

I turned to Kiran, grinning. "I think I know someone who could help."

EPILOGUE

ABRA

*M*y fingers trembled as they traced the space where a ray of light once cut through the air, seemingly without origin. When my hand fell limp against my side, fully whole, without even a fingernail disappearing into thin air, I let out a sigh I'd been storing up since that girl Asha had opened her mouth and that dreadful voice had bellowed out.

They didn't open it.

The fools didn't open it.

Though, by this point, I'd convinced myself that they'd tried.

Months ago, when I'd received that dreadfully tactless invitation from Calias, oozing in that gluttonous wax he liked to use—the one made from fae blood—I'd almost tossed it into the fire.

But then I'd seen where the treaty was to take place, and I'd vomited into the fire instead.

Rivre.

It couldn't be.

My servants had knocked on the doors to my office then. "Lady Abra, are you okay?"

They must have smelled my vomit. Or heard me retching. "All's well!" I'd called out. "No need to disturb me!" And they'd shuffled away.

Keeping my servants at arm's length without being cruel toward them was a difficult balance to strike. It wasn't their fault I was miserable, after all. It wasn't their fault I was hiding.

But they couldn't know I was hiding, either. That I'd forged a haughty demeanor to harden my face, to freeze my voice, to keep them away as much as necessary.

Of course, had I known they would eventually believe that I'd murdered my husband, I might not have bothered with trying so hard.

I did murder my husband.

Just not the husband they thought.

But that invitation, the chill it had sent up my spine, into my fingertips, was nothing like the magic I'd learned to craft for myself over the centuries. Not that this subdued form of magic that involved consuming a revolting draught every day of my miserable existence was anything like what I'd once possessed.

No, not possessed. Befriended.

Or so I'd thought.

My magic hadn't returned the feeling, apparently.

Though I was now beginning to wonder if it had finally found someone it preferred. A human, of all beings.

One I couldn't help but like, despite myself. So perhaps I understood why, after severing itself from me all those centuries ago, it had finally found companionship in her. In that girl, Queen Asha. The one who had sacrificed herself for her sister, then again for the King of Naenden and his brother. My heart twinged with mingled jealousy and pity for the girl. Pity, if she'd fallen in love with such a cruel being. Pity, for when the veil of affection grew thin from the incessant wear and tear of the beatings. Jealously, if it was in fact the case that she had succeeded in softening his heart, after all.

I had made a mistake the night of the Council meeting. Something ancient in me, something that beckoned to the female I had suppressed long ago, had come out to play. I had wanted to help her, to punish her captors for what I assumed had been abuse.

I should have used my poison on her instead.

Poison. A seamless change of pace for one who was once a healer. For who would better know the perfect combination of benign ingredients to turn a brew deadly? I sometimes wondered if my life would have taken a different path had I used that knowledge earlier, had I used it on *him*. Had I realized my potential only a few years earlier.

That was the thing about my magic, back when it had been mine. It hadn't simply given me the ability to heal wounds with my touch, to repair garments without a patch, to restore ruined objects to a state of newness.

It had gifted me with knowledge. Knowledge that pineberries and winter clove and salt from dehydrated tears, when boiled over a wormweed fire, would produce an elixir to reverse the effects of frostbite. Knowledge...along with a warning. That the removal of just one of these ingredients would accelerate the condition, could even cause the condition, if administered in the right doses.

Possessing the magic had been like having a map inscribed in my mind, one that detailed every possible interaction between elements, species, plants; the manners in which they might be crushed, mixed, boiled, seared to achieve a particular result.

The Old Magic might have fled, but it had left the map behind, branded into the cracks of my memory as clearly as the day I'd agreed to share my consciousness.

The map was how I knew I could fake possessing the Frost by stewing cannutgrawn gum and drinking the pungent tea from a goblet made of pure silver.

It was how I'd known a great many things that had kept me alive, unrecognizable.

The guilt of murdering Queen Asha would have been inconvenient, but it would have been a small price to pay to rid the Old Magic of its host. It was a picky thing, and I figured it would have taken it decades to find another suitable human worthy of taking up residence. But as it stood, the girl lived, and the power to open the Rip with her.

That was going to be a problem.

I probably should have let the Council see to her, finish her off. But then that sister of hers had waltzed right up to the King of Dwellen and spoken to him as if he were a toddler.

And I hated the King of Dwellen.

So I'd saved her sister's life, chosen not to meddle when, by some intervention of the Fates, the King of Naenden had saved her life.

He'd claimed he'd worked on her heart, forced it to beat again with nothing but his bare hands.

I wasn't so sure.

What I was fairly certain of was that Queen Asha and her sister boasted of greater character than I did.

It was strange. I hadn't felt less than superior to a human in a long time. Not since I'd first laid eyes on one, only to discover that their bodies were not nearly as equipped for this world as mine.

My first late husband had come to the same conclusion. There was a reason the humans had never had true control over their home since then.

I shook him from my mind to focus on the problem at hand. At least it wasn't as terrible as I'd assumed. When I'd received that invitation, glanced at the name of a place I'd shunned from my memory long ago, I'd known, I'd just known he was planning to open it. To unleash the Others on all of us.

My theory had only become more certain when I'd seen the girl, Queen Asha, in passing at the Council. Rumors of her Gift, as the fae liked to call it, had spread as far as Mystral, and I'd wondered myself if she possessed some Old Magic within her.

But then I'd heard her story. Heard her voice, and I'd known she had *my* magic. Not one of its brothers or sisters. Mine.

Well, not mine anymore. Not since it had harnessed the healing of the Rip to free itself from my body. It had made a deal with me—though I hadn't realized it at the time. Heal the Rip, gain its freedom.

A deal I was not about to let it revoke at Calias's party.

That was why I'd bribed one of Calias's servant to seat me next to the girl. It was a gamble, and rash, I knew that. The chances my magic wouldn't recognize me were slim, but I'd hoped that would turn out in my favor. That my magic would know better than to break its deal with me. That it would know, if it tried to open the Rip, I'd kill the girl before it ever got the chance. That those poisons would go straight into her drink, and that a human wouldn't simply suffer from a mild fit of vomiting.

I'd kill the girl, and then Calias would be next.

I just hadn't expected the girl would be so stinking likable. That she would remind me of myself. The version of me I once admired. Back before him. Back before I'd traded my soul for a son.

Back before I'd traded my son's soul for his life.

Farin's face, the face of his youth, his innocent smile, flashed before my eyes. My child, running free in the forest on a wound that should have been poisoning his blood, seeping the life out from him. If only I had understood then that allowing him to die would have been a mercy. If only I had understood that my desire to save him had been selfishly motivated, my inability to lose him due, not to necessity, but the pain that would have ripped through my soul.

The Fates would have rewarded me, then. They showed me just as much when he trotted around this new world on an ankle that should have spoiled with infection.

Instead, I traded both of our souls to his father, and the Fates chastised me in a way I'd never thought possible. They punished me by never ending it.

I traced my fingers back over the thin air. For a moment, my heart constricted in a wild euphoria, thinking perhaps my fingers would slip through. That, after all this time, they would catch my scent. That the Others would end my punishment, the way it should have ended years ago.

Except nothing disappeared, nothing slipped through to that dreadful place, and my heart sank like a ship flooding with relief.

No, I didn't want to die. Not yet.

I wasn't sure what I was waiting for—what I thought would heal my broken, wilted heart and make it alive again. A single mighty deed I could work that would erase what I'd done.

What could erase the fact that I had sold this world, all its people, over to the hand of my husband all those centuries ago? What could erase the fact that it was all in vain, that my boy would have lived anyway? That, in bringing his father to him in exchange for saving him, I had poisoned my child's soul.

That he hadn't been as strong as I thought.

That, in the end, his father had gotten to him.

In the end, he'd turned out worse.

My heart clenched, and I fought back the sobs. Not that I had to fight very hard. I mostly pretended to fight them now, only because I wished I could cry, let it all wash over me and cleanse me.

I supposed this was part of my punishment too.

Had the Fates brought me back to this place to taunt me? Had I known Calias's mind was shallow enough to use the Old Magic for an assassination attempt on the King of Naenden, I might not have bothered coming.

But he'd outsmarted me, if only in his lack of imagination.

Imagination.

The word pierced my heart.

At least Kiran had burnt him to a crisp. How that idiot Calias found the Rip in the first place was beyond me.

But, then again, I hadn't counted on his partner, that sickly looking half-fae that had made the hairs on the back of Queen Asha's neck stand up. That being who had slithered up to her any time she spoke of something she clearly shouldn't have. The one who thought I wasn't listening when he threatened her.

He had snuck out somehow, even though I'd been keeping a sharp eye on him. How he evaded me, I wasn't sure, but I didn't like the idea of it.

Now that I was sure the Rip was safely sutured, I would have to go after the servant. Something about his cunning eyes gave me the impression he was always the one pulling the strings. That he'd had greater plans for this place all along.

I groaned. Over the years, I convinced myself that I had made amends. That I'd repaid this place for the disaster I wrought upon it in my selfishness. That I'd slaughtered the monster I'd led to its gates. That I'd...

My throat closed up at the memory. I fixed it. I told myself I had, at least. I had obliterated the last dangling part of my soul by trying to make right what I'd done.

But I had clearly deceived myself. When the King of Mystral had courted me, I had thought the Fates were rewarding me. Convinced myself they had finally figured I had wandered alone, miserable, for long enough. That I was worthy of the smallest bit of happiness.

Then someone had poisoned my husband, and the whole world had assumed I'd done it. I'd known then that the Fates weren't finished with me.

"I closed it. I gave my magic up, let it free, to close it. To keep them safe," I whispered.

There was no answer.

"I...I..." But there was no use admitting the atrocity aloud. Not when the words would only strike me, and me alone.

This one last task. I'd complete this one last task, and then I'd lay myself to rest.

That servant, the half-fae, with the sneering eyes. He would unleash a host of Others on this world if he could. He'd unleash them thinking they would bend to his will. When he was done, he would leave Alondria without a root to feed himself.

He would have to find someone like Queen Asha to manage it. He'd have to find someone possessed with the Old Magic.

And there were others, siblings my sons and his companions hadn't known about. Strands of sentient magic that still roamed Alondria, slipping between hosts like a thief might jolt between shadows.

At least, that's what the rumors claimed.

I had a sneaking suspicion that conniving servant had heard them too.

I'd kill him first, if I could find him.

And if not?

I'd hunt them all down and slay them before he got the chance.

What was left of my tattered heart ached at the thought, though dully. My eyes burned, though without shedding tears.

This was my punishment for being too weak to do what I should have done centuries ago.

I'd kill the innocent to save the rest.

This was my punishment.

This was my purpose.

Perhaps the Fates would finally permit me to join them.

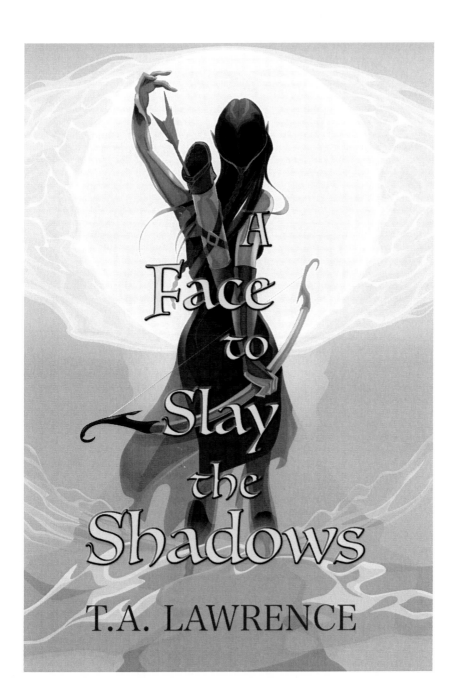

FREE PREQUEL NOVELLA

SIGN UP TO MY NEWSLETTER AT
TALAWRENCEBOOKS.COM

Rumors ripple through Alondria of an avenger of the weak, the innocent, the mistreated.

They say he stalks in the shadows, suffocates his victims with the flicker in his eyes. That, if you're unfortunate enough to catch him lower his hood, his will be the last face you'll ever see.

Of course, if anyone really knew that for sure, if anyone had ever escaped, they would have known better.

They would have known that the last face my victims ever saw...was a she.

Lydia is used to bringing reproach on the royal family. It's been that way ever since the day the midwife informed her father, the King of Naenden, that his wife had borne, not an heir, but a daughter.

What a shame.

With her father dead, Lydia has better things to do than sit around the palace and wait for her spoiled brother to run their kingdom into the ground.

Of course, a princess can't exactly travel alone without earning a *reputation*.

That's fine with Lydia. Because as long as the gossipers stay distracted spreading rumors of her indiscretions, they'll never imagine what she's actually up to.

But when Lydia happens across a petty thief she can't seem to shake, she violates her most sacred rule.

Never make a bargain you can't break.

ABOUT THE AUTHOR

T.A. Lawrence is the author of *The Severed Realms*, a series of fairytale retellings that feature mystery, danger, romance, and, of course, fae. T.A. Lawrence also writes the middle-grade series *The Astoria Chronicles*, the story of a girl who frequents a fantasy world through a portal in her neighbor's cotton field. T.A. lives in Alabama with her loving and supportive husband Jacob, who occasionally convinces her to leave the house.

ALSO BY T.A. LAWRENCE

Also in *The Severed Realms* series:
A Tune to Make Them Follow (Coming January 2023)

The Astoria Chronicles:
The Keeper of the Threshold (The Astoria Chronicles: Book 1)
The Secret of Atalo (The Astoria Chronicles: Book 2)

ACKNOWLEDGMENTS

To my husband Jacob, who didn't marry an author but loved me when I became one anyway. I can't wait to see all the versions of us the future holds, if the Lord wills it. To Mom, for keeping all the stream-of-consciousness journal entries I wrote to keep from falling asleep in the second grade. To Dad, for catching every time I misspell *judgment*. To Wilson, whose personality is not featured in this book as far as I'm aware. To Maria, every bit of protectiveness Asha feels for her sister is inspired by my love for you. To Amanda, for keeping my closet stocked with cute clothes because, between being an author and a speech therapist who wears scrubs to work, I don't think I'd treat myself to them if it weren't for you. To Tim, for your constant words of affirmation. To Karri, for my stunning cover. To Rachel Bobo, for advertising this book to every teenage girl who admits to you they have a love for reading. To Rachel Broadway, for being the only other person I've ever met who's read the book that inspired this particular retelling. To Meredith, for being my dreamer friend. To every person who took a chance on me by buying this book before it came out. To my ARC team, for binge-reading this book and making my dreams as an author come true.

Made in United States
North Haven, CT
17 June 2024